SINS
OF THE
MOTHER

Also available by August Norman

Come and Get Me

SINS OF THE MOTHER

A CAITLIN BERGMAN NOVEL

AUGUST NORMAN

CROOKED
LANE

NEW YORK

Published in the United States by Crooked Lane Books, an imprint of The Quick Brown Fox & Company LLC.

Crooked Lane Books and its logo are trademarks of The Quick Brown Fox & Company LLC.

Library of Congress Catalog-in-Publication data available upon request.

ISBN (hardcover): 978-1-64385-436-6
ISBN (ebook): 978-1-64385-437-3

Cover design by Nicole Lecht

Printed in the United States.

www.crookedlanebooks.com

Crooked Lane Books
34 West 27th St., 10th Floor
New York, NY 10001

First Edition: September 2020

10 9 8 7 6 5 4 3 2 1

To the mothers who bandage our wounds, kiss our boo-boos, and help us rise from our stumbles; whether or not we share the same blood, no one can judge your sacrifice.

1

T HE WOMAN SELLING Johnny his daughter back had only asked for
five grand.

Smart move.

One dollar more and he'd have headed to a hardware store for a tarp,
a shovel, and lime chalk.

Instead, the stack of twenties in his hunting jacket slapped against his
side with each step down the rough logging road. A lightning strike lit the
sky. Thunder rocked the mountainside seconds later, but no rain fell.

Dry lightning. Great.

Fire season didn't usually affect coastal Oregon, but Coos County
hadn't seen rain in a month, and the Siskiyou forest, less than two hours
south, had burnt like a furnace for the last week.

Not that he minded the threat of lightning-sparked wildfire or even
trudging uphill in the middle of the night's asshole, but had this bitch
asked for one dollar more, he'd have brought Gunner and Stupid Tom
along and taken care of her. Both of those boys were loyal enough, but
you didn't get a name like Stupid Tom 'cause you'd cured cancer. Five
measly grand kept the whole thing a solo expedition.

It also meant Johnny'd get Promise back without having to clean
some cult nutjob's blood out of his favorite camo gear.

He left the rough road for the last fifty feet of Douglas fir trees before
the firebreak, pulled out his monocular night scope, and swept the road
behind him. Nothing but his truck.

He turned back toward the break, a hundred-foot clearing from the base of the hill to the peak, then checked his watch: 12:27 AM.

One minute later, two feminine figures moved from the opposing woodland edge toward the clearing, one guiding the other from behind.

On foot, on time, only two; just like they'd planned.

Pocketing the scope, Johnny reached to the small of his back for his .45 and racked a round into the chamber. He hadn't killed anyone since guard duty at Abu Ghraib, and never a woman, but if this shit was gonna go sideways, he'd be ready. He tucked the gun into his waistband and walked toward the intersection.

Fifty feet from the clearing, he could see the pair approaching. Again he reached for his scope, but stopped when a flash of lightning showed them clearer. Promise stood in front, blindfolded and wearing bright-orange safety earmuffs. The older woman held a handgun down to her side.

He switched on a tiny flashlight and swung it back and forth.

Lady Handgun did the same.

They faced off at the opposite edges of the firebreak.

"What happens now?" Johnny yelled, competing with a roll of thunder.

The woman swung the flashlight to her left. "Put the money in the bucket."

The light's beam revealed a clothesline-style loop of rope strung from a tree at one side of the clearing to the other. At Johnny's end, a plastic bucket hung six feet off the ground.

The woman lifted one ear of Promise's earmuffs and gave a command. Promise reached up until her hand hit the rope and caught hold. The woman grabbed the other side of the loop and tugged.

The bucket on Johnny's end lurched forward a foot. In turn, Promise moved one step closer.

"The money," Handgun repeated.

"I get it," he yelled back.

He tossed the pack of cash into the bucket, then yanked Promise's side of the rope.

Everything moved another foot.

Then another.

A lightning flash cracked through the air, close enough that he could smell the ozone.

Johnny's eyes went temporarily red, and his ears shook with the latest burst of percussion.

"Let's get this done," the woman called.

He tugged hard on the rope again. "Shit would move faster if we both pulled."

She must have agreed. The bucket lurched forward times two. Now ninety feet remained between Johnny and his daughter.

Eighty-five, then eighty, seventy-five.

Then nothing.

Johnny pulled again, but no tug followed.

"What the hell?"

He let go of the rope, raised his gun, and reached for the night scope. The second the viewfinder met his eye, two bright flares blossomed across from him.

Muzzle flashes.

The bitch was shooting.

He dropped face first onto the logging road and returned two shots, careful to aim away from Promise's last position.

Hearing nothing further, he scanned the area.

Handgun's body lay crumpled where the rope loop met a tree. Promise remained in place seventy-five feet away, one hand still on the line.

A new figure, another woman, stood in the middle of the logging road facing Johnny, holding a gun in a practiced isosceles-triangle shooting stance.

Johnny dropped down, happy to eat a mouthful of dirt rather than face the volley of bullets that whizzed past. He shifted left, then fired two more times before yanking the scope up again.

The shooter was gone.

So was Promise.

He sprinted across the clearing.

Fifty feet past the firebreak, the road veered left. He stopped and scoped the area. Nothing on the road. He whipped around, caught the shooter and Promise running uphill through the woods, and started after them. The woman stumbled once, and Johnny saw a glint of light, like a reflection off falling metal.

New lightning, further now, revealed a moss-covered footpath leading over a ridge. Johnny gave it everything he had. No way he'd let his special girl go back to that cult. Two feet from the crest, he kicked something metallic. The shooter had dropped her gun.

He reached down with his left hand.

A jagged, solid object struck his right arm and spun him backward, sending his own gun into a clump of crisp ferns. He grabbed his wounded forearm and backed against a tree, warm blood trickling from elbow to hand.

A woman dressed all in red, maybe fifty or sixty years old, stepped in front of the fallen gun, holding a three-foot tree branch.

Despite the searing pain, Johnny brought both hands up in fists. "She's my daughter, you goddamned dog."

The woman pulled the branch back like a Louisville Slugger. "Then stop trying to touch her, you sick son of a bitch."

2

CAITLIN STARED AT the mausoleum's white marble columns and tried to recall the major earthquakes the century-old building had withstood. Northridge in '94, which she'd missed by two weeks while away at college; Sylmar in '71, four years before she'd been born; and the hundreds of tiny temblors that rattled the Los Angeles basin on a daily basis.

Either the Abbey of the Psalms had been built well, or the star power that had been laid to rest inside demanded the illusion of unfading glory. Since the cemetery's biggest names included Valentino, Chaplin, and other actors with credits mostly in silent films, the Hollywood Forever Cemetery received more tourists annually than family members of the deceased. Still, Caitlin's father had loved the quirky garden spot located less than two miles from the LAPD's Hollywood Division station, the cop shop where he'd spent most of his career, and had made plans for his interment there years before his passing.

"The good thing about cremation, Slugger," he'd said, over a bowl of kreplach soup at Canter's Deli, "is that there's always room for one more. And who doesn't want to hang out with Charlie Chaplin?"

Caitlin didn't need to check a directory or trace the plaques on the walls. She stepped into the Sanctuary of Hope, walked to the fifth panel, and sat on a stone bench.

"Happy birthday, Daddy," she said, reaching into her bag for the pack and lighter. She hadn't smoked a cigarette in four years, but her fingers still slipped the plastic wrap off the Marlboro Reds like a master

violinist tuning a Stradivarius and brought the lit bit of death to her lips
with the same steadied hand.

She took a single drag without inhaling to stoke the fire, then blew
the smoke upward, waving the cloud with her fingers and watching the
wispy tendrils ascend to wherever.

"Not much news to report, I'm afraid. Still not married. No kids. No
current beau, nor belle, in case you'd made any assumptions."

Her words echoed in the chamber of polished stone.

"Had a second book come out, and that went well. Still writing for
the *LA Voice*, though can't say how much longer that'll be a thing, especially with my newest editor. Paper's taking a weird direction, and our
advertisers are mostly nightclubs, prostitutes, and pot shops. Oh yeah,
pot's legal in California now, so one less thing to roll over in your ashes
about. I'm also running a lot—well, more than I was. Up to ten miles a
day, when I have the time."

She extinguished the cigarette on the marble bench.

"Quit these things, of course. I just miss you."

She took a deep breath and studied her father's plaque.

Matthew Bergman, 1953–2005, Father and Police Officer.

Rather than the words of the dull brass plate, she saw her dad on the
back porch of the West Hollywood apartment they'd had when she was
a sophomore at Fairfax High, and she could almost smell his end-of-
watch sweat and cigarette smoke merging with the annual jacaranda
bloom.

A harsh female voice brought her back to the present. "There's no
smoking in here."

Caitlin turned and saw a woman in her seventies dressed in old-
fashioned mourning black, veil and everything. She slid the open pack
of cigarettes behind her leg. "You smell smoke too? Someone must have
just passed through."

The woman's pursed lips softened as she looked Caitlin up and
down. "Dear, do you need help?"

"Help?" Caitlin smiled. "No, just talking to my dad on his
birthday."

The woman nodded, reaching into her purse. "I'm sorry for your
loss. I have five dollars."

It took Caitlin a second before she remembered that she was wearing a threadbare Army surplus jacket over a pair of oversized work pants. Even at nine in the morning, it would look like a heavy load in the middle of July. "Oh, I'm working on a story."

"A story?"

Caitlin ran a hand through the back of her hair. She never spent much time churching up her straight, chin-length mess, but today it felt particularly lifeless.

"About homelessness. I'm a reporter from the *LA Voice*. It's the free zine you see in grocery stores. Not the *Penny Saver* or the coupon thing, obviously, but the weekly newsprint magazine that handles hard-hitting LA news."

After four weeks of interviewing people living out of shelters, shopping carts, and cardboard palaces, she'd sent her story off to Stan Lawton, her editor for the last year. His request for follow-ups meant she had one more day on the streets.

The mourner took a five-dollar bill out and set it on a side table. "For your *story*, then."

Caitlin smiled. "Seriously, it's a ten-page exposé and will be in next week's issue."

"God bless you, dear," the woman said, then continued on her way.

Caitlin looked back to her father's plaque and broke out in laughter. "See, Dad? Life's going great."

She spent another three minutes in silent reflection, then stood, ran her hand across the cold marble wall, and walked out, taking the woman's misguided donation to a nearby homeless camp.

Back in her apartment an hour later, she edited her piece once again, sent Lawton the final draft, then stepped out to run a quick 5K around her neighborhood.

She'd just pulled off her shoes and started the shower when her phone chimed with his reply:

Sorry. Can't run the story.

3

C AITLIN SLID INTO the poorly lit restaurant's vinyl booth, knocking the tabletop hard enough to wake a seismic needle at Caltech.

Stan Lawton looked up, eyes wide, then fumbled his phone. "Bergman," he stammered, his mobile device bouncing into the shadows somewhere below. "What the hell are you doing here?"

"Relax, Stan. Don't have a coronary."

Caitlin snagged the phone with her foot, beating the spry-for-his-age sixty-two-year-old to pick it up, then noticed an image of an attractive woman in her early twenties on the screen, just above a social media profile.

"Nice." She slid the device across the table.

Lawton knocked over a basket of rolls to grab the phone, then glanced back toward the restaurant's entryway. "This isn't what it looks like. How did you know where I was, anyway?"

Caitlin *tsk*ed her tongue. "Your browsing history. You really need to change your password, or at least not keep it on a Post-it under the keyboard."

"But—"

"But your web searches weren't enough to know where you'd go? You're forgetting who you're dealing with. One, a woman—and women talk, Stan. Two, a reporter who happens to know every bartender in downtown LA. Three, the best damned investigative journalist on your staff—so why the hell aren't you publishing my homeless piece? And don't say the owner."

A Southern California real estate conglomerate had purchased the *LA Voice* twelve months earlier with the promise that nothing about the business model would change. Nothing did—for seven days; then Caitlin's editor for over a decade retired unceremoniously, and Stan Lawton arrived from a decorated career in Chicago, supposedly to maintain the same level of quality the *Voice* was known for. There'd been two rounds of layoffs since, and now, apparently, content oversight.

Lawton sat back in the booth. "I liked the story, Bergman. I really did. They felt—"

"Four weeks." Caitlin reached for the still-warm rolls that had tumbled into fair play, tore one in half, then continued, squeezing the soft bread in her fist to accentuate her words. "I spent a month living with the homeless thinking we might actually effect some change in this city, all for a story *you* approved."

He started again. "They felt—"

"Please don't say *they* when you mean *he*." The paper's *ownership conglomerate* had proven to ultimately consist of a single billionaire whose politics leaned so far right that a light breeze would carry him to the Texas panhandle. Caitlin dropped the roll to avoid winging it at her boss. "Our new overlord might be writing the checks, but you're the father of our little tribe, and we expect you to have our backs. Believe it or not, Stan, I was excited when I heard you'd be taking over. You were a hell of a journalist before you came to LA."

He smirked. "I'm not sure I do believe it."

She didn't slow down. "What's going in the issue if it's not my piece?"

Lawton glanced toward the door again. "The statehood ballot initiative."

One sharp laugh escaped Caitlin's mouth. "The three-states thing?"

For the upcoming fall ballot, a cadre of billionaires had proposed splitting California into three states, claiming that the new regions would be more representative of the inhabitants. Like everyone else, Caitlin guessed the move was an attempt to win additional conservative congressional seats through selective gerrymandering. Several booths away, the sultry growl of a bass-filled voice followed by a high-pitched giggle signaled a couple's enjoyment of their lunchtime affair, a not-so-subtle reminder that Caitlin's boss awaited a young woman in a restaurant known more for its discretion than its filet.

"Who even wrote the story?" she said. "Spill it, or your little meeting's going to turn into a livestream."

Lawton stifled a small laugh. "Bill Deets turned in a copy five days ago."

"Deets has only been on staff for two weeks. No way he pitched and wrote ten thousand thoroughly researched words in one week."

"No, Caitlin, he didn't—"

"Sonofabitch." Once again, Caitlin didn't need Lawton to fill in the blanks. "The owner is one of the three-states guys, isn't he? And Deets is his, what, copywriter? Jesus, at least tell me the article will have a *Paid Advertisement* warning on the header."

"You'll still get paid, Bergman."

She sat back. "Why wouldn't I? What are you trying to say?"

"Nothing. I don't know anything."

"That's the truth."

"No, I mean I have no idea what's going to happen. I don't know how much longer I'll have a job, let alone anyone else. You're young, you have options."

"I'm forty-three, Stan."

"Younger than me, and smart enough to play the game if you want to stay employed. Hell, I've got an idea or two you can knock out over the phone in time for this issue."

Caitlin threw her head back and let out a groan.

Lawton threw his hands up. "Fine, pitch me something less—"

"Meaningful?"

He sighed. "You're a hell of a writer, Bergman, but it is what it is. Now if you'll excuse me, I have an interview."

He nodded toward the exit. The young woman from his phone's screen waited near the hostess stand.

"We're hiring writers for the social media team. In fact, if you know anyone—"

"Sure." Worse than a May–December affair, Stan was hiring entry-level social masturbators weeks after laying off seasoned wordsmiths. Caitlin grabbed a nonmangled roll and a handful of butter packs, then climbed out of the booth. "I'll tell every kid I know you're looking for someone to cover the end of journalism, as long as they can fit it into two hundred and eighty characters."

CHAPTER

4

LAKSHMI STRAINED TO be heard over the dive bar's jukebox, another seventies tune, something by the piano guy who did the music from the *Lion King*. "Then I had to edit the whole piece again—for the fifth time. He's really a perfectionist."

The dark Hollywood bar smelled like fried foods and beer spilled so long ago that Marilyn Monroe could have stepped in it.

She watched Caitlin take another sip of her rum and Diet Coke. They'd been there since eight thirty, and Caitlin's rant about her homeless piece had subsided around nine. Lakshmi'd filled the last fifteen minutes venting about her own boss across town at NPR.

Finally, Caitlin replied, "But you're enjoying it, right? You're learning?"

"Not as much as I'd learn working with you."

She watched Caitlin consciously stop an eye roll, then politely glance toward the busy bar.

Too much. Don't scare the woman away.

Lakshmi cherished their semimonthly mentorship nights. Not only did they take place in Caitlin's favorite LA haunts, usually over greasy bar food or neighborhood taco trucks, but she got to absorb as much as possible of the woman's day-to-day life as a journalist. She grabbed one of the last french fries from the basket between them and tried to play it cool.

"Honestly, I spend most of my days showing David how to use his iPhone, not contributing to the stories in any meaningful way."

Caitlin smiled and nodded but seemed far away, hopefully still lost in her work BS, not annoyed. Lakshmi knew her own reputation. More than once in her twenty-three years she'd been labeled as *clingy, overwhelming,* or her personal favorite, *a lot.* Plus, there was the way she and Caitlin had met.

Two years back, as a student at Caitlin's alma mater, Indiana University, Lakshmi'd all but forced her to look into the disappearance of Angela Chapman, almost costing Caitlin her life. Still, when Lakshmi had reached out for a reference before moving to LA, Caitlin had given her a glowing recommendation, practically walking her into her current position at NPR. Maybe she was worrying too much.

Or should she say something?

She'd say something.

But what should she—

"You need to know the real world is going to suck sometimes," Caitlin said, stopping Lakshmi's runaway train of thought. "Bosses, assignments—"

"Paychecks," Lakshmi chimed in. Her current position paid about the same as the In-N-Out Burger down the street from her apartment.

Caitlin laughed. "Especially paychecks. But when the work really matters . . ."

She looked away without finishing her sentence. Lakshmi tried to follow her gaze. The best she could tell, Caitlin's focus fell somewhere between the jukebox and a dartboard, then settled on the lit flame of the red candleholder in the middle of their table.

Lakshmi's own eyes paused elsewhere, noticing a blonde with a pixie cut two tables away, the same girl who'd smiled at her from across the bar half an hour earlier. Any other night and she'd make an excuse to say hi, but she wasn't going to waste her Caitlin time trying to get laid.

"When the work really matters . . . what, Caitlin?"

Caitlin's eyes snapped upward, and she drummed the tabletop with both hands. "I gotta pee. Order us another round on my tab."

Lakshmi sat up straight. "Of drinks or fries?"

"Use your best judgment. Mine's off the rails right now."

Caitlin slid out of the booth and pushed her way through the crowded bar.

Lakshmi shook her head. *Bugger. I've scared her away.*

As insurance, she waved to their waitress and doubled down on both alcohol and fries. The times she'd been lucky enough to spend with Caitlin, Lakshmi'd never seen the woman abandon her favorite things.

She drained the last sip of her gin and tonic, then reached for her phone, partly to check for breaking news but mostly to not look lonely in a bar. What did people even do before mobile devices? In a small victory, the jukebox switched to a tune ingrained in her soul since birth. First, the Celtic-style fiddle intro, then the bass guitar kicking in with the beat—Lakshmi couldn't help but bounce along to *Come on Eileen.*

No sooner had Kevin Rowland started to lament a man named Johnnie Ray than Lakshmi was caught singing the lyrics out loud by Little Miss Pixie Cut.

"Someone likes oldies," the woman said, sliding into Caitlin's spot.

Lakshmi guessed five years older than her, maybe twenty-eight. She raised a finger. "First of all, Dexys Midnight Runners qualifies as eighties music, not oldies."

"I wasn't talking about the song," Pixie Cut said, "and you have a gorgeous accent. Where are you from?"

Though the timing was off, Lakshmi didn't mind the attention. She could play along until Caitlin returned. "Like the lads singing the lovely music you're interrupting, I'm a Brummie."

Pixie Cut looked confused. "What's a—"

"Birmingham, England." Lakshmi stressed her syllables in an exaggerated vocal caricature of someone from the West Midlands. Technically, her Indian-born father had moved her from the United Kingdom to Connecticut at the age of ten and the only Brummie slang she knew was from the internet, but American girls loved an accent and Caitlin was taking a while. "My name's Lakshmi Anjale. What's yours?"

5

C AITLIN PUSHED THROUGH the crowded bar to the back hallway's row of unisex bathrooms and waited for an opening. Her urge to use the restroom wasn't the only thing keeping her from the table. She knew Lakshmi was wasted in her position at National Public Radio, and even with the current situation at the paper, Caitlin could get the girl in the door with a one-line email. Hell, she'd be perfect for Lawton's social media position. But working in the same office would mean daily contact, not weekly, and Lakshmi was—

A bathroom door opened, and the right word wafted to mind— *intense.*

Caitlin took a deep breath and went in. Not the worst she'd seen, but definitely a multiple-layers-of-protective-tissue-over-the-flimsy-seat-cover situation. She lowered her pants and relaxed, scrolling through articles on her phone, but not really reading. Who was she to give a recent college graduate advice? She liked the girl but didn't know where her own career would be in a year, let alone the industry.

Her phone buzzed in her hand, knocking her thoughts back to the present but leaving her fingers somewhere else. She snapped her legs together, narrowly saving the falling device from a bath in the communal bowl, but like Stan Lawton hours earlier, moved too slow to prevent contact with the sticky floor.

"How's that for karma," she said, grabbing a wad of toilet paper and picking up the phone with two fingers. The incoming caller ID read

Coos County, Oregon. Caitlin swiped at the screen and answered in speaker mode.

"You've reached the one and only Caitlin Bergman."

"Miss Bergman," a male voice said, competing with the muffled noise from the bar's sound system. "This is Sheriff Boswell Martin in Coos County, Oregon."

Caitlin spoke loudly while wiping the screen. "Oregon? What'd I do now?"

She turned off the speaker option and held the possibly contagious handset to her ear. The phone didn't make her sick to her stomach, but the words coming through did the job.

* * *

She walked back toward the table, saw a young short-haired blonde next to Lakshmi. The pair looked perfectly happy sharing a fresh basket of fries. Caitlin changed directions, walked to the bar, and ordered a new drink.

"Hiya, Caitlin." Lakshmi left the booth and met her at the bar. "I have another drink at the table."

"I didn't want to interrupt. Who's your friend?"

Lakshmi smiled. "No idea. She came over the second you left, asked if you were my girl."

When Caitlin met Lakshmi in Indiana, the young woman had only recently come out. Now, in the liberal safety of the West Coast, Lakshmi embraced her sexual identity with pride.

"Better than asking if I was your mom, I guess."

"I wish." Lakshmi broke into a blush, but not because of anything romantic. Caitlin knew the girl had lost her mother early in a car accident. Lakshmi touched Caitlin's wrist. "I'll get her number and tell her to get lost. Come back to the table."

Caitlin took a sip of her new drink, anything to get the acidic taste out of her mouth. "I should get going."

"Wait, what's wrong? Is it about the article? I thought 'the real world is going to suck sometimes.'"

"I got a call," Caitlin said, spitting the words out fast, like time might give them more power than they deserved. "My mother's dead."

"Oh, Caitlin. I'm so sorry, but I thought . . ." The look on Lakshmi's face was more confusion than concern. "Why did I think your mother was already dead?"

Caitlin blew out a rum-flavored sigh. "Because that's what I tell everyone."

* * *

Not many therapists answered the phone at two thirty in the morning, but Scott picked up on the second ring.

"Just getting in?" He sounded unfazed and perfectly pleasant. Even if she'd been next to him in the Midwest, three hours ahead, Caitlin couldn't imagine being chipper at five thirty AM.

"Something like that. Sorry if I'm waking you, Scott. I didn't think you'd pick up."

She reclined on the somewhat-made side of her bed, careful to keep her boots off her comforter. The second her rideshare driver dropped her off at home, she'd smoked pot on her porch, but she still hadn't removed a single article of clothing.

"You know a great deal about the world," Scott said, his gentle smile obvious in his voice, "but apparently very little about seventy-two-year-old men. I've been up for forty-five minutes."

Even though she'd just burned through a bowl of West Hollywood's stinkiest legal weed, Scott's response brought Caitlin's first smile in an hour. She adjusted a pillow and sat up. "Still, you'll want to bill me double. This is a big one."

"I'll send an invoice today."

That was their joke. Technically, Scott Canton had retired from psychology decades ago. A Vietnam vet turned Black Panther, then social worker, then psychologist, then—in the least likely transition (or most likely, according to him)—poetry professor, Scott claimed as his current patients only a handful of veterans of Afghanistan and Iraq turned college students, and Caitlin, who'd had Scott as a teacher in undergrad. There had never been a dollar exchanged between them and never would be.

"So, my friend," he continued, "tell me what you couldn't tell your bartender this evening."

Caitlin kicked her boots off and onto the floor. Judging from the series of thumps, she'd knocked over one of her many stacks of books. "Maya Aronson is dead."

"I see." Scott said nothing else for a bit.

Caitlin reached for the plastic cup on her bedside table. Sadly, no water remained from the previous night. She tossed the cup toward her bedroom door. If she tripped on it later, she'd have to take it to the kitchen, which meant she'd probably wash it. "Did you hear what I said—"

"I'm very sorry for your loss," he interrupted, all sincerity. Scott was one of the few people who'd known that Caitlin's mother was still alive—or had been. "Tell me what happened."

She gave him the limited details: a woman's body had been found in a remote forest near the Oregon coast, and *associated documentation*—the sheriff had been vague about the meaning of the term—indicated that the deceased had a daughter named Caitlin Bergman.

"So you've reached the stage," Scott said. "No more parents."

Caitlin sighed. "No family at all, which is fine by me. Less disappointment all around."

"Bullshit." The man rarely swore outside his poetry.

If they'd have been in the same room, she'd have mimed clutching pearls. "Oh my, Professor Canton, such language."

"Family is what you make it, young lady. Don't have blood relations? Consult a list of people who answer the phone before the sunrise."

"I didn't mean—"

"There's your friend Mary, Mike Roman, Lakshmi—if you'd let her get close—"

His list continued and included some names she didn't remember ever mentioning to him. Not bad for someone she didn't pay.

"You're right, Scott, obviously, but you know what I mean. Now there's no one on earth who knows who my father is."

"Matthew Bergman was your father."

"Adopted."

"So what?"

"I still want to know—" Caitlin started, looking around the mess of her room and settling on a bookshelf where the cover of a mass-market paperback held together with rubber bands and tape showed a boy and a girl walking through the woods. "You don't get it. You're not adopted."

He laughed, but his tone carried a fair amount of fire. "White people are always talking about their lineage. You know, large subsets of American society were forced to make do without the benefit of a well-documented family tree."

"Fair point, but I still want to know who my birth father was."

"Not where your birth mother's been for all these years?"

Caitlin bit a jagged corner off the nail of her ring finger. "Well—"

"Or why she gave you up for adoption in the first place?"

She spit the bit of nail toward her window. "I mean, I guess I'd be interested . . . sort of."

Scott laughed again, this time clearly back to his smiling self. "If only you knew someone who had investigative skills."

Caitlin rolled her neck and shoulders. Her head hit the wall above her headboard with a thud. "It's not a great time to go up to Nowhere, Oregon. A reporter who's not on call is almost the same as a reporter who isn't needed anymore. I shouldn't be leaving work."

"Oh my darling," Scott started—one of the few men Caitlin would allow to call her *darling, honey,* or *angel.* "How good at your job do you think you'll be if the need to understand your mother—"

"I don't need to understand my mother—"

"Then don't try," he continued, "but it might feel good to tell her how you feel face-to-face, even if she can't reply. You won't be able to do that once the body is returned to the dust from whence it came."

Caitlin smiled at the idea of finally launching into the speech she'd rehearsed every year on her birthday. Neither rum nor weed had helped, but fifteen minutes on the phone with Scott had her convinced she was ready for bed, or at least motivated to change clothes and find a toothbrush. "I don't care what anyone says, Scott, you're pretty good at this."

"I try. Maybe take a friend along in case it gets emotional. How's your noble Roman?"

"Mike? He's off the radar. Well, in Mexico for a bit. I don't expect him soon."

"Perhaps young Lakshmi?"

"I've got this," Caitlin said, less bothered by the idea of Lakshmi tagging along than by how the young woman might view her mentor after hearing the torrent of obscenities she'd held back since birth. "All by myself."

"Of course you do. Call me when you get there."

Less than a minute after hanging up, Caitlin emailed Stan Lawton that she'd be gone over the weekend due to a family emergency. The next day, she paid way too much to fly into Portland, Oregon, rented a car, then drove south for three hours down the 5 freeway before turning onto a state road that wound along the Coquille River. She passed clumps of trailer homes and cinder-block churches scattered around tiny towns named more for function than vanity—Tenmile, Remote, Bridge—before arriving in the city of Coquille, the county seat of Coos County, Oregon.

CHAPTER

6

CAITLIN HAD SPENT forty-three years wondering if she'd recognize her own features in her birth mother's face. Would they share the same brown eyes, detached earlobes, or narrow lips? Had Mama Maya been responsible for her inability to roll her tongue or sit cross-legged? She ventured another look at the remains on the medical examiner's table, exposed only from the neck up, but saw nothing familiar. Jagged white chunks jutted from the distorted remnants of a mouth at unnatural angles.

"What happened to her teeth?" Caitlin said, her voice raised to compete with the whir of high-speed exhaust fans. The room smelled clinical, but hints of decomposition sneaked past the Vicks VapoRub she'd dabbed into each nostril. "Half are gone, and the rest . . . did something—"

"Probably knocked out with a rock," Sheriff Martin answered. The stocky fifty-year-old with the barrel chest carried himself like a bulldog, but his full gray goatee gave her the impression of a standoffish bear, wise and wary from surviving more than a few scrapes.

Caitlin looked past the sheriff and the corpse to the medical examiner, a box-dyed blonde near her own age who hadn't said a word since they'd entered the room. "Shouldn't there be bruising around the lips and the nose, then?"

The woman's latex gloves brushed against her scrubs with the forceful crossing of her arms. "Is she one of them, Boz? You know how I feel."

Caitlin had met the pair only fifteen minutes ago but could tell they had history. "One of what? A reporter? I cannot tell a lie. I am indeed an agent of the press."

The woman ignored her. "I won't help one of those dogs."

Martin held up a hand. "Leslie, if you can't maintain a professional—"

"Maintain this." The examiner left the room, the door swishing softly behind her loud exit.

Martin turned back to Caitlin. "Sorry about that. People around here aren't exactly comfortable with your mother's religious group."

Caitlin laughed. "You don't have Jews in Oregon?"

The sheriff blinked twice, started to say something, then stopped. Caitlin wasn't sure if his awkward reaction meant confusion or embarrassment. He jumped back in before she could decide.

"I understand it may be difficult, but do you recognize this person as your mother, Miss Bergman?"

Caitlin took another glance. The dead woman's hair, gray and beyond shoulder length, looked naturally straight like her own, but what did hair matter?

"Sorry, can't say."

He took the answer like he'd seen it coming. "How about tattoos or distinguishing marks?"

"She should have a pink clover-shaped birthmark on the back of her arm."

A long sigh escaped the sheriff's lips. "Excuse me for a moment."

He walked out the same door the medical examiner had taken.

Alone, Caitlin reached into her bag and pulled out the *Bitch Book*, a crumbling paperback whose real title, *She Taught Me to Fly*, she'd abandoned in her teens. Year after year she'd transformed the once-sappy coming-of-age tale into a journal of every word she'd ever wanted to say, scream, or punch at her mother, leaving a pulpy mess of multicolored pen strokes and torn pages behind. Peeling a rubber band off the well-worn cover, she ignored the slight tremble in her fingers and flipped to the page she'd dog-eared on her thirteenth birthday. She didn't need to read the words scribbled in blue pen between the lines of the publisher's original text. The angry cursive scrawl still came to her in dreams, but the moment required a formal presentation.

Or always had in her mind.

Now she wasn't even sure that the dead woman was Maya Aronson. She contemplated a peek under the beige drop cloth. Instead, her eyes drifted down to the only other exposed bit of skin: the feet.

The days of toe tags, gone. Someone had wrapped a plastic label, similar to a luggage tag, around the woman's ankle.

UD-0004.

Caitlin deciphered the code easily enough: the year's fourth *Unidentified Decedent.*

The door swung open and the medical examiner burst back into the room, followed by the sheriff.

"Not that it matters," she said, holding up her gloved hands, "but which side is the hemangioma on?"

Caitlin tucked the *Bitch Book* back into her satchel. "Hemangioma?"

The ME slipped her hands under the drop cloth. "Birthmark."

"The right," Caitlin said. "Why wouldn't it matter?"

Rather than answering, the ME shifted the body, exposing the bare backside.

"You could have warned the woman, Leslie." Martin stepped in front of Caitlin's view. "This body was found in the woods. Only a few days ago, but animals, insects, and weather—"

"I get it," Caitlin said, brushing him aside with confidence, then immediately wishing she hadn't. Patches of skin were missing from both of the dead woman's upper arms and lower back, and not from surgical precision. Any remnant of the cloverlike blotch of pink Caitlin had expected to see had been scraped to the bone. A quick rush of bile flooded her mouth. She swallowed hard and looked down toward the woman's waist, stopping at the hands. Neither had fingertips past the knuckles.

She stepped back, turned away, and took two quick breaths. "Wow, I get it now."

"Get what?" Martin said. "Is this your mother, Miss Bergman?"

Caitlin faced the man with a smile on her face. "I have no idea. I also have no idea why you called me. You obviously don't know this woman's name. So why did I fly from Los Angeles to Oregon to look at this dead body?"

7

CAITLIN TOOK A Kleenex from the sheriff's receptionist and blew the menthol from her nose. The medical examiner, district attorney, and sheriff's department shared the same building, so the walk hadn't taken long enough to get the smell of formaldehyde and decomposition out of her nostrils, or the sight of the poor woman's face out of her mind.

Sheriff Martin, a few steps ahead, waited by the open door to his office. "You mind the smell of pine?"

Caitlin looked around the department and saw a handful of deputies at desks, all looking up from their work. "Who doesn't like pine?" she said with a smile, entering his office and taking a chair.

Martin closed the door behind him, pulled a lighter from his pocket, and lit the kind of candle-in-a-jar the mall stores sold during the holidays. The pine worked on the scent in Caitlin's nose, but the image in her mind lingered. To clear it, she focused on the two flags displayed in frames on the wall behind the sheriff. She recognized Oregon's state flag but had never seen the other: a green rectangle with a gold circle and black lettering spelling out *THE GREAT SEAL OF STATE OF JEFFERSON* around two black Xs.

Caitlin pointed to the second flag. "Tell me about the State of Jefferson."

Martin let a small chuckle escape and took the chair behind his desk. "Technically, you're in it right now."

"As in?"

"It's a long story that has nothing to do with the reason you're here, but I'll give you the short version. In 1941, there was a movement to try to make a new state out of Northern California and Southern Oregon. They had some traction, but then the Japanese bombed Pearl Harbor and the whole thing fell apart."

Caitlin thought of the story going up in place of her homelessness piece in Los Angeles. "So the movement's over?"

Martin shifted his head to the side. "Now it's more of a feeling the people around here share. We're too far from Salem and Sacramento to get any attention, and we don't have a lot in common with the folks in Portland or San Francisco."

Caitlin laughed. "Or Los Angeles, I'm guessing."

Martin moved some papers away from his computer keyboard, knocking over a stack of glossy flyers. "That flag is just a gag the boys gave me. Now, about the body you were unable to identify."

"What's a 'dog,' Sheriff? I'm guessing your medical examiner wasn't talking about man's best friend."

"Call me Boz. Everyone around here does."

He held up one of the fallen flyers, showing his smiling face under the words *Re-elect Boz Martin, the Patriot's Sheriff.*

"Okay, Boz. What's a 'dog'?"

"Sorry about that, but Leslie's got a reason. Her daughter Lily went off with the Daughters of God two years ago, hence the 'Dogs.' They're also known as the Dayans."

"So they're a religious group?"

"They're a damned cult. Coos County has the same problems everybody else in Oregon deals with. We've got opioids, meth, spousal abuse, and drunk driving, but the Daughters of God are this area's local oddity. They moved here in the nineties, bought a bunch of overlogged land in the hills, and basically stayed up there. Unless they've pissed somebody off, most people don't even know they're here."

Caitlin remembered the tag and barcode around the woman's ankle. "And you think this dead woman was a member?"

"I have no idea, but ever since Leslie's daughter left her, she leans that way on any Jane Doe. We won't know until we make a positive ID, but the decedent was in her midsixties, and no woman of that age is missing within the surrounding counties. Does that match your mother's age?"

Caitlin double-checked the math in her head. "Maya should be sixty-five, but why do you think it's her? When we talked on the phone, you mentioned associated documentation."

Martin looked over at the door like someone might interrupt them, then leaned in. "We found a key."

"With the body?"

He glanced toward the exit again, then in the opposite direction toward the window looking out into the parking lot, before finally settling on his hands. He wasn't afraid of being interrupted. He was afraid of the words he had to say.

"In the body."

Caitlin slid onto the edge of her seat. "Inside the body?"

The sheriff looked up, embarrassed but able to meet her eyes. "Rectum."

Caitlin let a single, harsh laugh escape. "Nearly killed him."

Martin's eyes opened a mile.

"Or should I say *her*," Caitlin continued. "Nearly *wrecked her*. Of course, then the joke doesn't work, does it? Nearly *wrecked 'im*?"

The man's mouth drooped a bit, unsure which way to curl. Not everyone got her sense of humor.

"It's a coping mechanism," she said, snapping her fingers, then folding her hands in her lap. "Please continue. What did this keister key open?"

"A safety deposit box in a bank in Coos Bay."

"And what was in the safety deposit box?"

Martin scratched his temple. "Now that's where it gets weird."

"Weirder than a key in the butt?"

Again, the sheriff's face didn't know how to react. Caitlin wasn't sure she did either.

She sat up straight and aimed for professional. "Again, sorry. I know a woman is dead here, and this is obviously a tragedy. I'm dealing with something complicated. Actually, everything to do with my mother is complicated. I'll save my shtick for my therapist."

She cleared her throat and waved him on. Five seconds to a lifetime later, he continued.

"We know which bank it corresponds to, and the bank knows which box it opens. Your name is the only designated beneficiary, and you're listed as *daughter*."

That explained why he'd called her in the first place but not much else. "Well, you don't need me to open it. You got a search warrant and drilled it open, right?"

"Without a positive ID of this woman's body, we can't serve a warrant on the box. The owner's name matches a bank account but was from a fake ID. That is to say, it was opened more than two decades ago using what appeared to be a valid California driver's license, before they'd added the scannable magnetic stripe."

Caitlin sat back in her chair. That didn't sound quite right. "But I can open it?"

The sheriff nodded. "Because you're a beneficiary."

Another objection wanted to step forward, but Caitlin held back. Judging from the omission of any of this information over their original phone call, she could tell the sheriff wanted her there for a reason he wasn't ready to share. Of course, she'd failed to mention that she had no idea if she'd be able to identify Maya Aronson, dead or alive. They were both fishing. Time to see who had bigger bait. "What was the name on the account?"

"Sharon Sugar."

The name landed in Caitlin's stomach like a mouthful of worms. "That was her stage name."

"Her what?"

She reached into her bag. "My birth mother, Maya Aronson, gave me up for adoption in her twenties to follow an illustrious career in the adult entertainment industry, where she performed all kinds of acts under a stage name, most often Sharon Sugar. This would have been in the late seventies, early eighties."

She pulled out her worn paperback, flipped through the dog-eared pages until she got to a picture kept in place by two solid paper clips, then handed the sheriff a screenshot blown up from a video. After all these years, she didn't need to look at the photo to describe the all-natural topless brunette with big, curly hair in the style of the day. This particular image revealed a bright-pink birthmark on the back of the subject's right arm.

"I'm fairly certain this was her."

Martin studied the photo, then picked up another from his desk, a still taken of the corpse in the other room.

"Doesn't help much, does it, Sheriff?"

"Boz," he said, again. "You're not entirely sure?"

"Boz. I assume you'll want some blood or a swab."

Martin's eyes lingered on the photo. "We'll have to send your sample to the state lab, but that should take care of matters." He returned to her. "You haven't seen your mother since your birth?"

"Not in person. And from that angle, I don't really remember anything pretty."

Martin finally laughed.

Caitlin continued. "Of course, I looked her up from time to time. I think she left the industry in '85, was arrested in San Francisco in '89, then again in '90, back in LA. Possession, then DUI. Nothing after that."

Martin set the photos down. "Maybe what's in the safety deposit box will give you some closure."

"Maybe." Caitlin returned the photo to the *Bitch Book* and refastened its rubber bands. What would closure even look like? A photo album full of pictures of Caitlin taken throughout the years from a stalker's distance? Enough cash to quit work, maybe buy the *LA Voice* out from under the current regime? The name and location of her birth father? Regardless, the return flight she'd booked didn't head home until the next afternoon. "How far away is Coos Bay?"

CHAPTER

8

SHERIFF MARTIN OFFERED a ride in his SUV, but Caitlin opted to follow in the relative silence of her bright-green rental pickup. It wasn't that she minded the company of strangers—she'd never had a problem making small talk—but Los Angeles rarely provided a winding country road with little to no traffic through beautiful woodlands, and the size of the pickup meant she could look down on all the other cars like a god.

Twenty minutes later, they arrived in the town of Coos Bay, a picturesque isthmus dividing the Pacific Ocean from the namesake bay on the east. Rolling past fifty-foot piles of bucked and limbed Douglas fir trees outside more than one sawmill, Caitlin noticed they'd turned onto the 101, the same road that ran from Hollywood all the way to Seattle.

Like at home, signs advertised familiar fast food and coffee, but the tugboats and trawlers docked along the bay and the mom-and-pop shops offering fresh fish-and-chips reminded Caitlin more of New England.

The buildings, from single-story shopping centers to multistory office classics, had a built-in-1926-refinished-in-1980 feel, all weathered by rain and time. Caitlin counted several bar and grills lit by neon Pabst and Miller Lite logos, but the presence of sushi, Thai, and multiple Mexican places surprised her.

They turned past a two-story building whose white brick walls had been covered by three giant photo panels of Olympic runner Steve

Prefontaine. She was no Olympian, but Caitlin made a mental note to include the area in a future run, then shook her head. In her haste to pack, she'd left her running shoes behind.

The sheriff took a side street to a bank parking lot. Like the streets around the restaurants, the lot offered plenty of available spots. She took the space next to the sheriff's SUV and followed him to the door, where a uniformed officer from the Coos Bay Police Department waited. Martin introduced the man, who'd walked down from the city's station house, but Caitlin could tell the meeting was a matter of interdepartmental courtesy and neighborly friendship. After a bit of small talk, the officer walked back to his station and they entered the bank.

"Technically, I don't have a right to be there when you open the box," the sheriff said, after a teller had gone to retrieve the safety deposit container. "Since I haven't gotten a warrant, everything in that box is considered your private property."

Caitlin shook her head. "I want you around in case there's a mouthful of teeth and fingertips in this thing."

The teller returned and directed them into the safety deposit box vault. A long metal container sat on the table in the center of the room. Sheriff Martin opened a duffle bag and pulled out a camera, latex gloves, a handful of empty evidence bags, and one already-labeled Ziploc with a single key inside.

He turned on the camera and took a test shot. "Better glove up."

Caitlin wriggled her fingers into a pair of disposable gloves, pulled the key out of the bag, and slid it into place.

Martin raised the camera, hit record, and dictated the time, location, parties present, and a full disclaimer that he was there by Caitlin's permission.

Caitlin turned the key, took a deep breath, and touched the lid. "Let's see what's behind that dead woman's door number two."

She pushed the panel back and up.

No bats flew out, no overwhelming stench made her retch, no golden gleam made her avert her eyes.

"Huh," she said, underwhelmed.

Martin leaned over her shoulder. "So what is in the box?"

Caitlin reached for the first items. "Two California driver's licenses, both expired in 1998. The first would probably be how the account was opened." She handed him a faded plastic card with the name *Sharon Sugar*. "The other"—she paused and cleared her throat—"for Maya Aronson."

The faded photo showed the same face as the picture she'd given the sheriff, but here the woman was nearer Caitlin's current age, in her early forties. Instead of the made-up starlet of the adult video, Caitlin found herself looking at a carnival mirror image of herself. Maybe not the nose, but the eyes and the lips definitely came from the same family tree.

Martin handed her an open evidence bag. "Sorry."

"It's fine." Caitlin placed the licenses into the bag, then reached for the next item, a black spiral notebook. "Okay, this looks like a journal or diary."

She perused the contents. Handwritten entries followed dates. Definitely a journal.

Martin reached out. "If you don't mind, I'd like to requisition this notebook as part of a related investigation."

Again, the distinctions the sheriff was making between relevant evidence and Caitlin's property felt unusual. Despite the hair rising on the back of her neck, she nodded and handed it over. "As long as I get a copy."

"Of course," he said. "Just as soon as my forensics team checks it out."

Martin bagged the notebook, and Caitlin reached for the final item, a letter-sized envelope.

"Oh," escaped her lips. She shook her head, staring at the name written on the outside. "This is addressed to me."

It didn't feel like a pile of cash, nor a detailed photo scrapbook, but for the first time since her teens, Caitlin actually had a piece of communication directly from Mama Maya. Maybe there was such a thing as closure.

Suddenly aware of her mouth going dry, she opened the unsealed envelope and pulled out a trifolded piece of paper. Trembling, she straightened out the lined notebook paper and read the words to herself.

Caitlin,

I'm sorry this is the first letter I've ever written to you. Well, sent. I've written so many but never dared to bother you. Most of them said the same thing. I'm proud of who you have become and ashamed of who I was.

If you're reading this, I'm dead. Which means I made another wrong choice.

I trusted someone to be true.

They obviously weren't.

And you're the only one who might care.

The townspeople hate us.

The police can't be trusted.

The Daughters have been misled, and either the Light has gone out, or the Cataclysm awaits.

I can't count the mistakes I've made in my life. There are too many. The only good thing I ever did was to leave you with Matt. And maybe what I'm doing now. Maybe what I'm doing now will count when the names are read.

Though I have no right, I love you, daughter.

Be stronger than me, my crystalline bird.

Find the Five.

* * *

She watched Martin read the letter before placing it in with the rest of the box's contents. "What are 'the Five,' Sheriff?"

"What's that, Miss Bergman?"

"The letter mentioned 'the Five.' Any idea what that means?"

Martin shook his head. "Your guess is as good as mine. I don't know a lot about Dayan dogma."

"So what happens now?"

"You said your mother has a record. If we get any prints from the box, we'll match them up. Of course, unless we get DNA that matches our victim—"

Caitlin understood. "You still won't know for sure—legally, that is—that the victim is my mom. You'll need my DNA."

The sheriff already had a sealed tube in his hand. "If you would be so kind, swab this around your mouth."

Caitlin broke the seal, ran the sponge on a stick around her gums and cheek, then gave the sample back. "How soon will you know?"

"This has to go up to Springfield. Not sure how long it'll take them."

"Even though it's a murder?"

He cocked his head to one side. "If it was a murder."

For the briefest of moments, Caitlin wondered just how far her jaw could drop. "The woman's missing her teeth and fingertips."

Martin glanced away and broke down the camera gear. "True, but the cause of death was a blow to the back of the head. There's a lot of high drop-offs in these parts, lot of ravines. We might be looking at an accident—or even suicide."

Caitlin assumed the sheriff had heard the sound of her eyes bugging out of her head, because he turned back her way.

"I said *might*. Obviously, whoever messed with the body didn't want her identified, but that could mean anything. We're looking at all of the options. I'll let you know when we've got something."

More red flags than a communist parade went up in Caitlin's head. She didn't get the feeling Martin was a bad man, but she could tell he wanted nothing to do with the body found in the woods. But if that was the case, why bother calling her at all? And why was he handling this himself rather than delegating it to a deputy?

"Fine," she said. "When can I get a copy of the letter and the journal?"

"I can have them scanned by Monday and get you a downloadable link."

"And the originals? I'm old-school, Boz. I like to hold a book in my hands."

Caitlin watched him chew the answer over. Personal effects of murder victims typically stayed in evidence lockers until convictions were made. His treatment of the journal would indicate his seriousness about the investigation.

He snapped his hard-shell camera case closed. "Once we make the positive identification and get this whole nasty incident wrapped up, I'll make sure to mail it your way."

For a county sheriff, the man knew how to say as little as possible.

Caitlin walked toward the doorway, then reached for the bars of the open metal door that provided a second layer of protection behind the massive circular vault entry. As she slid one hand down the cold steel, her thoughts worked like busy little beavers, sending her into her tunnel.

Was she going to wait for a lab report on a sponge full of spit to find out what happened to her mother—as in, the biggest question of her forty-some years on earth?

Sheriff Martin didn't seem to give a damn, and Caitlin figured any attempt to learn about Mama Maya through fellow cult members would be an uphill climb. Plus, she had to make a decision about work soon: whether to stay and watch her beloved *Voice* slide into the world of biased propaganda or to kiss ass through her address book to find employment at some other soon-to-fail publication. That kind of big-ticket life-altering direction change would require a solid week of organizing her closets, painting the kitchen, alphabetizing the bookshelves, and every other variation of procrastination she'd prefer over making the call.

As logical and realistic as those nagging real-world points were, Caitlin knew they'd already lost to one stupid line from the letter.

Be stronger than me, my crystalline bird.

Back from the depths of her tunnel, she cleared her throat. "Save the cloud and print me a real copy. I'll still be in town."

Martin zipped his bag and stood up straight. "You'll still—"

"I've got some time before I need to get home. I'll reschedule my flight, find a hotel, and look around the state of Jefferson."

Normally Caitlin opted for a local bed-and-breakfast when on the road, but a low-budget name-brand place on the edge of the bay offered rooms for sixty bucks a night. Confident she could find something nicer if her trip turned into an extended stay, she checked in, threw her suitcase in the room, then walked to a downtown bar with a banner advertising happy-hour drink specials.

One cocktail and a plate of decent fish-and-chips later, Caitlin got out her laptop. Five minutes of background searches on the State of Jefferson brought her first smile in hours. Her homeless piece wouldn't make the next issue, but Caitlin knew she could knock out two thousand words about Jefferson that would complement the three-state piece with a few phone calls. She wouldn't change the world, but she might be able to expense her road trip—if Stan made room for the story. She typed up a pitch and shot off an email.

That done, she started down the other rabbit hole and typed *Daughters of God.*

The search, too generic, returned ten pages of results, but nothing referencing a cult.

She thought back to the other name Martin had mentioned, the *Dayans.*

As a Hebrew surname, she discovered, *Dayan* meant *a Jewish religious judge*, but in Sikhism, the word *Daya* meant *suffering in the suffering of all others, a state deeper and more positive in sentiment than sympathy.*

Neither corresponded to a mass-published theism.

What else was there?

Maya Aronson's letter mentioned *the Light* and *the Five*. Caitlin fought back a laugh. What religion didn't include light or numerology?

As in the bank, only one line in the woman's note carried any significance.

Be stronger than me, my crystalline bird.

"Screw you," Caitlin said, loud enough to turn the heads of the two guys at the only other occupied table in the place.

She held up her hand. "Sorry, my computer did a thing."

The men went back to their beers. Caitlin got the waitress's attention, ordered another drink, and tried not to think about the only other written message she'd ever gotten from her birth mother. The candles of her thirteenth birthday cake burned bright despite the years.

*   *   *

"What's this, a book?" she asked her dad, feeling the give in the only one of her presents wrapped with brown paper. She'd already opened the gift she'd really wanted, a new Sony Walkman cassette player. Better than the other models, this one had a built-in microphone that would let her record audio, like the reporters on TV.

"You'll make detective before I do, Slugger." Her father scratched his ear like he did when he had something uncomfortable to say.

Caitlin looked the package over. "Another Chandler? Or maybe MacDonald? I like how he writes women."

That got him to smile. "Why couldn't it be the new Sue Grafton?"

"Too thin to be a modern mystery," she said. "Feels flimsy, like decadent pulp."

He turned his blue Dodgers cap around. With the hat and his cop moustache, now the bushiest it'd been in years, her dad had a real Kirk Gibson thing going. Most of the men in the city did; the Dodgers were two games from the World Series. "What else do you see?"

She flipped the package over and found the paper barely held together by two lonely pieces of tape. She met her dad's eyes. "You didn't wrap this."

He reached for his pack of Marlboros, lit a fresh one. "Why do you say that? *Show your work.* You know, like you refuse to do in math class."

"The math in my class is so easy only idiots should have to show their work."

"You're a middle-schooler who does calculus for extra credit and never makes a mistake, Caitie. Your teacher thinks you're cheating."

"That dinosaur doesn't believe women are capable of reasoning. You're not like him, are you, Dad?"

He held his hands up in surrender. "Come on, genius. Let's hear some reasoning."

"Fine." She tapped on the package. "This is not your style. I had to cut into the other presents with a knife. This thing will slide open with a fart."

He gave her his best stern-dad eyes. Not the same as his serious on-duty look, because she could always see the smile ready to break free. "Caitie—"

"Sorry." She folded her hands in her lap and sat up straight. "I mean this package would blow open with a gentle summer breeze."

"Better," he said, taking a drag.

"From my butthole."

His laughter interrupted his exhale, and the whole thing turned into a coughing fit. "Oh my sweet girl, save it for your bat mitzvah."

Now she was the one with the serious face. "I thought we agreed I didn't have to do that."

"It's a rite of passage, Caitlin."

"For a religion neither of us follow."

"Being Jewish isn't always about believing in God."

"No, I get it, Dad. I watch *20/20*."

After watching the Israelis arrest Ivan "the Terrible" Demjanjuk—supposedly a notorious former concentration camp guard at Treblinka—in April, Caitlin rarely missed the news. Added bonus: Barbara Walters didn't take shit from anyone.

Rather than continuing the bat mitzvah debate, she went back to the package. "Aunt Rebekah?"

"No," he started. "It would be—"

"Pink. Right."

There weren't a lot of other adults in Caitlin's life at that point. Jane Bergman, her dad's ex-wife, had died in a car accident when Caitlin was seven. Jane had been the woman in her life until just after Caitlin's sixth birthday, when the up-and-coming defense attorney and LAPD officer Matt Bergman got divorced, but she'd never been Caitlin's mommy. Her dad had gone through several girlfriends since, but a single cop with a back-talking daughter living in a two-bedroom Hollywood flat didn't seem to interest the wannabe starlets hopping off buses every day.

"Why don't you open it, Slugger?"

Caitlin let the mystery go, slid her finger inside the loose flap, and unwrapped the paperback.

A boy and a girl walked through the woods under the title *She Taught Me to Fly* by Carol Rusnak.

"This doesn't look like a mystery."

Her dad rubbed his ear again. "Nope."

She flipped open the cover, surprised not to find any handwriting. Her father had written a personal message inside of every book she'd ever owned. "So who sent it?"

He cleared his throat. "Technically, you're a woman today, Caitie."

"Yeah, Dad, I've had my period for over a year."

He held up a hand. "And as a woman, I'm going to ask you to think about this as an adult." He took a final drag of his cigarette, blew out the smoke, and crushed the butt in an ashtray. "This book came from Maya."

Caitlin's cheeks flushed and her throat tightened. "As in *Mama Maya*?"

Her dad nodded.

She hard-swallowed. "So she's alive."

Of course, they'd discussed her birth mother over the years. She'd been told that a young woman, Mama Maya, not equipped with the necessary mothering skills, had given Caitlin's dad the ultimate gift and let him adopt her. The subject wasn't taboo, but it hadn't come up often. Nothing was known about her birth father, as that part of her birth certificate had been left blank.

Her dad cleared his throat again. "We've got a few hours until we meet your girlfriends at Star Lanes. Do you want to talk about anything?"

Caitlin brought the book closer to her chest. "I'm gonna read for a bit."

She took the paperback to her room and shut the door.

Two hours later, her dad came in.

Caitlin looked up, tears in her eyes. "Why would she send this? It's about a jerk who gets his best friend killed."

"I read it, Caitie. I don't think that's what it's about."

She climbed out of her beanbag chair. "No note, no letter, only two sentences underlined in the whole damned book."

She found the dog-eared page with the sentence highlighted in yellow and read. " 'Sitting by her side, he felt no stronger than Jenny's crystalline bird. The slightest bump from any direction, and he'd collapse in front of her, broken into a thousand pieces.' "

She shut the book and showed it to her dad.

"This book was written in 1978, three years after she left me with you. So it's not like it was even her book when she was young."

He nodded, looking over the cover. "Not everyone's as good with words as you are. Maybe Maya was trying to explain why she wasn't ready to be your mother."

Caitlin's fingers formed fists. "She's *not* my mother. I've never even met her."

Her dad looked down, took a breath, then looked back up. "If you could, would you like to?"

He knew where Maya was. Obviously. The package hadn't been mailed, so she'd handed it to him. They might even have spoken.

Had he known the whole thirteen years?

Had Mama Maya been out there, living some happy life without thinking of Caitlin for a single second? She felt another round of tears coming but made a fist and hit the top of her leg. She wasn't going to cry for a woman who couldn't even write a note in a book. She wasn't going to cry at all. Her dad had said it himself: she was a woman now.

"The truth," her dad started, "isn't one thing. It can be scary, no matter what side you're on."

She hit her leg again, harder. "I'm not scared."

The pain felt good, better than the emptiness in her chest, better than the acid in her stomach. Pain she could handle. And wasn't that everything she knew about the world? Even at thirteen, Caitlin knew that to be a woman was to suffer.

Her dad reached for her hand, stopping her before she could punch her other leg. "That's not what I'm trying to say, Caitie. Sometimes it's better to face the truth. It'll come out anyway. Better to get it over with."

"She didn't want to meet me," Caitlin said, pulling her fist out of her father's hands, the emptiness transforming into rage once again. Instead of hitting herself, she reached for a pen and scribbled on the book's cover, changing *She Taught Me to Fly* to *Bitch Book*. "As far as I'm concerned, she can die alone."

*   *   *

Swirling the last bits of ice in her second drink, Caitlin watched the light refract through the melting cubes. Ten minutes earlier, the glass had been full. Time, chemistry, and her own actions had taken their toll.

She reached into her bag once again. Roughly thirty years later, only thin strands of the once-firm binding of that original copy of *She Taught Me to Fly* remained intact. She grabbed a pen and flipped past page after page of text covered by handwriting in multiple colors of pen, finally finding an untouched section of original printed text near the back to write on.

Guess I was right about that whole die-alone thing.

She finished her cocktail, paid her bill, and retreated to her hotel room.

10

S TAN LAWTON REPLIED overnight, approving both the story and three days' worth of reasonable expenses. Caitlin had no problem finding people who wanted to go on record about the State of Jefferson, even on a Saturday morning. By nine AM, she'd eaten a continental breakfast and scheduled two interviews. The first, a phoner with a librarian in Salem, took half an hour and yielded a trove of historical info, both during the call and minutes later via emailed documents. The second, also by phone, saved her a five-hour drive south to Redding, California. Oddly enough, the radio DJ who hosted a weekly show on the subject of merging Southern Oregon with Northern California, opposed the Californian three-state initiative.

"They want to include the Bay Area in Northern California, like we have anything in common with those freaks."

"I'm assuming it's more about the Silicon Valley tax base," Caitlin offered.

"Don't need it. Jefferson can stand on its own—if we get both the northern California counties and Southern Oregon. We care more about freedom than taxation."

The DJ took Caitlin's info, promising to put her in touch with other Jeffersonians. Caitlin thanked him but wasn't sure she needed another source. What she needed was lunch.

She threw together an outfit of yesterday's jeans and a white button-down shirt, rolled up her sleeves, and grabbed her laptop bag.

Cloudless sunshine made the eighty-two degrees feel more like ninety, so Caitlin walked the streets slowly, peeking into storefront windows of antique shops and insurance agencies and then stumbling onto a local microbrewery, which offered far from the standard pub fare she'd expected. She ordered a bowl of roasted root vegetables on a base of pearled barley and two four-ounce samples of beer: a lager and a blond ale.

Back out in the heat, Caitlin regretted her choice of jeans. Rather than heading back to the main drag, she took a side road lined with shade-bearing trees that would get her back to the hotel's air conditioning, passing a sub shop, a tire place, and a barbershop with an old-fashioned red-and-white spinning pole.

Caitlin laughed, got out her phone, snapped a photo, and texted the image to Mary, her college roommate, now dean of a Big Ten journalism school. They'd only recently rekindled their friendship, and the previous talk with Scott had reminded Caitlin that friendship included actually sharing parts of her life on a somewhat regular basis. After spending the last month on the streets with the homeless, she'd certainly been slacking in her own communications department.

She followed the image up with a text.

Not sure if I'm in Oregon or time traveling.

Mary's reply came in seconds.

Either way, looks like you're back on the pole again.

The woman always made her smile.

Caitlin started to move on, but a handwritten sign taped to the glass door made her laugh out loud.

Closed. Too hot to work. You should go home too.

Oregon was growing on her. She snapped two pictures, shielded her phone screen from the sun, then checked which was better. The focus of the first looked soft, so she swiped to the second.

"No way." She put her phone down and turned one hundred and eighty degrees to the shop across the street she'd seen reflected in the glass door of the second photo.

The words *Daya's Gifts—Handmade Articles for the Home and the Spirit* had been hand painted onto the large picture window of an understated single-story storefront.

Her phone beeped with another text from Mary:

Where have you been anyway?

Faced with an opportunity to learn about the Dayans, Caitlin no longer felt the requirements of friendship to be as pressing. She typed a quick reply:

Going into an interview. More soon.

She crossed the street and tried the shop's door. A cluster of bells announced her entrance. Reclaimed pieces of furniture displayed various trinkets. A shabby-chic vanity held beaded necklaces and earrings. A non-matching bookshelf showcased geodes and pink salt crystals. Two tables in the center of the room had been covered with coarse-looking sweaters and scarves. The distant smell of old wood competed with the scent of diffused lavender and lemon oil wafting from a lit oil burner on the long counter in the back of the room, where a cash register sat, unmanned.

No blast of air conditioning cooled the room, but a small desk fan oscillated in a steady and partly effective arc.

Caitlin let the door close behind her. A woman dressed in a simple flat-red housedress emerged from a curtain behind the back counter.

"Welcome, sister. Come in out of the heat."

Cursed with unfortunate forward-jutting front teeth and flat brown hair, the woman gave Caitlin the distinct impression of a cartoon mouse.

"Thanks." Caitlin crossed her arms. "No AC, huh?"

The Mouse smiled. "We prefer not to unduly tax the earth."

Caitlin smiled back. "You don't sell T-shirts, do you?"

"No, but we do have dresses and shorts. As you can see, we create our own clothing, plus we make a line of healing oils and creams."

"*We?*" Caitlin said, as naïvely as possible. "As in your family?"

The woman folded her hands on the counter. "You're not from around here, are you?"

Caitlin laughed. "Los Angeles. You'd think I'd be okay with the heat."

The woman nodded but didn't say anything else.

Caitlin pushed on. "So there's actually a Daya behind Daya's Gifts?"

"Of course."

If the Dayans were supposed to proselytize, this woman wasn't doing her job. Caitlin made an effort to look interested in a stack of sweaters, despite how implausible purchasing wool in this heat wave might seem. She held up a heavy-knit gray pullover. "How much for this one?"

"How much would you like to pay?"

"I'm sorry?"

"If you'd like the sweater, simply tell me the amount you'd like to pay."

"Wow," Caitlin said. "Hard to believe you can stay in business like that."

"We thrive by the power of charity."

Caitlin returned the sweater to the pile and moved on to the only thing she might actually wear: shorts. "Cool, so you sell my credit card info or something, like a social media platform?"

The woman looked offended. "We don't accept credit cards."

"I was joking." Caitlin grabbed a pair of red shorts from the stack. "How about ten dollars?"

The woman smiled. "If that is what you consider those to be worth."

Caitlin checked her wallet, saw another five. "We can make it fifteen."

The woman reached under the counter and pulled a plastic shopping bag from a larger wad of bags, none of which referenced Daya's Gifts.

"They're reused," the Mouse said, "so we're not—"

"Taxing the earth, sure." Caitlin handed her the shorts and the cash. "Do you have any documentation or paperwork? I'd like to learn more about your organization. Plus, my accountant is always on me about my charitable deductions, if you can write me a receipt."

"I'm sorry," the Mouse said, looking to the side as she placed the shorts in the bag. "We ran out last week."

Caitlin thanked her, stepped outside, then walked back to her hotel.

Her phone rang halfway through changing into the new shorts next to her room's hard-working AC unit. She tugged the shorts the rest of the way, fastened the button, and answered the unknown number with a 541 area code. "Caitlin Bergman."

Sheriff Martin was calling from his private number. "Miss Bergman, sorry to bother you."

"What's up, Boz? Did something happen?"

"No, sorry to give you that impression. This is purely a friendly call. You seemed interested in Jefferson."

The cool air of the AC hit Caitlin's sweaty back, and chills ran up her skin. "I am, actually. Did someone tell you that?"

Martin stuttered briefly. "What? No, you asked about the flag in the office. Oddly enough, I had lunch with one of my reelection campaign donors today. When he heard a big-city reporter was curious about his favorite cause, he practically bribed me to put you two together. That is, if you have the time."

Caitlin reached for a pad of paper. "Sure, I'll give the man a call. What's that number?"

Martin laughed. "Oh, you'll want to meet Anders Larsen in person."

CHAPTER

11

"G UIDED BY THE Spirit, I have communed with Lily Kramer."
Standing over the Chair of Knowledge, Desmond Pratten
rested his hands on the girl's shoulders and smiled at the women seated
cross-legged on the white marble tile, the Daughters of God.

"After a complete yielding, she accepted the knowledge and moves
forward willingly, casting away her birth name, as must be done."

Dressed in their ceremonial red tunics, the fifty women present for
the ceremony raised their hands above their shoulders and spoke in unison. "We say good-bye to Lily Kramer."

At nineteen, Lily was the youngest of the Daughters by far, and the
only new recruit since the ascension of the Five. She glanced back at
Desmond, nervous but full of joy.

He nodded in encouragement.

She straightened her white gown, cleared her throat, and spoke.

"My sisters, my mothers, my family."

The confident woman's voice filled the Gallery of Light, absent the
terrible stutter from which she'd once suffered.

"I came to you broken and lost," she continued, "unable to stand on
my own. You welcomed and soothed me, anointed me with your love
and the Light."

The Daughters raised their hands once more. "You are unique, powerful, and necessary."

"Indeed," Desmond said, taking focus on the dais. "She is unique, powerful, and necessary, and her name shall be called on the last day."

He reached out his hand. "Stand now and speak the name to which you will answer when the Spirit calls."

Backlit by the golden glow of sunshine streaming through the gallery's twenty-foot wall of glass, Lily took Desmond's hand. Despite her year of labor around the compound as an initiate, he felt the unspoiled softness of the four-decade difference between their skin. Something to look forward to later.

"I say good-bye to Lily Kramer," she said. "From now, until the last day, my name is Eve."

"Eve," the Daughters repeated, rising to embrace her.

Eve broke out in laughter, which led to tears of joy. Desmond let go of her hand, and she walked into the sea of women to be loved.

It was good to see the Daughters happy. Not just happy, but hopeful, especially after the last two weeks. He wished he could share their optimism, but his thoughts kept coming back to Daya. Until she returned, he wouldn't be able to relax fully. The double doors at the end of the gallery opened, and Gwendolyn Sunrise entered, dressed in her outer-world business suit.

"Have I missed it?" she said, rushing to hug the newly named Eve.

Eve threw her arms around Gwendolyn's sizable frame. "Thank you, Sunrise. You're just in time for the Climb."

Desmond moved into the center. "That's right, my loves. Eve must prepare. Who will help this Daughter make the Climb?"

All of the women, including Gwendolyn Sunrise, answered the refrain.

"We climb God's Hill together, now and at the end of days."

Desmond kissed Eve's forehead, then raised his open hand toward the double doors. "I pray for your ascension."

Beaming, the young woman untied her dress and let the gown drop to the floor, leaving her in only white slippers.

She bowed once, then walked out the doors, the throng of Daughters following to escort her on the Climb.

Gwendolyn lingered. "The suite has been readied, including the—"

Rather than letting her finish the sentence, Desmond kissed her forehead as well. "Thank you, my love." Gwendolyn lived in his circle of trust, but he still didn't like hearing the words *erectile dysfunction medicine* out loud.

"There's something else. A woman visited Daya's Gifts."

Desmond smiled again, finally infected by the day's hope. "Another voyager?"

"Doubtful." Gwendolyn handed him a photo printed from a security-camera feed. "I wasn't able to get her name, but she looks familiar, particularly the eyes."

"Good lord." His smile disappeared. "Why is she here?"

"The sheriff brought her in to identify a body. Her name is—"

"Caitlin Bergman," Desmond said, the joy of the ceremony gone in an instant. "She's Magda's daughter."

12

CAITLIN TOOK HER time in the hotel shower, even though a Larsen Timber SUV idled in the parking lot waiting for her. Cooler, she threw on fresh clothes, grabbed her bag, and slid into the SUV's back seat, ready to let a local show her the sights.

The driver didn't speak much, other than to repeat what Dana the secretary had stressed over the phone: Anders Larsen couldn't wait to talk about the State of Jefferson. From the comfort of the chilled back seat, Caitlin watched the roadside snake up and down through mountains of dense forest broken occasionally by huge stretches of bare hillside where logging had exposed the land like a man's chest shaved for a surgery, naked and vulnerable. Every few miles, a side road would reveal a solitary home marked by an assortment of cars and their parts, all close to being absorbed by nature. More often a sign, or remnants of it, would advertise one of the many churches in the area. One in particular, a series of purple cards with yellow writing, caught her attention.

The first read: *Ever Wonder Why*

The second, five hundred feet later: *You Are Here?*

The third: *Ask Your Maker*

There was a fourth, something about Jesus, but she'd looked up past the last sign and watched the sun flicker through another stretch of fir and a lighter-colored tree, possibly hemlock, in a breathtaking mix of green and gold.

As beautiful as it was, all she could imagine at the top of each hill was a tiny cluster of huts where ex–porn stars like her very own maker knitted sweaters.

Stupid sign. It's too late to ask her anything.

After forty-five minutes of answerless nature, the SUV descended into a valley, crossed a rail line, and pulled into the parking lot of Larsen Timber, a massive three-story sheet-metal warehouse along a rail siding full of loaded flatcars.

A durable-looking woman in her thirties wearing a flannel over beige Carhartt dungarees waited on the sidewalk with a smile, unfazed by the oppressive heat.

"You must be Mrs. Bergman," she said, opening Caitlin's door. "I'm Dana."

Caitlin got out to the sound of a screeching saw blade. "The car wasn't really necessary."

Dana bounced ahead for the door into the building. "Try telling Anders. Have you ever seen a working lumber mill?"

"You're fully staffed on a Saturday?"

The woman laughed. "Well, I was at my son's baseball game when the big man called—"

"You didn't leave on my behalf?"

"Oh heavens, no. I love my son, but his dad can sit in this heat and still pretend to care. Anyway, last year's fire season led to a thinning grant, and we've been working double shifts six days a week since January."

They passed through an air-conditioned reception area, stopping briefly to put on neon-green safety earmuffs, then opened a door to the busy mill floor.

Dana shouted over the thrum of heavy equipment. "We do two-by-fours, one-by-fours, two-by-sixes—you name it. All sourced in state from responsibly managed forestland. Plus, the Chinese have been buying unfinished Doug fir as fast as we can pull it down."

"Impressive," Caitlin yelled back, following the path marked by reflective tape on the concrete floor. At least thirty men worked the line, ranging from forklift operators to board planers. Caitlin didn't know what any of the machines did, but they all looked modern and efficient.

The whole place smelled of sawdust competing with industrial lubricant.

They took a steel staircase up two stories, reentered the world of finished office space, hung their earmuffs on a rack of hooks, and stopped at an open doorway.

"Anders," Dana said, knocking on the metal frame. "Your reporter's here."

She moved aside with a smile, and Caitlin went in.

Anders Larsen's white hair gave way to the ruddy complexion of a man who'd spent a life of seventy years outdoors, and rarely on a golf course. His faded green button-down shirt and khakis looked fresh from a late-nineties L.L.Bean catalog. The office furniture matched the man. Rugged, no frills.

"Mrs. Bergman, so glad you could make it."

He leaned over his desk with his hand out and a smile that had never bought into the whole braces thing.

She shook his hand firmly, noticing the calluses she'd anticipated. "Actually, it's Miss."

He pointed to the chair. "Depending on how long you'll be in town, we can take care of that. I've got a whole company of stud-making studs. Please, sit on down, Miss Bergman."

She took one of the chairs in front of the desk. "Call me Caitlin. I understand the company's busy, but how come the boss is at work on a Saturday?"

"No place I'd rather be. Now, I hear you'd like to talk about Jefferson."

Caitlin pulled her phone out and started her recorder. "And I understand you're the man to talk to. This November, the people of California will consider the trisection of the state. How does the State of Jefferson come into the picture?"

Larsen rocked back in his chair and brought his feet up, landing his boots on top of his desk. "The whole issue comes down to the bane of our founding fathers: taxation without representation . . ."

Almost an hour later, the seventy-year-old still spoke with the enthusiasm of a college freshman majoring in political science. ". . . so we're left with what we've got here—a government *of* the people, but only *for* some of the people."

A knock on the open door behind them broke his train of thought. "Aw hell, you're busy."

Caitlin turned to see a taller, younger, and meaner-looking version of the man behind the desk standing in the doorway. Like Anders, he wore a rough-looking long-sleeved button-down. But unlike the boss, one sleeve had been rolled up to the bicep, revealing a mummy-like wrap of bandages starting at the wrist and ending somewhere inside the shirt. His eyes caught Caitlin's, and for the briefest of seconds, she thought she saw a look of recognition.

"Don't stand there yammering," Anders said. "I'm in the middle of something."

Around fifty, the man shifted his eyes away. A fine mist of sawdust gave his brown hair a salt-and-pepper look. "I'll come back."

"And waste my time twice? What's so important?" Anders motioned the man into the room. "Caitlin, this is Johnny, my boy."

Johnny Larsen shot Caitlin a nod, but rather than reaching for a handshake, he moved behind his father's desk and whispered. Caitlin made out something about "the BLM" and a town called "Powers."

Whatever he'd said made Anders just as angry as he had been happy to talk about statehood. "Bullshit. Did you tell them the whole point of starting now was to prevent a fire?"

The younger Larsen leaned in again, whispered; then both men looked up at Caitlin.

She had more than enough to work with but wanted a nice closing. "I've taken too much of your workday as it is, Anders. Let's finish with one last question. What do you want the people of California to think about when they head to the polls this fall?"

The son leaned back against the wall, one hand absently picking at his bandages, his eyes watching Caitlin's every move.

Anders sat up in his chair. "We're not a bunch of fringe-element nut-jobs shooting guns into the air. We're business leaders trying to make the best possible situation out of the gifts we're given. Unfortunately, the people making the rules live so far away they can't see that our towns and people aren't just losing the game—we don't even get to play."

Caitlin stopped her phone and packed up. "Thanks for your time—and the chauffeur."

Anders walked around the desk. "Of course. Unfortunately, the driver has to take me to my other mill. Johnny here can drive you back to your hotel."

Caitlin caught Johnny Larsen's eyes and smiled.

The man nodded but didn't look happy about his assignment.

"I'm in Coos Bay," she said. "Hope that's not a problem."

He beat her out the door. "I know where you're staying."

13

JOHNNY LARSEN'S TRUCK was no company SUV. The massive electric-blue F350 looked big enough to live in, but judging from the stickers on the midnight-tinted rear window, Caitlin wouldn't be welcome. One for the State of Jefferson, one Confederate flag, and one she didn't recognize but had a bad feeling about: *The Proud Sons of Oregon*. The high-gloss, decal-wrapped tailgate leaned more toward mainstream America: a belt-fed Browning M2 .50-caliber machine gun floated over the red-and-white stripes of freedom.

She opened the passenger door and climbed into a cloud of cigarette smoke, all the more potent on a hot day. Caitlin had smoked for fifteen years, but nostalgia was the last feeling the scent conjured.

Johnny had the beast moving before she managed to fasten her seat belt. If his bandaged right arm caused him pain, it wasn't slowing him down any. He pulled out of the parking lot and gunned the accelerator, taking the twisting country road like he could drive it blindfolded.

Caitlin kicked aside a plastic bag full of empty takeout containers and broke the ice. "I'd like to think you've got a really dirty tattoo under all those bandages."

The tiniest of smiles curled around his lit cigarette.

"Just an accident."

"Not work related, I hope."

"Motorcycle."

"Yikes. So what'd you tell your father to set him off? Something about the BLM and Powers?"

Johnny laughed. "Don't miss much, do you?"

He took the cigarette out of his mouth, exhaled, and glanced her way. "We're supposed to start cable logging a ridge south of Powers on Monday, but the Bureau of Land Management just declared fire season conditions in the region, so we gotta modify our equipment layout. Honestly, it's not a big deal, but the old man likes to pick a fight when he can. Makes him feel like he's still the swinging dick in these parts."

He took another drag; then silence.

A turn in the road sent the bag of takeout containers back toward Caitlin's feet. She foot-tucked the bag closer to the center console, but Larsen reached over and grabbed the trash.

"I got that."

On the bag's way past, Caitlin caught the image of a man with an ax over the restaurant's name. "The Lumberjack, huh? Any good?"

Johnny shoved the bag behind his seat.

"Good enough. Been in the family forever." He brushed his hand off on his jeans. "Bergman. What kind of name is that?"

That question had come up many times in her life, rarely without an all-too-obvious connotation.

"I've been told it means *mountain person* in German."

He nodded, eyes back on the road. "Figured it was Jewish."

And there it was. "Used to be plenty of Jews in Germany, even in the mountains. What kind of name is Larsen? Swedish?"

His eyes came her way again, but no smile this time. "Five generations, back to the beginning of Oregon. I'm very proud of my heritage."

Caitlin didn't need any other hints to guess the meaning of Larsen's *Proud Sons of Oregon* bumper sticker. They celebrated their proud *white* heritage. Nothing she liked more than forty-five minutes in the car with a white supremacist.

"I'm adopted," she said. "As far as I'm concerned, heritage is just a word for the sins of the generation before me."

At least the mother, she thought, but didn't say. This asshole didn't need to know anything else about her life. She lowered her window an inch to let the smoke attack something besides her eyes.

Johnny looked like he had more to say but reached for the radio, put on a country station.

Caitlin grabbed her phone and sent Lakshmi a text.

Want to make $30? Need interview transcribed. Tonight, if possible.

Lakshmi replied with a thumbs-up emoji and a message:

Send me the interview. I'll start now.

Five seconds later, the young woman called. Caitlin swiped the *Can't Talk Now* message.

Johnny turned down the radio. "Need to take that?"

Caitlin pasted the voice recording of her interview into the text thread with the caption *Will Explain Later*. "Nothing that can't wait."

They didn't speak again until they reached the hotel's parking lot.

She grabbed her bag and started her polite good-bye, but Johnny interrupted. "You didn't come all the way up to Coos County just to talk to the old man about Jefferson."

Caitlin's hand lingered on the handle, but she didn't get out. "Are you asking or telling?"

Even in park, Larsen's truck had the throaty growl of an animal ready to pounce.

"Heard about a body they found on the road outside the federal land."

The sheriff hadn't told Caitlin where her mother's body had been found. For some reason, she'd assumed it'd been in the woods. That a white supremacist with a substantially bandaged arm knew more about her reason for being in town than she did made Caitlin sit up straight.

"Heard from who?" she said, conscious of a surge of adrenaline.

Johnny laughed. "I hear everything in this county, like how some reporter from LA flew in to ID the body. That's gotta be you." Johnny moved his tongue around his mouth like it was responsible for setting up his next sentence. "You one of those Dogs?"

Johnny Larsen's tone, like the medical examiner's before him, said he had a serious ax to grind with the Daughters of God—or worse, a chainsaw.

"You're the second person around here to ask me that," Caitlin said. "Who are these people?"

He shook his head. "Bunch of wackjobs living in a compound in the high timber."

Caitlin forced a little chuckle. "What's their thing? Crystals, moon circles, the power of light?"

"Stealing little girls," Larsen said, deadly serious. "Those lunatics took my thirteen-year-old daughter. Whoever killed that old bitch did the world a favor."

Caitlin's inner journalist had competing questions ready to jump out. The rest of her wanted nothing more than to get into her hotel room and lock the door.

"Sorry about your daughter," she said, getting out. "Thanks for the ride."

She headed for the hotel lobby, painfully aware of the consistent rumble of the truck's engine behind her, proof that Larsen hadn't yet driven away. For a man who'd been hell-bent on setting a speed record from the lumber mill to the hotel, he wasn't making any effort to get back on the road.

She pushed through the lobby's glass doors but froze when someone called, "Mrs. Bergman?"

Caitlin turned to the employee behind the front desk, trying to hide the shudder that rolled down her spine. A young man with the remnants of active acne, he looked friendly enough in his blue vest. He couldn't have known that he'd been the third person in as many hours to assume Caitlin was married because of her age. He also couldn't have guessed how close he was to getting torn a new asshole.

"What?" she said through clenched teeth.

Even protected by three feet of solid counter, the kid took a step back. "Sorry, a cop came by earlier looking for you. He left you a package."

He stepped delicately back to his station, pulled a folder-sized package off a bottom shelf, and placed it on the counter top.

Caitlin let out a breath she hadn't realized she'd been holding, found a smile, and took the sealed brown envelope. "Awesome, thanks."

She stepped into the hall to her room, then stopped. The kid behind the desk wasn't the woman who'd checked Caitlin in, which meant someone had described her well enough for her to be recognized. Probably Sheriff Martin, but still—Caitlin whipped back toward the front door. The counter kid had disappeared into a cubby, but through the doors she saw Johnny Larsen's truck lingering in the parking lot, twenty feet from the curb. Was he lighting a cigarette, sending a text message, or was the man who heard about everything that happened in Coos County proving some kind of point? She tucked the package under her arm and walked back outside to see.

Maybe it was her timing, maybe not, but the second her foot left the curb, the truck backed out and roared away into traffic.

14

J OHNNY CUT INTO traffic, already on his phone.

"Are you kidding me? You really think some LA reporter gives a shit about Jefferson? Sounds like it's time you retire, old man."

Maybe it was the car speaker, but Anders didn't seem concerned. "Dana talked to her editor. She's legitimate. I think she might really help the cause."

Johnny laughed. "The cause? She's working with the Dogs. That bitch knows exactly where they've got Promise."

And those freaking eyes, he wanted to say. *Caitlin Bergman's got the same eyes as the one that jacked up my arm.* But nobody needed to know how wrong that night on the hill had gone, especially not Anders.

His father's voice dropped into the low tone he used when he wanted to seem like a hard-ass. "John, you stay away from that woman."

Used to be that tone of voice meant a beating, sometimes worse. Now it didn't mean shit.

"Stay away?"

"You hear me, son?"

A stoplight turned red and Johnny slammed the brakes, stopping both his truck and the string of curses ready to come out. No point in getting kicked out of the will after taking all those punches.

"Yes, sir."

He hung up and rolled down the window. The air coming off the bay smelled fresh, despite the hot-as-balls breeze blowing into the truck's cabin. What did Anders know about *the cause*? He'd spent Johnny's whole childhood bitching about the coloreds and the Mexicans but had been hiring seasonal illegals for the past five years 'cause they'd work for half the pay of a white man. Anders cared more about being the richest man in never-gonna-happen-Jefferson than fighting to keep Oregon in the hands of Oregonians.

Looking out at the water, Johnny remembered the first time he'd taken Promise out on the bay on his Boston Whaler, fishing and eating bologna sandwiches and exploring coves and inlets until sunset. Hearing her laugh, seeing her smile, all with the sun reflecting off the water—Johnny wasn't gonna give that up, and he definitely wasn't going to back off of Caitlin Bergman.

He reached behind his seat, pulled out the bag of trash from the Lumberjack, and threw it out the window. No one was gonna mess with his beautiful home.

CHAPTER

15

BEHIND THE LOCKED door of her hotel room, Caitlin slid the envelope's contents onto the bed's floral-patterned comforter. At first glance, she guessed there were a hundred pages of material printed on standard white copy paper, plus a thumb drive. The top page of the stack was a typed note on Coos County letterhead.

Miss Bergman:

While my office still cannot definitively verify that the body in question is your mother, we can confirm that fingerprints found on the notebook in the safety deposit box match those on file from Maya Aronson's prior arrest record. When the lab returns a verified familial DNA identification against your buccal swab, we'll be glad to return your mother's belongings. In the meantime, here's a copy of the entire spiral notebook, faster than expected. Hope that helps you get back to your life in Los Angeles.

Once again, the people of Coos County are sorry for your loss.

Caitlin had a lot to do. A shower, first of all, then some sort of dinner; then she'd write her State of Jefferson piece. She didn't want to get sucked into the handwritten journal of a dead woman, but sitting on the edge of the bed, her laptop bag still slung over one shoulder, she couldn't fight the urge to read the first entry.

* * *

How can I describe the feeling?

I want to get this down before the sensation fades, but my handwriting's shit and I'm not good with words.

I feel electric, wired, out of my mind, like coke and crystal got together with a handful of Ritalin and went straight up my nose. My whole brain is working, but not just my brain, my soul, if I have one.

He said I did. He said he could see my soul, trapped inside, burning bright like liquid gold.

He didn't even want to fuck. I mean, that's why I thought I was invited.

I'm messing this up. I'll start over. I don't want to forget anything.

It's seven AM on a Monday morning and I am sober as a nun.

February 15, 1993

I'd run into Bev on Friday at one of Larry F's parties in Calabasas. Bev looked amazing, skin glowing and everything, and she's two years older than me. Damned if she didn't look twenty-five instead of forty-two. I hadn't seen her in almost a year, figured she'd been back in Passages, or at least a county hospital. First time I'd seen her sober in a decade. Not that I was. Not with rails of blow on every surface, every flavor of Citron they made behind the bar, and two of the guys from Guns N' Roses jamming by the pool.

She invited me to this Valentine's Day party on Sunday, said I had to come. Honestly, I forgot all about it until I woke up around four the next day and checked my machine. She'd called to remind me, left the address, and said show up at seven PM.

Last year, we'd worked some parties together, oil shows for frat boys or businessmen, fetish dates for older types. I always walked away with five or six hundred bucks, sometimes more, so I figured I'd make enough to cover next month's rent.

Yesterday afternoon, I broke out the Thomas Guide *and my party bag and drove from my place in Encino to some narrow road off Laurel Canyon in the Hollywood Hills.*

I got to the top of the hill, drove through an open gate that led past a couple of eucalyptus trees, and parked on the grass next to ten other cars. No Porsches, one Mercedes—but like ten years old—the rest were shit boxes like mine. The house was a wood-paneled A-frame that perched over the edge of a valley looking west, and I could see the sun setting over the ocean past Santa Monica. I can't remember the last time I noticed the sunset. The mix of gold and pink and purple seemed impossible, like an Easter dress had caught on fire.

But it was almost seven, so I walked up a little wooden walkway to the front door and rang the bell. I can't say who I expected to answer, but I wouldn't have imagined the woman who did in a million years.

Short and at least seventy, this little old lady opened the door in a pair of slacks and a light sweater, her white hair pulled back in a ponytail.

"Happy Valentine's Day," she said, her arms out, like she was gonna hug me.

Her, this nice old lady; me in a pink halter, fishnets, and four-inch stilettos with a bag full of condoms, dildos, and lube.

"I think I'm lost," I said, cause yeah, duh.

She smiled and stepped closer, hugging me.

"We all are."

She smelled like flowers; not roses, but something light and pretty.

I told her Bev had invited me.

She let me go and looked up into my eyes. "I'm Linda Sperry. Welcome to my home."

My name slipped out, my real name. I have no idea why. It didn't even occur to me to lie to the woman.

"Maya?" she said, like legit happy. "We call my niece Daya. Please, come in."

The whole thing had a walking-into-a-trap feel, like I'd turn a corner and see all my friends and someone would announce another intervention, which would be bullshit, cause they're all worse than me, but I followed nice old Linda inside—and that's where I saw the orgy.

Well, I thought it was an orgy. Six people, two guys, four women, were all laying in a pile in a living room to the right. Except they were all clothed. Their hands traced each other's bodies, but hugging not tugging, and everybody had a blissed-out smile on their face. I didn't smell anything but incense, but the way they were moaning and laughing, they had to be smoking something.

I set my bag down and looked for a light switch. I'd worked parties like this before. Sometimes the vanilla crowd needed a pro to start the ball rolling.

"Dear?" Linda waited for me down the hall. "Beverly's out on the porch."

Again, I had no idea what to think.

We passed another room where a young woman played guitar and sang to a handful of other young women. The song sounded familiar, like "All You Need Is Love" by the Beatles, but on the chorus, she sang, "All you need is light. The light is all you need."

A sliding door led onto a massive porch with a mind-blowing view, except the twenty or so people seated on couches were watching a man, not the sun. I couldn't hear the guy from that distance, but his crowd listened like he had the secrets to life. Over on the right, Bev's blond head bobbed along with everybody else's, until he brought his hands together at his chest, smiled, and turned toward the remains of the sunset.

The people on the couches got up, some hugging, others stretching like they'd been there for hours. Bev scribbled something in a notebook, then closed her eyes.

Linda pointed me toward the porch. "Go ahead, dear."

I got two steps before Bev looked up, smiled, and screamed, "You made it!"

She jumped off the back of the couch and ran over, hugging me like we hadn't seen each other in years.

"I'm so glad you're here, Maya. Did you hear Desmond?"

I told her I'd just gotten there. "What is this place, Bevvie? I'm not exactly dressed for whatever this is."

Bev grabbed my hand. "It doesn't matter what you wear or don't wear here. Come on, I'll introduce you."

She tugged me toward the deck's railing, where five people surrounded the speaker.

"Desmond," she said, pushing through the others. "She came."

The lingerers parted and I saw the man, Desmond, for the first time. He was taller than me in my heels, and better looking than me on my best day—or most men I'd known—like one of those guys from the shaving cream ads. But his eyes—his eyes locked onto mine.

Gray, like a cloudy sky with a storm on the way.

"I'm Desmond Pratten," he said, reaching out with both hands.

I raised my hand to shake. "Sharon."

He took my hand with his right, then wrapped his left over my wrist. It only took a second, but a feeling of safety and comfort washed over me, like a weighted comforter on a cold night.

"I've been waiting to meet you, Sharon." He pulled me closer. "But that's not your name, is it?"

Not many people know my real name. Bev does, obviously, and for some reason, I'd told the Linda lady at the door. Besides that, it's the banks and the landlord. But here this man was, waiting to meet me.

"No," I stammered. "It's Maya."

He nodded, not letting go. "Yes, it is, for now. But I see something else burning inside you."

Normally I'd laugh at a line like that, but there, locked in his firm grip, I could only whisper, "What do you see?"

"Your soul. Hot, but damaged, bright like liquid gold."

My skin got warm, all over, and I started to shake. I don't know why. Bev and the others might have still been standing next to me, but I had no idea. "Liquid gold?"

He nodded. "Soon we'll let it out, and the light inside you will fill the heavens."

"I don't know what that means," I said, stuttering.

He let go of my wrist and put his arm around me, bringing me into a hug.

"You will, but first you need to know that he can't hurt you anymore."

I pulled back. "Who can't hurt me anymore?"

Those gray eyes looked at me, through me. "Your father."

I told him my piece of shit father had been dead for over twenty years.

Desmond's eyes held me in place. "In this world, yes, but not in your soul."

I don't remember anything after that.

They said I passed out, there in his arms. I woke later in a big, soft bed, still in my same clothes, next to Bev and two other women. A clock on the wall said it was just past five in the morning.

I tapped Bev until she opened her eyes. "What the hell is this?"

She smiled. "I don't have the words. Only the light."

She told me how I'd passed out, and how Desmond told everyone that my arrival meant a great new chapter had been begun in their story.

"I gotta go," I said, though honestly I'm not sure why. Just a feeling, like I needed to get back to some sort of reality.

I found my things on the floor near the door.

Bev followed me out of bed. "Will you come back?"

I didn't know then. I didn't know if the feeling was real, if anything that had happened made sense.

"Sure," I said. "Call me."

She smiled and hugged me. "Happy Valentine's Day, Maya."

16

"**D**AMN, MAYA."

Caitlin dropped the page onto the stack. In 1993, she'd been a senior in high school. Her mom had been living in the valley, maybe twenty minutes away, snorting coke and grinding on bachelor parties for money. Plus she'd known the guys from Guns N' Roses. Even at the dawn of grunge music, having a rock and roll mom would have been helpful around Fairfax High. That, or the smallest modicum of mother-daughter personal contact. Instead, Maya had met a man named Desmond Pratten and a woman named Linda Sperry who had a niece named Daya. Somehow, somewhere, all of that had ended with a body in an Oregonian forest.

It was too much to process.

She crammed the stack back into the envelope, then tucked the package into her suitcase. She had no idea how many years of Maya's life were captured in those pages but guessed they'd take longer than one night to get through.

The second shower of the day cleared her brain. She'd plotted a rough outline of her Jefferson story and felt ready to work, but as she stepped out of the bathroom, her eyes drifted back to her suitcase.

Too tempting.

She threw a blazer over her last clean outfit, grabbed her laptop bag, and went in search of dinner and dependable Wi-Fi. She passed several modern-looking places bustling with Saturday night crowds, ready to settle for the previous night's waterfront dive.

"Wait a second."

She pulled up her phone and took a chance, searching for a restaurant called the Lumberjack. For whatever reason, the Larsen family had inserted themselves into Caitlin's stay in town. After two decades in journalism, she knew that kind of interest in her work meant a fight was coming.

She thought back to when a group of girls in her high school had accused her of stealing one of their boyfriends, going so far as to publicly label Caitlin a slut, and the advice her dad had offered that night over dinner.

Don't let anyone back you against the ropes, Slugger. Take the fight to them.

It wasn't until the next day, after he'd talked the principal out of expelling Caitlin for breaking a girl's nose, that her father clarified that he hadn't literally meant to fight.

The Larsens knew who Caitlin was and where she was staying. Her dad's advice still rang true. *Take the fight to them.* The least she could do was see what years of their family tradition had brought the people of Oregon.

Four blocks off the main strip, an old-time wooden Paul Bunyan statue told her she'd found the right place. The solid eight-foot carving of the mythical lumberjack stood guard in front of a rustic side-alley bar. Pickups and motorcycles outnumbered sedans in the half-full parking lot, and the scent of burgers and fried onions wafted from an unseen kitchen vent. She reached for the doorknob, an actual ax handle, and entered to the sound of Mick Jagger singing about honky-tonk women over an infectious cowbell groove.

A handful of men with pool cues ran the trio of green tables to the left, a couple in their sixties occupied one of the ten red vinyl booths arranged in a U in the center, and a long bar ran the length of the wall to the right. Caitlin went that way, taking one of the many empty stools.

The bartender, a skinny but strong-looking brunette in her late fifties with more than a few tattoos poking out of her Harley-Davidson tank top, looked up from her phone.

"You here about the license?"

Caitlin laughed. "Not unless the license is a rum and Diet Coke, in which case, I'm here about a double."

The woman set her phone aside and reached for a pint glass. "Sorry, we don't get a lot of blazers in here. Usually they end up over at the microbrewery sucking down IPAs."

"I can't stand IPAs," Caitlin said, taking off her jacket. "I'm in town for a funeral."

"Sorry to hear that, hon."

"Thanks, but we weren't close."

The bartender reached for the rum on the shelf behind her and made the drink. Caitlin saw a familiar green rectangle behind the whiskey selection: the State of Jefferson flag once again.

"I don't want to sound like some insensitive out-of-towner," she said, pointing, "but what are your thoughts on the whole State of Jefferson thing?"

The bartender pushed Caitlin's drink forward with a smirk. "It's backwoods lost-cause bullshit, like the Confederate flag. But for some reason, these things have been popping up everywhere over the last decade."

Caitlin took a sip of her beverage. "Because people in these parts don't feel represented in Salem or Sacramento?"

The bartender crossed her arms and snorted. "More like every asshole needs someone to blame for their life not coming up roses."

The strong drink tasted more like a quadruple than a double. "Oh, I like you. I'm Caitlin."

"Hazel."

"Hazel, I need a burger, fries, and Wi-Fi. Any chance you've got all three?"

*　*　*

Half an hour and twelve hundred calories later, Caitlin had completed both dinner and a rough draft of her Jefferson piece. She checked her email. Right on time, Lakshmi had sent a complete transcription of the Anders interview. She'd also sent a three-line personal message:

What's happening with your mother?
Are you all right?
How are you working on a story right now?

Caitlin answered the personal message by sending thirty dollars through a money-transfer app, then compared the sections of the Anders interview she'd included from memory in her rough draft with what had actually been said. She made a single correction, then reread her piece. Of her three interviews, one read as neutral, the other two pro-Jefferson.

She went back to the bar, handed Hazel one of her official cards, and asked if she could use the woman's thoughts on Jefferson in the article.

"Quote me?" Hazel laughed. "Hell yes, all you want."

"Even though you work for the Larsens?"

Hazel shook her head. "I work for the Lumberjack. They pay me enough to make drinks, not to tell me what to think."

Hazel's contribution and another cocktail did the trick. Caitlin finished her piece, sent it off to Lawton, then visited the bathroom. When she got back to her table, a handwritten note waited where her dirty plate had been.

You should have a cigarette out back.

Caitlin glanced over to the bar. Hazel looked up from washing glasses and gave one slight nod toward the pool tables. Caitlin didn't know if he'd been there the whole time, but Sheriff Martin, in plain clothes, leaned over a table and racked a set of balls.

Caitlin slid her computer into her bag, left the booth, walked back toward the restroom, and took an exit out into to an informal smoking area. A plastic ashtray overflowed onto a stack of milk crates next to a ripe dumpster. At first she watched the door, expecting Hazel's arrival, but after a full minute she turned toward the dark parking lot. Floodlights revealed four cars parked directly behind the back door in a small lot butting up against an alley.

Further down the alley, near the loading dock of an old grocery store, Caitlin saw a red dot move up and down in the darkness. Shielding her eyes from the restaurant's lights, she made out a single figure standing at the edge of the lot, holding a lit cigarette. From the shape and height, she guessed it was a woman.

She got two steps into the lot before the restaurant's back door swung open behind her.

"Miss Bergman, is that you?"

She turned back to see Sheriff Martin lighting a cigarette.

"What are the odds," she asked with a smile, before shooting a quick glance back toward the loading dock. The female figure was gone.

Martin walked closer. "Out of all the places in town, how did you end up at the Lumberjack?"

"Walking distance from the hotel, Sheriff. How about you?"

"I live up the hill. You got the package, right?"

"Sure did, thanks."

"Sorry I don't have a definitive answer yet, but it looks like you can get back to your life in California."

Unlike the stench in Johnny Larsen's truck, the smell of Sheriff Martin's cigarette fading into the night sky made Caitlin think of her father, which brought her back to the reasons for the whole trip—both hers and whatever agenda the people of Coos County were pursuing. If Sheriff Martin could be trusted, he'd have to give Caitlin the same info Johnny had offered.

"I know you're off the clock, Boz," she started, stepping closer, "but where did they find my mother's body?"

His eyebrows went up, and he looked her over. "What are you doing out here near the dumpster?"

He'd answered her question with a question. Pro move.

"Smoking," she replied. "Where'd they find her? Road, woods, federal land?"

"Road," he said. "But in the woods and near federal land. I didn't take you for a smoker."

"But she hadn't been killed there, right? She'd been moved?"

Martin looked either impressed or suspicious. "Who have you been talking to?"

"Your benevolent donor's number-one son. Did the Dayans, or Daughters of God, or whatever they're called, really kidnap Johnny Larsen's daughter? And more importantly, did you set up that interview so I'd end up in a truck with him?"

"I know you're hurting, Miss Bergman, but I wouldn't get too involved in any of this mess."

"Did the cult take his daughter?"

He shrugged. "Pretty hard to take someone who's run away three times in the last year. That said, these Dayans are trouble. If your mother really was one of them, the best thing you can do is bury her and go on home. Speaking of which"—he stubbed out his cigarette in the ashtray—"I'd better get home to the wife."

She let him get five steps away before calling out again. "Was the key put in my mom's butt before or after her death?"

He turned back. "The report showed traces of lubricant and no signs of tearing, so we assume the placement was voluntary."

"Sheriff, you should never assume," Caitlin said. "It makes an ass out of you and my mom."

He laughed despite himself, waved, then turned around the alley corner toward the front of the building, out of sight. Maybe thirty seconds later, she heard an engine start and a car pull away. She looked back to the loading dock once again. Still no movement. She went back in and headed for the bar. Hazel had written the note, so she'd have an answer. Except Hazel wasn't there. A large man wearing a Ducks hoodie stood behind the bar, pouring beers for two young men with military-style buzz cuts.

"Hazel still here?" Caitlin said.

The new bartender pointed up to a clock. "Shift ended at nine. I'm all yours the rest of the night. What can I get you?"

Caitlin reached for her wallet. "Just my check, then."

He went to the register. "What was the name?"

"Bergman," she said, noticing the heads of the two young men whip her way.

A tattoo peeked out from under the sleeve of the nearest one's T-shirt, a banner wrapped around the words *Proud Son*.

The bartender turned back her way. "I don't see it here. Looks like Hazel took care of you."

"Sorry, I spaced." Caitlin shoved her wallet back into her purse. "Hazel said something about that before I went out to smoke. I meant I wanted to thank her for something we were talking about. When does she work again?"

"She'll be in tomorrow, but you don't have to leave."

"Stick around," the closest young man said, jumping into the conversation. "The night's just getting started. What kind of name is that—Bergman?"

Caitlin looked at all three men at the bar, then over at the men at the pool table, and realized she was the only woman left in the place.

"It means *gotta go* in German," she said, backing away from the bar. "As in, time for me to call it a night."

She left out the back door, walking as fast as possible without breaking into a sprint. Just as she neared the Paul Bunyan statue, a large blue pickup roared into the parking lot: the one and only Johnny Larsen. Back on the main strip, she stopped to see if she was being followed, but she saw neither the mysterious female waiting at the edge of the parking lot nor the bar's buzz-cut males of Aryan descent. In her hotel room five minutes later, she still hadn't decided if Hazel had sent her outside to meet the woman at the edge of the parking lot, to talk to Sheriff Martin, or to get away from a Proud Sons of Oregon meeting.

Too wired to sleep, she reached for her suitcase and read the second entry in her mother's journal.

CHAPTER

17

February 27, 1993

I WASN'T SURE HOW *to start this, then Daya—of all people—said I should just write to myself, my inner self, my true self. So hi, Maya. Hello, it's you . . . and your mind is completely freaking blown.*

It's Saturday and I'm in a campground in the Angeles National Forest, just up past Wrightwood. There's snow everywhere, so I should be cold, but I'm not. I'm melting, my whole body is on fire.

I haven't written since the first entry almost two weeks ago, so I'll start there.

After the Valentine's Day party, I lost my shit. Like, I sat in bed for two days, cordless phone in my lap, dialing Bev's number, getting her machine over and over. Once it stopped recording, I put on clothes and drove to her place in Van Nuys. She didn't live there anymore, but I didn't know, so I camped out in front of her door for a whole morning. The new renters chewed my ass in Russian until I figured out that Bev had ditched her lease, leaving most of her furniture and things behind.

I drove back to the house on Laurel Canyon and the place was empty, not a single car in the driveway. Still, I found notes—maybe fifteen or so— all taped to the door. One had my name on it.

Maya:

Your path to this point has been hard, but do not fear. You haven't missed your chance. Pack a bag with cold-weather, outdoor clothing, enough for a week, any food you have at home, and follow the map below. From here on out, the way will be easy. Though now you are alone, soon you will be with us. Now you are temporary, soon you will become absolute. Soon you will know the Light.

Desmond, the Guide.

Linda, the Seer.

Daya, the Future.

I drove home, packed what I could, then followed the instructions into the mountains northeast of Pasadena. I hadn't been up there since high school and had forgotten how many pine trees there are. Not giant redwoods or anything, but tall—a real forest compared to the rest of Los Angeles County. And the air? So fresh.

Two Dayans—that's what they're called—waited in the parking lot of a campground for voyagers like me.

"Your voyage has just begun," the first said, an ultra-tan surfer type in ski pants. "Follow the trail until you find your light."

"My light?"

The woman with him, an Asian girl in her twenties with hair down to her ass, pulled me close and kissed me on each cheek. "You can't miss it. Your soul brought you here. Let it guide you to your destiny."

"Sure, my destiny," I mumbled back. "But what is this place?"

"It's freedom from your past, from getting stuck in your regrets, from"—she laughed politely—"that look on your face."

The surfer pulled her away and into his arms. "Don't freak her out." His smile was bright and wide. "It's a retreat. Check it out. You'll love it."

I zipped my jacket and started up the trail, but turned back toward them. "But is it a—"

"Cult?" the girl answered with a laugh. "If it is, it's a really good one."

Maybe I should have turned back then. Maybe I would have if I was thinking, but I had to know who these people were, and why, out of all the people in LA, they wanted me.

Snow coated the hillside, but the sun was out. Five minutes up the path, I felt comfortable enough to unzip. By the time I got to the first big turn, I could hear music. By the second, laughter. When I got to the clearing at the top of the hill, I found the party—and the light. A giant bonfire, brighter than anything I could have imagined, reflected off the snow-filled trees and the fifty or so half-naked people dancing around in a sweltering ring. Sweaty, topless men and women, young and old, moved to music being played by acoustic guitars, a drum circle, and a pair of gorgeous male twins with flutes. The dancers touched each other's backs and shoulders, not sexually, but gently, like friends in half hugs, and every few seconds, someone would scream like they couldn't help themselves.

The circle spun, and I saw Bev, or at least parts of her. Her smile, her hair whipping around. I dropped my bag where I was, took off my jacket, and moved close to the dance, ready to join in.

A loud shrill buzz, like a gym teacher's whistle, stopped everyone in place.

"She's here," a voice said, soft and female. "Let's welcome her."

The whistle blew again and the dancers unfroze, turning toward me with excited smiles, like a huge group of kids ready to drag someone new into their game.

"Welcome, Maya," they said in breathy unison, sweat glistening on beards and bare breasts.

I didn't know what to do. Suddenly, I broke into tears. Something about all those people looking at me, smiling at me. It felt like total acceptance.

A figure pushed through the crowd. A brunette with long Pocahontas braids in denim shorts came up to me, smiling with her hands out and open.

"I'm Daya," she said, pulling me into her bare chest. "And you're finally home."

Daya was the same size as me, same body type even, though younger by a few years. I looked into her big brown eyes. "How can I be home? I don't even know what all this is."

She reached up and touched my temples with her fingertips.

"You don't have to know up there," she said, moving her hand down to my chest. "Your heart already knows."

Reaching for my bag, she led me toward a cabin beyond the fire. "Come. Desmond will decide if you are ready."

"Ready for what?"

Daya climbed the steps of the cabin, slipped off her pair of muddy moccasins, and reached for the door. "The knowing. Please take your boots off."

She entered the cabin, walked through the main room, and knocked twice on a closed door. "Wait here," she said, and went through.

I kicked off my boots and checked out the room.

A chintzy rug sat in front of a fireplace. I noticed a table and chairs, but they'd been pushed to the side. The rest of the room had been cut in half by a wall of canvases on easels, all facing the other direction. I peeked around and saw Linda, the old woman from the Laurel Canyon house, wearing a full-length smock, covered in paint.

I got her attention. The first time I'd seen her she'd seemed pleasant enough, but now, looking up from her palette of reds, oranges, and yellows, Linda beamed with energy and enthusiasm.

"You've made it." She set her brush aside. "I'm so glad. Please, come and look."

I entered her U of canvases and immediately noticed a trend: fires. Cities, houses, cars, schools—all burnt or burning in different ways, each with people writhing in agony. Hair burnt down to scalps, faces melting, men, women, and children. Seriously disturbing shit. One painting that really got to me showed a fireman with a hose running into a wall of fire ten times his size. No way he'd make it out alive.

The largest canvas, maybe four feet high by eight feet wide and only half finished, seemed to be the only scene of hope. In the upper left, a cloud of gray ash hovered over the remains of a giant city, maybe LA, and more of the same charred bodies littered the streets. In the upper right, feet of empty canvas away, a green forested mountain rose up to meet a blue sky, and a solid white beam went straight from the mountain to the top of the canvas.

Linda stood next to me, nodding toward the large, unfinished canvas. "Cataclysm."

I started to ask her what the hell that meant, but the door to the other room opened and Daya walked out.

"Desmond's ready for you."

She stepped aside and Desmond took her place in the doorway. He wore a full-body sarong, like one of the monks from the airport, but all white.

"Maya, thank you for finding me," he said, taking my hand as I entered. Either he or the cabin smelled like tea tree oil, strong, but clean. "And for starting the journey."

The room had a king-sized bed, but Desmond led me to a couch and sat next to me. Daya came in behind us, followed by Linda, who shut the door after her, even with a paintbrush still in her hand.

The women pulled up chairs and faced us. I looked over at Desmond and saw him watching me as well.

I smiled and they smiled, but no one said anything.

So I nodded, smiled even bigger.

They smiled back.

I started laughing, couldn't help it. They laughed too.

"What the hell is this?" I said. "What's happening here?"

Desmond reached toward me and placed his hand on my knee. "What do you think is happening here?"

I had no idea. That's what I told them, but they sat there, grinning, like they were waiting to hear me talk.

Linda leaned in. "Do you have a message for me?"

"A message? Like what?"

"Maybe something you saw in my paintings."

I laughed and looked around the room, almost expecting Geraldo Rivera to bust out from a closet, but no one else laughed this time.

Daya looked angry. "I told you it wasn't her."

"What wasn't me?" I said. "I mean, what am I not?"

Desmond pointed a calm but shushing finger Daya's direction. "Wait for the message."

He turned back toward me and smiled. Daya folded her hands and looked down. Linda scooted closer and leaned in.

I thought back to her paintings. "Honestly, most of your art scared me shitless."

Linda nodded. "Most, but not all?"

"I liked the big one, the unfinished thing with the green mountain on the right. Out of all of the places in the room, it was the place I wanted to go."

Daya looked up from her hands. Linda sat back with a smile. I checked out Desmond but couldn't read anything in those gray eyes.

Linda cleared her throat. "What about the left side?"

"Looked like LA," I said, "but like a bomb had gone off."

Linda gasped. Daya looked like she might cry. Desmond nodded and smiled.

"And so the message arrives," he said, like I'd just solved a big freaking riddle.

Daya jumped out of her chair and hugged me. Linda got up with tears in her eyes.

"Leave us now," Desmond said. The women left the room, not quite walking backward like I was the queen, but looking back every second or so to smile before closing the door behind them.

I stood up. "What the hell just happened? I don't know who you people think I am, but I'm no one special."

"Of course you are." Desmond left the couch and walked over to the open door of a bathroom.

I followed him, saw him filling a large plastic bowl in the sink. "I don't know what Bev told you people, but I don't have any money."

He reached for a small brown bottle and used a glass dropper to add several beads of oil to the water in the bowl. "We don't care about your money."

"Good, 'cause I might not even make rent this month."

He turned toward me, bowl in hand. I moved out of the way, and he walked back to the couch. "Please, sit."

"I'm not special," I said, no idea what he or they or anyone wanted from me. "I'm a bit of a freaking mess, in fact."

"Sit," he repeated, pointing to the couch.

I sat back down.

He knelt in front of me with the bowl at his side and reached for my socks.

"What are you doing?"

"Washing your feet."

"Washing my—"

He pulled one sock off, reached for the other. "That's right."

I've been fucking people for money for the last twenty-five years but had never felt naked once until I sat there with my bare feet in his hands.

"I'm no one special either," he said, lifting my feet and placing them gently in the warm water. "I was a humble yogi until I met Linda."

He told me how Linda had been having blinding headaches that nothing could touch. She'd been to all of the doctors, brain scans and everything. Turns out, Linda's kind of loaded, as in, super rich. Her late husband had created a missile guidance system, something to do with nukes during the Reagan years. Last year she came to one of Desmond's yoga retreats for help with the headaches, and everything changed for both of them.

"I'd taken her aside," Desmond said, massaging my feet in the water. "Like we are now. I'd never seen someone so twisted with pain, so racked with guilt."

"Guilt? Why would Linda be guilty?"

"The bombs. Her husband's death left her with so much money, but she couldn't use a penny without thinking about what each cent meant in the loss of human life."

He moved his hand up to my calf, still rubbing.

His touch felt great, but I was confused. "What bombs? No one's used a nuke since World War II, right?"

He switched to the other calf. "That's right." Desmond looked up and met my eyes. "I have a gift, Maya. I can help people with their pain, and sometimes, I can even see what they see."

"I don't know what that means."

"I know," he said, "but stay with me. Linda wasn't only suffering from headaches—she was also having dreams, nightmares even, every night. So I joined with her in something I call the Knowing."

"The Knowing?"

He lifted my feet out of the bowl and onto a dry towel. "Throughout my life, I've seen remarkable things through other people's eyes. Wonderful, magical experiences, but also horrible, shameful things. Like your father."

My throat choked up. "My father?"

"I see things," he repeated. "My visions are a gift that I use to help people heal."

I stood up. "What did you see about my father?" Nobody knows about my father. I never told a soul.

He rose as well but sat back in a chair. "In time. Now, you need to know what Linda saw every night. A city, full of life but not love, built on vanity and power, bursting at the seams, divided by lines of race and wealth."

"LA," I said. "No shit, right?"

"Right, but not just LA. She saw London, Paris, Moscow, Tokyo, Tehran, Mecca. All of the people in the world, all caught up in their own moments and movements, all blaming someone else for their problems. Then, the bombs came. Worldwide devastation, nuclear fallout, bodies strewn across the planet. From her house in the hills, she watched the people of Earth melt away, leaving only her untouched."

"No wonder she had headaches," I said, still not really sure why it had anything to do with me.

"But here's what she didn't know." Desmond folded his legs up and under each other on the chair. "Linda wasn't having dreams. She was having visions."

"Visions? Like, of the future?"

I expected Desmond to start laughing, like he'd been stringing me along the whole time, but he was serious.

"From the Spirit. Or as you might refer to him, God."

"Okay. I'm not really a God type of girl."

"Hear me out. God was showing her the end of the world."

I looked around for my bag. I'd been in bad situations before, dudes in shit hotel rooms with knives, someone hiding in the backseat of my car. None of that scared me as much as when someone started talking about visions from God. "Uh-huh."

"But he was also showing her there was time to save people. The special people."

"Sure, good to know."

"It's not just Linda. Daya also communicates with the Spirit."

I took a step away from the couch and his chair. "Cool family."

He wasn't blocking me or anything, but for a second I thought about making a run for it.

"She had a vision too. A vision of you."

"Bullshit." I turned back to face him. Enough was enough. "Why the hell would Daya have a vision about me? She into group sex or something?"

Desmond rose. "I understand, it's a lot to take in."

"So is a gang bang." I saw my bag by the door and went for it. "I don't know what I thought this place was. I figured you were all getting high and fucking each other and maybe I'd get to join in. But visions from God? I'm good."

"I can show you," he said, still behind me.

I turned back. "Show me what? There's no such thing as God."

"Ask Linda, or Daya, or any of those free souls dancing around the fire. I can show you."

He raised his hands. No prayer or anything, just open and up at eye level.

I didn't need some old man in the sky to tell me the meaning of life. Still, I set my bag down and walked back toward Desmond. Every asshole I'd ever met, from the guy with the knife to half of my producers, had backed down when I called them on their shit. I couldn't wait to laugh in his face.

"Fine. Show me your God."

I hadn't even stopped moving when he reached out for my head, one palm at each temple. All of my anger dropped away, and a wall of heat surged through my body. My vision went dark, then light, then suddenly I was somewhere else. I saw flames spreading out over the cities of the world, heard millions of voices in pain. That hell was replaced by a green mountain, where me and thousands of people, arm in arm, circled around a white column of light, brighter than anything I'd ever imagined, reaching up into the sky. One by one, the people of the circle leapt into the light and were carried up into the air. When it came to be my turn, I didn't hesitate. I stepped into the light and fell back so that I looked straight up into the beam to heaven. And there, at the top of the beam, a face waited. A face of kindness and wonder and wisdom and forgiveness. And it spoke—He spoke to me.

"Welcome, my daughter, your voyage has begun."

18

Lakshmi flagged down the more-of-an-actor-than-a-waiter who'd provided the bare minimum of service to her and her date. Red-headed Evelyn from Milwaukee had been in the bathroom for five minutes at this point. Lakshmi was starting to think the girl had skipped out the back door, maybe because she'd considered the same move herself every minute for the last half hour.

The waiter came her direction, then turned back to his station to retrieve her credit card receipt before finally making his way over.

"I gotta go," Lakshmi told the corn-fed next-Hemsworth-brother, grabbing her purse and getting up. "If a ginger who looks like she's afraid of math, science, literature, politics, and history asks about me, tell her I had an emergency."

"Shit, I forgot." The waiter reached for a notebook in his apron and read from the top page. "She told me to tell you, 'She had a great time, but it's a pass.' "

"Bloody hell." Lakshmi turned for the door, not sure which bothered her more: that the date she'd wanted to ditch had ditched her first, or that the waiter hadn't been able to memorize the simple message.

She still hadn't figured out life in LA, or at least online dating apps, or maybe dating in general, or life in the slightest. Sex wasn't a problem. Like with Pixie Cut, the girl she'd met on her night out with Caitlin. Lakshmi had learned enough about the city's scene to find company when needed—just not any meaningful connection. Evelyn, the runaway redhead, had seemed great through the app's algorithm, but sitting across from her, watching the girl eat sushi with a fork and talk about her search for a commercial talent agent, Lakshmi had been unable to find common ground. Now she was alone in East Hollywood on a Saturday night. Starting her walk back toward the Red Line train station, she had to remind herself that *Evelyn's not a girl; you're the same age.*

Maybe that was the reason she hadn't seriously connected with anyone. She'd felt so much older than everyone else ever since her first real love disappeared during sophomore year. Lakshmi had spent the rest of college looking for Angela, eventually getting Caitlin involved, only to discover that Angela had been held in an underground prison and tortured and . . .

Something Caitlin had said last year interrupted her descent into the past.

Not everything's that asshole's fault, kid. Keep moving and you'll be fine. Make the world a better place somehow.

Lakshmi shook the self-reflection away, double-checked the people around her at the intersection, then kept moving, crossing the street to the subway station. This time of night, the trains came every twenty minutes, and she'd missed the last one by five. She thought about finding Evelyn on social media and getting snarky, but she knew a more constructive way to kill time. Friendship always made the world a better place.

Caitlin answered the phone on the fourth ring.

"You don't sound intoxicated, and I don't hear a man's voice in the room," Lakshmi said. "Is something wrong?"

Caitlin's laugh brightened her night. "I'm reading. What's your excuse?"

Lakshmi filled her in on the latest disappointment. "What about you? Want to talk about whatever's happening?"

"I'm not sure I know what's happening," Caitlin said, then launched into the story.

By the time Lakshmi's train arrived, she'd nearly forgotten her bitterness over her Evelyn encounter. The date's letdown disappeared completely when Caitlin asked her to research the Daughters of God.

"Pop back a tick. You want my help?"

"I'm gonna try to figure out what Mama Maya was into up here," Caitlin said, "but it all started down there in LA."

Lakshmi got on the train, almost bouncing with excitement. "I thought Mike usually did the research you didn't have time for."

Caitlin and Mike Roman, a muscle-bound ex-Marine and ex-cop of few words, were close, and as far as Lakshmi knew, never in a romantic way.

"Roman's down in Mexico right now," Caitlin said. "Plus, he's more of a battering ram than a magnifying glass. I know you weren't exactly alive at the time, but want to look into a cult that started in LA in the nineties for me? I'll throw you some cash, maybe a little more than your transcription rate."

Lakshmi would have done it for free. "I'll start tonight."

CHAPTER

19

CAITLIN SNAPPED AWAKE, unsure why her heart was racing like she'd just sprinted a hundred meters.

Muted daylight streamed through the hotel room's window shade and the side-table clock read 8:43, seventeen minutes before her alarm would chime.

She reached for her phone but froze. Heavy pounding shook the door to her room. No one who worked in a hotel would knock that loud. Caitlin rolled out of bed in only a T-shirt and underwear, reaching for the pair of jeans she'd abandoned on the floor.

"Hey, bitch." The angry male voice on the other side of the door sounded familiar. "I know you're in there."

Caitlin grabbed the hotel phone and called the front desk.

"I need security," she said, pulling on her pants. "Someone's trying to break down my door."

"We don't have security," the clerk replied, possibly the same kid from the day before.

"Then call the police."

Caitlin hung up and slid her shoes on, unlaced with no socks.

Another barrage shook the door. "You think you can come to my county and jack me up?"

Caitlin placed the voice.

Johnny Larsen.

She didn't know how she'd pissed him off before nine on a Sunday but knew she didn't want to open the door. Larsen seemed like the type to argue with a gun in his hand, plus he'd figured out which room was hers, meaning he'd either bribed someone for the info or had someone watching her hotel.

"Sir," the same voice from the phone said, now in the hallway, "is there a problem?"

"Fuck yourself."

The pounding resumed.

Caitlin didn't travel with a curling iron, hair dryer, or anything heavy enough to weaponize. She inventoried the rest of the hotel room: a flimsy luggage rack, an ice bucket, and two eight-ounce plastic cups—one she'd used for water, the other still wrapped in cellophane.

The hotel clerk chimed in again. "If you're not a guest, I need you to leave the property."

Caitlin considered the window, but she knew no budget hotel would ever let a first-floor window open wide enough for someone to escape without paying.

"Not until I talk to this bitch," Larsen answered.

Screw this.

If Larsen had been waving a gun around, the clerk would have bugged out long ago. Caitlin went back toward the bathroom, where a solid-looking soap dish held an assortment of toiletries she'd ignored so far. She grabbed the dish, walked into her bathroom, pulled the shower curtain in front of her body, and threw the faux-sandstone block into the tub. Shards peppered the vinyl curtain when the dish broke, but one major chunk remained, a jagged three-inch triangle. She gripped the piece and went for the door.

"Sir, I've called the police—"

"That's it, dickhead," Larsen said, his voice moving away from the door and toward the clerk.

Caitlin pulled the handle and stepped into the hall. Larsen was ten feet down the corridor. The desk clerk stood ten feet further holding a broomstick in front of him, like a knight with a broadsword.

Caitlin raised the convincing end of the broken dish toward Larsen's back. "Who are you calling dickhead, fuck-stick?"

Larsen turned fast and wild, flaring his flannel jacket open. No gun shown on his belt, but the camouflage hilt of a hunting knife peeked out of a sheath.

Caitlin took a step back, ready to run. No need. At least three voices spoke in the hall behind her, one of which had to be a kid. Plus, the clerk wasn't going anywhere. Plenty of witnesses on hand.

Larsen's eyes went toward the new voices, then came back to Caitlin's improvised weapon. "The hell you gonna do with that thing?"

She squared off against him. "Whatever I have to. What's with all the noise?"

"The boys said I just missed some chick with a Jew name leaving the Lumberjack last night." He opened the palm of his right hand. "Want to explain why I found this shit in my truck this morning?"

He dropped a handful of something onto the hallway carpeting. From that distance, the ten or so little white bits looked like rocks.

Caitlin didn't have to move closer to know they weren't rocks. They were teeth, and where would anyone get a handful of teeth?

Larsen lowered his voice. "Think I'm going to jail for some dead Dog, bitch?"

So that was it. The man with the arm covered in bandages, probably covering up defensive wounds, had woken to find a mouthful of missing teeth in the bed of his truck. She laughed. "You do know you've just admitted you're holding the teeth of a homicide victim, right?"

He clenched his jaw and took a step in her direction.

"Come an inch closer," she said, "and you'll be the next body in the morgue."

Larsen's shoulders rose with a deep breath. For a second, Caitlin thought he'd really chance an attack, witnesses or not.

The clerk must have agreed. His broomstick snapped in half when it hit the back of Larsen's head. The big man fell face first with the solid thud of a three-hundred-year-old redwood.

CHAPTER

20

SHERIFF MARTIN ITCHED the side of his goatee with the back of his pen. "And how did you end up in the Lumberjack, again? Out of all of the places in the county?"

"My feet," Caitlin said, sitting back in the chair across from Martin's desk for the second time in two days. "The place looked like a dive. I love dives. Plus they had a State of Jefferson flag behind the bar."

The local police had arrived minutes after Johnny was knocked down. Then Sheriff Martin and a pair of deputies had followed to place the concussed but still-living Johnny Larsen under arrest for the murder of UD-0004. On the ride from the hotel to the station, Caitlin had told Sheriff Martin how her impromptu research project had turned into a legitimate story, then put him in touch with Stan Lawton for corroboration. It wasn't that Martin had interrogated her after the hotel surprise party, but as she'd given her account, his brow had furrowed deeper and deeper with each mention of her meetings with Johnny Larsen. At this point, she was worried his face might collapse.

"They had cheeseburgers, booze, and Wi-Fi," Caitlin stressed. "The whole thing was a coincidence."

"Right." He dropped his pen and shook his head in disbelief. "Coincidence."

Caitlin raised his headshake an eye roll. "Why were you there, Sheriff? Are you a Proud Son of Oregon?"

He absently reached for the fallen pen. "Well, I did grow up here, and I do feel a fair amount of pride in my state—"

"It's no Jefferson," Caitlin interrupted. "But are you a member of a white supremacist organization known as the Proud Sons of Oregon?"

Martin let out a sigh. "I am not, and calling them an organization is one helluva stretch. It's basically Johnny and two or three other assholes who wanted to get tattoos."

"But you happened to be in the same bar, maybe ten minutes before Larsen and his holes had their meeting."

"Just like you."

"Right," Caitlin said, bringing him full circle. "A coincidence. So do the bits of teeth found in the back of Larsen's truck match the empty mouth of the dead body?"

Martin found his pen again and doodled a series of circles on the yellow pad in front of him. "We've already sent them off, but it'd be pretty wild if they didn't. I think the best thing for everyone involved would be for you to head back to Los Angeles until we get our results."

"And when might that be?"

"A school shooting outside of Portland just jumped to the front of the line. From what they've told me, it could be weeks."

On her first day in town, Caitlin had thought Martin's goatee made him look like a wizened bear. Now her bear looked more like a pouting puppy.

"Is that before or after your next election, Sheriff?"

That put the man on his feet. "I've tried to take your grieving into consideration, Miss Bergman, but I've got work to do, and I no longer need your help."

Caitlin got up as well. "Hold on, Boz. I'm not trying to rock the boat."

"Coos Bay is a big town, but outside of it, this is a small county. I don't have to like everyone in the area, but I do have to live with them. You, on the other hand—" He opened his office door. "You can go on home now. We've got everything covered."

"There he is," a voice in the outer office said. "Don't tell him a thing, Miss Bergman."

Both Caitlin's and Sheriff Martin's heads whipped toward the open doorway. A pageboy cut of straight brown hair topped a short but full-bodied woman wearing a wine-red blazer over matching pants. The woman walked past a twentysomething deputy and met them both in the doorway.

"Damn it," Martin said, almost pulling the door shut in the woman's face. "Why are you here, Gwendolyn?"

"I'm acting as Caitlin Bergman's attorney. As such, I'm advising her not to say anything until we've had a chance to discuss recent events."

Caitlin stared at the older woman's determined expression and necklace of chunky wooden beads. "As I'm not under arrest, I have no need for an attorney. More importantly, who the hell are you?"

"Gwendolyn Sunrise." The business card she offered affirmed the unlikely combination of words. She broke into a smile so white and wide that Caitlin thought she'd been lost in the surf on a summer day. "I represent the Daughters of God organization and therefore am available to any family members in need of legal service." She turned toward Sheriff Martin, and her smile disappeared. "Desmond understands you've found both Magda's body and her murderer."

Martin took a step back. "Well, if Desmond understands it, it must be some sort of cosmically enlightened magic. I know nothing of the kind."

Ignoring his dig, Lady Sunrise turned back to Caitlin. "If you're not under arrest, then you're free to go. May I offer you a ride?"

The sheriff put a hand out. "Miss Bergman doesn't need a ride from anyone in your organization."

"Thank you, Sheriff," Caitlin said, grabbing her things, "but *Miss Bergman* can decide who she goes home with, if she's going home at all." She turned to the crimson-clad attorney. "Lead the way, sunshine."

The woman flashed that smile again. "It's Sunrise."

"Right," Caitlin said, almost squinting on her way out the door. "And this is a brand-new day."

21

C AITLIN FOLLOWED THE woman to the parking lot.

"I have a lot of questions, Gwendolyn."

Gwendolyn opened the back door of a ten-year-old town car painted nearly the same color of red as her suit. "Everyone does. I'll be glad to answer anything you'd like on the way to wherever you'd like to go."

"Coos Bay," Caitlin said, climbing in.

"Of course." She shut Caitlin inside.

Though aging, the car's vinyl interior, also the same shade of red, looked well kept.

A slender woman in her late teens waited behind the steering wheel. Caitlin made eye contact in the rearview. "Hello."

"Yes," the young woman said, not quite connecting. Her eyes moved away, not an aversion, but fixated on something behind the car.

Caitlin turned to look.

The lawyer in red, in transit to the car's passenger side, had turned back toward the government building. A woman in jeans and a polo shirt with dark roots poking through blond hair yelled from the sidewalk. Wearing no scrubs this time, Leslie Kramer, the medical examiner, started running toward the red town car.

Caitlin glanced back to the girl's eyes in the rearview and saw a high chance of tears in the forecast. She felt around the door for the control to lower the windows so she could hear what was being said but couldn't find a toggle.

The passenger door opened and Gwendolyn Sunrise got in. "Coos Bay," she said, slamming the door behind her.

The driver's eyes didn't leave the rearview.

Gwendolyn leaned forward and touched the girl's shoulder. "Now."

"Of course." The car popped into reverse with a lurch that sent both Caitlin and the lawyer toward the red vinyl of the front seats.

Just as they pivoted to face the main road, Leslie Kramer arrived at the driver's side window.

"Lily," she screamed, pounding on the glass. "I know you're in there. Talk to me."

"Go," Gwendolyn said.

Her daughter Lily ran off with the Daughters of God, Sheriff Martin had told Caitlin.

Now Lily Kramer, the girl behind the wheel, put the car in drive and hit the gas.

The thud of the senior Kramer's palm shook Caitlin's window, the woman struggling to keep up.

Caitlin leaned forward. "What is this shit?"

"A family dispute," Gwendolyn answered, her hand still on the driver's shoulder. "Stay in your center, Eve. I've got you."

Caitlin watched the medical examiner fall behind. "I don't know you people, and I'm not gonna be part of any sort of religious abduction."

Gwendolyn sat back like the moment had already faded into history. "Abduction? Eve isn't being kept away from anyone."

"Then have her stop the car. You said you represent the Daughters of God and some shit about how that means you help their families as well."

"That's right, Miss Bergman." Gwendolyn's hand went to the wooden beads around her neck. "Sometimes that means creating a safe distance from harmful family members. Eve's mother—"

"Calls her Lily, not Eve," Caitlin said. "Stop the car and let her talk to the woman, or let me out of here."

Gwendolyn held her necklace inches from her neck with one finger, shifted it from side to side twice, then let it drop, looking toward the front. "Stop."

Neither Lily nor Eve Kramer seemed relieved. "But—"

Again, Gwendolyn's hand went to the girl's shoulder. Her voice came out with the soothing calm of a spa commercial. "It's okay. She can't hurt you here."

The girl let out a deep exhale, then pulled the car over. Caitlin checked the rear window and saw Kramer bent over, panting.

"Back up," Gwendolyn said. "It'll be fine."

The young woman backed the car toward her mother and rolled a window down. Leslie Kramer jogged up and planted her hands on the windowsill.

"Lily? Baby, is that you?"

Lily kept her hands and eyes on the wheel. "Hello, Mother."

"Come home, Lily. Come with me right now."

She threw her arms around the girl's shoulders and pulled her toward the window, but Lily brushed her off.

"What do you want?"

"What do I want?" Kramer wiped tears from her eyes. "I want to see you."

Lily faced her. "Here I am. I'm fine, I'm happy, I'm safe. I have to go now."

"No, you don't," Leslie said, grabbing her wrist. "You don't have to do anything these people say. They don't know what's best for you."

Lily pried her mother's hand off. "I'm nineteen years old and am fully capable of deciding what's best for me."

She dropped her hand to the center console and the driver's side window went up, almost closing on the medical examiner's hand.

"Lily, no—"

The girl put the car in gear. "Move, or I'll run over your feet."

"Lily—"

"Good-bye, Mother," she said, then pulled away.

Leslie Kramer fell to her knees in tears.

Caitlin looked back to the driver, who once again found solace in the touch of Gwendolyn Sunrise's hand on her shoulder.

"It's not even noon on a Sunday," the girl said, fighting back tears, "and she's halfway through a bottle of Wild Turkey."

Gwendolyn patted her shoulder again. "You did great, Eve."

The girl wiped her eye, then focused on the road in front of her. "We'll be in Coos Bay in twenty minutes."

Gwendolyn sat back. "You see, Caitlin. We're not keeping anyone from their families."

"Sure," Caitlin said, her heart pumping from the exchange. "I get it. Let's talk about your group. Are you the Dayans or the Daughters of God?"

The woman smiled. "Our religion is registered as a 501(c)(3) under the name Daughters of God, but we tend to use both names."

"Why *Daughters*? Aren't there men in your group?"

"Perhaps I'm not the right person to answer your questions."

Caitlin held back her first thought: *You literally said you would be happy to answer any of my questions.* Instead she went with, "I thought you were at the sheriff's station to help me."

"One of our members is missing. I went there for answers, only to learn that she'd been killed."

"And you believe the dead woman is my birth mother?"

"Wasn't she? I understand you were brought here to identify the body. I'm sorry for your loss."

"Not much of a loss. I never knew my mother. I don't know anything about her life, and she didn't know anything about mine."

Gwendolyn Sunrise started to say something, then stopped and reached into a briefcase near her feet. She moved some papers aside, then came up with a framed photo of Caitlin. "Then how did I know who you were?"

Caitlin took the four-by-six frame and stared at a familiar black-and-white image. Her publisher had used that same press shot on the back of Caitlin's first book, almost four years old at this point.

"Your mother knew all about your work," Gwendolyn said, in the same calming tone she'd used on the girl. "She was your biggest fan."

Caitlin fought past the million ways she wanted to tell Gwendolyn Sunrise to screw herself and forced a smile. "Isn't that precious?"

Gwendolyn's hand ventured tentatively toward Caitlin's knee. "I can sense your anger."

"Picked that up all on your own?"

The look in Caitlin's eyes must have burned a hole in the lawyer's hand, because Gwendolyn withdrew toward her own side of the car. "Desmond can explain it better. He knows all things under the Light."

Caitlin set the frame in the space between them. "So Desmond's still alive?"

"Of course. He'd like you to come see him."

"Where? When?"

Gwendolyn laughed. "Whenever you feel ready."

"Not now," Caitlin said, stopping the knee-jerk "Right now" that had almost jumped out of her mouth. She hadn't found the car's window control yet, let alone the door handle. She didn't know *all things under the Light*, but she did know that hitching a ride to a cult's compound in an inescapable blood-red car without telling anyone had to be on every culture's list of no-nos. Still, the idea that Mama Maya had been keeping tabs on Caitlin's life had her mind racing with the questions she thought she'd stopped asking years ago.

Why did you leave me?

Did you ever try to come back to visit? To get to know me?

Who was my father?

Why wasn't he good enough?

Why wasn't I?

"You have my card," Gwendolyn said, flashing her full-mouth smile again, an instant reminder that the woman's last name was Sunrise. "Desmond can answer all of your questions."

CHAPTER

22

Once again, Caitlin waited in the hotel lobby to see how long the driver would linger. Unlike Johnny Larsen's truck, the Dayan town car left immediately.

"Can I help you, Miss Bergman?"

Expecting to see her broomstick hero, she turned toward the front desk, but a chubby man in his late thirties that Caitlin had definitely never met stood behind the counter. She knew the hotel staff probably gossiped with each shift change, but she didn't like that this complete stranger, like the employee the day before, knew her name.

She flattened her palms on his counter. "How do you know who I am?"

He stepped backward. "Sorry. Someone asked about you earlier, described you and everything."

"Who?"

"A woman," he stammered. "I don't know."

"A woman? Yeah, right." She stared the man down, but he either had no more words to give or was too scared to try them. She turned and walked toward her room. "I'm checking out."

First step: find a secure home base. She packed her bags and considered her options. Everyone in the county seemed to know where she was staying, even though she'd really only spoken to three people: Sheriff Martin, Johnny Larsen, and Hazel from the Lumberjack.

With a population under twenty thousand, Coos Bay was minuscule compared to LA. But combined with North Bend, the area became the largest metropolitan area on the Oregon coast. Not exactly a small town where everyone knew each other's business. Still, they knew a lot more about Caitlin's life than she knew about theirs. Might as well pick the spot with the most cameras.

By four thirty that afternoon, she'd unlocked the door to a suite at the Mill Casino Hotel and RV Park. By five thirty, she'd dropped two outfits with the front desk for laundry service and finished a goat cheese and spinach salad in a waterfront dining room. By six, she'd placed an order with a local marijuana delivery service. By seven, she'd grabbed the next entry of Mama Maya's journal, drawn a bath in the whirlpool, and lit a joint.

*   *   *

March 8, 1993

So much has happened. It feels like there's hardly time to write anything down.

I stayed at God's Hill, obviously.

I sleep in a massive tent with thirty others, though I'm right next to Bev. She's been my guide. There are four other tents like ours.

Actually, we don't sleep a lot.

It's all too exciting.

Every day, we wake to our morning song.

Daya stands near the prayer fire and starts.

The fire is dying, so come let me build
A light that can shine through to heaven above
So he'll see me trying, and doing his will
Building my fire with light and with love

(Linda wrote it, the song, I mean. It came to her in a dream. Not the end of the world dream, which we call the Cataclysmic Vision, but the Hopeful Morning, her message of joy.)

Soft, no mic or anything, but as soon as any of us hear Daya's voice, we join in. One by one, the song grows until the whole camp is singing. Once we're ready, we step out of the tent and head to the woodpile. We each grab a piece, take it to the fire, then form a giant circle, arm in arm. Then we spin like a galaxy around a massive star. Slow at first, just walking in a big circle, still singing our verse.

The drummers start pounding out a beat, and we speed up to match their tempo. We really get going, but no one falls. I don't think you can, because everyone else would just carry you, but you do get sweaty as shit. Then, either Desmond or Daya yells, and we come to a stop and start jumping in place. Each ring of the circle takes a turn leaping, all the way down from a squat to as high as we can make it, then the next ring, then the next, like we're sending a pulse out into the world. Finally, we all collapse in place and Daya announces the day's message.

Each day has a central mantra to meditate on, and each one has blown my mind so far. Like yesterday's—Allow yourself to be touched. *At first we all took it as an excuse to tickle or play with each other—there are some serious hotties here, both men and women—but by the afternoon, I could hear deep meaning in everything people said. Later, I cried when I found a handful of baby birds in a nest, helpless little things waiting for a mom to return with a meal.*

That was nothing compared to today's message: Your fear only protects you from your possibilities. *I thought about it all through first session.*

The people who've been here the longest have regular assignments, like food prep, laundry, farming, and all the stuff that keeps us going on God's Hill. I found out we're not actually on parkland up here, but right on the edge of the park on some old man's farmland. He lets us stay here if we work his fields, so most of the men are sent to work until the afternoon. For the rest of us, first session means we divide into Thought Clouds in the woods.

I swear, I feel like I'm eighteen again. We sing songs and have these talks, deep talks, about the meaning of life. Money, sex, drugs, God—nothing's off limits.

And the physical stuff. We move around so much. Sometimes we run, like we're playing tag. Sometimes we jump up and down for as long as we can, ten, twenty minutes. We'll chant the day's message over and over until the words are gibberish. Somehow that makes them stronger.

I passed out last week, woke up in my tent. But I had dreams. So strong. I'm dreaming every night. And my skin looks great. Like when I saw Bev's face at that party. I'm losing weight, too. Not in a bad way, but I feel so much stronger. I'm seeing muscles I haven't had since my days on the pole.

I feel so good.

There's so much more, but I've got to sleep. We're going on a midnight hike tonight. God, if I'd have written that a year ago, I'd have said no freaking way. I hated the woods, was afraid of them, even.

Now I know my fears were only protecting me from my possibilities.

* * *

Caitlin stood slowly. She'd been in the bath for half an hour, and either her high or Mama Maya's woodland adventure had brought a steady throb to her temples.

She toweled off and took the rest of the journal back into the bedroom. Her earlier attempt at a healthy dinner wasn't going to be enough. Room service promised her a large sausage-and-pepperoni pizza in under thirty minutes.

She grabbed the next page of Maya's journal, pulled the comforter from the king-sized bed, slid into the clean sheets, and went back to the woods.

* * *

March 17, 1993

Sex is my gift, not my curse.

Daya told me this today, a private message, just for me.

Sex is my gift from God.

Some are given wealth and prosperity. Some get the ability to sing or play an instrument. Some, like Linda, get dreams of the Spirit. Desmond gets the ability to channel and heal. Daya gets messages from communing with people.

I was given sex.

I am sex.

I'm crying. Right now, I'm freaking crying and it's crazy, because it's so pure.

I have been so ashamed for so long. Ashamed of how early the act came to me, of the hands that took me there, of the paths I followed.

Sex is my gift from the Spirit.

I am good at pleasing others. Not just good, I am a pro. Even now, at forty, I can make men and women see the light of life, feel the joy of God's creation.

"The horrible things that happened gave you empathy," Daya told me. "The ability to read lovers, to see where they hold their anxiety and to release them."

For years, I did so without enjoying it.

Not tonight.

Tonight I joined with Desmond and Daya.

No cameras.

No money.

No shame.

Just the three of us.

I've been fucking since I was twelve.

This was the first time I knew love.

* * *

"Gross," Caitlin said, shaking her head.

Not that she begrudged the woman a threesome. She'd made peace with her mother's lifestyle back in college, and sex was Caitlin's third favorite part of being a human being, right after french fries and pizza. But Mama Maya hadn't mentioned a shower or a bath since her initial foot wash, so a month of hot yoga in the woods meant no one in the sex party smelled like roses.

She flipped through the rest of the journal's pages and tried to estimate how long it'd take to finish. Longer than another joint and a pizza. A man had shown up at her door this morning, ready to kill. Last night, a woman had watched her from the edge of a parking lot. Somewhere in between was the story of a sheriff who didn't want to get involved, a missing teenager, and the Five, whatever or whoever they were. Tomorrow morning could go any number of directions, and she needed as much information as possible. Information, not the baggage she'd been dragging around for forty years. She needed someone to sift the data, not cry over past offenses, let alone read between the lines for references to a daughter named Caitlin. She hated to think it, or even say it out loud, but the words came out. "I need help."

She laughed, grabbed her phone, and found Scott Canton's number, but stopped. Her task would require the use of file-based research, and her warrior-poet therapist eschewed all things digital. Still, his voice appeared with a candidate as clearly as if she'd called. *Lakshmi—if you'd let her get close.*

Caitlin gritted her teeth until her cheek muscles hurt. She'd done her best to distance herself from Lakshmi's enthusiastic forays into friendship, insulating her personal life with a wall of professionalism. Having the girl read her dead mother's diary would knock that wall to pieces with a wrecking ball. Still, it needed to be done, and Lakshmi would jump at the chance.

What was the mantra Maya had written in her journal?

My fears were only protecting me from my possibilities.

Caitlin dialed her phone and got Lakshmi on the second ring. "Hey, kid, want to throw a hundred pages of extra reading on top of your research?"

Lakshmi laughed over the sounds of an active laundry room. "Yes, of course. I've found some general stuff about the group's formation so far, but nothing firsthand."

Caitlin fed her the limited names she'd found in the journal while uploading the contents of the thumb drive.

"My problem," she admitted, to both Lakshmi and herself, "is I'm basically skimming the pages looking for my name. Want to read about the adventures of my bisexual mom?"

Caitlin opened the door to room service and its warm box of cheesy self-satisfaction as Lakshmi happily agreed. Fifteen minutes later and three slices in, she returned to the journal, confident that Lakshmi would have the whole thing summarized in the next two days.

Giving herself permission to flip past the next few entries—Maya worked a farm, Maya and the others hiked Mount Baldy, Maya dewormed a goat—Caitlin stopped at an entry titled *My Real Name.*

* * *

June 6, 1993

My Real Name

I found out why I'm here tonight, or at least, how I was called to God's Hill.

It's my birthday. Not the day I came out of my mother, but my life-has-just-begun-to-make-sense birthday.

When did this start? February. Now it's June. Not everyone gets their birthday. Bev hasn't had one yet. But I did, and now I have a new name.

Magda.

I grew up Jewish, so Christ was the guy from Christmas and I'd never heard of Mary Magdalene, which is fine. Desmond says that all of the world's churches are right, in a way, though the emphasis on profit and real estate take them away from perfection. That's why we say both God and the Spirit.

Anyway, after today's morning song, Daya pulled me aside and told me I'd be given Desmond's word. It's been months since he's spoken to me. We've been together for sex many times, but Desmond hasn't given me any messages other than what I received when I first got to God's Hill.

I was nervous, nearly pissing my pants. That experience, that closeness to God, was stronger than any drug I'd ever tried, and I've tried most. I assumed I'd meet Desmond in his cabin, but Daya said no, I was supposed to follow the path to the top of the mountain by myself.

It was in the eighties, so by the time I got to the peak, I had a good sweat going.

Desmond sat on top of the Big Bounce, a twenty-foot trampoline some of the men had stretched between the trees, ten feet off the ground. He wasn't bouncing today. He sat facing the large, sweeping valley below the mountain with his eyes closed.

He looked so peaceful I almost turned back, but watching him rest, I realized I yearned to have that kind of peace, so I called out, "Teacher, may I approach?"

He opened his eyes, smiled, and nodded.

I climbed up and joined him on the Big Bounce, sitting as cross-legged as my hips allow, doing my best to match his posture.

Four months ago I would have started talking. Not this time. I inhaled the fresh air and waited.

"Linda's had a new vision," he said, still looking into the valley.

I hadn't seen Linda much over the last two weeks, but everyone said she'd been painting to the point of exhaustion.

"A migration," Desmond continued. "We're going to leave God's Hill."

My heart raced. I had no idea if that was a good or bad thing. "Is it the farmer?"

Some of the men had gotten into it with the local landowner. I didn't know why, but I'd heard the police were called, and I knew we weren't sending workers his way anymore.

"Oh no. This is a good migration, a growth, an expansion." He smiled at me. "And you're going to be an important part."

"Me?"

He put his hand on my knee. "I still remember the moment Beverly introduced us. You were everything she'd described."

I had to fight back a blush. "Why? I wasn't anything special, especially then. I mean, hot chicks in Hollywood are a dime a dozen, and I had really let myself go."

He smiled. "I don't mean your physical description. I mean how she'd described the woman in her dreams."

We'd been warned about interrupting Desmond when he was teaching, but I couldn't help myself. "I thought—"

He didn't look angry. "Yes?"

"When I first came to camp, when you showed me"—I paused, nervous to put it into words—"God's face, you said that Daya had been the one who'd had a vision of me."

Again, he smiled. "That's correct. Daya had told us of a vision she'd had of a strong, sexual woman who would help us reach God's Hill. She asked all of those present if they knew anyone who matched the description. No one had an answer, but the next morning, Beverly came forward and told me she'd had a dream. In her dream, you and she were together—"

Desmond never said fucking, *but that's what he meant by* together.

"—and people were watching, men and women, but they were ashamed, both of you and themselves. Instead of being scared, much as Beverly had felt, you went to each witness, putting everyone at ease, until all present had joined in. Out of nowhere, an explosion set the building on fire. Everyone panicked, but you grabbed Beverly, and she grabbed the others, and arm in arm, you led them naked through a wall of flame."

"Holy shit," I said, then quickly put my hand over my mouth.

Desmond laughed. "Indeed. On the other side of the flames, Linda, Daya, and I watched you all come to us, unscathed."

"Beverly dreamt all that?"

Desmond nodded. "Then you came to Linda's house, then here to us. Do you know the story of Mary Magdalene?"

I didn't. He explained how men throughout history had twisted the image of Mary Magdalene, possibly Jesus of Nazareth's thirteenth apostle, retelling her story as that of a prostitute who Jesus forgave and allowed to associate with his followers, a symbol of God's nonjudgmental love. But the church, being run by greedy men, had bastardized Mary's true story, hiding that she was just as trusted as the other apostles, and that she may have even been Jesus's wife on earth.

"Okay," I said, still not really following where he was going with this.

"In Daya's vision, this strong, sexual woman was known as Magda."

"Okay," I repeated.

Desmond put his arm around me.

"Don't be scared, Magda."

"I'm not Magda—"

"You are," he said, squeezing my shoulder, "if you let yourself be."

"What does that mean? What do I do as Magda?"

"First things first. You must say good-bye to Maya."

I asked how.

"You must tell me everything," he said. "The good and the bad, the best and the worst, so that we may celebrate Maya's passing."

"I'll be dead?"

"Oh no, you'll finally start to live."

Finally start to live.

Those words unlocked something in me, so I started with what I could remember. My father, and the way he hit my mother, then later me, then when Mom died, how his hits turned to softer hands that lingered instead of jabbed, though still just as painful. And I told him about the first time I stole, a box of candles from temple, how I tried pot in middle school, the first boy I kissed, then the first girl, and sex, and skipping school, and blowing my math teacher so I wouldn't fail, and prom, then how I ran away, then stripping, then coke and crystal, then porn. Each day was a constant search for new ways to get high, or at least to make my father's hands mean less.

Then, and I almost stopped there, but the words wanted to get out, I told Desmond about getting pregnant, the baby's father, and how I would have left it all to be with him, if only he'd wanted me, and about how hard I'd cried the day my daughter came, not from the pain, but because I'd seen her perfect, furious eyes, and I gave that child away. Then I told Desmond about how I'd thrown myself at men who passed me around, the diseases, the leases broken, the cars stolen, the time in jail for DUI, the times I should have gotten DUIs. I told him every single thing I could remember.

Finally, when the words ran out, he wiped my tears away, kissed my lips, and held me.

"Good-bye, Maya," he said. "You survived as well as you could. Magda has you now, and Magda will walk you through the flames."

I looked up at that beautiful man and felt so powerful, so full of joy.

"Unscathed," I said.

"That's right, Magda. The pure don't burn."

We stayed up there for another hour talking about the upcoming migration. He even asked for my thoughts on how we might recruit more members.

Maya was never asked for her opinion.

Magda has all kinds of ideas.

*   *   *

Caitlin sat up quickly.

Just like at home, her head banged against the wall above the bed's wooden headboard.

"Shit." She rubbed the tender spot.

Mama Maya, aka Magda, had unloaded a great deal in the last few pages, but only one thought circled in Caitlin's head.

Desmond knows the name of my real father—and according to the lawyer in red, Desmond wants me to come see him whenever I feel ready.

23

"THAT'S RIGHT, SCOTT," Caitlin said into her phone, keeping eye contact with the driver, Lily-call-her-Eve. "I'll be back in town tomorrow. Or, you know"—she waved toward the rearview from where she sat alone in the back of the town car—"call Sheriff Boswell Martin of the Coos County Sheriff's Department."

They said their good-byes, then hung up.

Eve looked back. "There's really nothing to worry about—"

Caitlin held up a finger and dialed Lakshmi. "Just a few more calls."

Twenty minutes later, she'd left her whereabouts with enough people that she felt 99 percent sure she wouldn't disappear on her way to the Dayan compound.

She checked the passing scenery. Like the route to Larsen Timber, the road wound through a deep forest of Douglas fir, hemlock, and red alder trees. Five minutes later, she realized they hadn't passed a single car headed the opposite direction. She knocked 10 percent off her return-unharmed estimate.

"Where exactly is your compound?" Caitlin said, finally. She'd called Gwendolyn Sunrise and agreed to meet Desmond first thing in the morning, and they'd sent the car. In her excitement, she'd neglected to fill in the details.

Eve's eyes returned to the rearview. "We'll be at God's Hill in twenty minutes."

"I thought that was in Los Angeles."

"It's wherever the Daughters gather," the young woman answered with a smile, "but you're right. We started in Los Angeles. How did you know?"

"I'm from there." Caitlin leaned forward, putting an arm between the driver's and passenger's seats. "Since we have some time, mind if I ask how you became a Daughter in the first place?"

"Some friends and I stopped into one of the wellness welcomes, and I got to talking with one of the messengers. They were there for me when no one else was."

Wellness welcomes and messengers.

Enough of the back-seat nonsense. Caitlin climbed up into the passenger seat.

"What's a wellness welcome? Do you mean the shop in town, Daya's Gifts?"

Eve flinched at the motion, but her smile returned when Caitlin settled in and clicked her seat belt. "That's the one in Coos Bay. There's Linda's Mountain in Coquille, Desmond's Dive in North Bend, Hope's Meadows in Dew Valley, and Magda's Treasure Chest in Bandon. They sell our craftwork, but really they're safe places where women in trouble can go."

Two things caught Caitlin's attention: that one of the shops was named after Magda, the name Maya Aronson had adopted, and that there were five shops total, as in, *Find the Five.*

She wanted to address both without appearing eager. "Is that what you were, Lily? In trouble?"

Caitlin saw the girl's hands tighten on the steering wheel. "I'm sorry. It's Eve, right?"

"My mother drinks," the young woman said. "Sometimes she drives drunk. She killed my brother. He was eleven. Since she works for the county, they called it a car accident, but no one bothered giving her a Breathalyzer. Maybe if they would have, she'd have seen how lost she was. I wasn't going to wait around to see what happened to me."

Caitlin nodded. "And how old were you? Fifteen, sixteen?"

"No way. The Daughters won't accept any voyagers under the age of eighteen. Desmond says they're not ready to hear the message until then. I'm the youngest one on God's Hill."

That made a third thread Caitlin wanted to follow. According to Johnny Larsen, his missing daughter was only thirteen. If the Dayans really lived by their rules, or at least the federal age of consent, the last thing they'd want around was a minor.

Eve seemed willing to talk. Maybe she'd talk about the Five. Caitlin had to be subtle. "So, five shops?"

"Wellness welcomes."

"Right. Maybe tomorrow I'll try to visit the other four, make a game of it."

Eve glanced over like Caitlin was the crazy one. "Sounds like a lot of driving."

Time to see if the words had meaning for all of the Dayans or just Mama Maya.

"Well, I'd be able to tell people I 'found the five.' "

That prompted a double take. "Why did you say it like that?"

A yellow arrow sign indicated a sharp turn up ahead, maybe five hundred feet.

Caitlin continued to play dumb. "Like what? 'Find the five'?"

"Do you"—Eve's voice lowered—"do you have a message for me?"

Caitlin pointed up ahead. "There's a turn coming."

The young woman didn't falter. "Something you're supposed to tell me?"

Caitlin tapped Eve's hand. "Look forward."

Eve glanced back, then hit the brakes, pulling the town car to a stop a safe hundred feet from the corner.

"Do you?"

"Do I what?" Caitlin said.

Eve smiled, then shook her head. "Sorry. You couldn't know what you were saying. Could you please get in the back seat? I don't want to get distracted again."

"Sure." Caitlin opened the door and walked around this time.

She'd hit on something, but she didn't think it was the number of shops. The Five loomed large in Dayan legend, but not enough for Eve to tell a stranger. She was open to a message, however—one that the messenger might not even know they were carrying. Caitlin thought back to her mother's journal and how Linda, Daya, and Desmond had waited for Maya to tell them something special. Was it a shared set of codewords, an openness to unseen meaning in the universe, or simply an interview technique designed to make the unassuming feel like they alone had a special power—similar to how Caitlin had asked Eve about the Five?

Once Caitlin had returned to her spot in the back, Eve got them going again. They rode in silence for the next ten minutes. Caitlin tried to check her email, but her phone's signal went in and out. She was about to broach the subject of the Five again when they pulled up to a gate.

"We're home," Eve said, pressing a remote control.

A solid-looking metal gate opened to one side, and the town car went through, following a paved asphalt road up a mountainside. Two turns later, they stopped at a checkpoint. The first entrance had reminded Caitlin of something from a Hollywood Hills McMansion: sleek and modern, but easy enough to jump over. This new gate, with its fifteen-foot razor-wire-topped chain-link fence, looked more like the U.S. border checkpoint at San Ysidro.

"Whoa," Caitlin said.

Eve stopped the car two feet from the gate but didn't reach for a remote this time. "It's for our protection."

One half of the gate swung two feet inward, and a woman in a red beret and uniform, more paramilitary than security guard, walked out with a semiautomatic rifle hanging from a shoulder strap.

Caitlin shook her head. "From who? Navy Seals?"

The guard completed a circle around the car. Unlike Gwendolyn Sunrise, or even Eve the driver, this woman didn't waste any time faking a smile. She walked back through the gate, and both doors swung open.

Eve drove through slowly, giving Caitlin enough time to notice a second armed guard sitting in a modern-looking booth, complete with video monitors of live camera feeds.

From there, the road zigged through heavy forest and climbed, then zagged and climbed even higher. A trailhead on the left, marked by white words painted over a red rectangle, caught her eye.

"What's 'The Climb'?"

Eve's smile returned. "All Daughters must make the Climb to God's Hill. Though the others are there for support, you strip naked and climb up a rugged path."

Caitlin thought of a hundred kung fu movies she'd watched with her dad. "Sort of a physical metaphor for the metaphysical?"

Eve looked unsure how to answer. "Don't know, but I thought I'd die. I was lucky to be surrounded by the Daughters."

Minutes later, they pulled into a clearing at the edge of the hill, where several large buildings with sheet-metal siding formed a U in front of four perfectly arranged acre-sized farm fields, each full of recognizable vegetables. Beyond the fields, ten or so cottages faced a three-story building constructed in the style of a farmhouse but wide like a college dormitory. Up the hill past the giant house, easily another three stories higher, a plume of white smoke rose from a bright fire.

Eve pulled into the first of the sheet-metal buildings, a long garage, open on one side. Caitlin counted ten town cars as they passed, all just as red as the one she was in. Besides that, she noted several all-terrain vehicles and a white Jeep Wrangler with KC bug lights on the rails.

They parked, and Eve came around to open her door. "Welcome to God's Hill, Caitlin Bergman."

Caitlin got out, instantly feeling the difference in temperature due to the change in elevation. She grabbed her laptop bag, empty except for a backup phone battery, a handful of pens, and a good old-fashioned notebook. She'd left her computer and her mother's journal in her hotel room.

"Which way do we go?"

Eve stepped in front and smiled. "Toward the singing, of course."

Caitlin laughed. Had it been there a second ago? She heard the voices now, singing the words Mama Maya had called the Morning Song.

The fire is dying, so come let me build
A light that can shine through to heaven above
So he'll see me trying, and doing his will
Building my fire with light and with love

Eve led Caitlin down a path that split the well-kept fields, the song's intensity growing with each step. Caitlin noticed others following them on the fringes, women in shades of red, some dirty from working in the fields, some from working in the motor pool.

Eve turned back, smiling at Caitlin and now singing along. Caitlin smiled in return, raising her eyebrows. It wasn't awful, but something felt off, like Christian rap or country music played on the cello.

As they neared the cottages, Caitlin flashed back to the passage in Maya's journal where she'd gotten to the top of the hill and a bunch of sweaty, half-naked hippies had hugged her to the point of tears.

She wasn't ready for that in the slightest.

More women in red came out and joined the procession, and Caitlin noticed a trend: not a single man in sight.

Finally they reached the area between the cottages and the giant row house, and the group stopped, forming a semicircle behind Caitlin and Eve, facing the house.

The front door opened and two women walked out, both armed and dressed in paramilitary garb like the previous gatekeepers. From behind reflective sunglasses, they scanned the crowd, then took their places on each side of the door.

The singing reached its peak volume and they finished the last line, stopping with the thunderous roll of a pair of hand-beaten drums.

Caitlin scanned the faces. Besides Eve, most looked to be anywhere from thirty to seventy years old, of all races, but with a similar body type, slim and durable. The women, maybe fifty in total, all wore simple shirts and pants in shades of red.

Making eye contact with more than one, Caitlin received kind smiles from everyone, until their faces looked beyond her toward the house.

She turned back just in time for the arrival of the one and only Desmond Pratten.

Just like in Maya's journal, Desmond wore an all-white sarong that covered his body down to his ankles, where a pair of leather sandals showed off pedicured toes. While he was obviously in his late sixties, his tan skin looked movie-star smooth, a result of either his unique way of life or a buttload of Botox and fillers.

He opened his mouth, revealing a bright set of perfectly aligned teeth, possibly veneers, and spoke in a loud, firm voice. "She's here. Let's welcome her."

Everyone present took one step forward, smiled, and said, "Welcome, Caitlin."

"Hey, ladies." Caitlin gave a little wave, hearing the clang of an alarm in her head—more wacky than terrifying, like a song by the Beastie Boys she'd loved in college. "Let's get funky."

24

LAKSHMI DIDN'T KNOW much about Pasadena, but the sprawling home surrounded by ten colors of roses and a wrought-iron fence seemed like the kind of place that kept a kennel of hounds to deal with front-door solicitors. She double-checked the address on her phone against the numbers welded into a rose in the center of the ornate gate.

Right place, just bigger than she'd expected. Much bigger. All the way bigger.

No one liked a drop-in out of the blue. She'd go back to the office and try the woman's phone again.

She returned to her car, reached for the handle, then stopped. The only number she had found went to a foundation's switchboard, and that hadn't gotten her anywhere.

"Sod it," she said, turning back to the gate.

A male voice answered before her finger made contact with the call box. "Well?"

Lakshmi drew her hand back. "Hello?"

"Hello," the voice answered, with as much disdain as the word could carry. "How can we help you?"

"Sorry, you startled me. I hadn't pushed the button yet."

"Cameras," the voice said. "They surround the property. How can we help you?"

Lakshmi straightened her blazer. Just the feel of the lapels in her fingertips reminded her why she'd started wearing it: Caitlin Bergman wore one just like it and Caitlin didn't take shit from anybody. "I'm here to speak with Beverly."

"Regarding?"

Lakshmi reached into her bag, pulled out a business card, and held it up toward the call box. "Our interview."

"To the right, please."

Lakshmi turned right but didn't see a camera.

"Too far," the voice chided.

Lakshmi split the difference slowly.

"Wait, NPR?"

Lakshmi pocketed the card. "That's correct."

If their cameras could read the words *National Public Radio* from that distance, they had also captured her name and phone number, which meant the voice behind the microphone could just as easily call her boss and ask why she'd dropped in on a mansion in the middle of her lunch break. An apology developed in her head but hadn't made it to her lips when the voice returned.

"Is this about the flowers?"

Lakshmi didn't answer out loud, because she wasn't about to start an interview with a lie, but her head's slight movement might easily have been misconstrued as a nod, if someone wanted to split hairs.

"Mrs. Chandler told us that was tomorrow."

The massive iron rose split in two as the gate swung inward.

"Follow the path to the garden. Mrs. Chandler will be right with you."

Fifteen minutes later, Beverly Chandler, née Beverly Bangs, the woman who'd recruited Maya Aronson into the Dayan community, entered the English-style garden through an arch in the hedge. Her untucked bright-pink blouse flowed over her white capris and the best pair of fake boobs Lakshmi had ever seen—and these on a woman in her sixties, no less. She'd never been into plastic surgery, but the benefits of being married to one of the field's pioneers were apparent in every inch of Beverly Chandler's curated features.

"I am so very sorry to have kept you waiting," she said. "I hate to admit there must have been a scheduling mix-up. My assistant said I have something tomorrow at this time with the Huntington people, and

I swear your office told me we'd wait until autumn to focus on the contest preparation—" She waved her irritation away and held out her hand. "But you're here now."

The sunlight caught the diamonds of the woman's tennis bracelet. "Beverly Chandler."

"Lakshmi Anjale."

Taking Beverly's smooth, well-lotioned hand, Lakshmi couldn't remember the last time she'd gotten a manicure or even clipped her nails.

Beverly broke out her smile again. "Would you like to see it?"

"Yes, of course," Lakshmi said, completely unsure what she was agreeing to. She didn't have a type exactly, but Vanna White had played a large part in her adolescent fantasies, and Beverly Chandler looked like she still had the skill to turn a girl's letters.

"Right this way."

Lakshmi followed her to a corner of the garden, where a three-foot fence protected a rosebush in its first weeks of blossom. Beverly opened a gate and crouched next to the plant, cradling the stem of the most brightly pink flower Lakshmi'd ever seen.

"I call her Springtime's Maiden," Beverly said. "She's a disease-resistant hybrid tea that blooms continuously from spring to fall, and so far she's a real climber. Just look at the pink color of the bud. By the end of the season, she'll be almost burgundy, like the end of a sunset."

"Beautiful."

Beverly raised her eyebrows. "Should we start with me in the photos, or just the Maiden by herself?"

"Mrs. Chandler—"

"Beverly."

"I'm not here about your roses."

"I'm sorry, I thought you were from NPR."

"I am, though I'm not working on a story right now."

"Well, then what—"

"Maya Aronson."

Beverly's smile disappeared. Suddenly, her once-flawless face looked very artificial, as though it'd been designed to smile perpetually. Anything less than happiness and the illusion melted like a cake in the sun.

"You may have known her as Sharon Sugar," Lakshmi continued.

Beverly took a step back, not noticing that her foot had dug into the base of her prized rosebush. "How did you get into my house?"

"I'm helping a friend. Please, Mrs. Chandler—"

Beverly's hand went to her back, then returned with a pair of pruning shears. "Get the fuck away from me." She looked toward the house and yelled. "Carl, get security."

"There's no need—"

"The Dayans found me, Carl. Hurry."

Lakshmi put her hands out in front. "I'm not a Dayan, Mrs. Chandler."

The pruning shears came between the two. "You won't get another second of my life. I'm not that person anymore." Beverly seemed close to tears.

The hedge wall rustled with someone's approach. A sturdy man in a polo shirt and shorts came through the gate, ready for action. He wasn't huge, but he was bigger than Lakshmi. She took a last chance.

"Maya Aronson is dead. I'm helping her daughter find out why."

Beverly relaxed slightly, took a breath, then rested her hand on the little fence. "Carl, please show this young woman out, and make sure she never makes it past my gate again."

25

"LET'S SPEAK IN the gallery," Desmond said.

Caitlin followed the sandaled man through a pair of double doors that led into a two-story great room lit naturally by its wall of hillside-facing windows. A high-quality glossy white tile covered the floor wall to wall, and a pair of chairs waited near the glass on a twenty-foot dais. One of the seats, a high-backed armchair with ornate gold-leafed carvings and tufted red velvet cushions, looked permanent; the other, a white, wooden folding chair, like it'd been set up for the occasion.

"I'm surprised you don't call this a throne room," Caitlin said, watching the man ascend the two feet of stairs up the dais.

He smiled and pointed her to the folding chair at his side. She sat, then saw the reason for the room's name.

Now facing the wall through which they'd entered, Caitlin beheld a massive collection of oil paintings, ranging from small canvases to giant murals. Even from fifty feet away, she recognized the scene depicted on the four-by-eight-foot work on the far-left wall as the painting Linda Sperry had shown Maya Aronson in the Angeles National Forest.

"I use this room for teaching," Desmond said, his voice resonating off the tile. He pointed out the windows toward the hillside. "The voyagers look upon myself and the Eternal Flame of Ceremony Peak, the path to the heavens." He turned back toward the gallery wall. "Whereas I look to them and the inspiration for all of this."

"Linda's paintings of cataclysm," Caitlin said.

The guru turned her way, tucking his feet up and under on his throne, still flexible after all this time. If he was surprised by her knowledge of the Dayan art world or even Linda's name, he didn't show it. "Yes, Caitlin. Cataclysm to be sure, but above all things, hope. Gwendolyn told me you had questions, but it appears you already know something of our ways. I'd be curious to know how."

Caitlin studied the man but held back the questions that came to mind: *Who does your Botox? Are they in town, or do you keep someone on staff?*

"A good journalist always does her research," she said. "But then, I'm not here on assignment. I'm here to learn about Maya Aronson." She watched his wrinkleless eyes for a reaction. "I believe you called her Magda."

Blinking twice, he pursed his lips. "So it's true. Magda has left us." He exhaled, touched his fingertips to his temples, then raised both hands toward the ceiling. "Good-bye, my darling."

"You two were close?" The artifice of her audience with the king had Caitlin in a fighting mood. She stood and stepped off the platform, walking toward the paintings. "That must have been nice. I never met the woman. What was she like?"

She didn't look back but heard his chuckle.

"Fiery, devoted, a true believer, and a shepherd of lost souls."

"Cool. Desmond—" She turned and saw him watching her, now on his feet. "Can I call you Desmond, or do you have a formal title?"

He smiled. "Desmond is fine."

"Great. Why'd your *devoted shepherd* get dumped in the woods? You Dayans don't believe in burying your dead? And I'm sorry, is it Dayans or Daughters of God? No one's really explained it to me."

"Each name is as good as the other to us. Feel free to use either." Desmond stepped down from the dais and walked toward her. "You carry a lot of anger."

Caitlin noticed the two women with guns waiting just feet outside the still-open double doors. "And your people carry a lot of firepower. So what happened?"

He held his hands up. "Caitlin, please. It must be hard finding out your mother was still alive—"

"Don't call her my mother."

"—and that she devoted her life to our unconventional way of living as a Daughter of God."

"Instead of reaching out to the daughter of her own body. Speaking of which, why are you not trying to convert me? To get me topless around the fire?"

"Conversion's such a Christian concept." His smile was probably meant to soothe. Caitlin felt only condescension. "The word itself implies a transition from one state to another, which implies a need to change key aspects of the self. I'm a spiritual guide, not a wizard."

"Good to know. How about Daya?"

The man's smile disappeared. "You've come to me for answers. While I understand you're a journalist, I don't feel that you're here to get to know our ways and beliefs."

Caitlin's fists settled on her hips. "I'm betting you're all a bunch of lunatics."

He nodded. "Those without faith are always the first to ridicule."

"I have faith," she countered.

"In the Spirit?"

"In actions. Here, now, in day-to-day life. It's organized religion I have the problem with."

"Then we are in agreement spiritually. Ask me what you really want to know."

"Fine." She squared off across from the man. "You knew Maya Aronson and her past."

"Better than anyone else in the world. More importantly, I knew the woman she became."

"Lucky you. How did you know who I was?"

Desmond's weight shifted to one side. "In person? Your eyes, of course. Looking at you is like looking into her soul. Moreover, Magda had me keep tabs on where you were and how you were doing throughout the years."

"Why? In case she might contact me one day?" She braced herself for some sappy platitude.

As if he'd read her mind, Desmond shook his head side to side. "No, I won't humor your ego and lie to you." He pointed out the window to the hill. "She needed to protect the work she was doing here. To do so, one must be free of their past lives. As long as she was sure you were safe, she could go on with her mission."

"Right." Caitlin felt her fingers form a fist. "Her mission of not being my mother."

Desmond shifted back to his center, his demeanor, day-spa calm. "She was very proud of who you've become. We don't often trust the media, but your work has exposed corruption and saved women around the country, tenets the Daughters of God adhere to above all."

"Cool, great tenets," Caitlin said, bouncing her fist off her leg. The anger bubbling inside threatened to overpower her logical thread. Why was she there anyway? She looked back at the wall of overwhelming end-of-the-world imagery, saw a firefighter dwarfed by an immense wall of flame. The image jolted her back into the game. "So you know the name of my father."

Desmond tented his fingers. "It's been some time since Magda and I spoke about her past."

Back in control, Caitlin gave Desmond another look. What was it about this man that made these women give up their lives? Good-looking, no doubt, especially imagining him twenty years younger, but he hadn't exactly tried to charm her since she'd walked in. If anything, he'd done the complete opposite of what she'd expected. Maybe that was the point. His lack of effort was almost a concession: *We both know I'm a fraud. Ask for what you want, and I'll give it to you so you can leave me to my bullshit fiefdom.*

But then, what if he really believed every word but knew to hide it from a skeptic like her?

She touched her temple, looked down, then looked back up like a thought had occurred to her. "Since the trampoline?"

His brow furrowed. "What about a trampoline?"

"You won't believe me." Caitlin stared out the window and up to the tendril of smoke rising into the sky. Time to play the game. Like Eve on the way there, the Dayans in Maya's journal claimed to have heard messages in visions and dreams. Caitlin could have a message of her own. "I had a dream. A man and I were bouncing on a trampoline, and I was telling him things about my life, my job, the men I've loved, the people

I've hurt. Then this guy stopped me and said he knew the one thing I'd always wanted to know."

Desmond moved closer, coming into Caitlin's view. "What did he say?"

"That's the problem. I woke up. But I knew what he meant, meaning I knew what the one thing I'd always wanted to know was. That dream's stuck with me for years. I never understood the trampoline. It's not like there was one in my life, but I came to believe it was a symbol for something holding me down. Now I'm here, talking to a man who knows more about my biological mother than anyone else in the world. Maybe I'm crazy, and I'm not saying you're the man of my dreams, but I have an irrefutable feeling that you know who my father was. Do you?"

Desmond studied her with the alertness of an eagle.

"I do," he said, his head cocking slightly to one side before he straightened himself. "Though the name escapes my memory. This was twenty years ago. Still, I'll have the answer in my notes. I'll retrieve this information on one condition."

"What's that?"

"I need you to describe Magda's body."

There it was. Desmond had finally revealed why he wanted her in his compound in the first place.

"You knew her better than I—"

"They won't allow anyone from my organization to verify—"

"Fine." She described the remains as she remembered them, lack of teeth and fingers included, but left out the part about the key and the journal. "I've given them a DNA swab. As soon as the lab runs their tests, it'll be official." She searched his eyes. At first, she took his reactions as genuine mourning; then concern morphed into calculation, and he turned quickly.

"Did you notice any marks or—"

"Hard to tell." Caitlin slowed the pace. "She'd lost a lot of skin on the arms and back."

He nodded like he'd agreed with a concept only he had heard. Again, his words came out quickly. "And what do they think happened to her?"

"Their first theory was that she fell in the woods and hit her head. Of course, that changed yesterday when they arrested a man named Johnny Larsen."

"I know about the Larsens. They've hated us for years, especially John. He must have killed her. He'd kill us all if they had the chance."

"Why? Do you have his thirteen-year-old daughter in this camp?"

Desmond looked up, then stepped back, his hands clenching and unclenching. "Not at all. She came to us, but we have strict rules. Adults only, above the age of understanding."

"So you sent her away?"

"Most certainly." His eyes clouded with a faraway look. "I'm very sorry for your loss," he said, then shook his head and turned toward the gallery wall. "Gwendolyn?"

As if she'd been there the entire time, Gwendolyn Sunrise walked through the open double doors. Desmond stepped off the dais and walked out, leaving Caitlin alone once again with the lawyer in red.

CHAPTER

26

Desmond took the stairs up to his suite two at a time, slamming and then locking the door behind him.

"A dream about a trampoline?" he said, digging through a dresser drawer. "Yeah, right. You can't shit a shitter, precious."

The reporter knew too much, too soon. Someone had talked, someone who knew about Magda's recruitment in the Angeles National Forest, Linda Sperry's visions, everything. He moved a row of underwear aside, pulled the satellite phone from the drawer, and dialed Daya's number.

Still no answer.

"Fuck," he said, hanging up.

Someone had obviously disfigured the body to prevent identification. So who was dead: Magda, Daya, or both? And which would be worse?

If Magda was dead, that meant Daya might still be out there but unable to return his call. Had the Larsen family grabbed her, looking for Promise? Some sort of ransom or swap?

Desmond went out the side door into Daya's adjoining room. Dark, like it had been for two weeks, and nothing was missing, or didn't seem to be. He opened her closet, pushed a row of clothes to one side, removed the wall panel, and entered the combination to Daya's safe.

The door swung open, revealing several bound stacks of cash. He counted quickly, found the same hundred thousand dollars he'd counted every day for the past week.

"Shit," he said, sealing the safe and returning to his room.

They'd had fights, sure, especially over the last year, but he couldn't—no, not couldn't, *wouldn't*—believe she'd cut and run after more than two decades together.

He went to his own closet's safe, repeated the search. Four hundred grand this time. Again, as expected.

No one had taken from either of the large piles of getaway cash, but there were ten more drops throughout the compound in places only the two of them knew.

He'd have to check them all, but first things first. He grabbed the phone again and dialed Tanner.

Six rings later, Tanner answered. "Shit, Desmond, is that you? I was—"

"Shut the fuck up." Desmond fished a black duffle bag out of his bottom drawer. "Have you noticed any suspicious activity on the Sperry accounts lately?"

"Hold on, man. I'm out on the deck and my signal's awful." Tanner sounded high. "How's it going, man? I hear there are forest fires in the county south of there."

"Tanner, get your shit together. Check the Sperry accounts for any activity authorized by anyone but you and me."

"Who else would . . . wait, do you mean like Daya?"

"Exactly like Daya. Call me back in five minutes."

Desmond hung up, switched the phone's ringer to vibrate, tucked it into the bag, then went on the hunt. He'd checked three locations, all intact, before Tanner called back.

"Nothing strange here, man. Should I be worried?"

Desmond cut him off, then went for the other hiding places, but saw nothing wrong.

So Daya hadn't run off—and the reporter from Los Angeles, Magda's daughter, couldn't say for sure whom she'd seen in the morgue, but they'd find out as soon as the DNA results came back.

At least one of his most trusted followers was dead. Maybe Johnny Larsen had killed Daya as well. Desmond had warned her not to mess with the Larsens, but Daya had been convinced she could squeeze them for cash.

Not a lot, she'd said. *Something small, five or ten grand. We're already sending the girl back. Might as well get something out of the deal.*

Desmond had tried to stress the bigger concern.

People like Anders Larsen have the kind of money to keep local law enforcement on their side. That five grand is nothing compared to the campaign contributions they make.

And now they'd left a body. No fingers or teeth, but a message as clear as day. *We can do what we want, when we want—and you're next.*

"Shit," Desmond muttered, standing outside the motor pool building. "Is this how it ends?"

He looked around the grounds, saw the fields and cottages, the row house, the path up the hill to Ceremony Peak. This had been his life since Los Angeles, all that he'd known for years. Beyond the occasional trip to Vegas with Daya to sit in hot tubs and blow off steam, he'd spent the majority of his life surrounded by these women and their needs— and man, had it been a wild ride. But Linda'd had to go and name a fucking date and cock everything up.

The end of the world was great as a concept. *You won't need your money anymore; give it to the group. You won't need your families anymore; come and work for me. Social rules mean nothing; give in to your body. Hell, give me your body.*

But put a date on the calendar, and shit was bound to go wrong. The day had come and gone over two years ago. The Daughters had survived, but only because of Daya's quick thinking—and ruthlessness.

Now she was gone, either on the run or dead. Without him, at any rate.

Could he be ruthless without her?

He thought of the last fifty Daughters. Some too old to return to the world they'd left behind, some too weak, a few who'd seen too much. It wouldn't be ruthless to follow the plan he and Daya had made. It'd be a kindness.

He checked the satellite phone's clock.

Just past two. Plenty of time to prep for the night's ceremony; then he'd have Caitlin Bergman returned to town with the information she wanted. If it really was the worst case, he'd need at least a day to set things in motion, far from prying eyes.

"Darling," he said, finding a Daughter washing one of the town cars. "Please gas up the Jeep and pull it around. I'm needed in town."

He walked away without waiting to hear her response. The women on God's Hill did what he said, no questions asked.

27

IT WASN'T THE first time Johnny Larsen had walked out of lockup, but this freedom felt much sweeter than after his DUIs. Two trucks waited in the parking lot. The window of his father's Escalade came down, and Anders started bitching.

"Do you have any idea how much money I had to move to bail you out?"

Johnny gave the old man a nod, saw his father's attorney and his own wife in the other seats.

"Be right back." He walked toward the second vehicle, Gunner's pickup.

Both Anders and the lawyer swore an ocean of blue streaks. Gloria just sat there like always. There'd be time enough to listen to each of their earfuls. He got in the passenger side of Gunner's truck. Gunner slapped him on the shoulder, and Stupid Tom handed him a Coors tall-boy from the back bench of the extended cab.

"What you got in mind, Johnny?" Gunner said.

Johnny took a sip of the Rockies. "No more messing around. We're gonna get Promise back before this gets out of hand. I need you boys to find the reporter."

"Why? You think she's got Promise?"

"She's working with the Dogs, no doubt in my mind, and either she knows where they've got her or knows someone who knows."

Stupid Tom leaned in. "I went back to her hotel. She checked out yesterday after the you-know."

Johnny laughed. "Good. She's scared. If she's still in our county, let's make sure she stays that way."

He gave them a list of places to cover and finished his beer, then returned to Anders's SUV for the lecture and ride home.

*　*　*

Gloria didn't say much, other than to ask if he wanted another beer or more fried chicken every five minutes.

Johnny pushed the last bits of a drumstick to the side of his plate. "Stop fussing. I need to think."

"John, I gotta say something—"

"Like hell you do."

He watched her look away and straighten a pile of napkins, like the house would collapse if the corners of perforated paper weren't lined up straight. She'd been that way for the last two years. Always looking a different direction and trying to fix something that didn't need fixing.

She turned back with a strained smile. "How about a slice of pie, honey?"

"Jesus, Gloria. I was in for one night."

"It's apple."

He dropped his fork. "Maybe later."

"What about . . . ?" She brushed her hair back to one side.

He looked up, actually caught her eyes. She smiled, maybe for the first time in a month.

He didn't believe it. "You want to fuck right now?"

"If you do, Johnny."

He stood up, pushing the chair back across the linoleum floor with a loud squawk. Gloria took a step back but didn't look away.

They didn't have a lot of sex, and when they did, Johnny made it happen. Most of the time, he got more action at the strip club near the lumberyard. Not that Gloria was bad looking, even at thirty-two. She hadn't gotten fat after Promise was born, and some days, when she didn't know he was looking at her, he still saw the sixteen-year-old girl who'd been there waiting when he got back from Baghdad, despite the dishonorable discharge. That girl had been down for anything.

He pushed his plate aside and reached for his wife.

Her eyes went wide, then looked away.

That sideways look made the whole thing bullshit. His open hand became a fist.

"Dammit, Gloria, what happened to you? You used to have fire, confidence. Shit, Promise is more of a woman than you now."

Her eyes flashed back his way, plenty of fire now. "Promise isn't here, John. You need to let her go."

"Let her go? That's my daughter you're talking about. My special girl."

Gloria hard-swallowed. Only seconds earlier, Johnny'd been thinking how she still looked good after all these years. Now, staring at her again, he saw creases, sags, and the beginnings of sunspots.

"She is, right?"

"Is what, John?"

"Sometimes I look at Promise and I don't see the slightest bit of me."

Gloria'd delivered Promise less than a year after Johnny'd come back from Iraq.

Now the woman looked pissed. "You know damned well that she's your daughter, Johnny Larsen. I've never even been with another man."

"You don't seem to care that she's gone."

"She's thirteen and she ran away. She'll either come back or she won't. There's no reason to go to jail over it. Maybe we should let her go."

He moved closer, both hands in fists now. "The more I look at you, I know damn well that girl isn't my blood."

As if sensing that his kettle was ready to boil over, Gloria reached for the plate he'd pushed aside and took it to the sink. "Maybe that's what you need to tell yourself."

He went after her, pulling on her shoulder. "What the hell does that mean?"

She looked away, then caught herself, and raised her eyes slowly. "To make what you do to that girl okay."

Johnny didn't see her eyes anymore. His fist struck right where they'd been. She fell forward over the sink, then back onto the floor.

He raised his hand again, towering over her. "What kind of mother are you?"

She kept her face covered, muffling her sobs.

He grabbed his jacket off the back of his chair. "I'm going out to get Promise."

CHAPTER

28

"THIS IS WHERE Magda slept." Gwendolyn Sunrise stepped aside to let Caitlin enter the room.

Still in the main house, Magda's queen-sized bed and simple bathroom reminded Caitlin of her previous hotel room, with one exception: no lock on the door.

"You're welcome to look through her belongings and keep anything that might be of sentiment."

Caitlin nodded to the woman, then started a lap around the remains of a life. She paused at a three-drawer dresser. "Mind if I—?"

Gwendolyn nodded back. "Anything."

The top drawer's stack of flowing blouses and slacks might as well have all been the same piece of rough red cloth. Caitlin was no fashionista, but even she shuddered at the thought of wearing the same outfit seven days a week.

"Spice of life," she said, more to herself than anything else.

Lady Sunrise took the opportunity to come closer. "What's that?"

"Variety." Caitlin slid the drawer closed and reached for the next. "So Desmond's coming back, right? I'm under the impression he's looking for information on my behalf."

"If that's what he said."

The second drawer held socks, T-shirts, and tank tops but no underwear. Not exactly the get-to-know-the-dead-woman experience Caitlin had hoped for, but it would kill time until Desmond returned.

She stepped back, checking out the rest of the room. A single-rod closet held two outfits on hangers: a flat-red dress, similar to the one worn by the woman from Daya's Gifts in Coos Bay, and an all-weather coat.

"What about the third drawer?" Gwendolyn said.

Caitlin had to hold back a laugh. Somebody obviously wanted her to find something in the third drawer. "I'm saving the best for last."

She opened the drawer to see her own face, or at least the back cover to her first book, a nonfiction investigation of LAPD corruption. The brand-new-looking copy sat on top of a pile of articles photocopied from her paper in Los Angeles.

"Oh, those shouldn't be in there," Gwendolyn said. "Desmond frowns upon non-Dayan reading materials. I guess Magda really cared about you."

Like the framed photo in the back of the town car the day before, the whole performance made Caitlin want to barf. Still, she reached for the props and played her part. "I guess she did."

She flipped through the pages, hoping for some handwriting or even some highlighting, but the copy couldn't have been out of a bookstore for more than a week. She slid the drawer shut, wondering why they'd bothered to plant the book and articles. Did they think the portrait of a proud mother would help Caitlin go away happy, or was this just a layer of protection?

Take the reporter to the guest room, put some shit in it to make it look lived in, then send her on her way.

Of course, the solution could be much simpler: nobody wanted a journalist digging through their secrets. "This is very sweet, but I was hoping for some of Magda's writing. Did she keep a journal or anything?"

"Oh no," Gwendolyn said, scandalized by the concept. "That wouldn't be allowed."

"Not even as self-reflection, part of experiencing religious growth?"

"We used to do so, but the practice stopped when Linda ascended."

"Ascended?"

Gwendolyn started to answer, then stopped. "We no longer journal."

Caitlin's hands tightened around the bag over her shoulder. She'd made the right move leaving the journal in the hotel room.

"Guess that's just the writer in me. No photos either?"

Sunrise smiled, once again fingering the chunky beads around her neck. "We don't have the same image consciousness as the rest of society. Simple living, lived simply."

"Sounds lovely," Caitlin said, noticing no jewelry or accessories anywhere in the room supposedly belonging to Magda. She tried something new. "Is the namesake here today?"

"The namesake?"

"You are Dayans, right? I've seen Desmond, but I'd love to meet the one and only Daya."

Sunrise's beaming demeanor went down a shade.

Caitlin played nice. "Unless she's no longer with the organization, hence the switch to the Daughters of God name?"

"Daya's still with us," Sunrise said, her smile back and brighter than ever. "But unfortunately, she's unavailable at this time."

Caitlin wandered toward the window. "Maybe later?"

"Possibly."

She sensed no possibility in Gwendolyn's use of the word. Even though the bedroom was near the middle of the building, she could once again see the plume of smoke rising from the top of the hill.

"What's up the hill? Barbecue?"

"We're vegetarians."

"Still, throw a little bit of sea salt, olive oil, and rosemary onto some potatoes and carrots, put them on a tray over a fire, and that's some good eating. Don't quote me on that recipe; it's something I got at a restaurant. I don't do a lot of cooking, do you?"

"I did when I became a Daughter. Cooking, sewing, digging ditches, latrines even. We all do our part."

"When did you join, Gwendolyn?"

"Oh, it's hard to remember a time before I was a Daughter."

"Sure, what lady likes to talk about her age?"

"The truth is, we believe that the past is something to learn from, then abandon. The Spirit sees us in each moment. In a way, we are reborn every morning."

"Hence your name," Caitlin said. "Sunrise, right? That's your Dayan name?"

"Why would you think—"

"Because Maya became Magda, Lily became Eve. It's been a while since I've looked over my name origins, but Gwendolyn means fair or white something, doesn't it?"

For once, Gwendolyn's smile looked real. "That's close. White ring."

"The white ring of sunrise," Caitlin said. "It's beautiful. Were you an attorney before you were Gwendolyn?"

"Not quite. I'd dropped out two semesters into law school. You might not believe this, but it was your mother who convinced me to finish and pass the bar."

"I don't know what to believe." Caitlin looked around the sparse room. "I dropped out of college a month shy of graduation, but she wasn't there for me."

"She couldn't have been, Caitlin."

"They had planes flying to Indiana twice a day out of LAX."

"That's not what I mean. Maya Aronson couldn't have helped you, because Maya Aronson couldn't help herself. Magda didn't become Magda overnight, and I didn't become Gwendolyn for years."

"I get it, but Magda forgot how to use a phone?"

"It's not that simple. You see—"

Caitlin wasn't letting up. "You don't get a signal up here either?"

"There are no phones on God's Hill, mobile or otherwise. We receive our messages straight from heaven."

"In town, though. She could have borrowed a phone, checked the computer at the library."

Gwendolyn played with her chunky beads. "Our rules forbid—"

"Screw it," Caitlin said, walking toward the door. What did she expect from her mother's friends? Gwendolyn Sunrise had probably left a dozen kids to join up with Desmond Pratten's hilltop circus—anything to feel special. "Want to show me where you make the sweaters and scarves?"

Gwendolyn hustled to keep up while pulling her walkie-talkie out. "Of course, I just need to—"

"Make a call first. Please do."

Five minutes later, the dogs and ponies had been arranged enough for Gwendolyn to walk them both from the main house to one of the sheet-metal outbuildings, where a dozen women in red sat at a long table covered with fabric, yarn, and sewing accessories.

Some sewed, some knitted, some might have been spinning gold for all Caitlin knew. The whole thing had a living-historical-village feel.

"No blacksmith?" she said.

If Gwendolyn was offended, it didn't show. "Not quite, but we do have a fully functional machine shop."

They toured that next, then a kitchen, cafeteria, and their medical center, then headed back through the central fields for a detailed look at the various fresh vegetables. Lots of ladies, cucumbers, and eggplant, but not a single man other than Desmond.

"Gwendolyn, I couldn't help but wonder, is Desmond the only man on God's Hill?"

"For over a decade," Gwendolyn answered, smiling like that was an accomplishment. "At first, we communed as both males and females, but the energy the men brought caused violence, jealousy, and complications."

"Complications? Like fights?"

Gwendolyn nodded emphatically. "Daya called them distractions from our mission. Since they've gone, we've risen closer to the Spirit than we ever imagined."

"Sure. Who needs the hassle?" Caitlin checked her phone. No signal, but the time was her real worry: 5:47 PM. "Can you see if Desmond has retrieved my information yet? I'd like to leave before it gets dark."

Gwendolyn stepped away with her walkie-talkie to relay the request. Caitlin couldn't be sure, but the plume of smoke at the hilltop seemed more active than before.

She returned moments later. "Desmond regrets that he has been unable to find his notes yet. He's confident he'll locate them tonight after our services. Of course, if you'd like to come back another time—"

"I'll wait."

"Wonderful. In that case, we're about to meet for dinner. Since you're not a Dayan, we can't invite you to share our meal, but we can have a plate made for you."

Caitlin had no intention of eating their food. "I've got a granola bar in my bag. I'll just wander around the grounds."

"Maybe you'd prefer to wait in Magda's room?" Gwendolyn's question ended in the right punctuation, but the tone implied little to none of the interrogative tense.

"Even better." Caitlin followed the crimson queen back to the main house.

"Can we get you some water?" Gwendolyn said, perched in the doorway once again.

Caitlin pulled a still-sealed store-bought bottle of water from her bag and plopped down on the bed. "I'm good. How long do you think it'll be?"

"No more than an hour."

"Great, do you—"

The shutting of the door ended their conversation.

Caitlin didn't mind. She needed a break to process the day's events. A lot had changed since Mama Maya signed up, and no one was offering the whole story. The physical copy of the journal was back at the hotel, but Caitlin had added the scanned version to her phone's digital library. She ripped open a granola bar and went back in search of the truth.

CHAPTER

29

February 16, 1996

I'M LOOKING AT *the previous pages and am at a loss for words. I haven't written in or even looked at this notebook for two and a half years. In fact, this is just about the three-year anniversary of my first voyage to Linda, Desmond, and Daya.*

I'm so happy to have started this journey. I look back at poor Maya, struggling to pay her bills, loaded with self-doubt, juggling pills and booze and guilt, and can't believe how far we've come. Not just me, all of the Dayans.

We left the hills near the Angeles National Forest and returned to Hollywood using Linda's house as a base of operations. Desmond placed his trust in my judgment, and we began a recruiting phase that grew our numbers from under a hundred to over a thousand, and our property holdings to ten locations in four cities. LA, Santa Monica, Santa Barbara, and San Francisco. I don't mean to take credit for what has always been the Spirit's plan, but I do feel joy for my part in the movement.

It all started out of the realization of my gift. Bev and I returned to Hollywood, but not for porn. We started simple, taking a van full of girls to the clubs to see what would happen. In the beginning, we'd end up with a handful of guys happy to return to whatever afterparty was going on. But it wasn't only guys. There's something infectious about our energy. So pure, so confident, so sexy. Like my first night at Linda's house, the pickups were blown away by the vibe. It wasn't for everyone, but the right ones heard the message and felt the love. Some men even contributed money toward the cause, especially if it meant time with a lady or two. I can't believe I once felt shame for this natural invitation.

Tonight is our last night in California. Tomorrow, all four cities' worth of Dayans will move to a hilltop compound in Oregon, our new God's Hill, the one from Linda's vision.

This feeling is electric, this mood is pure.

We are the Light.

Soon we will be the Light on the hill.

Soon we will all be with God.

*   *   *

February 17, 1996

Holy freaking shit.

We met at Linda's house last night. No one had seen her in weeks. At dusk, thirty of us gathered on the front lawn around the fire pit. I assumed Desmond was going to give us a message before we made the move to Oregon, and he was, but just as he began, Daya pushed Linda out of the house in a wheelchair.

Her voice was weak, but her words were clear. "I know the time," she said.

Everyone knew what she meant.

Desmond looked as surprised as the rest of us.

"You didn't tell me—" he started, but Linda launched into her latest vision.

"I won't be there," she said, "but the Spirit's power will be an awful force. Not awful as in terrible, though the destruction will be worldwide, but awful as in an occurrence every bit as miraculous as the earth's creation, but in reverse. Insects, tortured by years of man's pesticides, disappear. Animals, creatures we were meant to hold dominion over, die off, ravaged by infections caused by the chemicals we put into the water and air. But when nature turns on man, instead of begging for forgiveness, instead of clinging to the land and simple life like we do every day, man will look at the dying forests and fields, and the oceans full of garbage, and turn on each other."

At this point, Linda's voice no longer sounded weak. Her cheeks turned red as she gripped the arms of her chair.

"They'll start with religion. Wars about who knows God best. Then they'll fight for power over technology. The biggest bombs, the smartest killing machines, the fastest computers. Each country will claim ownership instead of sharing, fearing each other instead of growing together. They'll find hate in accents and sexual behaviors, fear in every foreigner. Then, mired in hate, they'll fight for the last scraps of food and access to clean water. That's when God will come, that's when it all ends."

Linda snagged a hankie from the sleeve of her sweater and wiped the corner of her mouth.

We all took a collective breath, sure she had finished her message, but she struggled up to her feet. Daya moved around to catch her in case she fell, but Linda pulled her shoulders back and yelled.

"February seventeenth." Her clear voice cut through me like she was inside my head. "In the year of our Lord's return, two thousand and sixteen. Twenty years from today."

I felt like I'd been punched in the stomach. Looking around, I knew we all did. Except maybe Desmond. He looked angry.

"Linda." He reached out and touched her shoulder. "Surely you can't know the exact—"

"The seventeenth," she repeated. "I will not see this glorious day, but you will, my beautiful children."

She stepped forward on her own, walking toward the fire pit.

"In the past, every time I saw this scene, I watched from the top of the mountain, our glorious God's Hill, but not this time. Now I looked down through a shaft of pure white, down from heaven. As the world burned around the Dayans, your faces turned up to me. And as you called to me, I heard a voice, His voice. 'Don't despair,' he said. 'The Dayans will not suffer. Daya and Desmond, Magda and Beverly—' "

I couldn't have spoken at that moment if I'd been commanded to. We all clung to every word Linda said.

" 'You know their names?' I said unto God. He laughed, a gentle, pure laugh of a summer day. 'Their actions, my child. While the world around them bickered and destroyed, your people built, called to others, lived in my purity and splendor. Now call to them, Linda. Bring them here.' "

I was crying now. We all were.

Linda reached out to us. "And so I did. I called to each of you, and up you came. As the mortal world burned, we joined hands and sang in joy. When the last of us arrived, everything went white, and I knew I was return-ing to this time and this body. 'Wait,' I said, struggling to stay in the moment. 'They need to know the date so that they might prepare as many voyagers as possible.' Before my eyes opened, His voice spoke one last time. 'The age when you first saw the hill. That age, from this day.' "

Linda looked into the fire, then turned back toward everyone. "On my wedding night, the first sleep of my honeymoon and the consecration of my marriage to gluttony and avarice, I had my first vision of God's Hill. I was twenty years old then. The Cataclysm will come on February seventeenth, two thousand and sixteen. The Dayans will ascend while the world ends."

In our heads, we all took a collective breath, floored by the weight of her vision. That's why no one caught her when she collapsed.

"Please," Desmond yelled. "Give us space."

He lifted Linda's unconscious body into the wheelchair, and he and Daya wheeled her into the house.

Minutes later, Desmond returned and told us Linda was sleeping soundly, and that we should all do the same.

So we went to our beds, speaking for hours about the date determined to be the end of all days, before finally falling asleep. Near three in the morn-ing, I woke to a gentle hand on my shoulder. Daya put a finger to her lips and motioned to follow her. Quietly, we went down the hall to Linda's room.

A single lamp was on, and I could see Linda in her bed, her head toward the wall, the back of her white nightgown visible, with Desmond standing beside her.

"How is she?" I whispered. "Do you need anything?"

Desmond rose with a smile and met us at the door. "Yes, Magda. We have a big day tomorrow, and Daya and I should sleep. Would you do some-thing for us?"

"Anything."

"Stay here, in case Linda needs anything."

"Of course," I said, ready to lie on the floor next to her bed.

"You won't need to be in the room," he said, handing me a pillow. "But if you could sit in the hall where you can hear if she calls out and make sure that no one tries to disturb her, you'd be giving us an amazing gift."

Daya nodded through a tired smile. "We only need three or four hours, then we'll be back."

Gladly accepting the assignment, I closed the door and sat up against it so no one could possibly go near without going through me.

When Desmond returned hours later, no one had.

"Let's check on the patient," he said, opening the door.

We tiptoed inside, careful not to make any noise.

But when I saw the bed, I couldn't believe what had happened.

"Where is she?" I said, not whispering at all. The bedding lay crumpled like it'd been slept in, but she wasn't there. It's only a small bedroom, maybe ten by ten feet, no bathroom, one closet.

I checked the closet, and under the bed, then the windows. The dual sliding-glass panels looked out over the city, but the curtains were drawn and the screens were intact. Plus, I couldn't imagine Linda climbing out, then somehow putting everything back in place.

Desmond fell to his knees, laughing.

I was freaking out. "What are you laughing about? She's fucking gone."

He shook his head. "Not gone, Magda. She's ascended." He looked up at me, tears in his eyes. "It's a miracle."

CHAPTER

30

"ARE YOU KIDDING me?" Caitlin swiped her phone shut and walked to the bathroom to pee. *If the next entry has Linda making appearances three days later, some Israelites named Matthew, Mark, Luke, and John have a winning plagiarism suit.*

"Is this really who I'm related to?" she said, talking out loud again, the thought too ridiculous to keep in.

She flushed the toilet, washed her hands, and then got her phone out. No signal, no Wi-Fi or Bluetooth networks available. She settled for the time: 7:12.

More than the hour the lawyer had estimated.

Caitlin grabbed her bag and went for the door, lightly pushing on the wood. Apparently, her touch was too light. The door didn't give. She pushed harder, but the door, the one without a lock, wouldn't budge.

What have I let you stupid fire-worshiping witches do?

She pounded on the surface. "This shit's not cool."

No one answered.

Don't freak out. Not yet.

Caitlin had spent the early years of her career covering the downtown LA crime beat, which meant multiple trips to the infamous Men's Central Jail, which had exposed her to locks other than standard dead bolts. Either the Dayans were using their God's juju to keep the door sealed, or they'd installed electromagnetic locks that were controlled from the hallway.

She looked the door up and down. Sure enough, a metal plate on the doorjamb met the surface of the door. She didn't remember any technical specs from her old jailhouse tours, but she doubted her chances of overpowering the door were any better than those of the seventeen thousand men crammed into Central.

"Who's the stupid witch now?" she muttered.

Seriously, no need to freak out. They know you're expected back in town tomorrow. They know people know where you are. They're just keeping you from wandering the grounds while they do whatever it is they do.

She'd said it to herself, so she mostly believed it. Still, two years ago in Indiana, she'd promised herself she'd never sit in a cage again.

She crossed over to the window she'd looked out earlier. Solid and sealed, no way to open it. The sun was nearly down, but dots of light stretched from the fire at the top of the hill down toward the building in a steadily moving line of handheld candles.

Must be the services Gwendolyn mentioned.

But surely they wouldn't all be there at the same time. Not in a compound guarded by women with semiautomatic rifles.

Think, stupid. What did Deputy Swagger say?

Back at Central, a short deputy who made up any difference between his and Caitlin's height with swagger had spent five minutes showing off the small bit of the jail's security he commanded.

Electromagnets need electricity. Take away the spark and the bond fails. Just like the bedroom, know what I mean?

Caitlin had let him mansplain away, all the while using the cell phone he should have taken from her to snap exclusive photos of a video monitor showing a high-profile inmate. Of course, jails had backup generators, and he'd gone on and on about the difference between fail-safe and fail-secure. Jails and banks used fail-secure, meaning if the power was cut, the door locked automatically. Commercial properties used fail-safe. If you could cut the power or even disrupt the surface of a strike plate, the magnetic field would dissipate and the bond would fail.

She opened her bag, found her *Bitch Book*, and turned to the picture of Maya Aronson.

"What did you get us into?"

She tapped the photo and slid one of the paper clips off the edge.

She couldn't disrupt the lock until it was open, but once it was, a simple bit of metal might stop the bond from resealing.

So how do you get someone to open a door they don't want to open?

The Dayans might love their hilltop fires, but Caitlin doubted they liked them indoors.

She ripped an early page from the book, grabbed her lighter from her bag, and found the smoke alarm. A minute later, standing on top of the bathroom counter, her offering from the *Bitch Book* gave off enough smoke to bring the magical screech of the alarm. She climbed down, left the pages burning in the sink, slung her bag over her shoulder, and waited by the door with the paper clip in hand.

For a second, she contemplated attacking whoever came through the door. Beyond growing up aware of the constant dangers facing women due to her dad's job, Caitlin had spent a year in her twenties learning Wing Chun. She didn't come close to mastery, but she had learned to defend herself. She also knew that the odds of stripping a semiautomatic rifle off an opponent and walking away unharmed were in the winning-lottery-ticket range. She clung to the paper clip and pushed an ear against the door.

Despite the alarm, she was able to hear footsteps approaching, then the tiniest of buzzing noises. She grabbed the door handle and pulled.

A woman in red tumbled through the doorway. As she was easily four inches shorter and twenty pounds lighter than her, Caitlin again considered drilling her first responder in the throat. Instead, she put a foot into the open doorway and reached out her hand to help the woman up.

"The door was stuck. We must have pulled at the same time."

The woman's eyes, startled at first, calmed as they met Caitlin's smiling face. "Where's the fire?"

"Top of the hill. Is it time to meet with Desmond?"

Cursed with unfortunate forward-jutting front teeth and flat brown hair, the woman shook off her disorientation, giving Caitlin the distinct impression of a stunned mouse. It took a second, but Caitlin recognized the same woman who'd sold her shorts in Daya's Gifts two days before.

Mouse Girl looked around the room, then settled on the smoke rising from the sink. "What happened here?"

Still in the doorway, Caitlin ran the paper clip along the doorjamb. Nothing happened. Of course. The strike plate wouldn't be magnetized once the door had been unlocked. "Yeah, sorry. I dropped a cigarette onto something I was reading, then myself. I can't even explain it, really. Just me at my most awkward."

She pulled the door back and forth, waving the air with her hand. "I thought it was out, then the alarm started going off. So what's with this door? I pulled and it wouldn't open. You didn't lock me in here, did you?"

The mousy woman waved her hand over the alarm, and the shrill noise cut out. "There's no smoking in here."

"It was my last one anyway." Caitlin pushed the door all the way open and faced into the hallway. "Is Gwendolyn almost done with the ceremony? I've got to get back to town."

Still no one around; no door-release switches on the wall either. Either her guard had a handheld remote, or . . . Caitlin looked out into the hall above the door and saw the white plastic dome of a motion sensor.

"She'll be back soon," the Mouse said, walking Caitlin's way. "Desmond was almost finished."

"You were up there, at the top of the hill?"

Mouse shook her head. "Just down the hall."

"Cameras, huh?" Caitlin moved aside so she could return to her post. "Smart thinking. That way you can do your job without missing out. You sold me shorts, right? In Daya's Gifts?"

In the hall, the Mouse broke into the fakest of smiles, almost to the point of weasel. "Please don't smoke again."

"Sure thing." Caitlin stepped back into the room, palming the paper clip instead of sliding it against the jamb. "And thanks for coming to my rescue. Sorry you missed part of the ceremony."

The Mouse remained in place until the door shut completely. Caitlin dropped to her knees, put her ear against the door, and listened to the woman walking back the way she'd come. Seconds later she heard the slight buzz and faint pop of the electromagnetic lock coming back to life.

She wasn't worried about the paper clip anymore. First she opened the drawer of red clothing and picked a red blouse and drawstring pants that would cover her outfit. Then she went to the tiny closet area, pulled the flat-red dress off a wire hanger, and twisted the end of the hanger until it was straight.

Finally, she pulled two things from her bag: another page from the *Bitch Book* and a brand-new stick of gum. A few chews of Peppermint Extra stuck the paper to the end of the coat hanger, and a single push of the paper and hanger under the door caught the eye of the motion detector, unlocking the door.

She stepped into the hall, but no alarms went off. Five closed doors down to her left, the sound of Desmond's televised voice emanated from an open doorway before a marked exit with a crossbar push panel. Caitlin walked to the right, passing two open doorways to darkened rooms similar to the one she'd been in, motion sensors and all. Another exit waited at the far end of the hall, but a hundred feet from the door, a pair of excited female voices came from an opening on the left.

"But no one's seen her for weeks."

"What else could it be?"

Caitlin stepped back and hid just inside the closest dark bedroom as the women passed.

"But Daya, really?"

A third voice, the Mouse down the hall, joined them. "What are you doing? We can't leave our stations."

"Are you kidding? He's going to tell us about Daya."

The other voice spoke in agreement. "I need to be there."

There was a pause; then the first woman spoke again. "We're going. Stay if you like, but we need to know."

Caitlin heard the clang of the far door's panic bar and the sounds of people walking outside before the exit clicked shut again. She took a deep breath and looked down the hall.

Of the three, the loyal Mouse still lingered in the guard's station. The volume of Desmond's voice doubled to the point of distortion.

"*. . . an event so special, that God is sending each of us a message we can't ignore . . .*"

The broadcast cut off completely, leaving only the Mouse's shuffling sounds behind.

"I'm coming, Desmond," the woman said. The door clanged open again, then closed with a satisfying click.

Caitlin ventured another glance into the hall. No one around. Whatever was happening at the top of the hill was too big to miss.

She could run. Away from the row house, through the fields, past the yarn barn, into the motor pool—maybe find some keys, take a car, drive away. Unguarded, she could also explore the grounds, find Desmond's records, maybe even her mother's actual room.

But how could she?

A cult was performing a secret ceremony. Her inner journalist wanted to know what the hell was happening at the top of that hill. Pulling even stronger, her thirteen-old-self needed to know why they'd abandoned the greater world, their careers, and their loved ones.

She counted to ten, then walked down the hall and out the door after them.

CHAPTER

31

Some people went to shit after a six-pack. Johnny just felt focused. Nobody'd found Bergman yet, but he had a guess where she'd be—at the top of the hill with the rest of the Dogs. While he'd been thrown into lockup for nothing, Leslie Kramer had seen the reporter riding away in a Dayan town car with that lawyer of theirs—and Caitlin Bergman was the daughter of the bitch who'd ruined the Promise handoff.

Which meant Promise had never come down from that hill.

He'd been to the Dogs' front gate before, close enough to know they carried serious firepower, not to mention maintained a stable of red town cars and a few white Jeeps. Even with his buzz, he knew better than to shoot his way in all by himself without knowing the lay of the land. With Gunner and Tom driving the county in search of Bergman's truck, tonight was all about recon. Of course, he'd fuck some shit up if the opportunity presented itself.

He parked on the same logging road from the week before, then hiked to the site of the failed exchange. No sign of life. He crossed the firebreak and moved onto the edge of the Dayan property. Without the flashes of last time's lightning, he had to search to find the way, barely more than a buck trail over pine needles. He took the narrow path slowly, once again checking the way with his scope every hundred feet. After half a mile, he picked up the pace. Nobody'd be guarding this approach. That was why the bitch had picked it in the first place.

Another quarter mile of serious hill humping led to a stretch of paved road. He wiped a line of sweat off his forehead and blew a quiet belch. He could have been louder. The only sounds beside his heavy breathing came from the wind rustling through the timber. He considered moving onto the road but caught the path's wider and more traveled continuation on the opposite side.

A wooden sign, white lettering over a red triangle, read *The Climb*. Fifty feet further up the trail, another sign read *Only You Can Save the Daughters*.

"Fucking-A right," Johnny said between huffs. "I'm coming for you, Promise."

32

MORE THAN ONE path led up toward the fire, each walkway lit by store-bought tiki torches; citronella, judging from the smell. Caitlin crouched behind a row of bushes to wait until the Mouse caught up with the other guards.

Fifty feet up the hill, she found a spot where she could see most of the group from the safety of a clump of rocks. Desmond stood on another raised dais, this one a foot-high brick semicircle ten feet in front of the largest bonfire Caitlin had ever seen. Below him, dozens of women in red sat on the ground, all attention on his words and movement. "And in her name, we ask for unity within the Light."

The women reached out to each other, joined hands, and raised them toward the flames.

"Linda," they chanted. "All-seeing, benevolent mother. We ask for your guidance on our path."

Their heads dropped, and Desmond continued. "Through vision and painting, through dream and nightmare, Linda set our course for our journey here to God's Hill."

Caitlin kept back a smile. According to the story she'd read, Linda's *great vision* had ended more than two years ago with a cataclysm that didn't happen, yet there they were, chanting along like every word was golden.

"She rose," they said. "Her gift passed to Daya."

Desmond took the verbal baton and ran. "And Daya continued Linda's ways, through words and through deeds. The Dayans grew, focused and purified."

A woman on the far right raised her hand, and the female chorus spoke as one. "The men were sent."

"Away for purity," Desmond offered.

"Away by design," the chorus answered.

"And you became—"

"The Daughters of God."

Desmond clasped his hands together. "You are the Daughters of God, the ones who ascend on the last day, called by name, and known to all."

They joined in. "Unique, powerful, and necessary."

Desmond again: "Ready to build God's new world. Others have faltered. Others have doubted. Linda's day came—"

"And went," they answered.

"A testament to your progress, a sign that the Dayans' work pleased the Lord, extending the time on earth. And then, the Five. Doubts, each and every one, but Daya stopped them, shared her vision, and—"

"Their doubts disappeared."

"The next day?"

"The Five ascended."

"Exactly. Which brings us to now, my daughters." Desmond looked side to side, taking his time, as if to make eye contact with every woman present. "I started our fire with a message from Daya. Her words, comforting and hopeful as they were, were not the entire message."

Caitlin shifted back onto her heels, the words circling in her mind. *The Five ascended.* Like Linda Sperry, five other Daughters must have pulled a disappearing act for five times the miracle, sometime after *Linda's day.* Convenient, since that whole end-of-the-world-thing hadn't happened.

The echo of Desmond's voice turned her focus back toward the fire.

"You may have noticed I've been absent this last week," he continued. "Not physically, of course, but if we've spoken, you know that I've been less than generous with my time."

He gazed into the fire, then sat on the rock wall at the back of the dais.

"This journey has had its travails, to be sure, but none perhaps as dire as this past week. As I'm sure you've heard, our Magda is gone. Sadly, I cannot say she has gone in the tradition of Linda and the Five. Her body was found beaten and disfigured. As expected, the local police seem unwilling to find those responsible. In times like these, even my faith is tested. Magda, who witnessed Linda's ascension, who has done so much, has been a shepherd, a guide to so many, lost to the hands of hatred and ignorance."

Maybe Desmond's tears were real, maybe it was the smoke, but he wiped his eyes and stood again.

"My daughters. This pain, like the pains we all fought and cast off to be here on God's Hill, this new pain threatened to pull me down. Then Daya, sweet Daya, came to me last night."

The women in red shifted noticeably at the second mention of Daya's name.

Desmond raised both hands. " 'Do not weep for Magda,' she told me, 'for I have seen the way.' "

He shifted direction slightly, as if performing the conversation between the two. " 'The way?' I asked. 'Magda was not with us when she left, so her name will not be read. She will miss the Light.' "

The women nodded along with this, as if familiar with the concept.

"Daya touched me then, both hands at my forehead—" He looked out at them. "You know of her gift to heal."

Again they nodded.

" 'My love,' she said. 'Magda will not be lost, nor cast off, for the Spirit has shown me the way.' I felt a calm course through my body, the pure beam of light that many of you have felt when hearing a message. 'This loss is not a tragedy, but a painful gift, as when a mother dies in childbirth. For Magda's death means a rebirth for the Daughters.' "

He pounded on his chest. "At this, my heart beat pure and I knew she spoke a divine message of light, but there was something else, a slight shadow. 'Like before,' my sweet Daya said, 'there is a cost to this step in the voyage.' "

Desmond dropped to his knees. "She didn't need to say the words, my daughters, this woman I have known from step one of the path. She kissed me, our lips met in a mix of tears and laughter, and we both knew what it meant. 'Listen for your name, my darling,' she said, and touched my forehead again."

Desmond wiped away a new set of tears, then looked up to face the gathering. "I closed my eyes, seconds only, wiped away tears as I'm doing now." He nodded, smiled, then sniffed. "And when I opened my eyes, Daya was gone."

An uproar spread through the crowd.

Desmond stood and raised his hands to the fire. "That's right, my daughters. To save Magda, Daya has ascended."

Caitlin watched the message spread from face to face. She saw the Mouse whisper to the woman at her side, Lily, the medical examiner's daughter, who smiled ear to ear. Gwendolyn Sunrise herself stood and started jumping up and down. In a few seconds, all the women joined her.

"Assholes," Caitlin muttered to herself.

He just said one of you got murdered and the other disappeared and you're giving him a standing ovation.

She backed away from the rocks and had started down the path when the singing began.

The fire is dying, so come let me build . . .

So many voices, and so happy, and so fucking out of their minds.

Caitlin didn't know what to do anymore. She didn't want to be caught there in the open, but the idea of being locked up again was just as daunting.

Screw it. I'll look for Desmond's records.

She took the steps quickly, returning to the main building's side door and slipping inside. The sound of singing from the nighttime revelers, loud and close, froze her in place. She looked left and saw the monitor of the unmanned security station broadcasting the hilltop scene. Her body let a huge shudder escape in relief. She moved another five feet down the hall before a thought occurred—the Mouse had turned off the set before abandoning her post. Not only was it on again, but the volume was turned up to the point of distortion. Something else—the hallway's lights were off.

Shit. Someone else must be here.

Caitlin slowed to a stop, debating which would be better: voluntarily readmitting herself to the locked room as if she'd never left, or playing dumb to whoever she might run into in the hall, claiming that whatever turned off the lights had opened her door.

She took two half steps in the direction of her former detention cell, then stopped when a door at the far end of the hall popped open and a shaft of bright light splashed into the dark corridor.

New debate: turn around, open the side door, and risk running into the hillside partygoers, or sprint forward to the middle of the hall and take the left turn, heading out the main doors?

The singing from the monitor behind her turned into random conversations. The meeting had ended. So far, no one had come through the open door. She jogged forward, as soft footed as possible. When she was ten feet from the intersection with the main-entrance corridor, the light at the end of the hall darkened, and someone backed into the hallway holding a box of paper work. Caitlin's jog became a sprint. As the far door swung shut, the silhouette of a woman with long hair and an assault rifle slung around her shoulder turned Caitlin's way. Caitlin took the corner and surged forward, aiming for the double doors to the outside.

"Caitlin Bergman, wait," the woman called.

Too late. Caitlin burst through the double doors and sprinted through the now-dark compound toward the motor pool.

I'm screwed were the only conscious words that came to mind, everything else on autopilot. *You've seen too much and they know you got out, which means they know you've seen too much.*

She'd find a car; if not, hide in the woods, get back to town. It was more a lizard-brain survival formula than a plan, but it was all she had.

Just past the cottages, the squawk of a walkie-talkie sounded somewhere behind her. She doubled down on her speed, despite someone's excited voice yelling words like "Inside the perimeter," "Stop them," and "Shoot if you have to."

She took a hard right into one of the four fields, diving behind tomato plants held up by trellises. She crawled toward the dark tree line at the side of the field, aware of the sounds of more than one person running, but not in her direction. She froze, sure anyone within a hundred feet would hear her heart thumping away like a marching band's drum line.

So far, so good, lizard brain—or at least, not so bad.

More voices came, both across the air and out of a radio.

". . . possibly more than one . . . up the southern entrance, near the Climb . . ."

She didn't remember everything about her tour, but the southern entrance and the Climb were both beyond the buildings where Eve had parked the town car, and downhill.

Whoever the guards are chasing isn't me.

She peeked above the tomato plants and saw two women in red run past the buildings at the end of the fields. She looked back toward the main house and cottages, saw no one else.

That meant her path to the motor pool was open.

She started that way again.

Somewhere between the rows of spinach and a crop of beets, the concussion of an explosion blew her off her feet. Her head rang like a tenth-round bell and her eyes streamed tears. The sheet-metal building that had housed the fleet of red town cars erupted into a ball of flame.

Seconds later, she rolled onto her knees, faced away from the wall of heat, and tried to stand.

Didn't work the first time.

She tried again, got a leg up, then the other.

Shouts came from the direction of the hill.

She listened for another lizard-brain instruction. No basic survival guidance this time.

She turned back toward the fire.

Plenty of room on the left of the fire to get to the road.

She started that way, but stopped.

A figure dressed in green camouflage was sprinting her direction, backlit by the wall of flames.

Caitlin spun around and started running through a field of cabbage.

Lights from the hill danced her way through the trees. She looked back, saw her opponent still in pursuit, but not nearly as fast as her.

Caitlin didn't care if the Dayans found her now. They'd see whoever had blown up their garage right behind her.

She dug in, bursting into a sprint, but her foot landed the wrong way on a cabbage, and she hit the ground hard.

Again, she forced herself up, getting in two weak steps before a tackle from behind knocked her back onto the ground.

Pain overrode her awareness, and she flailed her arms, making contact but not changing the dynamic. Someone was dragging her backward, despite the shouts of the approaching Dayans and the earsplitting thunder of a semiautomatic rifle firing round after round over her head.

33

THREE OF THE Guardians surrounded Desmond in a close formation, clearing the halls of the main house and ushering him into the
living room of his suite.

One of the well-armed women remained by his side; the other two
stood in the hall, ready to die protecting his life.

Desmond paced, nervous not about his survival, for the early reports
said the attack had been resolved, but because the foundation of everything he'd built was crumbling.

His guard handed him a walkie-talkie. "Gwendolyn."

Desmond took the radio to the bedroom, closing the door behind
him. "Sunrise, go secure."

He switched the radio's channel setting and waited.

Gwendolyn chimed in. "Desmond, are you safe?"

He ignored the question. "Who attacked us? Is it Larsen?"

"We don't know. Whoever it was only hit the motor pool, then left."

Desmond ran his fingers through his hair, grabbing a bit and yanking. "But the lights. Why did we lose half the lights?"

"Some circuit breakers tripped. They're back up now."

He let go of his hair, then tapped his fingertips against the side of his
head.

Think, damn it. Control this situation or you lose it all.

"What about the fire?" he said, trying to sound collected.

"Contained, but we lost most of the town cars, and the water it took to put the fire down drained tank number two."

Desmond threw the radio against his bed and let every swear he'd been holding back for the last two decades escape in a torrent, then picked up the walkie again.

"Is the Jeep okay?"

"Which one?"

"The only Jeep we have, darling."

"Desmond, I know very well we have two white Jeep Wranglers. I purchased both last year—"

"Were the Jeeps harmed in the fire, Gwendolyn?"

"No," she answered. Then, "Wait. I've been told there's only one on-site. Where could the other have gone?"

Desmond's hand covered his mouth and the response that wanted to come out. The other vehicle, *Daya's Jeep*, had been gone as long as she had.

He took a breath and started again. "Gwendolyn, is there still one Jeep in working order on the hill? Yes or no?"

"Yes," she said, "and two of the tractors were untouched. Do you think the attacker took the other Jeep?"

He rolled his neck from side to side. "Belongings are unimportant. The safety of the Daughters is paramount. Double the number of Guardians."

"Already done."

"Of course it is. True to your name, Sunrise, you bring the good news of rebirth once again."

Gwendolyn didn't have Daya's unflinching steel or Magda's sexual energy, but she lived to serve.

"One more thing," she added, "and I'm sad to say it isn't good news—"

"Just say it."

"Caitlin Bergman is gone."

"As in, she ran away?"

Desmond let up on the radio's send button and heard the sound of Gwendolyn's wooden beads clacking together.

"Sorry, Desmond. We just don't know."

He let the radio drop onto his bed. The plastic receiver bounced once, flipped over, then rolled off the side of the comforter, hitting the carpet.

"Fuck me," he said, heading toward his bathroom. He undid the sash around his waist, dropped his sarong, and sat on the toilet with his eyes closed, waiting for any type of relief.

They'd been attacked before. Estranged family members, jealous husbands, outfighting with townspeople, infighting with each other, a horrible case of the clap. All of those problems had been solved with cash, manipulation of the legal system, or a round of antibiotics. But he'd had Daya by his side for every battle.

Where the hell are you, Fireball? This is no fun without you.

He opened his eyes, half expecting to see her standing there, laughing and pulling him to bed—the other half expecting to find her holding a knife to his throat. What he saw in the mirror was an old man on a toilet who didn't want to play the game anymore.

He also saw light coming from under the door to the adjoining suite. He jumped to his feet, kicked his sarong away, and opened the door to Daya's room. A single lamp lit the far corner, away from the closet and the safe, close to Daya's desk. Naked, he moved close enough to see that the top drawer of her filing cabinet was open and a large block of files was gone.

CHAPTER

34

L AKSHMI STARED AT the menu, swore under her breath, then ordered the Huntington Rose Garden Tea Room's traditional service for thirty-seven dollars. After the twenty-five she'd dropped on admission to get into the botanical gardens, her unpaid adventure was adding up and she hadn't heard from Caitlin, other than a one-line text this morning:

Okay, back in town.

On the other hand, her view into the herb garden's clumps of green bushes and lavender sprigs divided by red brick paths reminded her just how little time she'd spent enjoying Southern California's beauty. That plus a genuine peacock strut through the grounds, as if that happened every day—which, she'd learned from her server, totally did. Judging from the more than twenty glorious birds she'd passed roaming the camellia garden on her way in, peacocks owned the place.

The other plus: she'd be able to hear every word Beverly Chandler and her companions shared at the table behind her. The ladies of the Pasadena Botanical Society had been in a closed-door session in the nearby Virginia Steele Scott Art Gallery since two o'clock, but their website's event plan included high tea at four.

By the time Lakshmi had slathered her first scone in clotted cream and raspberry jam, the well-dressed ladies who lunched had filled the eight-top behind her with the buzz of afternoon rosé and the reflected light flashes of enough diamonds to fund a small army. Rather than risking a look back, Lakshmi snapped a series of photos with her phone, then scrolled through the results. Sure enough, Beverly Chandler sat at the head of the table, facing the rest of the women and the wall to Lakshmi's left.

Having failed so miserably in her previous attempt, Lakshmi wasn't there to corner the woman. Instead, she'd reveal herself in time and see if Beverly came to her. She put in a pair of earbuds for show, spread her version of Maya Aronson's journal on the table in front of her, and reached for a truffle egg salad phyllo cup.

Salty, flaky, delicious. For a second, she disappeared into one of the few happy memories of her childhood. Her mother, both a first-generation immigrant to England and the wife of a surgeon, had gone out of her way to learn to prepare any and every variation of English tea service treats, and Lakshmi had been her taste tester, scone after cucumber sandwich after biscuit. She chased the delightful bite with a sip of the loveliest cup of tea she'd had since moving to America, closed her eyes, and tried to remember her mother's smile. The image came, but Lakshmi knew it was more amalgam than memory, pieced together from photos in albums rather than snapshots from her ten-year-old mind. She often wondered what their adult relationship would have become. As great as her mother had been, would she have supported her lesbian daughter? Not just gay, unmarried and gay?

She sighed, reached for a tiny quiche, and got back to work. Since the majority of Beverly and co.'s conversation dealt with botanical gossip, Lakshmi planned to spend the time with Caitlin's mother on top of God's Hill.

* * *

January 1, 1997

What an amazing new year. Last night, we lit the flame on God's Hill. Not just another fire, but the Eternal Flame, a fire that won't go out until February 17, 2016. Obviously, I haven't written since Linda's ascension back in February. We've all been so busy.

Following that night, our move was put on pause so the miracle could be communicated to those not present. Desmond and I went from Dayan house to house, city to city. I met voyagers that I'd recruited, and even ones that my recruits had recruited. All the while, Daya led a team to Oregon and oversaw construction.

*   *   *

Lakshmi skipped ahead through the construction phase. While it was impressive, she doubted Caitlin cared about their water filtration system or windmills. She stopped when she found a reference to the woman behind her.

*   *   *

Daytimes brought the hardest physical labor I've ever performed, but the nights were wild times of joy. Music, dancing, laughter, sex—something about the daytime exertion made the evenings that much sweeter. We all grew closer to each other and the Spirit.

Well, not Bevvie. I mentioned our numbers were around a thousand when we were in Los Angeles. Roughly one hundred didn't make the move. Another hundred made the move, but either found the work too hard, or their faith too weak, and they left as well.

My Beverly, the reason I'd found the Dayans in the first place, was one of those.

It started after Linda ascended.

When I was touring with the story, Bev had followed Daya up north with Tanner, one of her recruits. Tanner seemed nice enough, and devoted to the Light, but once I arrived, I realized he and Bev had been pulling away from the others, mostly pairing off.

One night, during Desmond's ceremony, Bev started crying.

"We honor Linda," Desmond was saying, "by forging this place of her dreams, this tower of her vision, so that she might call us on the final day."

It wasn't unusual for one of us to cry through Desmond's messages, but Bev sobbed out loud, enough for all of us to look her way.

Desmond continued, "Even then, on that final day—"

"February seventeenth," we answered.

"Linda will see those who made it to the top, through purity, simplicity, and honesty, and she will call our names."

Again, Bev cried loud enough to draw attention, and Daya got up and took her aside. After five minutes, Daya returned, but Bev didn't, so I went to the barracks and found her facedown on a bed. She pulled away like an abused dog but relaxed when she saw it was me. "Bevvie, come back. You'll miss the message."

"I know the damned message," she said. "The world's going to end and we'll be okay, as long as we follow the Light."

I'd seen other voyagers break down. I'd broken down.

The weight of the world is a lot to carry.

I rubbed her shoulders. "The voyage for the ultimate reward is perilous—"

"Don't spout Light Paths to me, Maya. Not you, of all people."

I pulled back at hearing my before-name. "It's Magda—"

"No, it's not. It's Maya-fucking-Aronson, or Sharon Sugar if someone needs a blow job."

"It's Magda," I repeated. "Desmond named me."

"Because of a dream I had, dumbass."

Her words hurt, but I knew the need to wound others was often part of the breakdown.

"But you had that dream, Bev. No one else. You."

Bev shook my hands off her shoulders and faced me. "It's not real, kid. Any of it."

She got up, walked toward the door, then looked back one last time. "Don't get me wrong. I had fun, but I'm done with all the bullshit."

Tanner waited outside. Bev melted into his arms, and they walked away toward his room.

We all get weak from time to time. I hoped that Tanner would bring her back to her center, but the next morning, both were gone.

By noon that next day, I'd formed a Re-welcome Team to bring them back, but Daya arrived at camp minutes before our departure and told us the news: the car that Beverly and Tanner had taken was destroyed by a logging truck. No one could have survived the accident.

I mourned my Beverly, but her death only strengthened my resolve. If she'd stayed pure on God's Hill, she'd still be alive.

*   *   *

"Do you really work for public radio?"

Lakshmi pulled her earbud out and turned away from the journal. She'd glanced back only once during the entire hour and felt confident Beverly hadn't seen her looking. Since nothing actually played through her headphones, she'd heard the shuffling of the group's departure hugs and had planned on bumping into Beverly on the way out, but here the woman was, all alone, once again flawless in pink, this time a tasteful sundress. Two other people sat at a table in the far corner, but no one from Beverly's group remained.

Lakshmi didn't bother feigning surprise. "I'm slightly more than an intern and slightly less than everything else, but they do pay me."

Beverly shook her head, then reached for the check on Lakshmi's table. "Then this is on me."

The waitress got the message from only a nod and a series of hand gestures.

"So you've decided I'm not a Dayan, Mrs. Chandler?"

"You sat here the whole time without singing, masturbating, or pulling a gun. No way you're a Dayan." She signed a credit card slip and closed the waiter's checkbook with a crisp snap. "The Japanese garden is lovely in the afternoon. Shall we?"

Lakshmi caught up with the spry socialite on the sidewalk outside the door.

"I have to apologize," Beverly started, leading Lakshmi through a gate, down a wooden path surrounded by bright-green bamboo, and into a refined area devoted to the plants and lifestyle of the Japanese countryside, "but had you shown up at my house and said you wanted to talk about my life as Beverly Bangs, I would have broken open a bottle of wine and gotten out the film projector."

She stopped at a stone bench with an exquisite view of another tea house, this styled in feudal Japanese, and brushed the bench before sitting on the stone.

"But the freaking Dayans. Even twenty years later, there's still a part of me that's up on that hill. It's Lakshmi, right? Lakshmi Anjale?"

Lakshmi nodded. "That's right."

"Indian?"

"I was born in Birmingham, England, but my parents were from India."

"As Lakshmi was Vishnu's wife, I assume you were brought up as a Hindu?"

Lakshmi held back the shudder that ran through her shoulders, not because of the religion itself but because of how her father, Dr. Anjale, refused to embrace any of its peaceful messages. It'd taken her years to understand that he would have applied the same strict conservative values to any theology on the planet, but the damage had been done. "I was."

"I'm less familiar with the surname Anjale, but I believe it's close to *gift* in Sanskrit, right?"

Lakshmi laughed. "I have no idea. I'm not big on Sanskrit."

Beverly smiled. "I've been around. A spiritual wanderer, I like to say. I grew up Protestant, tried Buddhism, dabbled in Scientology, spent half the nineties with the Dayans, and eventually found a happy medium."

"Are you still—"

"Religious?" Beverly looked out toward a water wheel that spread ripples across the surface of a koi pond. "I prefer spiritual."

"Do you believe in God?"

"I believe in love, Lakshmi. Do you?"

"Not with the girls I've met in LA."

A chuckle escaped Beverly's serious demeanor; then business mode returned. "This is all off the record." She wasn't asking. "No recordings and no notes. I'll answer your questions, but if anything said here today ever comes up on the radio, in writing, or even in some bullshit internet forum, my lawyer will sue you and every other Anjale he can find all the way back to India."

"Brilliant, thanks," Lakshmi said, more excited about the concession than the threat of legal action. "Before we begin, why the sudden change?"

Beverly cocked her head to one side and smiled. "As I said, I left part of myself up on that hill. I've never been strong enough to go back and get it. The least I can do is help Maya's family understand what it was like. Ready?"

Normally Lakshmi would both record and take notes, letting the act of writing solidify the words in her mind. She commanded herself to remember every syllable. "When you are."

Beverly looked down at her spotless nails. "What would you like to know?"

Given the constraints, Lakshmi went big. "What happened to Linda Sperry's body?"

A small gasp of surprise escaped Beverly's lips. "Most people start with the basics. Why'd I join? Did I know it was a cult? What were the orgies like? Why did I leave?"

"Okay," Lakshmi said. "Why did you join?"

Beverly tapped Lakshmi on the leg. "Midlife whatever. I was drunk and high most of the time, and I was pissing away the money I'd made in an industry I was both ashamed of and too old for. Then a friend invited me to a party and I met Desmond Pratten."

"Did he show you the face of God?"

Like the first time Lakshmi'd mentioned Maya Aronson in the woman's rose garden, Beverly looked shocked. "Who have you been talking to?"

Lakshmi told her about Maya's journal, though not the way it had been found. When she finished, Beverly looked amused.

"Hard to believe a diary survived this long, especially after Linda died. Once we got to Oregon, Daya went out of her way to destroy all written records. But that's not what we were talking about."

A hummingbird buzzed past, stopping to inspect a cherry tree months past its bloom.

"Should have been here in March," Beverly said, facing outward, leaving Lakshmi unsure whether she'd addressed her or the bird. "Sakura season is heavenly."

"Mrs. Chandler—"

"I never saw the face of God, Lakshmi. Not the first time Desmond tried to share his 'knowing,' not later with Daya, not ever." Beverly laughed slightly. "But Maya, first time out of the gate, 'I saw the face of God, God touched me, I get a new name.'"

"Forgive me for saying so," Lakshmi started, "but you seem a bit—"

"Jealous? Oh yes, I was. I wanted that experience like a flower wants the sun. Everyone who got the 'knowing' said it was better than sex. And it answered any question."

"Like what?"

"Like, is there really a God? If there was, that meant that everything Linda said would come true. And you have to remember, Linda said the world would end in the horrors of nuclear fallout. So yes, I was jealous that Desmond took to Maya so quickly. I only got her involved because I needed someone I knew to see if I was crazy or not. She showed up and became Magda all of a sudden."

"Is that why you left?"

"I left because it was all"—she looked around, checking the sidewalk, then lowered her voice—"a giant load of crap. After three years, I finally figured it out."

She stood and stretched out. Lakshmi rose as well. They walked down the path toward the Japanese tea house. "Because of Tanner?"

"Wow, you really do know everything. No, I left because of your first question."

Lakshmi had almost forgotten the first thing she'd asked. "Linda's ascension?"

Beverly nodded. "Oh yes, our sainted Linda, the woman who predicted the very date the world would end. The night before we were supposed to move to Oregon, she gets up off her deathbed and says her bit about the end of the world. Man, did that piss Daya off."

Her hand rose to her mouth, as if the words had escaped on their own and she wanted to grab them back. "I need to watch myself. The polite society of Pasadena has expectations. I can't afford to break character." Her hand returned to her side. "Have you ever felt you're two people, Lakshmi? One public and one personal?"

"Only my entire life," Lakshmi answered, suddenly back in a car with her father in her teens, an immigrant in America's Connecticut with no mother and a sexual awakening that couldn't be explored. She looked around the serene garden, remembering that she finally had her own apartment and the freedom to be whoever she wanted. Hell, she'd even seen a peacock an hour before. "Until moving to LA."

"Good for you." Beverly squinted against the sun. "I often wonder if it's a holdover from my time on the hill. The need to be happy, to understand, to do as I'm told despite every logical thought in my brain. We lied so much and so often. It's how we got what we wanted, even when lying to ourselves."

Lakshmi felt they were veering off topic. "So the night Linda ascended—"

Beverly fell back into her story. "She made her big speech, and Daya and I pushed her back into the house. Daya started screaming at the woman, about how her dream would ruin everything, but Linda kept repeating the date. Daya told me to go and get Desmond, so I left the room and waited in the hall, not sure if I should go back in, until Desmond came back out with a 'sacred' mission."

"A what?"

" 'Linda needs her plants,' he said. I knew what he meant, of course. Even near the end, Linda spent her days either painting or planting, and she kept a collection of potted plants on the porch below her balcony. She'd planned on taking them to Oregon to seed the original fields. Long story short, since I shared a horticultural interest, I got to spend half an hour carrying potted plants from the balcony to the study."

"Through the house?"

"No, the study had a retractable set of stairs that led down to the hillside porch below the balcony. So I traipsed back and forth, bringing pot after pot. Each time I'd see Linda, I'd ask how she was. Daya would pat Linda's hand and say she was improving, but I didn't see any difference. Eventually, they told me she'd fallen asleep. They even credited the fact that I'd brought fresh lavender into the room, said I was helping."

"And where was Maya in all of this?"

"No idea. I didn't see anyone but Desmond and Daya at the time. Finally, after the last plant was up, they told me to get some sleep. I went over to the bedrooms, took a shower, then fell asleep."

"When did you wake up?"

"When everyone started screaming about the miracle. I went down the hall and heard the story, how Maya had seen Linda laying in her bed in a white nightgown. Daya mentioned that they'd moved Linda to her bed after I'd gone to sleep."

"But you didn't believe them?"

Beverly laughed again, shaking her head. "No, I did. It made sense to let the old woman sleep in her bed. It wasn't until a month later that I remembered how Linda'd been wearing a light-purple nightgown that evening. Lilac, she would have called it, not white."

Lakshmi didn't see the significance. "Surely Maya could have seen lilac and called it white, right?"

"Oh yes. That's what I assumed. But later that morning, when I mentioned we should take Linda's plants to God's Hill, Daya told me the plants should stay there, with Linda."

Lakshmi's jaw dropped. "You mean, you think Linda is buried on the property?"

"She sure as hell didn't ascend."

"Who owns the property now?"

"No idea, but Desmond would never let Linda's house fall into someone else's hands."

Lakshmi did mental math. Driving to the hills over West Hollywood from Pasadena in the middle of rush hour meant over sixty minutes of white-knuckled traffic.

"Any chance you remember the address?"

35

CAITIE, USE YOUR BRAIN.

Matthew Bergman never used the phrase *use your head. Heads are just bone cages for the brain*, he'd say. *Your brain's got everything you need to stay out of trouble.*

"What about head butts?" Caitlin said, possibly aloud. She wasn't sure. Her brain was sending mixed messages.

Message one, she'd awoken in a small wood-paneled room, fully dressed in Dayan red on top of a neatly made single bed. Her brain made peace with this setting. She'd been on God's Hill, then the explosion, then hands. Someone had brought her here.

Message two was the troublemaker. Her father sat on the end of the bed near her feet. Maybe forty-five, wearing a gray sport coat over a white button-down, slacks underneath, his LAPD detective badge clipped on his belt, he lit a cigarette and exhaled.

"Head butts will hurt you just as much as whoever you're hitting, maybe even worse. It's a bad gamble, used only in life-or-death situations."

"Is that what this is, Daddy?" she said, her words slow and chunky.

"You tell me, Slugger. Use your brain."

"I miss you, so much."

"Me too, but we don't have time for that. Assess the situation—and show your work."

Caitlin tried to prop herself up but lost to dizziness. "Well, I'm talking to my dead father, so I've either got a head wound, possibly from a head butt—"

"Or?"

She lay back down and ran her fingertips over her scalp. No damage, but the sensation sent ripples of pleasure down her spine.

"Or I'm super high," she said with a giggle. "Sorry, Daddy."

He smiled. "Nothing to be sorry about, kid. I mean, a woman of your intelligence needs to lay off the weed in general, but you're gonna be fine if you get out of here."

Hearing his voice again, being in his presence, brought a warmth across her whole body, and she smiled until tears formed in her eyes.

"How are you, Daddy?"

"Don't worry about me, Caitie. Assess the situation."

"But you're here. Can you stay?"

He shook his head. "Sorry."

"So am I."

"What do you have to be sorry about?"

"I went looking for Mama Maya."

He laughed. "Of course you did. What'd you find?"

The good feeling disappeared. "She didn't want me."

He shook his head. "Maya wasn't ready to be a mom. That doesn't mean she didn't want you."

The tears started to flow. "She didn't want me, even when she cleaned up her life. She never wanted me."

Her chest convulsed and she shook through the tears. Whatever trip she was on had taken a turn, and vomit came out with a cough.

"Turn your head," her dad said, "or you'll choke."

Caitlin's head lolled to one side, and more vomit came. "You don't have to do this," she said between the heaves.

Hands grabbed her face and brushed vomit from her cheek. "Try to breathe."

"You're not even my real father," she said, then her stomach took over again.

"Don't die on me, Caitlin."

She opened her eyes to look up at her father's face. But Matthew Bergman wasn't the one keeping her from suffocating on her own sick. She blinked twice, now seeing a young woman, roughly the same age as she'd been when she received *She Taught Me to Fly* for her birthday.

"You're gonna be okay," the face said, though her eyes said anything but. "You're gonna be fine. Promise."

"You promise?" Caitlin thought, maybe out loud, maybe not.

"Promise," the girl repeated. "I'm Promise."

CHAPTER

36

"You sure it's her rental, Tom? I mean, you're positive?"

Johnny knocked his AC up a notch and sped up to fifty. He hated crossing bridges, always had. The green girders of the McCullough over the North Bend Channel had been there for years, but that didn't make him feel any better and he hadn't slept much.

Tom's voice came through the speaker loud enough to make Johnny lower the volume, his ears still aching from the previous night's explosion. "You said to find green pickups. I got a Dodge Fifteen Hundred with Washington plates and a Hertz sticker in the window."

"How about a white Jeep?"

Seconds after the Dayan motor pool went up, he'd seen the reporter running through the field. Then all hell had broken looser, a firefight had ensued, and he'd dived into the woods. He'd had his own retreat to worry about but had caught sight of a white Jeep Wrangler tearing ass in the opposite direction with Caitlin Bergman in the passenger seat.

"Shit, I don't know," Tom said. "You only said to look for the Fifteen Hundred. You want me to check the whole lot again?"

"Sit your dumb ass on that truck, Tom. I'll be there in five."

"Don't you have to work today?"

Johnny hung up and gunned it off the bridge into North Bend.

Two stoplights and five minutes later, he pulled into the casino's parking lot.

Sure enough, Stupid Tom had located Caitlin Bergman's rental truck. Johnny parked behind Tom's two-tone sedan and hopped out.

"I looked around," Tom said, sliding off the back bumper of the 1500. "I didn't see any Wranglers."

"Let's go." Johnny started walking toward the hotel's check-in desk. For once, Tom hadn't fucked up. Maybe he wasn't the world's biggest dumbass.

Tom caught up. "What are you thinking?"

"Your cousin still working in housekeeping?"

"Far as I know."

"She working today?"

Tom shrugged. "Why?"

Still a dumbass. "'Cause she can tell us what room number Bergman's in, and we can sit on the room and the truck until she goes somewhere. Come on, stupid. Let's get this bitch."

CHAPTER

37

THE WASHCLOTH FELT good, warm, but not too wet. Like the tongue of a big dog lapping at her cheek. Then her ear.

Caitlin hadn't had a pet since high school, and even then it wasn't hers. She and her dad had watched a golden Lab for a month. Another pity case. Someone on the force had been shot and the dog needed to be walked and fed. Matthew Bergman never turned down a misfit in need of a home.

She turned her head to the side, and another warm lash scrubbed her cheek.

Of course, once she'd become a journalist, she hadn't had the time to care for an animal. Not even a cat. She barely remembered to feed herself.

Still, nothing beat the feeling of unconditional love. She opened her eyes, expecting a giant tongue and a case of puppy breath. Instead she saw a gun.

"Hold on," she said, trying to focus.

A scared young brunette in a gray T-shirt and jeans, maybe in her teens, backed away from Caitlin with a washcloth in one hand and a pistol in the other.

Same brown wood paneling on the walls, probably the same girl she'd seen earlier.

Caitlin sat up. "Where am I?"

Right, she'd vomited and a girl had been there to save her from choking.

"Don't move," the teen said, her hand shaking slightly under the weight of the gun.

"Where?" Caitlin squinted against the light streaming in from the corner of a window covered with flattened cardboard boxes.

"You're safe." The girl dropped the washcloth and reached behind her for a doorknob. "I thought you were dead."

Caitlin shook her head and noticed her senses fighting to keep up. "They drugged me and I puked."

The girl turned the knob, and the door opened an inch. "I didn't know how much to give you."

Caitlin pushed off the mattress with one hand. "You drugged me?"

Standing would be hard, but she was able to get one foot on the ground, the other knee on the mattress.

"Sorry," the girl said, then stepped aside enough to slip out the door and lock it behind her.

"Wait." Caitlin's dream from before suddenly made sense. "Promise, I'm not going to hurt you. I'm not a Daughter of God."

That brought no response other than footsteps on wooden flooring walking away.

Great, trapped behind another locked door.

First there'd been Johnny Larsen pounding on her hotel room door. Then there were the Dayans and their magnetic locks. Now a thirteen-year-old with a gun.

Dizzy or not, this shit was getting old.

Caitlin got to her feet—bare, she noticed—and stepped toward the door. The knob was nothing special, just a simple thumb-turn lock that someone had turned around. Fully sober, she'd have the strength to break out. She followed the doorjamb up and found a light switch, but no light appeared.

The window was next.

Caitlin shuffled to the corner of light and pulled on the cardboard duct-taped to the window frame. A rectangle folded up and revealed a sheet of plate glass divided into eight sections by wooden lattice. She let the rectangle fall back down, then struck the cardboard with her palm.

The first section of glass tinkled out of the frame, and fresh air found its way into the room.

"Hey," the girl yelled from the other side of the door. "What are you doing?"

Caitlin moved her hand up a section and struck a second time. Again, the sound of broken glass meant success. She bent down and peeled the cardboard up. Wherever she was, it wasn't God's Hill. Bright sunshine showed over a grassy lawn that looked crisp and weeks past cutting. Either way, two or three more panels and she'd be able to crawl out.

She pulled back to strike again, but the doorknob rattled behind her.

"Stop it," Promise said through the door. "Don't you know we're hiding?"

"You might be hiding. I'm locked in a freaking closet." Caitlin turned, expecting the barrel of a gun.

Instead, the girl let the door open all the way. "Fine, come out or whatever. Just be quiet."

Caitlin followed her out into what looked like a storeroom. Trinkets, bottles of lotion, and stacks of homemade clothing lined shelves. An open doorway revealed a single bathroom and a second door that looked like it led outside.

"Is this Daya's Gifts?"

"No, that's in Coos Bay." Promise walked through the shelves and peered between two curtains before turning back to Caitlin. "There's food on the counter. I've got to check the front."

The girl disappeared through the curtains. Caitlin looked around, saw a half-eaten pack of peanut butter crackers on a counter, and stuffed one in her mouth.

"God, these are good," she said, more crumbs than intelligible words.

Promise answered with a shush from the other room.

"Seriously," Caitlin continued. "I'm gonna finish these. How is this happening? How did I get here?"

The curtains moved and Promise backed through, the gun in her hand once again.

"There's a truck outside," she whispered.

Caitlin moved toward her and matched her volume. "That's okay, right? This is a store."

Promise shook her head. "It's been closed for a month. No one should be here."

She crouched, her eyes still on the front of the shop. Caitlin followed her down to the floor, more sober every second. "But you have? Is this where you've been hiding? Who's been helping you?"

"Back door," Promise said, a command, not an answer.

Caitlin nodded and they backed up, eyes still toward the front, then Promise turned and tiptoed the other way. At the end of the first row of shelves, something tripped her and she sprawled out on the floor, the gun tumbling to her side.

Caitlin stepped closer but was caught by a hand on her shoulder. She spun fast and whipped her forehead forward.

Bone met bone and Caitlin saw stars.

"Butts," she said, falling back onto her ass like a toddler. She squinted the pain away and looked up at a carnival mirror image.

A woman roughly her own size and shape sat gripping her forehead under a mess of long gray hair. She lowered her hands to reveal a pair of brown eyes that might as well have been taken out of Caitlin's own skull.

"Didn't anyone ever tell you that head butts hurt, Caitlin?"

Caitlin wiped her own forehead, aware of a warm rush of blood staining her fingertips.

"Mama Maya?"

38

Mama Maya Aronson, rocking full-on Linda Hamilton–in–*Terminator 2* arms, left Caitlin sitting in place and went over to check on Promise.

"I'm sorry I tripped you. I saw the broken glass and assumed the worst."

Promise got to her feet and cast a sulky look Caitlin's way. "She freaked out."

Caitlin got up on her own, only slightly irritated that the woman seemed more concerned about Promise Larsen than for her own daughter. "You drugged me and locked me in a closet."

"So my dad wouldn't find us," Promise answered, bending to retrieve the handgun and stuffing it into the waistband of her jeans.

"Girls, calm down. No harm done."

Promise crossed her arms.

Caitlin caught herself mirroring the teenager's pout. "Wait, what the living hell?"

She dropped her arms, reached up to wipe another streak of blood from her forehead, and tried to take in the moment. After all this time, her mother was alive and right in front of her. How many days had it been since she'd stood in the medical examiner's office, ready to give the speech she'd been planning since her thirteenth birthday? Five, six? Here was Maya Aronson, Mama-freaking-Maya, very much not dead. Any part of Caitlin that had been buzzed now sizzled like a downed power line.

She held out her bloody hand and let her words run free. "Hi, by the way. I'm Caitlin Bergman, you know, the baby you abandoned forty years ago. What's your name? Maya? Magda? Sharon Sugar? I've only ever heard from you from a note in a bank vault. Nice invite, by the way, that key up a dead woman's butthole? Classy. Made my bat mitzvah invites look like they were glued together by a lonely thirteen-year-old raised by a single cop."

The words hung in the air, a challenge to be answered.

Mama Maya turned and walked down the row of shelving. "We don't have time for this."

"We don't?" Caitlin followed hot on her heels. "I thought you were freaking dead. Like, isn't that the reason I'm here in the first place, because the mother I never had dropped dead? Don't the dead have eternity?"

Maya turned quickly enough that Caitlin flinched and brought her hands up in defense. The woman only held up a scarf, then used it to dab the blood on Caitlin's forehead. "I go by Magda now."

Inches from her mother, Caitlin stared at the deep lines cut in the woman's tan face and saw more of herself than the twenty-year-old porn star she'd imagined for years. She reached up and met Magda's hand, taking possession of the scarf. The anger she still wanted to unleash suddenly checked itself. Beyond the physical appearance, something else messed with her senses: a smell, primal and familiar. She tried to place it but only came up with her own apartment.

As if she sensed the moment of détente, Magda turned and tossed a key ring to Promise. "I was followed but lost them at Bullards Beach. Get the rifle while I move the truck."

Promise caught the key with ease. "Is it him?"

Magda moved around Caitlin and headed for the front room. "One of the others, but you can bet he'll be here soon."

Caitlin had gone from inconvenient to invisible. "Hold on," she said, seconds behind the action.

Promise opened the back door and ran outside, her heels digging hard into a crushed-stone driveway. Caitlin followed Magda in the opposite direction into the main room, where a bright-green pickup truck sat visible through the front window.

"That's my rental car," she said. "What is happening right now?"

"I checked you out of your hotel." Magda held out a key fob. "Pull the truck around. We've got to leave."

CHAPTER

39

J OHNNY HAMMERED ON his truck's horn, then tore onto the right shoulder to pass some slow asshole.

The speed limit was fifty-five.

He pushed eighty.

He had fifteen minutes to make up.

Tom's cousin had walked them up to the room, only to find a house-keeping cart in the doorway. Johnny'd sent Tom to the parking lot while he and the cousin checked out the computer. It took another ten minutes for the cousin to convince security to rewind the external cameras and see the green truck turn left out of the main entrance.

On Johnny's command, Stupid Tom tore ass in that direction, leaving Johnny to sprint through the casino to his own truck to play catch-up.

In classic Stupid Tom fashion, he'd found the truck a mile south of the casino only to lose her when she looped through an RV campground. Instead of using his brain, he'd spent another ten minutes checking the parking lots down by the lighthouse.

Johnny didn't need to search the park to know where to look. The Dayans had a gift shop in Bandon.

He sent Tom in the right direction and hauled ass to catch up.

By the time he rolled into town, he was five minutes behind Tom, and Tom was pulling into the shop's parking lot. If the women were there, they were in for some trouble. If not, Johnny'd put the word out. The Proud Sons didn't have many core members yet, but they had like-minded friends in the county who would look out for that green truck.

40

SAFE AT A stoplight three miles away, Caitlin checked the rearview again, then reached down to squeeze her right heel into her canvas tennis shoe. Promise held the left in the back seat, next to Caitlin's open suitcase. Magda, assault rifle in her lap in the passenger seat, looked side to side.

"Run the light."

Caitlin laughed. The events of the last fifteen minutes had driven any drug-induced sluggishness from her system. "Sure, let's attract attention. Between the firearms, the teen runaway, and the dead woman, a traffic stop will make everything better." She looked back at Promise. "Gimme that one."

The girl complied, and Caitlin leaned over to put her other shoe on.

"Green light," Magda said.

"Yeah, yeah."

"Caitlin, we need—"

"Don't." Caitlin sat up, hit the gas, and drove through the light. "You didn't teach me how to drive, you don't get to tell me how now. Where's my phone?"

Promise held up Caitlin's iPhone. "It's dead."

"Then we charge it. Give me my bag."

Promise sent Caitlin's laptop bag forward. Magda intercepted the satchel. "I'll do it. Take the next right."

To Caitlin's surprise, Magda connected the correct cable to the truck's console. "No calls."

"Bullshit."

She grabbed the phone and unlocked the screen. The truck's console connected via Bluetooth immediately, and a series of chimes came through the speakers.

Magda sat back with the shock of a caveman who'd just seen a time traveler appear in the middle of the hunt. "What's happening?"

Apparently, the charging cable was the extent of her technical knowledge.

Promise reached out and touched Magda's shoulder. "Voice mails and text messages. People have been trying to reach her."

"I thought you told them she was okay."

Lost in the list of missed calls popping up on the screen, Caitlin looked back at Promise. "Wait, what did you do?"

"Your face," Promise said. "I tried to get into your phone for a while but couldn't get past the pass code. Then I remembered some phones had facial—"

Caitlin swore to herself. Usually she turned off the facial recognition when on assignments in case her phone fell into the wrong hands, but that need hadn't even occurred to her here. "And you held it in front of my doped-up face. Gross. Then what did you do?"

"I couldn't get into your email—"

"You're damned right." Rather than relying on the standard app, Caitlin used an encrypted program that required a separate password independent of the phone's standard features.

"—but I was able to send texts, so I sent a few simple messages."

Caitlin pulled the truck onto the shoulder.

"We can't stop here," Magda said.

"Just did, dead woman." Caitlin looked through her text threads.

Promise had sent five text messages, one to each of the most recently active threads. They all read the same thing: *Okay, back in town.*

The girl leaned between the front seats. "You don't seem to have many friends."

"I've got friends, little girl. We're just too cool for text messages."

"Please," Magda interrupted. "We have to get going. There's only a few ways to get where we're going, and this truck sticks out."

"I'm sorry," Caitlin replied. "Maybe we should rent something more appropriate. Big red limousine, maybe?"

"Drive."

"Fine." Caitlin pulled back into traffic. "Where are we going, anyway?"

Magda pointed toward the right. "Back to God's Hill."

Promise's outrage beat Caitlin to the outburst. "What? We can't."

"We have to find the Five."

Caitlin laughed. "No way. I'm driving us straight to Sheriff Martin."

Magda started to reply, but again Promise's teenage terror won the race to respond. "He'll make me go back."

"Your dad's a dick," Caitlin said. "I get it, but Martin will take care of you."

"Why? He didn't last time."

"There's no time for debate," Magda said. "If we don't find the Five, the Daughters will live in falsehood."

"What does that even mean?"

Magda ignored the question. "Turn left at the next intersection."

Caitlin reached a T in the road and, according to a sign, turned left toward Coquille. "What does 'live in falsehood' mean?"

Magda shook her head. "To live in falsehood is to follow a false path. To follow a false path means they'll miss the signs. Those that miss the signs cannot recognize the Cataclysm."

Caitlin sighed. Whether it was still the effects of whatever they'd drugged her with or just overall confusion, she had no idea what to do.

"Who's my father?"

Magda slapped the dashboard. "Did you hear what I just said?"

"Yes, you complete fucking stranger. What's it have to do with me?"

"They'll all die without the Light. Fifty Daughters will die, lost and wandering, because of Daya. Because of the Five."

Caitlin's hands tightened around the steering wheel. Out of all the ways she'd imagined meeting this woman, none of them had included an absurd rant about a phony religion. The same words she'd said on her thirteenth birthday came back to mind. "They can die alone for all I care."

Magda sat back, her eyes sending fire Caitlin's way. "I can't believe Matthew Bergman raised a daughter to say words like that."

"Maybe it's genetic and I got it from the mother who abandoned me, or whatever random casting-couch sperm donor happened to knock her up."

Magda's anger dropped down a notch. "I don't know what I expected when I wrote that letter—"

Caitlin laughed. "And shoved a key inside a dead woman—"

"—but I see now that—"

"—and cut off her fingers—"

"—I've asked too much—"

"—and the teeth. You knocked the teeth out of a woman's skull—"

Magda yelled. "Yes, yes I did. I had to. There was no one else. Daya was going to sell this girl."

"To Johnny Larsen? Her father?"

"A fucking child molester. And Daya knew. For five grand."

Caitlin caught Promise Larsen's eyes in the rearview. The quick glance away was all she needed to know that Magda was telling the truth.

Magda continued. "I knew then that Daya couldn't be trusted, that she'd gone against everything the Daughters stood for. And if that was true, what else might she have done? Desmond looks to her as the Seer, the heir to Linda's gifts—"

"Right. Didn't Linda Sperry predict the world would end on February seventeenth, two thousand and sixteen? I don't have my calendar on me, but I'm pretty sure her sight might not have been twenty-twenty."

Magda took a breath. "I don't expect you to understand. And now I see I shouldn't expect you to drop your entire life to help me. If you'll drive us to God's Hill, you can leave and never look back. But I have to save the remaining Daughters, and to do that, I have to find the Five."

Caitlin shook her head. "How? There's an armed guard tower on the only entrance to the place."

"There's a northern gate that hasn't been used since the ascension of the Five, when the road was lost in a landslide. It's unguarded and safe. I came down that way with you."

"Right, and why were you there, anyway?"

"To protect you. I've followed you since your arrival, but between evading the Larsens and taking care of Promise, I hadn't been able to make contact. I tried once in Coos Bay outside a bar—"

The woman in the parking lot of the Lumberjack.

"—then again at your hotel—"

Before I checked out. The clerk said a woman came in asking about me.

"—but I couldn't afford to linger around the casino. When I saw the Dayan car leave the parking lot, I returned to God's Hill."

"And let me get locked in a freaking cell?"

"Where I knew you'd be safe. With you in the containment room and everyone else at Ceremony Peak, I was able to look for proof that Daya also lied about—"

"The Five, right." Caitlin remembered the woman backing into the hallway of the main house, holding a box of papers. "That was you."

"I know what you do for a living," Magda said. "You find the truth, help people in need. I thought it was a sign that you might help the Daughters."

Caitlin stared at the woman, realizing that ever since she'd gotten the sheriff's call, she'd secretly hoped for some magical reunion. An after-school special where her long-lost mother had been pining for her special daughter, but a witch or international law or a crazy mix-up at the hospital had meant the only obstacle to their shared happiness was a chance encounter at a drugstore. Except the woman sitting next to her didn't want to make up for lost time or braid each other's hair. She wanted to abuse her neglected familial relationship to solve some cult-based drama.

Caitlin shook her head. She wasn't going to learn anything about her birth mother, dead or alive. "I don't understand any of this shit and I don't really care. Who is my real father?"

Magda looked out the passenger window, then glanced back at Promise, finally returning her gaze Caitlin's way. "If you help us get back there, I'll tell you everything you want to know, and you can go on with your life like I really was the dead body on the road."

CHAPTER

41

EVEN IN THE metropolis of Los Angeles, Lakshmi's GPS dropped in and out on the twisting hillside road. Luckily, the mansions on either side of Linda Sperry's estate displayed ostentatious address plates, meaning the gate of faded red wood at the top of the hill had to be the only way in and out of the former Dayan compound. She parked on the narrow road's shoulder, then inspected the entrance. Not only were there no obvious security features, but the hasp of the rusted padlock hadn't even been closed. One slight touch and the door yawned open with the creak of ungreased hinges. She took a calming breath, then stepped onto the driveway.

The cell phone in her front pocket rang louder than a car alarm.

"Bugger," she said, one hand over her now-pounding heart. She answered in a whisper. "Caitlin? Sorry I haven't rung, but I have so much to tell you."

"Lakshmi—" Caitlin started, but her voice cut out.

They played the who-has-a-worse-connection game for three volleys before Lakshmi took charge.

"Caitlin, I'll ring you back in a few. If you can hear me, Beverly Bangs is alive."

She hung up, set her ringer to silent, then stepped through the gate. Similar to the description in Maya Aronson's diary, the driveway veered to the right through a grove of eucalyptus trees, opened up to a grass clearing, then continued until the corner of a house came into view.

Peeling paint, dead grass, and a wheelless red limo on cinder blocks—the whole thing had a zombies-will-come-out-of-the-woods-any-second feel.

She checked her phone: 6:47 PM.

Maybe the zombies were at dinner.

The center of Linda's former hillside home, a two-story A-frame with a sixties vibe, brought together two much-less aesthetically coordinated additions of single-story row housing. If not for a mountain of swollen trash bags lazily piled feet from the front entrance, the place would have seemed deserted.

Sunset wasn't far off. If she was going to do something, she'd better get it done.

She broke into a sprint, crossing the hundred-foot distance to the closest side of the house in seconds. Back against the wall, she listened for movement but heard only her own rapid breaths. The remains of a vegetable garden filled the space between the house and the property fence, though any semblance of organization had lost to the combination of predatory weeds and neglect.

At the garden's edge, a well-trod trail of hardened dirt led around a clump of bushes. Lakshmi tiptoed down the path and peeked. Both row house additions stood on solid ground, but the original A-frame and its deck jutted out almost thirty feet, cantilevered by massive support beams that met concrete foundations on the hillside below.

A stairway of natural stone led down the steep incline to a strip of land under the house's massive deck. Beyond that, the hill continued uninhabited and wild for hundreds of feet before meeting other properties and a twisting road. If Linda's flower garden was still down there, Lakshmi couldn't see it from her current position.

She considered running around the other side of the house for another vantage point, but the rev of a car's engine coming down the driveway made her heart rate spike again. Someone was home.

She went for the stairs. Halfway down, she saw the strip of land under the pilings, a rectangular patch of green surrounded by smooth stones. Unlike the garden above, this bed looked fertile and well kept, but no one was growing flowers. After the two last flights of stairs, she came out onto the plateau to face a ripe crop of marijuana.

"Well done, Linda," she said, looking around. Under the deck, maybe two stories up, exposed pipes and ductwork ran the length of the house.

The slide of a glass door and a sudden flurry of steps on the deck above meant whoever'd been in the car now walked directly above her. She ran for the cover of the deck and wedged herself against the hillside, a mix of loose dirt and some sort of failing anti-erosion concrete. Sure anyone within the state of California could hear her chest heaving, she inhaled once and held it.

A male voice called out from above. "I can see you, and I've got a gun."

So much for holding her breath.

"Come out into the clearing, nice and slow, and put your hands up and shit."

Lakshmi raised her shaky hands and walked out, feeling dumber than she knew how to describe.

A man with long, gray hair and the effortless tan of a lifetime surfer looked down over the barrel of a shotgun. "Who are you, and why are you dicking with my garden?"

Lakshmi's mouth went dry. A thousand responses came to mind, but all seemed ridiculous. The only one that stuck was a question: *What would Caitlin do?*

She let air fill her lungs, relaxed her shoulders, then smiled at the man with the gun. "Desmond sent me."

He loosened his grip on the shotgun, using one hand to shield his eyes from the setting sun. "Why?"

Bullocks.

Lakshmi's mind raced through the bits she remembered of Magda's journal for something she could use. "To see the site of the miracle, of course."

After a couple thousand seconds, the old surfer lowered the gun. "Well, shit. Come up the stairs."

Turning back the way she'd come, Lakshmi tried to hide the release of tension from her body.

"Not those ones," the man said, pointing directly below his feet. "The fire escape."

She turned back to the underside of the deck. Previously hidden either by adrenaline during her first glances toward the house or by a shade of light-brown paint that blended with the dusty soil, a steel cat-walk ran the width of the A-frame. A door banged open, and a metal staircase unfolded in two segments, coming to rest along the hillside.

She brushed dirt off her pants, then climbed the aluminum stairway until she reached a metallic mesh wall. Turning right, she found another set of steps leading up into a room with a desk and a bunch of dusty books.

The surf bum sat in a crusty faux-leather chair, his shotgun down at his side, his fingertips drumming on the edges of cracked fabric.

"Welcome," he said, forcing a smile, then adding, "voyager."

Lakshmi stepped up through the opening, a square trapdoor with a brass ring in the center. The room smelled like fast food, weed, and the gas of a man who lived alone.

"Brilliant," she said, doing her best to summon Dayan enthusiasm. "A fire escape from the study to the hillside."

"Yeah." The surf bum cleared his throat. "Linda had the architect hide the whole thing, 'cause nature or whatever."

He glanced sideways at a framed picture of Linda Sperry in her mid-fifties, then looked away, hopefully embarrassed. Someone had drawn ridiculous breasts and nipples over the photo with a red Sharpie.

Lakshmi looked around the room as if it were paradise, despite the stacks of magazines and newspapers covering the furniture. "And this was her study? It's glorious."

"You said Desmond sent you," he said, nodding to the couch.

Again she tried to play confident, sitting back onto the one exposed section of sofa. "He did."

The movement of the cushions began a newspaper avalanche her direction. She managed to stem the tide with her elbow, but a month's worth of headlines ended up on the floor, cascading toward the edge of the trapdoor. The wooden square dropped to the floor with a bang, sealing the exit.

He didn't seem bothered by the mess or the noise, but something was making him uncomfortable. "Why are you really here?"

Lakshmi hated how far she'd sunken into the old couch. Athletic as she was, getting up would take more than a second.

"Lakshmi," she said, shifting her weight forward. "That's my name. It means—"

"Why?" he repeated.

"As I said, Desmond wanted me to visit Linda's room, so I could—"

"See the miracle." He reached down to his side, near the shotgun. "Right."

Lakshmi scrambled to her feet, ready to fight, but the man's hand had picked up only a phone, a concept suddenly just as frightening as a gun.

He stood as well, bringing the phone with him. "I gotta hear it from Desmond."

"Cool," Lakshmi said, after a painful gulp. "Mind if I see—"

"Knock yourself out." He took a step backward while dialing, then leaned down to grab the shotgun before moving into a hallway, his eyes watching her the whole time. "On your left."

Lakshmi followed, grinning like an idiot, then turned toward a closed door.

She looked back, saw him nod again, still watching, then turned the knob enough to feel for a lock on the other side of the handle. It wouldn't stop a shotgun blast, but a locked door might give her a few seconds to think of a way out. "Do you mind if I sit in here alone?"

He just waved at her. "Fucking hills," he said, giving his phone a shake, then stepping further back into a great room. Apparently, Lakshmi wasn't the only one with a spotty connection. He'd have to go outside to get a good signal.

She didn't have much time. A paranoid man with a gun was about to figure out she wasn't supposed to be in that house. She closed the door and locked herself inside Linda's room: ten by ten, a full-sized bed in the corner, a tiny side table next to the wall, and dual-sliding windows looking out on the sunset.

Magda had said she'd looked under the bed the night of her miracle, so Lakshmi did the same. No sign of a trapdoor like the one in the study.

Bloody hell.

She reached for the side table, a three-foot oval draped with a red tablecloth, and raised the fabric.

Oh thank you, sweet Vanna White.

Just beyond the plus-shaped table base, a brass ring waited for the challenge.

She moved the table aside and revealed the secret of Linda Sperry's ascension. Another set of emergency stairs led down to the catwalk and almost directly into a metallic mesh wall. She went down and pushed on the wall. The entire frame swung open with a creak and a cloud of dust, revealing the same fire escape she'd climbed into the study.

Neither Beverly nor Magda had ever known a second set of stairs led down to the garden, all because Linda Sperry'd had her homebuilder blend the fire escape into the natural surroundings.

Lakshmi stumbled down the hillside steps, her eyes on the decking above. The climb back to the road, uphill toward a man trying to get a better signal, would be risky. She knew another road existed downhill, hundreds of feet through scrub brush. She counted to three, then started running.

Passing the crop of weed, she heard the clang of the study trapdoor popping open once again.

Faster, she willed herself, jumping down three feet of a ridge. The sun had nearly set and darkness was falling. Maybe she could hide.

The bangs of feet on metal steps made her *maybe* highly dubious.

"Stop it, kid. Right now," the surf bum shouted, not far behind.

He was in his sixties, right? She was young and agile.

The distinct *chk-chk* sound of the shotgun being racked cut any age disparity in half. Still, if she could lower herself over the next—

Nope, that's a twenty-foot drop.

She caught herself before tumbling over a ridge.

Only two choices now, both stupid: jump and risk horrible injury—or surrender.

"Tanner, stop," someone called from above. Someone feminine, familiar.

Lakshmi turned back to see the surf bum, Tanner, staring uphill at a blonde in hot pink aiming a handgun in his direction.

"Jesus," he said. "Is that you, Bevvie?"

"Drop the gun," Beverly Chandler said. "Lakshmi's with me."

42

JOHNNY FINISHED HIS beer and signaled for another. No one had seen shit for the last four hours. Gunner had dropped by after his shift at the mill but left for dinner with his girlfriend. Tom had bailed an hour later for his bouncer job at the Bachelor's Inn, leaving Johnny alone in the Lumberjack on a low simmer.

Hazel twisted the cap off a Coors Lite and brought it over. "What's got your panties in a bunch, John?"

Johnny shook his head. "Mind your own business, unless you've seen the bitch?"

Hazel put her hands up in surrender. "We don't have many rules at the Lumberjack, but even we wouldn't let a girl as young as Promise in here."

Johnny took a good pull. "My daughter's no bitch. You think I'd talk about Promise like that? What kind of man do you think I am?"

Hazel reached for a pair of dirty glasses and dunked them in her sink. "You say the word *bitch* so much, most people would guess you breed terriers."

"Most people should keep their mouths shut." Johnny finished his beer. "Promise is an angel. It's those Dogs that got to her. A bunch of freaks poisoning her mind against her own family."

"Un-huh." Hazel turned back his way. "So who's this bitch then?"

Johnny gave her a nice long stare. Hazel didn't look away. Not like his wife.

"That Jew reporter that was in here Saturday night." He tossed his empty bottle into the trash can beneath the wait station. "Brunette in a sport coat, carries herself like a man."

Hazel shook her head, reached into the cooler below the bar, and came back with a fresh beer. "Must have been after I left."

"Right."

Johnny walked his new bottle to the pool room. Hazel was full of shit, but he wouldn't press her until his dinner was delivered.

Two regulars in their late sixties played the closest table, leaving two other tables wide open.

As he reached for a pool cue, a small growl escaped Johnny's lips. Would have been nice if some strangers had the run of the room. He wanted to punch someone out. Instead, he racked a triangle of balls and broke, happy for the loud pop of that initial impact.

"So this is what you do on a sick day."

He didn't have to look away from the table to recognize the grating sound of his father's voice. The five-ball dropped into the far-corner pocket.

"You gonna fire me, sir?"

Dressed in a Bandon Dunes polo, the shirt he wore whenever he wanted to remind people that he'd bought his way into every country club in the area, Anders shuffled over to the old-timers at the first table and handed them a twenty. "Why don't you boys have a round of the good stuff on Larsen Timber?"

The pair took the hint well enough, leaving them the whole room. Maybe Johnny'd get to punch someone after all. He fixated on the red three, inches from the far bumper and the side pocket. "You gonna buy me a round of the good stuff too?"

He took the shot, but the three bounced shy.

Anders raised his voice. "Look at my eyes when you talk to me, boy."

Johnny straightened up and turned toward his father, conscious of the solid feeling of the lightweight pool cue in his hand. One good swing would take the old man off his high horse, maybe out of the saddle altogether.

"Yes, sir. How can I be of service?"

"That sarcastic tone's what got you thrown out of the Army. I've paid you double what they did ever since the Battle of Baghdad, and I'll be damned if I'll let you talk to me like that."

Johnny took a step toward his father. "How are you gonna stop me?"

Inheritance be damned. It'd feel good to knock the endless gripe out of the old man's mouth.

Anders took a step back but didn't soften. "I'll stop the payment on your bail, you ungrateful shit, and Boz Martin will throw your ass back in county lockup. Hell, maybe that's where you belong. I sent Dana by your place to fetch you, and she said your missus looked like she got hit by a Trakloader."

Johnny took another step closer. "You gonna tell me how to handle my wife, Daddy? I learned from the master, after all."

Married three times, the old asshole wasn't walking the high road. The first wife, John's mother, had died on his eighth birthday after a nasty fall down the stairs of the Larsens' single-story ranch. Wives two and three had left on their own after a few rounds each, both too scared to go after the man's money. Johnny was about to throw that in his face when Anders sat back into an open booth.

"I'm trying to figure out what the hell's going on with you, son. Sit down and talk this out."

Johnny squeezed the cue one last time, then tossed it onto the table, grabbed his beer, and joined Anders in the booth.

Hazel delivered his burger and a Scotch for the old man, and Johnny caught Anders up on the day's events.

Anders ran his hand through his remaining hair. "And what were you gonna do if you caught up with the reporter?"

Johnny chewed the last bite of his burger. Usually he liked the food at the Lumberjack, but something about this meal made him feel like someone had wiped their ass with his bun.

"It's not the reporter. Well, it might be, but not just her. Tom said the woman driving the truck out of the casino had long gray hair. Sounds like the bitch who jacked up my arm and took Promise."

Anders sipped the last of his J&B. "Answer my question. What were you gonna do?"

"Whatever it took to get Promise back."

The old man shook his head. "In the middle of Bandon, where any tourist on their way to the Dunes could stop by at any second, and only one day after you spent the night in jail for publicly threatening Caitlin Bergman. Shit, son. That's no kind of plan."

Johnny finished his beer. "It is what it is."

"It's murder, you simpleton, and that's a one-way ticket to life in prison."

"Nobody's gonna give a shit about one more dead Dog."

"Don't be stupid. That reporter is known, nationally. She's got ties to law enforcement, including the feds. Dana told me as much before the interview, and she learned all that just from a web search." Anders stopped and stifled a cough. "Of course, if our big-city friend was to be caught in some kind of accident . . . Hell, if they all were, I doubt Martin would look too close. Especially if his people were tied up with wildfire evacuation notices."

"Wildfires? In Coos County?"

Anders nodded. "If you'd have come to work today, you'd know that the BLM issued a cease-work order for the Powers ridge project. Whole area's basically a tinderbox."

"But that's down southwest, other end of the county from the Dogs' compound."

Anders finished his drink. "And a fire down there would threaten a lot of homes. If you and a few boys you trust with your life happened to find Promise right before a second fire were to start up north—"

Johnny chimed in. "Away from any major structures—"

"—somebody'd have to prioritize."

Nodding, Johnny thought about the area around the Dogs' compound. Most of the surrounding land was government owned, some tribal, no schools or churches, none of his people. "We go in, find Promise, set a fire to take their attention, and get out quick. Without anyone coming to their rescue, the Dayans would be fucked. Assuming Promise is still there."

"Even if she's not," Anders said, sliding out of the booth. "Still far enough from any decent folk to matter." He stood. "Wind's picking up and there's a full moon tonight. I'd better get home."

Love wasn't a word that came to mind, but Johnny smiled at his father's weathered face and felt as close to the man as he ever had.

"Good-night, sir. You drive carefully."

* * *

Half an hour later, he met Gunner in the parking lot.

"We're taking your truck," Johnny said, walking around to the passenger side.

Gunner raised an eyebrow, then shut his half-open door when Johnny got in. "If you say so. Where to?"

"Just past Powers. You bring your kit?"

Gunner backed the truck up and took off out of the parking lot. "Got both my Armalite and the Rock River."

"How many rounds?"

"Case of two twenty-three for the Rock River, and five boxes of five fifty-six. Of course, the Rock will shoot both."

Johnny popped his Zippo and lit a cigarette. "What about the tracers?"

Gunner shook his head. "Shit, I only got a box of twenty left. Are we going to war or something? 'Cause I would have brought my vest."

"Not yet, and twenty tracers will be more than enough."

Almost forty minutes later, the pair parked Gunner's truck off a logging road one mile from the ridge Larsen Timber hadn't been able to log. They left one of the AR-15s and most of the ammo locked in his cab and humped through the woods in the dark, lit only by the moon.

"This is good enough," Johnny said, stopping just before a dry drainage ditch that marked the edge of the plot. "Give me that thing."

Gunner pulled back, offended. "Hold on, John. This is my rifle and my ammo. I feel like I ought to do the shooting."

"I didn't want to dirty your hands."

Gunner laughed. "You told me to bring an assload of firepower to a bar in the middle of the night. I figured my hands were gonna get wrist-deep in shit."

Johnny didn't really care as long as the job got done. "Well said, brother. See if you can hit that clump of fir, midway up. But only two rounds."

Gunner flicked the laser scope on and raised his rifle.

Johnny covered his ears with his hands. "Burn that shit, Gunner."

Gunner pulled the trigger for a single shot.

A bright red arc of glowing phosphorus streaked through the night sky and landed close to the point Johnny had pointed out. Within seconds, a larger glow burned from the landing point.

"Hit it again."

Gunner repeated the motion, hitting twenty feet farther. The round struck a tree, then fell sideways into the brush, still bright red, until seconds later when the red turned white and orange.

"Shit," Gunner said. "Look at those fuckers burn."

Johnny slapped him on the shoulder. "Send two more a hundred yards to the left, then let's get out of here."

"Yes, sir." Gunner swung the rifle to his left. "So what is this, an insurance thing?"

Johnny was already five steps down the path. "That's exactly what it is."

CHAPTER

43

MAGDA WOULDN'T EAT anything from Caitlin's favorite fast-food spots, so Caitlin bought sub sandwiches for herself and Promise and a salad for her mother at a shop built into a gas station outside Coquille.

Mother.

The word felt so awkward in her mouth, foreign in her thoughts.

My mother eats only organic non-GMO foods.

My mother grows her own produce.

Well, she does. My mom and her kooky woodland friends live off the grid on top of a mountain.

She checked the gas station parking lot. No sign of trouble. The attendant, a bearded man in his forties, waited by her truck. She handed him her credit card and hopped in. Since all of the gas stations in Oregon were full-service, Magda and Promise waited on a bench in a dark city park two blocks away. The attendant handed Caitlin her card and receipt without incident or even a second glance.

She pulled to the side of the lot and tried Lakshmi's phone but got voice mail again. This time she left a message with the highlights: "Mother alive. Missing runaway found. Driving the pair back to compound. If you don't hear from me by tomorrow morning, call Sheriff Martin and tell him everything."

She considered calling Martin herself, but Promise's earlier fears still carried a fair amount of weight. If Caitlin took Promise to the cops, they'd either put her in the system or return the girl to her parents. Neither option sounded like the right choice at the moment, nor did the equally possible third outcome—being accused of kidnapping a minor. Caitlin decided to get Magda back to the hill; then they'd have a realistic talk about Promise's choices.

She pulled into traffic and returned to the edge of the dark park where she'd left the pair. Seconds later, Magda and Promise climbed in.

"I cooked," Caitlin said, pointing to the supplies.

After they agreed on basic directions, Promise dug into her dinner, taking down a bottle of Coke in feverish gulps. Magda gave the plastic fork that came with the salad a dirty glance but still single-used the single-use polystyrene to shovel in sustenance.

"How'd you become Sharon Sugar?" Caitlin said, taking a left onto a dark country road, her mouth finishing a bite of turkey sandwich.

Magda almost choked on her salad. "Sharon Sugar is dead."

"Not to me. She's been with me my whole life. My mother, the porn star. How'd that happen?"

"The past is unimportant. All that matters is our presence in the present."

Caitlin felt her anger bubbling up again. "Are you saying I'm unimportant? Because your past is driving your ass around right now, in the presence of the present."

Magda closed the top of her salad container. "I'm talking about the salvation of the world and the souls of those on God's Hill. That's a little more important than how Maya got into porn."

"Well, according to your directions, we've got more than half an hour in the present where you can't do anything about that."

"Fine." Magda shoved her to-go container down next to her feet. "Maya Aronson had a father, Daniel Aronson."

"Wow, that's the first time I've ever heard anyone talk about my grandfather."

"And you should thank the Light for that. Daniel Aronson had too much in common with Promise's father. Do I need to say more?"

Caitlin shook her head no.

"Maya was lost at the end of high school and turned to substances and older men. First came the dancing, then the tricks, then the offers to do both at the same time for more money, just in front of a camera."

Magda shuddered and turned back toward Promise. The teenager had fallen asleep in the back seat seconds after finishing her sandwich. "Look at her, out cold already."

Caitlin studied the way her mother watched over the young woman. Her first reaction, jealousy. But looking again, she didn't think she was seeing a mother's gaze but rather the reflection of hindsight.

"Tell me about Promise."

Magda took a sip of water. "To tell you about her, I have to start with the Five."

Caitlin sighed. "Fine, tell me about the Five."

Magda started her story. Two of the Five had barely been Daughters. Maybe four years total between them, both under thirty; both had run from abusive men. The other three were key players over the age of fifty: a clothing designer, a construction engineer, and a doctor who'd been with the group from the beginning.

Caitlin jumped in with something she'd heard Desmond say.

"'Doubts, every one of them.' What did they have doubts about?"

Magda's eyes snapped open. "The Cataclysm, of course."

"The one that didn't happen."

"I don't know if you can imagine that day, Caitlin. All of us huddled around the fire, preparing to meet God, to finally be called up. Desmond walked among us, passing out the Calm, trying to keep us from running into the fire."

"Wait, what's the Calm?"

"An enhancer," Magda said, like that would make sense. "Those who were anxious took a cup of the Calm."

Newsreel images of Jonestown played in Caitlin's head. "Christ, it wasn't Kool-Aid, was it?"

Magda waved Caitlin off like she was the one spouting nonsense. "An herbal mixture of chamomile, lemon balm, and valerian root. Daya made it from our gardens. It's what Promise gave you last night."

Caitlin slowed for an otherwise carless four-way stop. "But the world wasn't on fire. Didn't that bother anyone?"

"The world *was* on fire," Magda answered with a frown, her eleven lines deep and distinct enough to make Caitlin steal a quick glance in the mirror and check the area above her own eyes. "Years of drought, almost two decades of war in Iraq and Afghanistan, hurricanes, tornadoes, flooding, coral bleaching, melting ice caps, ocean gyres of plastic waste, class warfare, refugee crises in Syria, Africa, South and Central America—"

Caitlin couldn't help herself. "The presidential election?"

Magda nodded. "To us, the world sat ready to burn."

Caitlin hated that every word of their logic made sense. She continued down the asphalt road, her headlights the only source of light besides the full moon.

"We sang and danced, disrobed and presented our naked bodies to heaven, spent the day rejoicing. Then, as the sun set, we readied ourselves with prayer and meditation."

Part of Maya's journal came back to Caitlin. "Linda's wedding night, right? You were waiting for night to fall and the world to end."

"That's right. Hand in hand, we circled the fire, waiting for the clouds to part and let God's pure light shine down. Then, Daya fell."

"As in, fell down, physically?"

"It wasn't uncommon in our circles, though I couldn't remember Daya ever stumbling, let alone collapsing. We rushed to help her, but she got up quickly and yelled for Desmond."

The road took them through a stretch of flat land where someone had wedged a tiny cattle ranch up against a stream. Magda stopped talking, her eyes glued to the possibility of confrontation. Two trucks sat in the driveway of a trailer home, the only light coming from a TV visible in an unshaded window. Seconds later, heavy trees surrounded the road and took back the night.

Caitlin prompted her mother. "Daya asked for Desmond, you were saying?"

Magda relaxed and continued, " 'The Knowing,' Daya yelled. 'I need the Knowing.' This was unusual. Those of us who'd had the Knowing experience with Desmond knew that the ceremony was only done in private, often alone in nature. But Desmond stepped forward and placed his hands on Daya's temples."

Magda took another sip of water. "She started shaking so hard she almost fell again, then froze in place and started speaking. The high-pitched words from her mouth sounded different than the low, husky voice I'd known for over twenty years, but familiar. After three or four words, I knew it was Linda, speaking through her, to all of us present."

Caitlin's eyes rolled so hard she was afraid she'd pull the truck off the road. For the last two minutes, Magda had presented herself as a rational human being. Now she was talking about spiritual possession with a straight face.

Magda continued, oblivious. " 'My lovely Dayan voyagers,' she called out. 'I see you and know you.' And then she named us, Caitlin, every one of us, without hesitation, even those who'd joined after her ascension. 'The Spirit has seen your sacrifice and good deeds. God sees your naked bodies, your gorgeous, clean souls, and the acts you have performed. Rejoice now, for you have done the impossible. You have stayed the Cataclysm. Desmond, the Guide, has brought you here. Daya, the Future, has become the Seer. Cling to them. Continue your labors, for every task you complete saves the world from the fire for one more day.' "

Caitlin glanced over to gauge Magda's seriousness. The tear rolling down the woman's cheek said she believed every word of her story.

"Daya collapsed again, falling into Desmond's arms, sound asleep. We took her back to her quarters, and she slept for two full days."

"Her speech ended the party?"

Magda smiled. "Oh no, her speech started the party. Have you ever known true ecstasy, Caitlin?"

A blush formed on her cheeks. Was this the moment her birth mother was going to give her *the talk*?

"I don't lay back and take it, if that's what you're asking."

Magda shook her head. "I'm talking about loving with the full force of the maker coursing through every fiber of your body. We'd saved the world. *We* did. One man and one hundred women, naked and penitent and penniless. After years of sacrifice and dedication, the fate of the world had been decided by misfits, mess-ups, and even ex–porn stars. Do you believe in God?"

If Caitlin had to choose between talking about sex or God with Magda, she'd prefer sex. "I pop into temple for funerals and weddings."

"I don't mean organized, western God. I mean the one true source, the answer in the dark to every question, the eternal. The voice that's there in the flowers and the soil and the breeze."

Again, Magda seemed headed for nonsense. Caitlin needed to know why the woman had dragged her into this mess after years of silence. "Yeah, I've heard the wind in the willows whisper Mary and seen the one set of footprints. How does your glorious God orgy involve Promise and her father?"

If Magda was annoyed, she didn't let it show. "Months went by, and people started leaving. One at a time, no problems. A week later, three of the younger women left quietly in the night. While this was sad, it wasn't unheard of. We prayed for them but accepted that they must follow their own paths."

"Must not have been sleeping in the main house, huh?"

Again, Magda ignored her. "Then the Five stood up at an evening ceremony, said they'd packed their things, and that they were leaving in the morning. Desmond spoke, saying he understood their doubts, how mankind has learned to distrust gifts of purity, but if they wanted to leave, he wouldn't stop them. Of course, by leaving, they knew what we all knew: when the day did come, their names would no longer be called."

"And having your name called is important why?"

Magda didn't answer, maybe lost under the weight of the concept. Was that the fear keeping a village of women on the top of a mountain, the reason she couldn't wait to get back?

Caitlin prompted her once again. "Okay, after the big talk, you went to bed and—"

"The next morning, they were gone."

"Sure, makes sense. That was the plan."

"No, Caitlin, only their bodies were gone. Not their clothes or belongings. Their bedrooms looked the same as they had the days before."

"Still not getting it."

"Daya emerged that morning, rejoicing in the work of God. 'They've ascended,' she said, telling us how she and Desmond spoke with the Five after the ceremony, asking them to meditate in their beds and decide in the morning. Our lawyer, Gwendolyn—"

"I know Gwendolyn Funtimes," Caitlin said.

"She stayed in the same bungalow with the Five, all night long."

"Like you did, outside Linda's door."

For the first time, Magda looked over at Caitlin with a slight smile. "You did read my journal."

Caitlin fought back the answer that came loaded and ready to fire. *You shoved a key in a dead woman's butt and left a note with my name on it. You're damned right I did.*

"Parts," she said instead. "Are you saying the women disappeared?"

Magda nodded. "Ascended."

"And became *the Five*."

"I know you don't believe—"

Caitlin held a hand up. "Let's not stop for that. What happened next?"

"When everyone heard, doubts flew out the window and the departures stopped. Once again, we all walked the same path toward the Light."

"Until Promise showed up."

"Yes." Magda's eyes returned to the teenager in the back seat. "I was working a wellness welcome, and she arrived with a note."

"What, from a teacher?"

The Dayans often received referrals, Magda explained. The people of the county didn't all agree with their ways, but whenever a woman needed refuge, a whisper network of trusted allies showed them a way to God's Hill.

"And who referred Promise?"

Magda's brow furrowed. "Our allies are sacred, Caitlin. They often come from dangerous situations themselves."

Caitlin hid a smile. Her mother and she shared a common belief after all: one should never betray a source. Still, she had a feeling she knew someone in the Larsens' periphery who would notice a thirteen-year-old in trouble. The woman who'd slipped her a note in the Lumberjack the same night Magda had tried to make contact: Hazel, the bartender.

At first Magda had hesitated to shelter Promise, due to her age. "But I recognized the signs, both in her actions and in God's will, so I presented her to Desmond for initiation."

44

"I T WAS AMAZING," Promise said from the back seat, still lying down but obviously awake. "I felt so safe. And I learned so much."

Magda put the journal back in the bag. "Try to sleep, Promise. We'll be there soon, and we may not get to rest overnight."

The girl sat up and leaned between the front seats. "Kind of hard when you keep saying my name. How far now?"

She reached for Caitlin's phone, stared at the screen, then put it back in the console. "Your signal is bad. The map shows us just outside of Coquille. That was like an hour ago."

Caitlin took her phone back. Sure enough, no signal. How many turns had it been? She was supposed to drop the pair off, but how was she going to find her way back?

She turned toward Magda, fighting off a sudden surge of anger, more at herself than her mother. She'd jumped face first into the woman's story, completely losing track of the big picture, not to mention her surroundings. Because of what? Her need to get to know this woman who cared more about Promise Larsen than her own daughter? "Was this part of your plan?"

Magda looked confused. "What do you mean?"

Caitlin shook her head. "To get me out in the middle of nowhere in the middle of the night—"

"It's not the middle of the night," Magda answered, "and I know exactly where we are."

"—knowing damned well I won't have a clue how to get back to civilization."

"Relax, Caitlin, I'll draw you a map—"

Caitlin's hands strangled the steering wheel. "Don't call me that. You didn't name me."

"Of course I did."

"Matthew Bergman named me Caitlin—"

"Because I asked him to—"

"—after his great-aunt Catherine."

Magda crossed her arms. "Right. His Jewish great-aunt with the name of a Catholic queen."

Caitlin's father had told her all kinds of stories about his great-aunt. "That's right."

"Bullshit. Caitlin Flaherty was my best friend in high school. I spent every second I could at her house until some junkie knifed her in MacArthur Park."

"My ass."

Promise spoke up. "Guys?"

Magda continued. "She was the sweetest girl I'd ever known, and some crackhead robbed her while we were waiting for fake IDs."

"Hey, guys," Promise repeated, louder.

Caitlin laughed. "Great, I'm named after a crackhead."

Promise tapped on Magda's shoulder. "The light."

If the girl thought some random Dayan reference would calm either woman down, she was wrong.

Magda was almost yelling. "That's not what I said. Her parents packed up and moved to Calabasas or some-fucking-where, and I never saw them again. After that, everything went to hell."

"The headlights," Promise yelled. "There's a car coming."

Caitlin's eyes had been fixed on the road in front of her but somehow still missed the flickering lights coming down through a grove of trees to the far right, maybe half a minute away.

"Shit," she said, looking for a shoulder.

Magda brought the assault rifle up. "Kill the lights and pull over."

"No way," Caitlin said. "You get down and we'll drive right past."

"It'll be too late."

Caitlin looked over and growled. "Get. The. Fuck. Down."

By the grace of God, or the Light, or the righteous anger pulsing through Caitlin's veins, her jacked-up, gun-toting mother sank down into her seat.

Caitlin held her breath and concentrated on the road before her, hyperalert and ready to floor the accelerator if necessary. She eased into an uphill curve toward the right at the same time the opposing vehicle came down the hill.

The other driver clicked their high beams to standard, revealing a fifteen-year-old blue or black sedan with a primer-gray hood carrying a man behind the wheel and a woman in the passenger seat.

If either of them cared about Caitlin's truck, neither showed any interest during the two brief seconds of passing. Caitlin continued up the hill, and the sedan's taillights disappeared into the night.

"No big deal," she said, her held breath escaping with a little less control than she'd hoped.

Promise rose and looked behind them. Magda sat up like she hadn't been prepared for a battle.

"There's a gate on the left at the top of the hill. Drive past until you see a break in the trees. We'll get out there."

"Fine," Caitlin said, ready to be done with the whole thing.

She slowed near the top of the hill until her headlights caught a reflector stuck to the edge of a yellow metal gatepost. After another hundred feet, the dark gap of a dirt road broke through the tree line.

"Looks like the party's over," she said, turning off the main road into the darkness and stopping the truck twenty feet into the forest.

Promise started gathering her belongings.

Magda stayed in place. "There are so many things I want to say—"

"My father," Caitlin said, not letting the woman steer the conversation anymore. If their time was short, she wanted at least that one question answered. "Who was he?"

"You have to understand. I made a promise—"

"Not to anyone who's ever given a shit about me. Who was he? Another porn star? Some random bar hookup? Mick Jagger? Who?"

"I know I haven't been there for you, but I promised I'd go my entire life without telling anyone this secret."

"You told Desmond. In your diary, you said you told Desmond."

"That was a cleansing between me and God. This information won't help with your anger. I'm sorry I involved you in any of this. After you helped that girl in Indiana, I thought maybe now you'd be ready, maybe even able to join me on my voyage—"

Whether out of disbelief or pure ego, Caitlin couldn't help but interrupt. "You read my book?"

"Both."

A warm smile came to Caitlin's face.

Magda reached into a bag at her feet. "Then I read this."

She pulled out a familiar paperback: Caitlin's torn copy of *She Taught Me to Fly*, the one with a lifetime of resentment scribbled across its pages. Her smile cooled in an instant.

"You're not ready for the voyage, Caitlin, just like Maya wasn't ready to be your mother." She shook her head. "Like *I* wasn't ready to be your mother."

Her hand lingered on the door handle. "I'll pray that we'll meet in the Light, my crystalline bird, and in that Light, you'll know that not a day went by that I didn't love you, as much as I could." She squeezed the handle, and the truck cabin's light came on. "Until then, forget you ever found me."

"Damn it," Caitlin said. "Close the door."

"It's better this way—"

"Shut the door." Caitlin reached over and yanked the door shut. "That car's back."

She'd caught the distant glare of headlights as a flash in her side mirror coming from the same direction as they had. Since nobody'd been behind them for miles, the other car must have turned around.

She overrode the truck's auto-light function and drove up the dirt road in only the moonlight that spilled down through the tall trees.

Branches whipped against the large truck's windows, and more than one lurch convinced Caitlin she might end up purchasing her rental rather than returning it with a broken axle, but after what felt like an hour-long minute, Magda grabbed her arm.

"There, drive around back."

The road broke out of the tree coverage into a clearing serviced by a paved road, undoubtedly linked to the yellow gate at the bottom of the hill. What looked like an unlit one-room cabin sat at the end of the clearing, separated from the forest by a narrow strip of grass on one side.

Caitlin took the truck around the cabin, where a detached sheet-metal garage stood, open and empty.

"Pull in and shut the door," Magda said, already half out of the truck.

The sixty-five-year-old hit the ground running with her assault rifle in hand, looking as deadly as any soldier Caitlin had ever known. The woman vanished around the cabin before Caitlin had the truck in park.

"Promise," she said.

"The door," Promise answered, popping out of the truck almost as quickly as Magda.

Caitlin killed the engine and got out, aware of her heart pounding through her chest. Promise stood to the left of the door, trying to untangle a length of chain from a metal holder.

"It's looped," Caitlin said, joining her and taking over, lifting the loop of metal links over its restrainer. When it was free, they both tugged on the chain, working together to lower a retractable roll door inch by inch.

The door fell faster than Caitlin expected, racing toward the garage's concrete floor with a loud whir until slapping down on the pavement, leaving the women in total darkness.

"Shit." Caitlin patted her pockets for the phone she knew she'd left in the truck. "We need light."

She took a step toward the truck, but Promise grabbed her. "Wait, listen."

Caitlin tried to pick sounds out over the quick pace of their breathing. Sure enough, footsteps crunched through dry grass.

They held each other in the darkness.

There was another gun in the truck, the handgun Promise had used in Bandon, plus light, bags, and her phone. Still, Caitlin couldn't move from the spot.

A door in front of the parked truck opened with a loud crack and a rectangle of moonlight, then Magda stepped inside. "It's safe, for now. They drove up past the gate but turned around at the washout."

Promise ran across the room and fell into Magda's arms. Caitlin watched the old woman comfort the girl yet again. For whatever reason, this time didn't hurt as much.

"The washout," she echoed, remembering Magda had said the Dayans had abandoned the northern entrance after a landslide. "So I'm driving my truck back down that hillside."

"Unless they're dumb enough to come up after us in a car," Magda said.

Promise raised her head but didn't leave Magda's arms. "If they're my daddy's friends, they're dumber than that. You should stay the night, Caitlin."

Caitlin shook her head. "I should go now. Worst case, they follow me, expecting you to be with me, then leave when I head to the airport."

Magda put some distance between herself and Promise. "That's not the worst case, and you know it."

"Either way, it gives you more time."

Magda shifted her weight from hip to hip. Even in the dim light of the garage, Caitlin saw a look she instantly recognized as skepticism on her mother's face, having made the same face many times.

Caitlin crossed her arms. "I can take care of myself. I've done it my whole life."

Promise looked up at Magda as if she expected a fight.

"Fine." Magda handed the girl the assault rifle. "Promise will scout the trail to make sure it's clear."

"She's thirteen—" Caitlin started, stopping when the girl ejected the gun's ammo cartridge, studied the number of rounds in the clip, then slammed it back in place.

"There's a bluff to the left of the trail, before the switchback," Magda said.

Promise spun toward the door. "I know."

"Two shots fast if there's trouble."

"Got it," the girl answered, already out in the night sky.

"Don't you dare engage," Magda called after her.

Caitlin couldn't be sure, but she might have heard Promise reply one last time with a single word: *Duh.*

"Unbelievable," Caitlin said. "You're gonna send that kid down a hill in the middle of the night with an assault rifle."

Magda turned toward the door. "Somebody's got to draw you a map."

CHAPTER

45

DESMOND CHECKED THE satellite phone's history.

The cleanup of the previous night's incursion and motor pool fire had kept him busy all the way until his evening ceremony and unable to break away from the nervous women. He'd missed Tanner's call from Los Angeles by two hours.

He tore through the bag that kept the phone's charger, found the instructions Daya had left for retrieving voice mail, then entered the code.

Tanner's message lasted only five seconds.

"Shit, man, there's someone here, and she says you sent her to see Linda's room. Call me back now."

If there'd been any doubt in Desmond's mind as to whether his world was going to end, Tanner's brief warning sent it up in a puff of smoke. A day after Magda's investigative reporter daughter—who knew way more than she should about the organization—broke out of a containment room and stole crucial financial files from Daya's office, someone, a woman, had shown up at Linda Sperry's LA home. If they knew about the money, they'd know that Linda Sperry still received, and even cashed, checks from her husband's investments, despite being dead for years. Plus, Caitlin Bergman had been on-site. Who'd talked? Who'd broken his trust? The newest initiate, Eve, the medical examiner's daughter?

They'd lain together after the Climb, as he did with all new Daughters. Had she regretted the experience? Their age difference? His performance? He'd been distracted, and even the blue pills hadn't helped.

Perhaps Promise Larsen? Had she figured out Daya's reckless scheme to extort her father? Did it even matter?

Daya was gone, most of the Daughters as well. The ones that remained were years past their beauty or worse, succumbing to the pitfalls of age, and the local police seemed to be letting the Larsen family get away with murder.

The Dayans were done. It was time to pull the cord, grab what could be grabbed, and get out of the God business. But what to do about his Daughters, the witnesses to it all? Sure they were loyal now, but would they stay that way when confronted with Linda Sperry's body, or the Five? Eventually they'd realize how they'd gifted their money away, cut off their families, and betrayed their marriages, all because of a man named Desmond Pratten.

With Daya gone, the only person who knew his true identity was his lawyer, Gwendolyn Sunrise. In no way did he question her loyalty, but who knew what the others had divined over the years. There were only two ways this could end if he stayed around—either in prison for embezzlement or in prison for murder. At his age, what would be the difference? As for the Daughters, wasn't an end to all things what they really wanted?

He reached for the bottle of Mexican Valium in his safe, pocketed two for himself, then placed the rest on a cart near the door.

The TV in his bedroom, the only set on God's Hill, had shown nonstop coverage of a spreading wildfire for the last hour and a half. He grabbed a multitool from his desk drawer, then followed the coaxial cable from the TV to the closet, where the satellite signal entered the room. One firm snip and the aerial coverage of the bright-red flames in the dark night turned into a solid rectangle of blue.

He replaced the tool, reached for a walkie-talkie, and requested the presence of Gwendolyn Sunrise.

Minutes later, he showed her the signalless TV.

"What does it mean?" she said. "Is this another attack?"

Desmond took the woman in his arms. "No, my beautiful Sunrise. Nothing can attack us now. A nuclear device has been dropped on Los Angeles."

Her eyes went wide.

"And not just LA," he continued, "but Moscow, Tehran, Mecca, London, and Paris."

"Does this mean—"

He nodded. "A wildfire burns to the south of us and will be here soon."

A shudder shook Gwendolyn's body.

"Don't be afraid, my love." He lifted her drooping chin with his finger. "This is the day we've worked so hard to see."

Gwendolyn's fear transformed into enthusiasm.

"The Cataclysm is here?"

Desmond lowered his head until their foreheads touched. "And we must ready the Daughters. I didn't want to create jealously among the others, but Daya told me one other thing before she ascended."

He kissed her forehead.

"You are to be the shepherd, Sunrise. You will administer the Calm, both in liquid form and in spirit. You will walk the Daughters into the Light. That is, if you're willing."

She threw her arms around Desmond, crying in joy. "Tell me what needs to be done, and I will make sure every single Daughter hears her name tonight."

CHAPTER

46

THE DAYANS HAD outfitted the cabin more like a construction trailer than the ranger station Caitlin'd expected. A series of maps lined one wall, though there was nothing she could use to get to town. The large, professionally drafted charts featured every bit of the God's Hill compound, from the roads in and out to the flow of water down various elevations.

"Watch the window, Caitlin, not the blueprints."

She glanced back at Magda, who scribbled on a pad of paper under the narrow beam of a pocket flashlight, then looked back out the single window.

Moonlight revealed both the paved road in front of the cabin and the rough path they'd taken up the hill in her truck.

"How bad was this landslide or washout or whatever?" Caitlin said, trying to ignore the constant sway of the trees on both sides of the road. Heavy winds made every bit of the forest look like trouble. "With all the equipment you ladies have, why not just fix it?"

Magda held up a hand. "I'm doing this from memory, you know."

"I mean, you built all of this yourselves, right?"

Magda answered without looking up. "Daya sold the paving equipment after the Five ascended. The mixer, our bulldozer, even the screed."

"What's a screed?"

Magda looked up, smirking. "About ninety thousand dollars used." She returned to her feverish scribbling.

"I just need to get back to the Five," Caitlin said, "meaning the I-5 freeway, not your Five." She laughed. "Look at us, we both have a Five in common."

"Almost there. I don't want you to get lost."

"As long as I get back to a phone signal, I'll be fine."

They returned to anxious silence. Caitlin blinked hard twice. She wasn't sure how many hours it'd been since waking up stoned, but a headache was forming behind her eyes.

Magda broke the silence first. "Do you have any children, Caitlin?"

Caitlin looked back. "What? Me?"

Magda put her pen down. "Sure. Ever married?"

"No marriages, no kids. Why?"

"From your phone history, I thought maybe you had a daughter named Lakshmi."

Caitlin laughed. "Not exactly."

"A friend, then?"

"I look out for her."

Magda tore the piece of paper from the pad and stood. "I'm glad for you. The joy that comes from looking after someone else is the Spirit's gift to us all."

She stepped closer and held out the paper.

"I'm sorry Maya couldn't give that to you."

"Me too." Caitlin took the paper, a rough map next to an ordered list of street names and turns, and tucked it into her laptop bag. Her fingers brushed against her worn paperback. "About the book in my bag."

"That Maya gave you when you were thirteen?" Magda said.

"Yes."

Magda raised a finger to her cheek and scratched lightly. "Maya was two months out of rehab. Do you know the twelve steps, Caitlin? Step nine?"

"Something about apologizing to the people you've wronged."

A swell of wind whipped around the cabin, and the whole building settled like it'd taken a deep breath. Magda looked up, took her own calming inhale, then continued. "Direct amends. Of course, what Maya didn't know was that she still hadn't faced her past with God's eyes and the full clarity of the Light, but she tried—"

"You sent a book." Caitlin refused to refer to the woman in front of her in the third person.

Magda nodded. "She'd called Matt. He wasn't hard to find. They met at that deli on Fairfax, the one with the bar called the Kibbutz Room. I don't remember the name—"

"Canter's," Caitlin said. Her father's favorite lunch spot.

Magda smiled. "That's right, with the pickles. He still looked great. Older, and with one of those ridiculous cop moustaches, but healthy and happy enough. Did you know they went to junior prom together?"

Caitlin had heard that part of the story. Maya Aronson had asked Matt Bergman to prom, but two hours into the date, the girl's father had shown up and made Maya leave.

Magda's smile faded. "Anyway, Matt told Maya about you, and how smart you were, and how much you loved to read. She'd never read much but wanted to get to know you, to impress you even, so she bought a copy of the only book she knew anything about. Rehab had been hard, especially that first month, so Maya tried to busy her mind with any book or newspaper they had at the center. As far as she was concerned, *She Taught Me to Fly* was the best book she'd ever read." She let a small laugh out. "Maybe the first."

"So you—" Caitlin stopped. This time, she let the third person correct the second, partly because it felt easier to keep Magda talking, possibly to make it easier to hear. "Maya sent me a copy?"

Magda moved beside her and faced the window. "She showed up at your dad's apartment with a copy, but he didn't let her in."

"Didn't let her in? Wait, when was this?"

Magda didn't hesitate. "October tenth, nineteen eighty-eight."

"That was—"

"Your birthday. Of course."

Caitlin looked over, confused, or amazed, or both. Her brain and heart fought over the right term for the feeling, finally settling on dumbfounded.

Magda raised an eyebrow. "You came out of my body, Caitlin. No matter how much of Maya I've forgotten, I've never forgotten your birthday." She shook her head and laughed. "They wouldn't give me anything for the pain."

Caitlin caught the slip into the first person but tried to hide any reaction. Magda continued like she hadn't noticed either.

"You were early, and honestly, everyone thought you'd come out stillborn. I wish I could tell you I took care of myself during the pregnancy, but—" She turned away from the window, looking back into the cabin. "Maya spent two months on crank before she knew she was pregnant. Even after she knew, she didn't exactly stop. You came during the seventh month, very much alive, and despite everything Maya had done to herself, you were healthy. Thank the Spirit."

Caitlin started to speak but found she had to clear her throat first. "And you gave me to Matthew Bergman."

Magda nodded.

Caitlin wanted to get into so much more of the backstory, including putting a name to her birth father, but her heart was stuck on that day.

"Until I turned thirteen, when he turned you away."

Magda let out a sigh, nodding again. "You were at school. Maya showed up way too early. Matt wasn't even there."

"Then how—"

"She wasn't sober. That's how weak Maya was. Two days after she'd met Matt for lunch, all the way to step nine, she threw out everything she'd worked for."

Magda looked up. Even in the dark, Caitlin saw tears forming in the corners of the woman's eyes. "Someone must have called about the junkie passed out on the front porch, and Matt rolled up, still in uniform." She blinked the moment away, but the tears still came out. As did Mama Maya. "I don't know what I said, if I even made sense, but he calmed me down, told me to come back another time, when I was sober." She sucked in a sharp breath but couldn't stop a sudden sob from shaking her frame. "He was right," she said, before a second gasp rocked her again, "so I left that note." She wiped her eyes and caught her breath. "Did it even make sense?"

"Did what make sense?"

"The note I left in the book."

Caitlin could tell the woman was in pain, but if Maya, Magda, or who-the-hell-ever thought two highlighted lines in a kids' book would have made everything better, she wasn't going to pat her on the back and say yes.

"The crystalline bird thing?" Caitlin fought with her clenched jaw. "Nope, never really understood it."

Magda sucked back some snot. "No, the note, on the outside of the wrapping."

Caitlin shook her head. "There wasn't a note. Just the brown paper."

"Matt must have thrown it away." Magda turned back to the window. "Well, he was the sober one."

Caitlin touched her shoulder. "What did it say?"

"Doesn't matter. Maya didn't have the words then." Magda raised her own hand and met Caitlin's at her shoulder, giving it a gentle squeeze. "I need to show you the files. They're in your truck."

"Files? What files?"

Magda turned and walked toward the cabin's back door.

"Financial records. Proof that Daya was stealing from the Daughters by moving money around in the names of the Five, after their ascension."

Caitlin followed after. "Wait, what about my father?"

CHAPTER

47

THE WOMAN MOVED fast for her age. By Caitlin's first step out of the cabin, Magda had already entered the garage and started raising the door.

Caitlin caught up. "Did Matthew Bergman know who my father was the whole time? Was that what was in the note?"

Magda had the door halfway up. "We don't have time. If you want to stay the night, I can tell you everything."

"Bullshit, Magda. This is the deal. I got you here, so you have to tell me who my father was."

Magda didn't let up on the chain, hand over hand. "Matt was your father."

Caitlin grabbed the chain, stopping the process. "That's what everyone keeps saying, and I get it. He was amazing. He never did anything wrong and I'll always love the man, but I need to know. Who is my biological father?"

Magda looked away, then looked back, meeting Caitlin's eyes. "Everyone does something wrong, even Matt Bergman."

Once again, Caitlin felt her blood rise. "You make someone else raise your baby, and you're gonna badmouth—"

Magda turned quickly and knocked Caitlin's hand off the chain. "I was twenty-two. I'd already done a few films but was still dancing at the Tropicana and turning tricks when the manager wasn't looking, or even when he was. I didn't do it sober, either. Coke, speed, you name it, one of us always had a vial or a pipe. So one Thursday, the LAPD raided the place. Two of the girls were under eighteen, and we all ran for it. I ended up in the bathroom, topless and struggling to toss an eight-ball, when the stall door opened up and in walked my junior prom date, Officer Matt Bergman."

"Bullshit."

"He threw a shirt over me and walked me out. The whole time, I think he's gonna throw me in the truck with the rest, but he snuck me into an alley and let me go, told me to call him that night."

"To call him?"

"He went back in for my purse and whatever, so I called him to get it back, and one thing led to another. We finished what we never got started back on prom night."

Caitlin almost laughed. "You had sex with Matt Bergman?"

"Sex? We fucked in the back of a squad car off Mulholland."

In the past week, Caitlin had learned her birth mother was part of a doomsday cult, then dead, then alive, then that she handled modern weaponry like a Green Beret. Each one of those surreal discoveries made more sense than the idea of her dad, the fountain of wisdom and enforcer of laws, banging a stripper in an official LAPD vehicle.

"But he was dating Jane—"

"Actually, they were engaged."

"And you—"

"Had a gift."

"But he—"

"Was a man, Caitlin. A young man whose high school sweetheart fucked like a pro."

Caitlin hard-swallowed a breath. "So you?"

Magda nodded, then started pulling the chain again.

Caitlin's hands fell to her sides. "Did he know?"

The door neared the top.

"Of course he did."

"But he didn't—" Caitlin felt a weight on her chest. "I mean, he didn't even sign the birth certificate." She watched Magda tie off the chain. "He would have, he would have claimed me—"

"He couldn't. Whether or not he told Jane, and he obviously didn't, he had a future in front of him. Twenty-three, working his way up at

LAPD. No one was going to promote the Jewish guy fucking the porn star who turned tricks on the side. I mean, did it never occur to you that he'd been able to adopt you so easily?"

Caitlin pulled the truck's key fob from her pocket and squeezed the button. The truck unlocked and its lights flashed twice. She had everything she needed to leave, but none of it felt right. "You're lying. My dad's not—" She stopped herself from saying *my father*. It made sense, of course. It even felt right, except that he'd never told her. His love of the truth wasn't just why he'd loved being a police officer but also, when he was faced with the less-than-ideal realities of his job from day to day, one of the reasons he'd encouraged Caitlin to become a journalist. "I mean, he didn't do things like that."

Magda raised an eyebrow, then looked away. "Fine. The man was a saint."

Caitlin squeezed the plastic in her hand again. Her head didn't know what she wanted, but her hand sure felt like it wanted to punch somebody.

"You're full of shit, Magda."

Magda nodded. "Maya Aronson was full of shit, and dope, and booze, and whatever else brought her quiet. That's why she couldn't be your mother, and that's why she's gone. I'm Magda, and I walk in the truth of the Light. Even if that means you'll never be my daughter, I have others, and they need my help. You should get going."

Caitlin moved three feet closer. As many years as she'd spent hating Maya Aronson, she doubted she could bring herself to hit the woman. Magda, on the other hand, was asking to get the bitch knocked out of her.

A loud gunshot stopped Caitlin halfway from the truck to Magda.

Five frozen seconds later, a second pop followed.

Caitlin turned toward the truck cab.

"No," Magda yelled, pulling the chain off its restraint and letting the garage door spin down to the ground. "It's too late for that."

CHAPTER

48

They met Promise in front of the cabin. Winded, she handed Magda the assault rifle.

"Only two so far," the girl said between breaths, "Stupid Tom and Tammy, that girl who lives down the street from him. Tom was climbing the trail when I fired, Tammy stayed with the car."

Magda pulled the gun's magazine and double-checked the rifle. "Did they run?"

"She did, but Tom just kept going up the hill. Faster if anything."

"Good." Magda shoved the mag back in.

Caitlin tightened the strap of her laptop bag. She had no problem leaving her suitcase or even her rental truck on the hill, but her laptop was another story. "How is that good?"

"Instead of staying to protect her, a man with a gun left a woman with a car all alone in the middle of nowhere. She'll be willing to take you back to town. If not, hit her over the head and take her car. I'll distract the idiot in the woods, you run down the road. The washout can be tricky, so stay on the logs to the right."

Caitlin nodded. She had no idea what was happening, but any plan sounded right. "Fine. Let's go, Promise."

Promise looked confused. "What? I'm staying here." She looked at Magda. "Right?"

Magda touched the girl's arm. "Of course."

"Bullshit," Caitlin said. "You said you'd keep her safe, no matter what. How is leading a teenager through a mountainside firefight safe?"

"I'm not afraid of Stupid Tom," Promise said, "and I can handle a gun."

Caitlin reached for the girl's other arm. "You know damned well that your dad's on his way. We've got to get you away from this place right now."

Promise shifted away. "But Magda said she'll protect me—"

"She says a lot of things." If Magda hadn't mentioned Daya's files, maybe Caitlin would have left Promise in her care. Instead, she pulled the girl back her way. "Magda's a liar. That's what the Dayans do. They lie to get whatever they want. She lied to get me to Oregon, not to finally have a relationship, or to get to know her only real daughter, but to look into whoever killed the Five. I didn't do it, and she still hasn't found them, so she lied about my father's identity, just now, to keep me here, to get me to look into, what, embezzlement?"

Staring at Magda's determined face, she answered her own question.

"No, not embezzlement. She got me here knowing that I can't stand the idea of a world that treats women like sidewalks, the idea that someone brutally mutilated a helpless, peace-loving sister and dumped her in the forest."

Magda looked back to the woods, maybe for threats, maybe because Caitlin finally saw the truth.

Caitlin grabbed both of Promise's shoulders. "Magda didn't read my books because she wanted to know me but because she needed to know how best to use me. She betrayed Daya to save your life. Without proof of Daya's corruption, she can't go back to Desmond and the Daughters. If she can't go back, she can't ascend on the day of the Cataclysm, which is more important to her than you or I ever will be."

Another look Magda's direction told Caitlin she wasn't just close to right; she'd hit a bull's-eye with a cannon.

"She's lied to you the whole time, Promise, making you believe that you can't trust the police, but you can. I'll make sure that you can. If not here, then I'll take you with me."

Promise looked back and forth between the two, a pendulum of doubt.

Magda broke the stalemate. "Caitlin's right," she said, letting go of the girl's arm. "I'll move faster on my own."

She raised her hands to cradle Promise's face. "You are protected by the Light, Promise Larsen. Wherever you go, the Spirit will follow." She looked over at Caitlin. "And though she doesn't believe in the Light, Caitlin will take care of you."

The girl looked over at Caitlin with tears in her eyes.

Caitlin took her by the hand. "Your father will never touch you again. Now let's go."

"Caitlin," Magda called. "You may not understand me or believe me, but I'm doing this for you."

Caitlin turned back. "I believe"—she gave her mother one last look—"that you believe that's true. Good-bye, Mama Maya."

* * *

She led the girl down the dirt- and branch-covered asphalt as fast as humanly possible, no conversation, no playing back her last interactions with Magda, only the thought of getting Promise to safety. The single-lane road cutting halfway into the hillside looked neglected rather than damaged. After two switchbacks, they came to the washout, though *landslide* might have been the more accurate term. For forty feet, the pavement had given out and the land beneath had slid down the hillside. In addition, several massive trees and boulders from the hill above the road had fallen down into the chasm, giving the impression of an avalanche that had cascaded into a sinkhole. Dangerous, but even in the moonlight, it seemed hard to believe it was irreparable.

"Follow the logs," Caitlin said, pointing to a fallen tree toward the right of the collapse.

Promise went first, stepping past a tree's exposed broccoli-stalk clump of roots and onto its two-foot-diameter trunk. The girl's weight did nothing to the tree, and the only sound of falling dirt came from the spots where her hand briefly touched the sloping hillside for balance.

"It's safe," she said, doubling her speed, then hopping onto a second log ten feet from the other end of the washout.

Caitlin stepped on after her. The log felt secure enough.

Down the hill to her left, a burst of gunfire echoed through the night.

Seconds later, someone returned two shots with a handgun.

Caitlin moved fast, one hand out to her right. Twenty feet in, she noticed that Promise stood on safe land, staring down the hillside.

"What is it? Can you see them?"

The girl shook her head. "It's a light."

Caitlin neared the intersection of the two logs, then steadied herself to climb onto the second. Again, the impasse showed no sign of shifting. She joined Promise at the edge.

Promise pointed down at a small circle of dim light. "Do you see it?"

Caitlin caught her breath. Twenty feet down, under a clump of rocks half covered by dirt, a two-inch circle glowed the same color as the moonlight.

"It's a mirror," Caitlin said.

"Why would a mirror be down there?"

"I think it's a car. Can't tell in this light." Caitlin looked down the road. Like the previous section, several tree branches covered the pavement, but it seemed safe enough. "Whatever it is, it's no help to us now. Let's go."

They'd gone another quarter of a mile when a second volley of gunfire broke through the otherwise silent night.

"Further this time," Caitlin said, concentrating on a break in the pavement two hundred feet further downhill. "The road's just down there."

They sneaked their way to the edge of the trees at the driveway's intersection with the main road.

The same sedan they'd passed half an hour earlier, blue with a primer-gray hood, had parked in the opening to the path they'd taken the truck up, lights on but engine not running.

"Is that Tammy?" Caitlin said, pointing to a single woman pacing in front of the car, eyes up the path.

Promise nodded. "She got fat."

"She's not fat." Caitlin sighed. "She's pregnant."

"So we're not going to be able to hit her over the head, are we?"

49

L AKSHMI CHECKED HER binoculars again. For the last three hours, she'd seen waves of LAPD officers come and go from the Sperry property, first in uniforms, then in suits, then in coveralls. Originally she'd watched from the top of the hill past the entrance, but she'd quickly realized she needed to move if she was going to see anything useful. So she'd driven down past the gate, fighting the temptation to simply stop and tell the officers the parts of the story she knew.

This was about helping Caitlin, not telling the story. Plus, giving the officers anything would lead to questions about Beverly and also Tanner, and Beverly had insisted that neither should be involved.

"Why?" Lakshmi'd asked. "What's so special about a man you haven't seen for twenty years—who held me at gunpoint, I might add?"

After explaining that Tanner's shotgun had never been loaded, Beverly answered, "You don't know how hard it was to leave that life, to give up all that you held dear, the people you'd loved, to know that they were still under the control of Desmond and Daya."

After they'd run away from God's Hill together, Beverly had abandoned him and latched on to the first wealthy man she could to find some stability. Without her guidance, Tanner had returned to Linda's house, only to be recruited by Desmond to become a caretaker of sorts, to *get the mail* as he called it, monthly financial documents in Linda Sperry's name that he would forward to God's Hill in exchange for free rent and a thousand dollars a month.

"I owe him, Lakshmi," Beverly had added, watching Tanner pack his few things into a trash bag and load them into the trunk of her Mercedes. She'd convinced him to disappear and was prepared to supply financial help to make that happen. "Your showing up in my garden reminded me that I owe them all."

Beverly hadn't wanted lovable but dim-witted Tanner to be the fall guy when Linda Sperry's body was found. Since the other stipulation of his deal with Desmond included that he always have something growing in Linda's flower bed, both Beverly and Lakshmi agreed that her remains had to be six feet under a crop of weed. Ultimately, Lakshmi conceded that the man seemed worthy of a head start. An anonymous call to the local police from Tanner's throwaway phone would lead the authorities toward Linda Sperry's bones easily enough.

Hours later, following the winding road down into a canyon, Lakshmi'd found a vantage point that revealed most of the property's backyard. Eventually, a team of technicians set up shop around Linda's hillside garden, their movements marked by the dancing dots of flashlights but no big floodlights or tents.

By eleven at night, the flashlights and vehicles had disappeared. Either they'd found nothing, or they'd found enough to come back in the light of morning.

Lakshmi drove east toward her apartment and, more importantly, toward cell phone service. A single message from Caitlin popped up. She played back the voice mail.

"Mother alive. Missing runaway found. Driving the pair back to compound. If you don't hear from me by tomorrow morning, call Sheriff Martin and tell him everything."

Lakshmi sent a text at the first stoplight she hit, then pulled over and called Caitlin's cell for her turn to go straight to voice mail.

She let it go until she got back to her apartment in Koreatown. First thing in the door, she powered up her laptop and checked her email, sent another text, and called again.

Still nothing. Caitlin had literally said not to worry until the morning. Was she obsessing? She'd done this before, not just with Caitlin, but in relationships, or more accurately, relationships that had failed because of a ridiculous number of phone calls and texts.

On the other hand, it'd been hours since their failed call, and Caitlin might need to know about both Beverly Chandler's version of things and Linda Sperry's body, especially if she was going back to the Dayan compound. Now there was no answer.

Lakshmi could handle being called pushy. She could even live with losing her mentor for overreacting. But if her fear of being called obsessive meant someone hurt Caitlin Bergman, she'd never forgive herself.

Where is that number?

Lakshmi looked up Caitlin's text from her trip to the Dayan compound, found and called the number of the Coos County Sheriff's Department, got the automated switchboard, and chose accordingly. A man answered after two rings.

"Sheriff Martin."

"Really?" Lakshmi said. "It's almost midnight."

"I should say the same thing. Who is this?"

Lakshmi explained who she was and how Caitlin had mentioned going away with the Dayans.

"Just what do you think I can do about it, Miss—?"

"Anjale, Sheriff. Someone needs to tell Caitlin that Linda Sperry's body has been found, well, is going to be found—"

"I have to stop you right there. The reason I'm answering the phone right now is that my whole department is out giving evacuation notices. Half of the damned county is on fire, and it's moving fast. I don't have time to be Caitlin Bergman's answering service. If I were you, I'd make sure I was good and safe tonight."

"I'm in Los Angeles," Lakshmi answered.

"Then stop wasting my time."

"Bugger," she said, double-checking her phone. Sure enough, the man had hung up on her.

CHAPTER

50

"TAMMY," PROMISE LARSEN said, running out onto the road. "Thank God you're here."

The pregnant woman turned fast, her third-trimester belly leading seconds ahead of her nickel-wide eyes, her right hand clutching a lit-up cell phone. "Promise? Is that you?"

Promise closed the distance in seconds, throwing her arms around Tammy. "You've got to get me out of here. Do you have a gun?"

"What? No," Tammy stammered, the expectant mother not much older than the teenager. "Where's Tom?"

Promise ignored the question, sticking to the plan. She took the phone from Tammy's hand and stepped toward the car. "Does this thing work?"

Tammy reached out for her phone. "Not out here. Where's Tom?"

Caitlin jogged out of the woods, looking back like she might be followed. "He rescued us from the Dayans. Let's go."

Tammy took two steps back, her belly one. "Who the hell are you?"

Promise pulled the woman back her direction. "That's Caitlin. She saved me."

"I thought Tom saved you."

"He saved us both." Caitlin reached for the driver's side front door, found it unlocked. "But we've got to move. Tom wants us to get help."

Promise grabbed Tammy's hand and yanked her toward the back door.

Tammy's eyes lingered on the hillside. "I heard shooting. Is he okay?"

"Okay?" Caitlin got in the driver's seat, found keys still in the ignition, and started the car. "The father of your baby is a real American hero. Get in."

Promise opened the door and ushered the pregnant woman into the back seat.

"Stupid Tom's not the father," Tammy said, her eyes following Promise around the outside of the car. "I might be a tramp, but I'm not an idiot."

Promise turned away, powered down Tammy's phone, and got in the passenger side. "Then what are you doing with him?"

"I needed a ride home from the club and he's into preggos; then all of a sudden he gets a call from your daddy and we take this freaking detour. What the hell is going on?"

Caitlin looked at the pregnant nineteen-year-old stripper in the back seat and decided the woman could handle the truth.

"Dumbass Tom is Johnny Larsen's stooge. Johnny Larsen's into teens, and he doesn't care what their last name is. We've got to get Promise out of here before he shows up."

Tammy's face glazed over with a look too strange to read. "You're that reporter, aren't you? The Jew they were talking about?"

Good lord, what a time for random antisemitism.

"Yes, Tammy. I am the legendary Jewess Caitlin Bergman."

"You stood up to Johnny Larsen at some hotel," she said, almost in reverence. "Got him thrown into jail? Tom said the Proud Sons were out looking for you. Of course, there's really only three or four Proud Sons, but you're the one they're looking for?"

Caitlin didn't love where this was going, but girl code was stronger than race, right? "That's correct, Tammy, and now I'm going to take this car and get Promise somewhere safe. You got a problem with that?"

"Yeah." Tammy reached for the door.

Would she run? Call Johnny Larsen?

Caitlin reached for her own handle, ready for anything.

The young woman pointed to the passenger seat. "I need to sit up front. The seat belt's better for the baby."

Caitlin breathed a sigh of relief. After Tammy and Promise switched seats, she pulled out toward Coquille.

Tammy reached for Caitlin's arm. "Where are you going?"

"Sheriff's office. We'll be safe there."

"Not tonight we won't. There's a big-ass wildfire moving north. Everything southwest of Coquille's being evacuated, and half the roads are closed. That's how come me and Tom were taking this way in the first place. Turn around. I'll get you back to Coos Bay from the other side."

Caitlin pulled a U-turn and gunned it. As fast as she took the turns, she still had thirty minutes of driving to debate where to go. The sheriff was out, for now. Her first solution: rent the girl a hotel room. Too risky. Caitlin wouldn't know which hotels had employees that might know Promise, or worse, Johnny Larsen. Plus, the girl had run away before.

"Tammy," she said, thinking out loud. "Any chance Promise can crash at your place?"

"Hell no." Tammy checked her own attitude and came back apologetic. "Sorry, it's just you don't mess with the Larsens. Shit, I was gonna tell Tom you held me at gunpoint just so I don't get my ass beat." Her hands slid down around her belly. "Or worse."

"Stupid Tom would hit a pregnant woman?"

Tammy raised her eyebrows toward the back seat. "If her daddy said to."

Caitlin started to ask Promise about other options but caught herself. The less Tammy knew, the safer all around. When Caitlin's phone chimed with voice mail alerts ten minutes later, she fought the same urge again and didn't listen to her messages.

The sound didn't go unnoticed, however.

"Hey, Promise," Tammy said, turning to the back seat. "Gimme my phone."

Caitlin watched Promise's eyes in the rearview. The girl didn't look worried.

"I don't think it's working." Promise handed the cheap model over. "Still says no signal."

"No signal?"

Tammy stared at the screen, tapped a few options, even went so far as to give the thing a shake. "What the shit?"

"Maybe it's the fire," Caitlin said. "Sometimes cell towers are on top of hills."

Tammy looked more concerned about her nonfunctional phone than she had about abandoning Stupid Tom. "But yours works. Who do you have, Sprint?"

"Is that who you have?"

Tammy nodded.

Caitlin smiled. "Then I've got AT&T. It'll probably start working when you get home."

Tammy spent another confusing minute squeezing her buttons before looking up. "Damn, turn here."

The signs of civilization returned in the form of a church, a liquor store, and a work truck headed the opposite direction. Two turns later, they stopped at the edge of Tammy's trailer park.

Tammy promised she'd tell Tom that she'd freaked out when the shooting started and took the car herself, but she also pressed Caitlin for cash in a way that suggested a streak of entrepreneurship that might supersede gender.

Caitlin doubted the twenty she gave her would outbid Johnny Larsen's wallet or fists. She waited to say anything else until Tammy walked away, Promise had claimed the front seat, and they'd pulled back onto the road.

"What'd you do to her phone?"

Promise's mouth curled into what was almost a smile. "Reset the carrier setting. She'll probably figure it out. Maybe not."

Caitlin didn't want to count on maybe.

"Does your dad know anyone on the Coos Bay police force?"

"If he doesn't, they all know Grandpa Anders."

"And your grandfather—"

"Is rich."

"Gotcha." Caitlin followed a sign toward North Bend. A few cars passed heading the opposite way. She suddenly felt very aware that the car she was driving was neither hers nor inconspicuous.

"What about your mom?"

Promise's response came out almost twice the volume. "My mom?"

"Maybe if I told her about your father—"

"She'd what? Grow some balls?"

Caitlin took a breath. "She knows?"

Promise looked away, scratching at the peeling finish of Stupid Tom's side panel. The car was old enough to have roll-up windows. "She knows."

"And she stays with him?"

Promise turned back Caitlin's way. "Not every woman's as strong as Magda."

Caitlin started to respond to that load of shit, but the road narrowed toward a mass of green metal girders that made up the bridge into North Bend.

Then who can be trusted to watch this girl while I decide what the hell to do?

Even if ninety-nine thousand, nine hundred and ninety-nine of the hundred thousand people in the county were perfectly normal, law-abiding, nonpsychotic superheroes, Caitlin had no way of knowing who in the thirteen-year-old's life could be trusted.

"Promise, who helped you get to the Dayans in the first place?"

Promise looked away. "I shouldn't say."

Caitlin made her guess. "You don't have to. I know it was Hazel from the Lumberjack."

Promise's shrug wasn't a ringing endorsement, but it wasn't a sullen denial either.

"She helped me too," Caitlin continued, her intuition turning her earlier assumption into the only thing that made sense. "The night I went there, she tried to help me meet with Magda, but had to scare her away when she saw your dad's friends come in."

Promise's eyes returned to the front windshield. "She's all right. Her son's a hottie."

Caitlin was happy to hear a normal sentence come out of the teen-ager's mouth. "Hazel's got a son?"

"Tammy's age. He's in the Army. We used to all go down to the dunes to watch him ride dirt bikes."

"Like BMX-style?"

Promise actually laughed at that. "Motocross. Like the X Games. He was sponsored and everything."

Caitlin pulled over, found her notes from the Lumberjack, then dialed Hazel's number. Luckily, Hazel answered. Even luckier, she gave an address.

They left Stupid Tom's stupid car a mile from their destination, then crept through the shadows and side streets of a hilltop neighborhood overlooking Coos Bay, finally knocking on the side door of a single-story house.

Hazel opened the door a crack, looked around, then hurried them inside.

51

Promise hadn't been kidding.

Hazel's two-bedroom house had more framed pictures of her son Ryan in neon motocross gear than furniture.

"Where's your stuff?" Hazel said, bringing them each a glass of water and setting a box of Wheat Thins on the living room coffee table. Promise reached out for the crackers like they hadn't eaten hours before.

"Back on the hill," Caitlin said. "With my rental truck."

"And Magda," Promise said, through a mouthful.

Caitlin nodded. "Everything went to shit."

She told Hazel most of what she could remember, stopping only to gulp down water.

Hazel brushed a strand of Promise's hair back. "You girls have really been through it. So what's your plan?"

Caitlin sat back on the couch. "First thing in the morning, I get ahold of the sheriff. If he doesn't answer, I go to the state police. If they don't bite, I go to the FBI."

"Like any of them will care," Promise said. "Only the Daughters know the way to the Light."

Caitlin popped a stack of crackers in her mouth. "Hiding from life in the woods isn't the way to anything but mosquito bites."

Hazel patted the girl on the back, then reached for a TV remote. "Better check on the fire."

Two channel changes later, the screen displayed a scene Caitlin knew all too well from summers in California. A field reporter stood at the base of a hillside neighborhood behind a line of police tape and the flashing lights of a fire truck. Further up the hill, beyond the last house, a bright wall of orange flames snaked through the darkness. The station switched to overhead footage taken earlier in the evening. A massive SuperTanker plane dropped flame retardant on one of many hot spots in the rapidly advancing firestorm. The camera, obviously mounted on a helicopter looking down on the SuperTanker, pulled back to a wide shot, shrinking the massive plane to the size of a crop duster and revealing a miles-long hellscape of unconfined fire.

A graphic at the bottom of the screen read *Three Percent Contained*.

"Good lord," Hazel said. "They're barely making a dent."

Caitlin took a gulp of water. "I imagine Oregon's used to fires like this."

Hazel shook her head. "Not around here, not for years."

Promise stared at the screen and muttered something under her breath.

Caitlin touched the girl's leg. "What's that?"

Promise stood up. "It's the Cataclysm."

Hazel laughed. "The what?"

"I need to be there," Promise said. "I need to get to God's Hill."

Caitlin stood up to meet her. "Not tonight, you don't."

Promise pointed at the TV. "But this is the Light."

"No, it's not, Promise. Those women are insane. Magda is crazy."

"You're the one who's crazy." Promise's words came out soft, but the look in her eyes screamed bloody murder. "You think you're just gonna drop me off at the police station and everything's gonna be all right? Or my mom's just gonna leave my dad? Magda said she'd take care of me, and she did. Magda said I'd be safe under the Light, and I was. It wasn't until you came to town that everything went bad. You're the one who's crazy."

"Maybe I am," Caitlin said, her own voice raised. After days of dealing with a cult, her not-dead mother, and white supremacists, a teenager was going to drive her to violence. "Or maybe I'm just tired and need to catch like four hours of sleep in a safe place."

"There is no safe place."

"Girls," Hazel said, turning off the TV and stepping between them. "I don't think the world's going to end tonight. Maybe tomorrow, I don't know, but tonight, you both should get some sleep." She took Promise by the arm. "You can sleep in Ryan's room. There's clean sheets, and I think I have extra toothbrushes. I don't know about you, but I can't stand going to bed with a dirty mouth."

Maybe it was because Hazel had raised a child, or maybe she just had the calming skills of a bartender, but Promise relented to her demands like a regular who definitely wanted to return in good favor.

"I could brush."

Hazel walked her down the hall.

Caitlin reached for her phone; text messages, voice mails, and emails all waited for her replies.

"I got a charger for that," Hazel said, returning with an unwrapped toothbrush and a travel-sized toothpaste.

"Thanks." Caitlin nodded toward Ryan's bedroom. "There's no weapons or anything in his room, are there?"

Hazel shook her head. "Not unless she can swing a motorcycle helmet. He's got like twenty of those."

"Good. I need ten minutes to make some calls."

Hazel picked up the remains of their snack. "You go right ahead. I'll get you a towel and some sheets of your own. This couch folds out into a queen."

"You're an angel, Hazel."

Hazel waved the praise away. "I help when I can."

Caitlin watched the woman go, then finally got to her phone. She'd listened to only half of the first voice mail before she dialed Lakshmi and hit connect. Between rings, she checked the time: 1:37 AM.

Good God, Hazel really is an angel.

Lakshmi answered on the third ring. "Caitlin? You're alive."

Caitlin laughed out loud, surprised by how happy she was to hear the young woman's British accent on the other end of the phone. "And you're awake."

"I don't know if I'll ever sleep again. So much has happened."

"I know the feeling." Caitlin sat back into the couch. "Tell me everything."

They traded stories for almost ten minutes.

Caitlin stretched out, finally kicking off her shoes. "I can't believe you did that, all by yourself."

Lakshmi sounded apologetic. "I know you said I only needed to look into Beverly Bangs, but when I didn't hear from you—"

"I'm not mad."

"You're not? I thought maybe that was why you weren't calling back. In the past, I've been a little, you know, pushy—"

"Stop."

"—and I've tried too hard—"

"Seriously—"

"—and I know I've asked a lot of you, just moving to LA without knowing anyone, like you're my family or something, asking for help to try to get a job—"

"Shut up, Anjale."

Lakshmi stopped talking.

"I'm not mad," Caitlin continued. "Far from it. I'm amazed."

"Amazed?"

"Good God, yes. Amazed and proud. Good freaking job, kid. Great job."

Caitlin could hear the girl's blush through the phone. "Oh, well, it really was the least—"

"And you are part of my family. Inasmuch as I have family. I mean, you answered the phone at almost two in the morning."

"Well, it was you."

They both stopped there. Caitlin realized she was smiling and wondered if it'd been her first of the day.

"Of course"—Lakshmi broke the pause—"you do have family now. Your mother's still alive."

"Yes, she is. Her and Beverly Bangs Chandler."

Caitlin thought about the pieces. She'd really let Magda have it up on the hill, but now, with the gunfire in the distance, she found herself thinking not just about her mother but about all the women in red living in their alternate reality. Even in the modern world, scientists couldn't convince everyone on the planet that the earth was round. What would it take to get her mother and her well-armed friends off that stupid hill before they all ended up unrecognizable in the forest?

How can I break through to someone who thinks they've seen the face of God?

As tired as her brain cells had to be, one good idea managed to surface. "I know Beverly said she wanted to stay off the record, but do you think she'd record a message?"

"What kind of message?"

"Something I can play for Magda. She's been told that Beverly and Tanner died in a car accident because they tried to leave God's Hill. If Beverly could tell her something only the two of them would know—"

"That's brilliant," Lakshmi said. "I'll call her first thing in the morning."

"Me too." Caitlin relaxed into the cushions. "Call me in the morning as well."

Lakshmi assured her she would, then hung up.

What a day.

Every muscle in Caitlin's body ached like she'd competed in an Iron Man competition. A shower would help, sleep even more. The next morning, she'd get Promise help. After that, with a message from a dead woman, she'd go back to God's Hill and give her mother another chance. As angry as she'd been an hour before, she still had a mother. As long as she was alive, there was a possibility the two of them could have a relationship. And if she could bring Magda down from the mountain, maybe others would follow.

The sound of Hazel returning caused Caitlin to full-on yawn, a sign she'd fall asleep in seconds, but the look on Hazel's face cut Caitlin's assured slumber short.

"What is it?"

"She's not in the room," Hazel said. "Did she come out here?"

Caitlin reached for her shoes. "Crap, is there a back door?"

"Yeah." Hazel started that direction. "You go out front. She can't get far on foot. I'll get my car out of the garage."

The loud roar of an engine, the kind a high-performance motocross bike might make soaring over a sandy dune, erupted somewhere in front of the house, then howled away down the street.

"Shit." Caitlin slipped her shoes on. "Let's go."

Hazel looked around the kitchen counter. "Where the hell are my keys?"

Caitlin got up to help her look but already knew they weren't going to catch a girl who wanted to be on time for the end of the world.

CHAPTER

52

JOHNNY CHECKED HIS watch. Almost two in the morning, and the last he'd heard from Tom was hours ago.

Gunner tightened the straps of his Kevlar. Once they'd gone miles from Powers, they'd stopped by Johnny's for more gear. Each carried a semiautomatic assault rifle and ammo.

"Wind's picking up, John. I'll be damned if I can't smell the fire."

Johnny slid two more loaded clips into the top left pocket of his BDU-style tactical pants. "That shit's in your nose hairs."

Gunner put a finger to a nostril and cleared a passage. Some of the snot made it onto the clump of ferns at his feet, the rest onto his sleeve. "No way, we started something big."

"Guess the forest service should have let us log."

"Yeah, but what if they trace the tracers?"

"Back to you?" Johnny laughed. "Bought them at the gun show, didn't you?"

"Yeah, but—"

"Relax. Nobody at those things is tracking ammo. You ready for this?"

He handed Gunner a night-vision rig. No discount monocular this time.

"You're letting me use your ATNs?" Gunner said, taking the goggles.

"Military grade, for real work. This might get dirty."

"Cool."

Johnny watched Gunner adjust the straps and turn the goggles on. "I mean it. There's a good chance we walk out of here with blood on our hands."

Gunner put a finger up and emptied his other nostril. "You mean, like we might have to rough some bitches up?"

"I'm here to get Promise, even if we have to leave some bodies behind."

Gunner pushed the goggles up, revealing his eyes.

Johnny didn't see a hundred percent conviction. "They ain't from here, Gunner, and they ain't like us."

Gunner nodded. "Yeah, you're right."

Johnny still didn't feel like Gunner was all the way on board. "You help me get Promise away from those Dogs, I'll give you ten grand."

"Damn, John, of your own money?"

"What's money compared to my daughter?"

Gunner flipped the goggles back into position. "Shit, I'd have done it for five."

53

Hazel offered to drive her all the way to God's Hill, but Caitlin insisted that as a local, the bartender would be more valuable making the case to the sheriff in person first thing in the morning. Instead, they settled on a ride to Stupid Tom's car.

Armed with the map Magda had drawn, Caitlin aimed the stolen sedan back toward God's Hill. She plugged her phone charger into the cigarette lighter, turned the car radio on, and let the auto-seek function search station by station until she hit a talk channel providing nonstop fire coverage.

She had no idea how fast a motocross bike would go, nor what kind of mileage it might get, but still doubted she'd catch Promise. Undoubtedly, the girl knew a thousand faster ways to get back to the Dayan compound than Caitlin ever would.

Mixing with a handful of cars on the 101, she passed through North Bend at the speed limit, then floored it over the bridge out of town, causing her phone to fall off the seat.

"Right, the phone."

Too many moving pieces, not enough time, not enough sleep.

Caitlin turned the radio down, reached for the phone, and made a call on speaker.

Lakshmi answered. "You're not calling to take back that whole 'good job, well done' thing, are you?"

"No, but don't wait till the morning to call Beverly."

She filled Lakshmi in on the latest development, then hung up. Maybe Beverly Chandler would answer Lakshmi's late-night call, maybe she'd return the call first thing in the morning, maybe not at all.

Caitlin was in her tunnel, too many thoughts to think, not enough time to explore a single one. Usually the feeling hit at the beginning of a story assignment, the moment where she compartmentalized all of the moving pieces, then broke them down into a spreadsheet to identify common qualities and disparities. But this wasn't a story, this was life, and every line item carried a lifetime of weight.

Plus, the nighttime driving.

And the rapidly advancing wildfires.

And the knowledge that she'd soon outrun her cell phone service.

She returned to the phone, dialed another number.

"I can't speak too loudly," Scott Canton said, his voice hushed, "for I might scare the fish."

Caitlin laughed. "Seriously? You're fishing before the sunrise?"

"My friend, at my age, every day is about the sunrise."

She knew from experience that Scott's *fishing* meant sitting in a boat on a lake and reflecting on nature.

"Thank God someone is sitting somewhere enjoying something."

"Thank God?" Scott said, his voice now full volume. "You must have had some week. Tell me everything."

Caitlin let the items floating in her tunnel out into the open, a flow from memory to memory. Scott followed her thoughts enough to comment occasionally and even guide her when she veered off topic. Finally, when she'd emptied every bit of her mind, he took over.

"Sounds like you may die tonight, young woman."

His words almost caused her to swerve off the road. "What the hell, Scott? Is that supposed to help me?"

He laughed. "Hear me out, for I might die in the next five minutes, here in this boat. We all can—"

His voice dropped out for a few words, but he was on a roll, so Caitlin didn't interrupt.

"—I don't mean this as a bad thing, or an alarm, but as a spiritual reminder. To live on this earth is to die on this earth. We are all bound for the same fate, and the timing is rarely preordained. In your case, you've told me the situation, the players, and the stakes. After all that, you still have chosen to return to a fight from which you could walk away. As your friend, I want nothing more than to tell you to turn around and leave those people to burn in the fire they created. Be assured, I'm going to call the local police—"

Again, the signal dropped a few words.

"—but as a one-time soldier, I understand your choice. I know the feeling of the calm before the battle."

Caitlin recognized an upcoming turn in the road as the way to Tammy's trailer park. "Great, Scott, so any advice other than don't die?"

"Of course. Make—"

This time, the signal loss had to be addressed.

"Scott, I'm losing you. What did you say?"

"I said, make peace before you go to war."

Hoping to boost the signal, Caitlin pulled the phone off the charger and set it on the dashboard. "Yeah, I don't think these assholes are going to want to shake hands and walk away."

"Wouldn't that be nice? No, of course I mean make peace with your past, then walk into battle with a clear head and a true heart."

"My past, huh?"

"Can you forgive Mama Maya? Can you forgive your father?"

"If she's even telling the truth."

"Whether she is or isn't, can you accept that the man you've told me so much about may have been flawed?"

"Dad didn't break the law," Caitlin said. "He was the law."

"Surely, but was he the letter or the spirit?"

"Of the law?" Caitlin double-checked the air-conditioning control on the car's console. She had it cranked, but sweat still soaked her back. "If you mean, am I familiar with the law enforcement concept of the terms, I am."

"Growing up Jewish, I doubt you know Second Corinthians."

"Is that the 'Love is kind, love is gentle' wedding thing?"

Scott laughed. "Not quite. It's a plea in one of the apostle Paul's letters, saying basically to see the forest through the trees. Without going into the fine points of semantics, years of translation—"

Caitlin jumped on that. "Or centuries of corruption and manipulation of text by men to keep women subservient?"

"Getting to my point," Scott continued, "it's widely accepted that Paul said, 'The letter kills, but the Spirit gives life.' Meaning, don't get caught up on whether you should stone someone for telling a lie, as the letter of the law would demand, if the lie was told to get people out of the valley before a flood. Surely the act of saving their lives would honor the spirit of the law more than nitpicking who did what for what reasons. If not—"

His voice stopped.

"If not, what, Scott?"

She waited for an answer but got none.

"Scott?"

She picked up the phone, saw the *Dropped Call* warning. Once again, her phone had lost signal.

She looked down at the map. Her next turn would take her back to God's Hill, maybe ten minutes at the most. She turned the stereo's volume back up but got only static. A twist of the knob left her with only the sound of the car speeding along the wooded road and her own thoughts.

"I know my dad was flawed," she said, "but could he have lied to me for—"

She stopped, picturing Matt Bergman once again in his prime, and spoke directly to him. "Is it true? Did you know you were my real dad every day of my life until you died?"

She listened for a response but got only tires on asphalt as the road rose into the hills.

It didn't add up. The man fought injustice every day of his career.

"You ended in Internal Affairs, for God's sake."

Still nothing.

"Speaking of you, God. Care to chime in?"

The road took a sharp turn to the left, then another to the right. When she straightened out, a flurry of gray specs hovered over her windshield and in front of the headlights.

"If that's your answer, I don't care for it."

From years of Los Angeles wildfires, Caitlin recognized the sudden flurry falling from the sky as ash, not snowflakes. It also meant the wind carrying the firestorm from the south had turned her way.

Her headlights happened upon a roadside reflector, then another, and finally the yellow metal gate.

"Fine," she said, parking Stupid Tom's car in the same place she'd found it. "My mother was a porn star, an addict, a prostitute, and joined a cult. My father may have been a liar who couldn't admit he'd knocked up a porn star, all to protect his career and marriage."

She reached for the limited bag of supplies she'd brought from Hazel's house, rummaged past the bottles of water, and came back with a foot-long Maglite-style flashlight.

"I come from stupid, lying people who made dumb decisions for dumber reasons."

She opened the door and immediately tasted the smoke in the air.

"Which makes me the perfect candidate to save Promise from doing something idiotic."

CHAPTER

54

"I THOUGHT WE AGREED not to talk," Beverly Chandler said, the gravel of three in the morning in her voice. "Have they found Linda?"

Lakshmi led with an apology. "Sorry about the hour—"

"I'm not asleep. Tell me."

Lakshmi told Beverly Chandler everything she knew.

Beverly listened intently without commenting, then sighed. "Where are you now, Lakshmi?"

"Koreatown," she said. "My apartment."

"No, the address. I'm sending a car."

"A car?"

"I'll meet you in Burbank in an hour. We'll take my plane into North Bend and do whatever we can."

"Beverly, all Caitlin needs is a message."

"Are you kidding? For more than twenty years, the Dayans have been waiting for the end of the world. Now a wildfire is moving toward God's Hill. Those women won't leave until they see the face of God or burn alive. They don't need a message, they need evacuation."

55

ESMOND STEPPED BACK and looked at the luggage on top of his bed.

After all the years, his life boiled down to two suitcases' worth of shit.

Well, not complete shit.

He'd spread slightly more than eight hundred grand in cash between the two bags under layers of regular street clothes, not Dayan-made sarongs of red and white but jeans and T-shirts bought from the nearest Walmart. He'd forgotten shoes, actual honest-to-goodness tennis shoes made with real leather and closed toes, but would put a state between himself and Oregon before he bothered to shop again.

He had one American passport under his legal name, and two under an alias he'd purchased in the nineties. Both had been renewed multiple times without issue, despite the latest in biometrics. If he couldn't get to a border in time, he had driver's licenses from Oregon, Washington, Idaho, and Utah, and enough credit cards to advance another hundred thousand.

What else?

Right, the license plate.

He looked over at the wall of monitors, glancing past the images of the fields, barracks, and God's Hill, and confirmed the Jeep still waited just beyond the machine shop.

The second after his call with Tanner, he'd triple-checked that the vehicle had been gassed up, then filled an extra twenty-gallon can. If he got to the 5 freeway, he'd make it to Washington without being seen by an attendant at one of Oregon's full-service stations.

He pulled the bottom drawer out of his dresser, set it on the carpet, ran his hand along the trim until he found a large manila envelope, and shook the contents onto the floor.

Two license plates, one Nevada, the other Arizona; one for him, the other for Daya when the day came.

"Sorry to make the trip without you, my darling," he said, grabbing both and zipping them into the first hard-shelled suitcase. He lifted the bag off the bed, his muscles straining against the weight. Years of having other people waiting at hand hadn't left his own body in great shape.

Screw it, once he got to Canada, he'd get a truck stop massage. After that, maybe a whole brothel in Mexico or Thailand.

He reached for the second bag, but his eyes caught on movement from one of the monitors.

Not the wide-angle view of Ceremony Peak, though he could tell the work of the faithful progressed, but from the front gate. A blur of neon green passed by the guard tower without definition. Unmanned since midnight, the tower's camera didn't focus in time for Desmond to make out what had passed. A second monitor came to life, the camera just outside the machine shop, then the one looking down on the fields.

A teenager rode a motorcycle at full speed toward the front door of the Spirit's Estate.

"Fuck me."

Everything had been fine until Magda brought Promise Larsen to God's Hill. Here she was again at the worst possible time. Where Promise was, her father was sure to follow.

Desmond zipped the second bag, then wheeled both toward the door.

He'd moved everything just outside the Gallery when the front doors of the Spirit's Estate opened and the girl walked inside.

"Desmond? Where is everyone? Did I miss the Light?"

He turned toward her, pushing the bags into the darkened room, and opened his arms.

"You have returned to us just in time. Come, Promise, join me in the Gallery."

CHAPTER

56

CAITLIN CONSIDERED THE two paths: the paved option leading to the landslide and the mix of dirt and rocks she'd driven the rental truck up through the woods. She'd need the rugged path on the way out, and some familiarity with the hard-to-see trail would be helpful, but it was pushing three in the morning. Her tired legs demanded she take as much pavement as possible.

She flicked the flashlight on and started up the road, noticing that the heat remained oppressive, even at the high altitude. The only saving grace was a strong wind whipping through the trees, intermittently sending swaths of cool air her way. More branches had snapped since she and Promise came down the road, a sign of how brittle the towering forest had become.

By the time she reached the fallen trunks of the landslide, sweat ran down her back and two words bounced back and forth between her ears: *tinder box.*

She moved the flashlight along the hillside, tracing the route she and Promise had used over the mass of dirt and rock. She could repeat the process easily enough, starting on the smaller, secondary log, then hopping down to the sturdy primary beam. Four feet onto the closest tree, she swung the flashlight across the chasm to the other end and stopped when the light tripped across a small, iridescent triangle. Not the reflective surface Promise had pointed out earlier, this small flash four feet below the opposing ledge of remaining pavement looked familiar.

Caitlin advanced, keeping her light's beam on the steps in front of her. Climbing down to the larger tree trunk, she swung the flashlight toward the area under the ledge again.

"Shit," she said, finding not only the original triangle but a second one two feet lower down the landslide. The iridescent triangles she was seeing were from the backs of running shoes.

A body lay sprawled on the hillside, motionless, facedown and aimed downhill.

She took another ten steps across the log. Twelve feet from the safety of the opposing ledge, Caitlin could tell the body was a man. A handgun had fallen from his hand, maybe ten feet lower than her current position.

"Hey," she said.

A gust of wind blew through the canyon, louder than her own voice. Bits of dirt from the hillside rolled down past her. She steadied herself, looked again.

The flashlight revealed blue letters over a white T-shirt: *F.B.I.*

"What the hell?" she said, crouching. Another glance showed the words *Federal Bikini Inspector.*

The body she assumed was Stupid Tom didn't move.

Neither did she.

Chances were, Magda had killed Tom seconds after Caitlin and Promise took his car. Then again, her mother wasn't the only woman packing heat on the mountain. Caitlin had no idea who'd put Tom in the landslide. Hell, his name was Stupid Tom. Maybe he'd fallen all by himself.

Still, she'd spent every year of her life yelling at people in movies who passed by free guns without picking them up. She ran the light over the area.

Sure enough, a clump of rocks two feet down led to a solid block of asphalt. She could climb down alongside the body, grab the gun, then get back up.

First things first. She lowered herself into the clump of rocks, then grabbed an avocado-sized stone and gave it a toss.

The stone landed an inch past where she'd aimed, square in Stupid Tom's lower back. He didn't shift or make a sound. Flashlight in hand,

Caitlin leaned against the soil and slid down to the large chunk of asphalt.

"Tom, are you alive?"

Again, no answer. Not that she wanted one. She dropped into a squat, the chunk of asphalt wobbling beneath her feet, inches from Tom's head; the gun was two feet further down the hill. She swung the light over Tom's back again. No sign of chest movement, especially not with the red blossom of blood near his left shoulder.

Easing one shoe off the asphalt, Caitlin lowered herself another foot. Again, dirt followed her down the hill. She trained the light on Tom's head with one hand, then reached for the gun with the other. Inch by inch, her hand crept along, her eyes shifting from the pistol to Tom's head. Finally, she connected with the butt of the gun, one finger, then a second, and pulled.

Maybe it was a gust of wind, maybe the moving dirt, but as she got control of the handgun, she looked back up and saw Tom's head move.

Not open eyes or moving limbs; just hair, blown by the wind.

"You've gotta be kidding me," Caitlin said, bringing the gun up to her chest in relief. The shift in her weight caused a shift in the chunk of asphalt. She fell backward, her head aimed downhill, her legs hitting the rough soil behind her.

"No—"

The word didn't stop her body, nor the soil above. As fast as she slid, the chunk of asphalt followed her down. In seconds, she'd fallen eight feet down the landslide, coming to rest where a grouping of stones had wedged against a still-standing tree trunk. Her hands went up to protect her head, but the asphalt chunk hit lower, bruising rather than wounding her back.

"Sonofabitch," she said, listening to the cascading dirt. Something else was gaining momentum.

She turned uphill, then wished she hadn't. Stupid Tom's corpse washed over her with a cloud of dirt, diagonally covering her legs.

Caitlin brushed the rough soil from her mouth and gasped for air. Once under control, she did an inventory. Her right hand still had the gun; her left still held the flashlight, though partially buried. She freed her hand, pulled her legs out from under Tom's body, and sat up.

She looked up at the pale, cloudy sky, saw flakes of ash still falling like Shitmas morning, and laughed. "There'd better be bullets in this thing."

She pulled back the automatic's slide, ejected a single unused round, and released the clip.

Empty.

She searched the dirt for the single ejected cartridge, brushed it off, slid it into the otherwise empty clip, reloaded the gun, then sat back, one arm falling onto Tom's body. Definitely dead. He would never inspect another bikini.

She swung the flashlight around to plot a way back up.

To her right, the uphill ledge would require a forty-five-degree climb up obviously loose soil. To her left, the downhill ledge could be reached somewhat easier through a pile of solid-looking boulders.

At the base, feet from her current position, the light reflected back at Caitlin.

"No way."

She stood and moved closer.

The flashlight's beam revealed a dark rectangle over a V of red paint. She moved the light left and saw the rectangle of a mirror, the same mirror she and Promise had seen earlier. A Dayan town car had been buried at the base of the landslide, and not accidentally.

Caitlin moved closer, brushed dirt from the dark rectangle of tinted glass, and tried to shine the light inside.

No good. She took the butt of the gun and struck the window, breaking an orange-sized hole into the safety glass.

The contents of the town car might have sat there for a year, but sealed inside the glass and metal, a smell of stagnant decay somewhere between mildew and cheese hadn't escaped until now.

Caitlin retched once, hard, then patted her pockets for her phone. Recording a video, she raised the flashlight and her camera phone and looked inside.

A red seat back visible to her left and an intact window several feet in front of her meant she was looking into the back seat. She coughed again, spit a mouthful of stomach acid to the side, then turned her camera slowly to the right, her hand shaking with each degree of rotation.

Despite the addition of light, the red of the opposing door's side panel faded from dark crimson to a brownish black. She exhaled a held breath, looked down at her screen, then let her eyes follow the flashlight's beam back through the opening. A dank, black film covered the paneling and what had to have been an explosion of sludge at some point.

"No," she said, aware that *sludge* couldn't describe the mix of scattered blood, mold, and worse. Her heart knew that not only had someone been killed in this car, but at least one body had been buried without modern funeral rites or preservation and sealed within. Fighting the tremble in her hand that threatened to rock her entire frame, she continued her slow pan to the back bench.

A group of red lumps in the same hue as the latest in Dayan fashion huddled in a pile in the far corner. Sections of black and bits of white appeared near seat belt level where hands might once have hung from sleeves. As she tilted her light up slightly, deep-brown and black patches revealed how wounds and natural decomposition had stained or eaten through fabric.

Taking another quick breath, Caitlin realized she'd started crying at some point. Tears ran down her cheeks, but something wouldn't let her wipe them away until she saw the inevitable.

Slightly below window height near the top of the back seat, the light landed on three white blobs, instantly recognizable as the form inside every human head: skulls. Thankfully, the size of the opening in the window prevented Caitlin or her phone from seeing too much definition, but the closest skull, still loosely attached to a mass of long gray hair, told Caitlin she'd seen enough. What once had been a forehead was now a forgotten woman's last testament. The dark gape in the center of the white bone was too perfect and intentional to be anything but a bullet hole. She turned the camera left toward the front seats, where two other huddled masses had been left to rot.

Caitlin stopped the camera, stumbled away from the opening, and folded over at the waist, trying to breathe or think or just live. Less than a week before, she'd been able to handle the toothless corpse in the medical examiner's office. Minutes before, she'd brushed past Stupid Tom's cooling body without a second thought, even when he'd fallen on top of her.

This was different.

This was malice aforethought, planning and execution, cold-blooded murder, conspiracy, and the reduction of five lives to nothing more than a verse in a religious ceremony and a detour sign.

Caitlin had found the Five after all.

Looking up at the ash-filled sky, she wasn't sure if the information would help or hurt her, or if she was missing some last cosmic warning to turn and run. All she knew was a hot fire had started inside her, and it wasn't going to go out until she kicked somebody's ass.

57

Edging around the side of a sheet-metal building blackened by a recent fire, Johnny motioned Gunner toward the next structure.

"What?" Gunner whispered. "You see somebody?"

Maybe Stupid Tom wasn't the only one who needed a nickname. "This," Johnny whispered back, repeating the motion, "means you go that way. I'll cover you."

"Oh yeah, right, like ninjas."

"Like in the military, dumbass."

"Yeah, cool. Do it again."

"Do what again?"

"The ninja thing."

Johnny shook his head and repeated the gesture a third time.

Gunner broke into a sprint toward the next sheet-metal building, then turned and threw his back up against the wall. The only remotely ninja-like aspect of his approach was that his impact made the same sound as a gong knocked off its pedestal. Gunner threw his hands up like it couldn't have been helped.

Johnny swore under his breath, then ran past Gunner to a dark opening in the next building, sweeping his AR around what appeared to be a machine shop. Plenty of tools, nobody working them at four in the morning. He advanced toward the moonlight pouring in through a window.

"Gunner, get in here."

Gunner joined him at the window, looking out over a long field leading to a series of cabins.

"Shit, John. This place is bigger than I thought. Where do you think they've got Promise?"

"No idea. We go house to house."

"Cool." Gunner started toward a door leading to the field.

"Gunner."

"What?"

"Try being fucking quiet this time."

Gunner opened the door. "Like a ninja."

He ran full speed, stopping at the edge of the field behind a row of tomato plants. Johnny started to follow, then stopped. A red metal gas can sat next to an industrial generator. He grabbed the can, felt enough liquid sloshing around to cause some trouble, unscrewed the cap, and poured a trail from the generator to the door.

"Gunner," he whispered. "Another insurance plan."

He pointed to the tree line at the far left of the fields. "Meet me there."

Gunner nodded, then started running.

Johnny poured a ten-foot trail out the door, then jogged right, away from both the building and Gunner, leaving a trail of gasoline through the grass behind him.

Once the can was empty, he went toward the tree line, catching up with Gunner behind a clump of trees.

"You want to light the place up?" Gunner said, offering a cigarette lighter.

"Not yet. First we find Promise, then we hit that line with a tracer, cut off their road out of here. You and I will hump back down the trail the opposite way." He pointed toward the main buildings. "Here on out, stay in the trees, but keep your eyes up the field. We ought to be able to sneak past."

Johnny started running; Gunner followed. They stopped just past the end of the fields, not far from the clump of cabins.

No one sounded an alarm. Not one light came on in the cabins.

Gunner put his hand on Johnny's shoulder. "You think they're gone or something?"

Johnny shook him off, jogged over to the closest cabin, sidled up to a shaded window, and peered through a gap in the curtains. Four beds, but no one home. He looked back at Gunner, shook his head, and pointed to the next cabin. Gunner repeated the process, got the same result. They stopped taking turns and split up, meeting on the other side of the cabins.

Gunner tilted his goggles up. "Maybe they evacuated 'cause of the fire we started out in Powers."

Johnny looked up toward the main row house. The only lights in the compound came from the four spotlights near the three-story roof line, but beyond the building, up to the right, the gray sky glowed brighter. All the running had his heart pounding, but Johnny heard something.

"Do you hear music?"

Gunner nodded. "Sounds like singing."

He pointed to a neon-green motocross bike left on the steps of the main compound. "What do you think about that?"

Johnny looked back across the empty fields. "Let's go see."

The closer Johnny got to the top of the hill, the less he needed the night-vision goggles. He tilted the rig back and wiped sweat away from his eyes.

This close, the singing they'd heard from the cabins came through full volume, forty or fifty voices, all singing the same words:

The fire is dying, so come let me build
A light that can shine through to heaven above

Johnny left the path, climbing rocks to a clump of bushes that looked down on a clearing.

So he'll see me trying, and doing his will
Building my fire with light and with love

From his vantage point, he could see a large semicircle of women moving back and forth around a towering fire, but that didn't mean he understood what his eyes were taking in.

Gunner joined him seconds later. "Holy shit, John. They're all naked."

"Yeah," Johnny said, trying to make out faces.

The circling women changed directions and started a new verse.

The world here is ending, the story come true

We'll all join the Spirit on this night
But don't worry Daughters, there's nothing to fear
You've earned the gift of the Light

Gunner nudged him with an elbow. "And they're not all old. You think they do this every night? 'Cause I'll come back with a camera."

"Shut up and look for Promise so we can get the fuck out of here."

"Cool, but I might have to rub one out."

Johnny pointed to a woman at the far end of the circle, still in a red smock, holding an assault rifle every bit as deadly as their own. "Keep your head in the game."

He brought up his own rifle and eyed the circle through his scope. A full-bodied brunette with a bowl cut wearing nothing but a beaded necklace climbed onto a platform at the edge of the fire pit.

The singing stopped and the women broke the circle, gathering to face the speaker, their bare backsides to Johnny and Gunner.

"Daughters," the woman said. "The night has come. An hour ago, fires had reached the south side of the Coquille River. Our time approaches. Even now, Desmond prepares in silent reflection. Soon he will come to shepherd us into the Light."

"As it was told," the women answered, "so shall it be."

Gunner looked over at Johnny. "What the fuck is this?"

Johnny shook his head. The best he could do: "Cult shit."

The woman pointed over to a table, where another naked woman poured liquid from a large silver decanter into a single chalice. "Now, one by one, oldest to youngest, each will step forward and take the Calm."

"Stop."

The crowd of women turned all at once, looking off to their right at whoever had just yelled. Every woman there broke out in a scream of joy.

The big woman stepped down from the pedestal and followed the swarm of women to the opposite side of the fire, shouting, "Magda's alive, Magda's alive."

Johnny put the scope back up to his eye as the new guest brought the crowd toward the pedestal. A fully clothed woman holding an assault rifle pushed through the clinging hands.

"Holy shit," Johnny said. "It's her."

Gunner strained to see. "Who?"

"The bitch that took Promise."

"The reporter's mom? Do you see her too?"

Johnny held out his hand. There was no sign of Caitlin Bergman, but she'd be here. They'd run from the casino in Bergman's rental truck, then the Dayan shop in Bandon. Last thing he'd heard from Tom was that he'd passed the truck on the road leading to the compound's back entrance hours earlier.

The Bitch and the big woman were talking, and the Bitch didn't like what she was hearing.

"Where?" she yelled.

The big woman pointed down the hill toward the main house, and the Bitch pushed through to the downhill path, then ran down the steps.

A few started to follow, but the big woman called out to the crowd. "Daughters, rejoice. Magda has returned in time for the Light. Come now, line up for the Calm so we are ready when she and Desmond return for the calling of the names."

The crowd, some crying, others smiling ear to ear, turned away from Magda's departure and formed a line near the silver decanter.

"Damn, John. What the hell are they doing?"

Johnny got up into a crouch. "You stay here and keep watch. I'm going to find Promise. Anything goes wrong or you think I'm in trouble, run back to the field and light this place on fire. I'll meet you at the trucks."

"What if I see that reporter? The one that got you busted in the first place?"

Johnny pat Gunner on the shoulder. "I'll give you an extra ten grand if Caitlin Bergman catches lead poisoning."

CHAPTER

58

DESMOND WATCHED THE young woman's finger trace the brush marks of Linda's largest painting, the four-by-eight canvas that had built God's Hill: *The Cataclysm*. As paintings went, it truly was striking.

"It's really happening," Promise said, lost in the scene.

As a prophecy, Desmond would have preferred to have Linda dream of a tropical island with loose tax laws and looser extradition treaties.

He tented his fingers in front of him and nodded. "Yes, my child. The time is upon us."

On her solemn look of acceptance, he returned to his work at hand. Daya had always made the Calm in the past, but Desmond knew the recipe well enough, including Daya's plan for administering the last batch.

The key ingredients of the standard recipe: chamomile, lemon balm, and prescription Valium pills, crushed into a fine dust. The batch he'd sent up the hill had double the Valium and a generous portion of Walmart-brand rat poison. Plus sugar.

He looked up at the teenager. "How much do you weigh, darling?"

"Ninety-eight pounds," she said. "But I've been running a lot. Does that matter?"

Her eyes shifted back and forth, unable to directly return his gaze. He knew the look well. Even now, at the end of the world, the young woman needed approval from someone, anyone who would tell her how special she was in the scope of things, how *consequential*.

He couldn't resist.

"It does matter," he said, his face solemn, his eyes fixed on her flawless face.

Her hands went together near her waist, fingers twisting fingertips, hips shifting slightly side to side. The agony of sitting under judgment, the need for release.

He knew the girl's damage, the abuse she'd faced at her father's hands. He could drive an empty vessel like Promise Larsen as long and as far as he wanted, but he didn't have time to mess around.

He blinked once, then broke into a smile. "It's the perfect weight. You truly are a Daughter of God."

Her body went loose, hands down to her sides, chest raised, the relief of inclusion apparent.

Desmond crushed two Valium and added the dust to the shaker. One would calm her down, two might put her to sleep. Even at his age, he could handle her frame.

Ninety-eight pounds.

Only ten pounds lighter than Daya had been the night they'd met at a strip club outside Reno. Daya had known the art of the tease, the agony and release, and she'd seen his bullshit coming a mile away. If it hadn't been for her one hundred and eight pounds of cunning, he never would have approached Linda Sperry, and God's Hill would have stayed the fever dream of a guilt-ridden defense contractor's widow.

"My crazy aunt thinks she talks to God," she'd said, grinding away, "and she's got more money than sense."

"Maybe what she needs is to meet God face to face," he'd answered, fondling Daya under her G-string, neither of them even slightly concerned about breaking the strip club's no-contact policy, the first of many rules they'd break together.

Now lost without Daya's guidance, Desmond's hand hovered over the box of powder beneath the counter as he weighed the ultimate question: send the girl up the hill with the rest, or find a use for her?

"It's time for the Calm," he said, omitting the poison and emptying the shaker into a paper cup.

He stepped out from behind the counter and met the girl at the dais. She looked up at him, hopeful but trembling.

"And I'll be with Magda?"

He held the cup out in front for her communion. "Magda's spirit waits for you in the Light."

The girl raised the cup to her lips and drank, eyes closed.

He placed his hands on her shoulders and walked her behind his throne, directing her to sit up against the wood, facing the windows.

"Come, my child, let us prepare you."

He had enough cloth napkins under the counter to fashion a blind-fold. Once the Valium kicked in, he could direct her to the Jeep. A willing teenage servant would be useful when police were on the lookout for a silver-haired man named Desmond.

An angry female voice called from the entrance. "Desmond, we've been betrayed."

Magda.

Desmond whipped around toward the door, not because he didn't recognize the voice but because he didn't believe she could still be alive. That meant the body in the morgue had been Daya all along. But where had Magda been? Working with her daughter? Protecting Promise Larsen? And why had she come back now?

He moved beside the chair, fell to his knees, and threw his arms up to the sky. "Now, at our final hour, my Magda has returned, as the Spirit said it would be."

Magda entered, gun slung around her shoulder, moving fast, determined, like he'd seen her so many times over the years. She stopped feet from the dais. "The Daughters are at Ceremony Peak drinking the Calm. Why, Desmond?"

Desmond's mind raced. Magda seemed furious, but not necessarily at him. "You know why, my miracle of miracles, for the Light has come this time. Have you seen the news out in the world?"

Magda shook her head. "I've been hiding, keeping Promise safe from her family."

Of course she had. Knowing of her own father's abuse, he should have foreseen that Magda would never let a girl return to that kind of life.

Promise stood up from behind the chair. "Magda?"

The girl stumbled slightly, then jogged down the dais toward Magda, collapsing into her arms. The Valium had kicked in.

"Why are you here?" Magda squeezed the young woman.

Promise buried her head in Magda's chest. "To be with you at the end."

Magda looked Promise in the eyes. "Sweet girl, this isn't the end."

"But the Cataclysm—"

"Is upon us," Desmond said, stepping down toward them. He didn't know what Magda wanted, but she'd always needed the Light. Maybe he could turn this. "We are surrounded by fire, as Linda foretold, and Daya in her place. The world has fallen to nuclear war."

"But Daya was false."

Desmond turned to hide his surprise. He'd expected an accusation, but not at Daya's expense. "Daya ascended, my love. As we soon will."

Magda shook her head. "Daya didn't ascend, and she never will. She corrupted the Daughters."

"Corrupted? How so?"

"It's hard for me to tell you, my guide, my heart, my teacher, but Daya's been stealing money, cashing checks that should have gone to the families of the Five."

"Magda, you can't know—"

"I have proof. Files she kept in her office."

Desmond stepped back. Caitlin Bergman hadn't stolen the files from Daya's suite after all. Magda had—and she still wasn't linking him to any of it.

"This is all so disturbing," he said, not completely a lie.

"There's more," she continued. "When you said to send Promise away, back to her family, Daya tried to sell her back to Johnny Larsen, knowing damned well what he'd been doing to the girl. It's why the Larsens are attacking us."

"I don't believe it," Desmond said, stepping back onto the dais, raising both hands.

"Believe it, asshole."

Following Desmond's eyes, Magda spun around toward the door.

A man in camo gear, body armor, and night-vision goggles stood in the doorway. Unlike Magda, his gun was very much in his hands. "So where's my five grand?"

CHAPTER

59

CAITLIN HEARD THE singing before she saw the light of the fire. The road she'd followed up from the washout had come to a winding stairway, obviously the way to the peak, before continuing toward a loop that looked like it circled the compound and joined up with the southern entrance.

She sure as hell wasn't going to take the long way. The hundred feet of stairs took her up to the edge of the ceremonial fire circle on the opposite side as her first visit. Once again, the Dayans surrounded their eternal flame, and damn were they naked.

Ten to fifteen women lay on the stone wall circling the fire, eyes closed. Another twenty milled along the edges of the plateau. The rest stood in a line near the fire, singing and waiting to be served a beverage from a silver decanter by a woman Caitlin recognized by bare ass alone. Even from twenty feet away, she could see where Gwendolyn Sunrise's sun didn't rise.

No sign of Magda or Promise, but near the other side of the plateau, one woman, her old friend Mouse Girl, remained dressed in red with the ultimate accessory: a firearm.

If Promise wasn't here, she might be locked in one of the holding rooms in the main house. Maybe the long way was the only way. Caitlin turned back toward the stairs, but a sound behind her, neither singing nor speaking, caught her attention: coughing, or rather gurgling. Someone was choking.

She looked back to the circle, saw the chest of one of the supine women on the rock wall heave. A mess of white foam flowed from the woman's lips to her shoulder.

"She's choking," Caitlin yelled, rushing into the clearing. Surprisingly, no one even noticed her approach. She got her hand under the woman's head and turned her onto her side. The woman's closed eyes didn't open, but her mouth did. Curdled chunks of white and red replaced the stream of foam.

"Help," Caitlin yelled, trying to clear the woman's airway.

The volume of the singing lessened as some of the voices dropped out. A young woman said, "Look, it's Magda's daughter."

A handful of voices answered her. "Blessed be the Daughters."

Caitlin turned back toward the crowd, saw Lily "Eve" Kramer looking her way.

"Help me," Caitlin repeated, and Lily ran over, naked and smiling like a puppy in its first dog park.

"Caitlin, you made it. I hoped you would."

"Lily, this woman's sick."

Lily's smile took a hit. "It's Eve, remember?"

Caitlin grabbed Lily's cheeks and turned her toward the chunks of blood-filled vomit. "Eve, Lily, who-the-fuck-ever you are, snap out of it. This woman's dying."

Lily's eyes widened. She took Caitlin's position, propping the unconscious woman's head up, then nodded. "It's only the Calm. As long as I help her breathe, she'll be fine when the Light comes."

Caitlin took a step back, noticed the feet of the next closest woman and their odd blue tint. She reached out and touched a bare foot.

Cool, not ice cold, but not the normal warmth of a healthy body next to a roaring fire.

Caitlin turned back to Lily. "Have you taken the Calm?"

Lily shook her head. "Not my turn yet."

Caitlin looked back at the line, saw twenty women still waiting for a drink, meaning almost as many had already sipped from Gwendolyn Sunrise's blessed cup.

"It's poison," she yelled, pushing through the naked women toward the serving station. "You're drinking poison."

The singing finally stopped, and all the women, especially Gwendolyn Sunrise, turned toward Caitlin, not angry or scared but with complete wonderment.

"You came back," Gwendolyn said, the ceremonial chalice in one hand. "And you've seen the miracle. Magda lives."

"Magda lives," the others boomed, smiles on every one of their faces, even Mouse Girl.

Caitlin pushed through the smiling nudes, closing in on Gwendolyn Sunrise. "Where is Promise Larsen?"

Gwendolyn only smiled. "Not here, and that is truly her loss, for the world burns—"

"As foretold," the Daughters finished.

"And the Light comes—"

"For the pure."

Gwendolyn threw her arms wide. "Led by Desmond the Shepherd."

The still-standing Daughters raised their hands toward the sky. "Father, brother, lover, guide."

Caitlin moved close enough to Gwendolyn to smell the woman's sweat. "And where is your shepherd?"

"Preparing his soul."

Caitlin reached for the cup in Gwendolyn's hand. "Did Desmond drink from the Calm?"

Gwendolyn handed her the cup freely. "Of course."

Caitlin threw the cup on the ground. "It's fucking poison. You're drinking poison."

Gwendolyn calmly bent over, retrieved the cup, and smiled once more. "It's only poison to the unsure. A soul of white can enter the Light. Only the pure won't burn."

She raised her hand.

The women repeated the phrase. "Only the pure won't burn."

And again. "Only the pure won't burn."

Caitlin didn't know how much time she had or what their reactions would be, but she couldn't let one more woman drink poison. She lunged for the silver decanter, knocking it off the table and into the fire.

The smiles dropped from every face on the hill, even Gwendolyn's. Mouse Girl reached for her rifle. Caitlin pulled Stupid Tom's handgun out of the back of her pants and beat Mouse Girl on the draw. Everyone took two steps back. Besides the gun in Mouse Girl's hand, Caitlin saw two more assault rifles on the ground near the stairs to the compound.

"Where's Magda?"

The faces all looked for leadership. Gwendolyn Sunrise raised her hand, and everybody who had taken two steps back moved one step forward.

Caitlin couldn't shoot them all. Hell, with only one bullet, she couldn't shoot more than one, but she might be able to stop them. She raised the gun into the air to fire a warning.

Someone beat her to it.

And their shot wasn't a warning.

A copper-smelling mist soaked Caitlin's face. She opened her eyes and saw a red mess of tissue where Gwendolyn Sunrise's raised hand had been.

The naked lawyer screamed in pain. Everyone else turned away from Caitlin toward the outcropping of rocks looking down on the flat plain.

Mouse Girl raised her rifle and fired.

"A man," she screamed, then fired again.

Caitlin saw someone dressed as a soldier scramble away from the same point she'd used three nights before, running down the lit path toward the southern side of the property with Mouse Girl in close pursuit.

In seconds, two of the sweaty nudes had grabbed the other assault rifles and joined the chase. Additional gunshots and screams followed, and the remaining women broke into confused yelling.

So much for the Calm.

Caitlin didn't waste any time. Elbowing the wandering Daughters out of the way, she ran down the path as well, not after the assailant but toward the compound's main building. Halfway down the steps, she heard another burst of gunfire, then saw a streak of red sail through the sky over the fields. Seconds later, the Dayan machine shop exploded in a ball of flame.

CHAPTER

60

LASER SCOPE ON, Johnny scanned the large room left to right, saw only Promise, the Bitch, and the silver-haired nutjob in the toga. He stopped the red dot on the nutjob's forehead and called over to Promise.

"Daddy's here, my special girl. Time to go home."

The Bitch pushed Promise to the side and went for the AR strapped to her back.

Johnny swung his rifle left, pulled the trigger, and caught the old woman in her shoulder, spinning her one hundred and eighty degrees and knocking her onto the floor, face first. Her gun hit the tile and bounced, falling six feet further.

"No," Promise screamed, throwing herself over the fallen woman.

"Move, girl. I'm done with this shit."

Silver-haired nutjob moved closer but froze when Johnny's laser point returned to his chest, hands up again. "You can have her."

Johnny laughed. "Says the asshole shitting his pajamas."

"You can have any of the women. Take your pick."

He couldn't believe what he was hearing. "What the hell are you talking about?"

"You like them young," Nutjob said, a shake in his voice. "Take Lily Kramer. She'll do whatever you want. They all will. Anything I tell them. Not just one at a time. Anything you can dream of. No one else has to die."

Johnny walked toward Promise and the Bitch, his gun still aimed at Nutjob.

"I haven't killed anybody, you sick fuck. She's alive."

He bent down, grabbed the woman's AR, ejected the magazine and tucked it into his pocket, then aimed the second rifle a foot higher than Nutjob's head and pulled the trigger. Nutjob collapsed with a scream, but the bullet went through the giant window facing the woods.

"Damn," Johnny said, tossing the empty AR across the room. "Kind of thought that thing would shatter."

He reached down and grabbed Promise's arm. She reared back and threw a punch, but her arm flailed wildly, and he was able to pull her away from the woman on the floor with less of a fight than he'd expected.

A growing pool of blood spread onto the white tile underneath the old bitch, but her chest moved up and down.

Promise swung again, her fist bouncing weakly against Johnny's Kevlar vest. He shoved her hard, and she tumbled in the other direction.

He looked back at Nutjob, saw the man had gotten up and moved toward the door.

"What'd you give her?"

Nutjob froze again. "Valium. She'll be unconscious in a minute."

"Good."

What to do about the Bitch?

He could put a bullet in her head, probably should, but that would leave Nutjob as a witness, which would mean he'd have to kill Nutjob as well and hope their exit fire made the whole thing go away.

He wiped a bead of sweat from his brow, looked over at the daughter he'd been hunting for six months, and decided he'd take those odds.

He raised his rifle. No need for the laser at that distance, but it felt good to see the dot on the back of the Bitch's head.

A loud bang filled the tiled chamber, and Johnny reached for his back. He twisted around, saw Caitlin Bergman standing in the doorway with a handgun, and returned fire.

61

CAITLIN SPUN BACK into the hall as Johnny Larsen's assault rifle went semiauto, barely avoiding the stream of bullets tearing into the hallway's drywall. She knew she'd made contact, but obviously his body armor meant she'd only pissed him off. She ran to her right, checking each door she passed.

Locked.

Locked.

Locked—no, wait.

She grabbed the third door's handle, slammed her shoulder into the wood, and tumbled into the room, landing on her knees. No sound of Larsen behind her, but she reached back and thank-the-freaking-Spirit found a dead bolt to lock. She turned back to the office-type room, saw a window and door on the opposite wall.

Another burst of gunfire rang through the halls, followed by what sounded like a waterfall of shattering glass.

The gallery's windows.

Caitlin pressed herself to the window. No good. The straight line of the building meant she couldn't see more than a few feet.

She opened the back door a crack and peered outside. Not only had the two-story gallery window completely shattered and fallen, but Johnny Larsen had walked out the opening with Promise slung over his shoulder, headed toward the far end of the building. He stopped short, turned back toward the gallery, reloaded his rifle, then fired once.

The bright glare of red tracer fire lit up the night, piercing one of the building's second-story windows. He turned to the opposite end of the row house and fired again. This time, the tracer landed where the building met the ground, and the red flame turned orange as the dry grass took the incendiary's invitation.

He's setting the building on fire.

Caitlin ran back across the room, undid the dead bolt, and returned to the long hallway. Past the entrance to the gallery, the one and only Desmond Pratten awkwardly dragged two giant suitcases toward the far exit.

She'd heard enough of Johnny Larsen's conversation to know that Magda was wounded, maybe even bleeding to death. Still, with a hilltop of women choking on their own vomit, Caitlin couldn't let Desmond get away.

Her dad's words came back in a flash.

Take the fight to them, Slugger.

She gritted her teeth and started running. By the time Desmond turned in her direction, she'd dropped the asshole like those name-calling bitches in high school. He went down and onto his back, his head striking the tile floor with a solid thud.

His hands flew up in defense, but Caitlin knocked them aside, straddled his chest, and whaled on his face, hammering with the heels of her fists. After a dozen solid hits, Desmond's nose had crunched more than once, his hands had stopped fighting back, and his blood painted Caitlin's fists.

The clarion call of a smoke detector blared suddenly down the hall, then another, then a third. Chest pounding, she got up.

Desmond's foot flew up into her stomach, knocking her against the hard-shell suitcases. Both she and the bags sprawled across the hall and Desmond ran past, kicking her again on the way. Before she could get to her feet, a door slammed somewhere down the hall behind her. She pulled herself up and looked around. No sign of Desmond. She took a step, kicked something plastic on the floor: a cell phone with a two-inch antenna.

A satellite phone.

Apparently, the no-phones-on-God's-Hill-mobile-or-otherwise rule didn't apply to Desmond Pratten. Caitlin's own device had never gotten a signal, but a satellite phone would do the trick. She hit the power button, dialed 911, and prayed the phone could make a connection.

An operator came on the line. "What's your emergency?"

Caitlin ran toward the gallery and tried not to laugh. "You might want to get a pen."

She gave the woman the directions she'd followed from Coos Bay, the number of women who might have ingested poison, the explosion of the machine shop, and a brief description of Johnny Larsen shooting tracer fire into the building.

"And my mother's been shot," she added, squatting next to Magda's body and turning her over.

"Your mother?"

Whether from the upstairs rooms, the outside air, or both, thick smoke wafted into the gallery. Caitlin coughed, then brushed the hair away from her unconscious mother's face. "That's right. Please send all the help you can."

She pocketed the phone, then dragged Magda toward the open window, struggling to lift the muscular woman over the two feet of broken glass.

"Leave me."

Caitlin looked down, saw Magda's open eyes.

"Are you kidding? You're not even hurt that bad."

She managed another fifteen feet before setting Magda down on the stone walkway, away from the burning grass.

"You're bleeding from both sides of your right shoulder," Caitlin said, helping Magda sit up, "which I believe they call a through-and-through, so less chance of infection if we can stop the bleeding."

"Desmond was just as false as Daya." Magda's head lolled toward the hilltop fire. "You don't need me, Caitlin. You never have. The fire is coming, and I'll slow you down."

Caitlin bent over, put her arm around Magda, and stood, helping her mother to her feet.

"Maybe I didn't need you, but that doesn't mean I didn't want you. You're here and I'm here. Johnny Larsen has Promise, and she needs us both."

The fight came back to Magda's eyes. "Where did he take her?"

Somewhere past the main house to their right, an eruption of gunfire answered that question.

62

JOHNNY FIRED ANOTHER burst at the last place he'd seen a pair of top-less chicks with rifles. A thick cloud of smoke made it hard to tell if he'd hit anyone, but no one shot back. He hadn't seen Gunner yet, but the trail of gasoline he'd left from the machine shop had definitely gone up. With the wind whipping all around, the fire had spread, not only to the fields, but all the way to the clumps of cabins, and Promise's body was weighing him down. Plus, his back ached like someone had shoved a spike into a kidney.

He covered his mouth, took as deep of a breath as he could, and ran toward the tree line he and Gunner had taken on the way in. A gust of wind came through, blowing both smoke and embers toward the trees. Small patches of undergrowth already smoldered. He passed the cabins, the fields, and what was left of the machine shop. Luckily, the fire hadn't spread to the remaining buildings or the trees along the southern entrance where they'd left Gunner's truck.

He rounded a sheet-metal building, saw the road out but no sign of Gunner. Instead, a single white Jeep Wrangler waited, soft top, no windows, and no one inside. No telling if the keys were in it, but he'd pass it on the way down the hill regardless. He took another deep breath and ran.

Fifty feet away, the wind shifted to the south, and he found himself fighting through a cloud of ash and bright-orange embers. He slowed, coughing his way across the last twenty feet.

Unlocked. Lucky break. He set his AR down and slid Promise into the passenger seat. Even luckier, a set of keys waited on the dashboard.

Eyes still closed, Promise shifted in the seat. "What's happening?"

"I'm taking you home, beautiful."

"No." She shook her head, her eyelids fluttering irregularly.

Johnny grabbed the keys and aimed for the ignition, but Promise's hand slapped down on his wrist, and the keys ended up on the floor mat.

"Don't say no to me." Johnny belted the girl with the kind of slap he used on his wife. "Not after what I've been through to get you back. You'll see. It'll be like it was, Daddy and his special girl."

He slid the AR onto his lap, felt the pistol in his leg-strap holster dig into the underside of his leg. He loosened the strap, raised the rig to his upper thigh, and shifted the gun so the butt was easily accessible. Finally, he bent down for the keys, got them in the ignition, started the Jeep, and turned on the headlights.

"You freaking bitch."

Ten feet away, Caitlin Bergman, covered in dirt and blood, sat on a neon-green motocross bike with a handgun aimed right at Johnny's face.

CHAPTER

63

"DON'T MOVE, LARSEN."

Ash and embers whipping around her like a snowstorm, Caitlin extended the kickstand and got off the back of the motorcycle, keeping Stupid Tom's gun aimed at Johnny's face. Her only bullet had pancaked against his body armor, but he couldn't know that. Since the bike would carry only one and Magda's shoulder made it too risky to double up, Caitlin had ridden ahead, confident that Magda would be along on foot any second with a real gun and real ammo. The plan was to find Larsen, not confront him, but she'd seen him empty his hands to drive and took a chance. Now here she was, armed only with her mouth.

Johnny's right hand dipped slightly below the steering wheel.

"What'd I say, asshole?"

Caitlin stepped forward with the bravado of someone with bullets to spare.

His hands returned to ten and two, and Caitlin moved closer to the driver's side. She could hear the Jeep's engine running but didn't know if he had the manual transmission in gear. If he wanted to drive forward, he'd have to go over the bike. She stopped to his left, five feet off his side mirror.

She blinked her watering eyes, fighting back bits of ash. "If you move again, you die."

"Easy there, Bergman."

Another gust of wind swept through, and Caitlin yelled to make sure Larsen heard every word. "Take the keys out of the ignition and throw them over the side."

"Or what?" Johnny said, no fear in his voice.

She took another two steps, ending nearly perpendicular to his door. "Or this all ends now."

"Yeah?"

She could see Promise's head but not much else over Johnny's arms. Caitlin doubled down on her bluff. "You're damned right."

Larsen ground his teeth. "I say you're full of shit. If you were gonna shoot me, you'd have done it already. Now that bitch I shot in the big house," he said with a slight smile, "the one that looks like you in twenty years, but with a backbone? She'd have dropped me in a second, just like she did that Daya chick in the woods."

That Daya comment was his attempt to bait her, but Caitlin settled herself, holding the gun in the modified Weaver stance she'd learned from her father, her firing arm straight, her supportive arm bent at an angle.

"'Course," Johnny continued, "if you have to shoot me, you might miss and hit Promise, which would make this whole shit show pointless, wouldn't it? Head shots are harder than they look, especially with all this crap in the air getting in your eyes, and you already know I'm wearing Kevlar."

He wasn't wrong. Both of them blinked back watering eyes, and Caitlin's chest ached from all the smoke. She kept her words tight to avoid the coughing fit that wanted out. "The keys, asshole. Right. Fucking. Now."

"Sure," Larsen said. "You're the one with the gun."

Johnny's right hand lowered toward the ignition. He froze there, smiling. "You should have killed me."

Her bluff had failed. Caitlin pivoted right and ran toward the Jeep's back bumper but wasn't fast enough.

A crisp gunshot boomed from the front seat.

She fell into the dirt, waiting for her body to light up in pain, but only the spots where her shoulder hit the ground registered. She crawled behind the Jeep, expecting a second, third, and ninetieth shot to follow, but nothing happened.

A deep breath gave her the courage to look through the back window of the Jeep's soft-top. Johnny Larsen sat slumped against the driver's side door. Promise fought with her seat belt, opened the passenger side door, and stumbled out, carrying her father's pistol.

"I'm not your special girl," she said, eyes still on her father's body, "and I won't go home. Ever."

Caitlin reached out for her. "That's fine, Promise. You don't ever have to."

Promise turned Caitlin's way, blinking between consciousness and someplace else. Caitlin opened her outstretched palm and moved her fingers until the girl's eyes tracked her movement. "You saved my life, kid."

She lowered her hand slowly toward Promise's arm.

Promise's head turned as she seemed to make the connection. Her shoulders shook and she lowered the gun. "You saved mine, Magda."

"Close enough," Caitlin said, bringing the girl into a hug.

She couldn't be sure how long she stood there with her arms around the young woman. Seconds, minutes; the moment felt eternal, like Caitlin's whole life had led to this one embrace. What did family mean, or love? She closed her eyes, sure that if she passed out there in the swirling smoke and woke bathed in light, she would regret nothing.

The sound of Magda running onto the road from behind a building broke the moment. Caitlin opened her eyes. Sound asleep, Promise did not.

Magda carried an assault rifle Caitlin hadn't seen before. "Sorry I was late. He wasn't alone."

Caitlin didn't see anyone in pursuit. "Do we need—"

"His friend won't be a problem." Magda opened the Jeep's front door and pulled Johnny Larsen's dead body out. "It's time to get to the Hill for the calling of the names."

CHAPTER

64

Wedged in the passenger seat with Promise, Caitlin tried to convince Magda the world wasn't ending.

"But the hill isn't surrounded by fire, Magda. It's only on this entrance, and that's only because Larsen set it. Promise needs medical attention."

Magda shook her head and swung the Jeep around a corner. "Desmond said it was only Valium when he was—"

The words trailed off. Riding either adrenaline or shock, Magda pulled the Jeep around the side road that bypassed the main compound, despite her wounded shoulder, and aimed for the stairway at the base of God's Hill, starting a completely different thought.

"You've seen the winds, Caitlin, and the rest of the county. The fire will spread quickly. This is how it happens."

"How what happens, Linda's dream? That was all bullshit. You said so yourself, Desmond is just as false as Daya. Plus, he poisoned the Daughters."

"What you saw was the Calm," Magda yelled. "You don't understand. They were in a relaxed state—"

"Listen to me, Magda. You're in shock. I saw them suffocating on their own vomit, not tripping out on some 'calm.' Half of them were already dead, as in beyond help, and they're all going to die if we don't get them out of here."

They took a turn that forced Caitlin against the door. Out the wind-shield, she could see that the trees surrounding the compound were now ablaze.

Magda still didn't seem concerned. "The signs are here, the time is right."

Caitlin grabbed the handle above the roll bar to keep from slipping. "But you know this is bullshit. Hell, you said it yourself in your note to me. The Daughters are corrupt. Daya tried to sell a thirteen-year-old girl to a child molester. Desmond left you to die in the gallery after begging for his life while offering to pimp out every woman on the hill."

"It's not about Desmond or Daya, Caitlin. Can't you see that? It's about meeting the Spirit in the Light and ascending, like the Five, like Linda."

"I found the Five."

Magda rolled her eyes. "I've searched all of God's Hill, for months. They're—"

"Under the landslide, in a town car, all dead, completely unascended. I've seen them, five bodies; at least one of them was shot in the head. Either Desmond or Daya murdered them, probably both. It's why they sold the paving equipment, so no one would try to repair the road."

"You don't understand, Caitlin."

"No, I fucking don't." Even after hearing Desmond Pratten try to sell Lily Kramer to save his own ass, her mother wasn't going to abandon her crazy faith. "How can you still believe any of this shit?"

Magda rounded a corner. "Because I've seen the face of God. I've seen this day before. In the Knowing."

"The Knowing—"

"You were there, Caitlin."

"I was where?"

"Just like now. You were older, and you were there, and you forgave me—"

"Stop."

"—just like you did tonight—"

Caitlin grabbed Magda's arm and pointed ahead. "Stop."

A football field away, two burning trees had fallen over the road. Magda brought the Jeep to a stop.

"I saw the face of God, Caitlin, and you were there. Even if Desmond and Daya were false, Linda was true from the beginning, and she ascended." Magda opened her door and got out.

Caitlin reached for her own handle. "But Linda didn't ascend either."

Magda appeared at Caitlin's side of the car, either oblivious to the last statement or just unable to hear it. "We walk from here. Can you lift Promise?"

Caitlin nudged the teen. "We have to walk, kid."

Promise woke enough to stumble alongside under Caitlin's arm. The fallen trees, each around two feet in diameter, glowed with ribbons of flame, but Magda managed to find safe sections they could cross. Another five hundred feet would take them to the stairs to God's Hill. A quarter of a mile downhill past that would get them to the garage where Caitlin's rental truck waited. What did it matter if Magda was determined to die?

The freaking satellite phone.

Caitlin paused with Promise, reached into her pocket, grabbed the satellite phone, and dialed Lakshmi's number from memory.

Once again, the girl answered in the darkest hour of the night. "Brilliant, Caitlin, you're alive."

"Debatable," Caitlin answered, her and Promise trailing ten feet behind Magda. "I know it's not the morning, but were you able to get the message I asked for?"

"I can do better than that. We're on our way there now in a private jet. Beverly?"

Somewhere between laughter and prayer, Caitlin waited until an older woman's voice came on the phone. "This is Beverly Chandler."

Caitlin covered the handset. "Magda, stop. Before you climb those stairs, you need to talk to someone."

Magda turned, staring first at Caitlin like she was insane, then focusing on the phone in her hand. She walked over and took the satellite phone.

"Hello?"

Caitlin heard the first exchange.

"Maya, is that you?"

Magda took a step backward, tears in her eyes. "Bevvie?"

Would it be enough? Would twenty years of mental programming keep Magda locked in her twisted reality, or would the woman's mind break on the side of a burning mountain?

Seconds later, Magda fell to her knees, crying, but still talking on the phone.

Something had broken, but Caitlin didn't think it was Magda. She pulled Promise a few feet away, giving the women a minute of privacy.

Finally, Magda walked back over, her face red, her eyes a mess, but no tears visible. Caitlin knew the look well enough. Just like she herself had done on her thirteenth birthday, Magda had turned her sadness to rage. She handed Caitlin the phone.

Lakshmi waited on the other end. "We'll be at the North Bend airport in two hours," she said. "Stay safe."

Caitlin made sure Lakshmi had as much information as possible, then hung up.

Magda resumed her walk toward the stairs like a bullet hadn't passed through her shoulder. "We've got to get the Daughters out of here before they all burn to death."

65

THE TRIO'S ARRIVAL at the top of the stairs didn't seem to surprise even one of the remaining Daughters. Despite the smoke-filled air and the ground littered with naked, unmoving bodies in rank pools of bodily fluids, fifteen women held hands in a semicircle around the still-raging fire. Led by Gwendolyn Sunrise, her stump of a hand wrapped in a bloody T-shirt, they sang out the words to another one of their songs with the artificial joy of a high school show choir.

Even at the darkest hour
Even on the ending night
We will harness love's pure power
And rise up into the pure light

Caitlin propped Promise against a waist-high rock wall, the strenuous activity having taken its toll on the drugged girl—and, she had to admit, her. Magda broke through into the center of the group.

"Daughters, listen to me."

Gwendolyn raised the held hand of the woman on her good side and doubled down with another verse.

Other voices may conspire
To come and take you far away
But only true believer fire
Can save you on the final day

"My sisters," Magda continued, pleading in front of the semicircle, "my friends, my family—"

Gwendolyn let go of her neighbor's hand and stepped forward, her good palm open and out, her wounded hand dripping blood. "You're in pain, Magda. Join us and prepare."

Caitlin watched the eyes of the others. Only a handful actually tracked the actions of the two women. The rest had the glazed-over, bloodshot eyes of kids who'd spent twenty straight hours watching cartoons after downing two liters of Mountain Dew. She recognized Lily Kramer and Mouse Girl, now naked and unarmed, among the bedraggled survivors.

"No," Magda said. "Tonight is not the night. Desmond has abandoned us."

Gwendolyn smiled the idea away, shaking her head. "As was foretold, even on the last night, the seeds of doubt will be sown."

"These aren't the seeds of doubt. Linda Sperry did not ascend."

"Of course she did," Gwendolyn said. "You were the witness to the miracle—"

"Because I didn't know there was a stairway under the house. Beverly Bangs is alive—"

Caitlin saw the name register on Gwendolyn's face, but nothing from the rest of the crowd. From the age difference between Sunrise and the others, Caitlin guessed many had joined after Beverly left.

"But not here," Gwendolyn answered, turning back to the Daughters. "Water not the seeds of doubt, for they are—"

The response came. "The roots of diversion."

"And the roots of diversion grow?"

"The tree of temptation."

Caitlin saw desperation cloud Magda's face. After all those years of chanting along, even teaching the words, she stood helpless.

"Caitlin has seen the Five," Magda said, waving her over. "She's found their bodies, not far from here. Tell them, Caitlin, please."

Caitlin waded into the women and met their eyes. She saw exhaustion—surely most were close to collapse—but also fear and doubt, even in bloody Gwendolyn Sunrise, who sneered at Caitlin's approach. Only fifteen women remained on their feet. That meant over thirty were dead. The remaining women weren't going to leave willingly; to do so would mean the destruction of their entire realities, beliefs so strong that they were willing to stand naked on top of a mountain in front of a fire during fire season.

"She's not a Daughter," Gwendolyn said. "She doesn't even believe in God."

"It's true." Caitlin climbed up onto the rock wall circling the Eternal Flame and faced the women. "I'm not a Daughter."

She looked down, saw Magda, helpless and alone.

"I came here looking for a mother. A woman I thought had abandoned me, a woman I hated for years, without ever having even met her. I came with doubts, laughing at your ways and your songs, ready to bury my so-called mother with a final *fuck you*."

Gwendolyn Sunrise nodded, as if she'd been right all along.

"And then I met a few of you—"

She pointed at the naked lawyer. "Gwendolyn, a natural leader and true believer. What kind of strength must it take to stand there, bleeding and in shock?" She moved on to Lily Kramer. "Eve, the youngest, but with a heart of pure gold and dedication."

She pointed down toward the main compound.

"Then I met Desmond. Our time together was short." She looked at Magda, remembering Maya's first meeting at Linda Sperry's house. "But I felt something I had never felt before. He touched my wrist—"

Recognition passed through more than one face.

"—and something happened in me. Something opened. Then Desmond said something to me I'd never even considered. I didn't hate my mother, Magda, who, as confused as she is right now after having been shot by one of the intruders, has always been a pure follower of the Light."

Magda looked dumbfounded. Caitlin didn't slow down. "I didn't hate her, I hated myself. The weakness in me. The cravings I had, the desires, the complete lack of someone who could tell me I was special." She pointed around the circle. "You've all grown up wanting. You've all suffered. Yet here you are, at the end of it all: giving, pure, and ready, without fear. Well, Desmond spoke that truth and touched my wrist, and something happened to me."

Caitlin thought about Scott Canton's advice, about the letter and the spirit of the law.

Don't get caught up on whether you should stone someone for telling a lie . . . if the lie was told to get people out of the valley before a flood.

Fighting these women and their beliefs wasn't going to do anything but send them deeper into their foxholes.

"I was terrified," she continued. "I ran away from the compound, broke out, blew up the motor pool."

Another look of recognition crossed the faces.

"And that's when my miracle happened. I fell asleep. When I woke, my mother stood over me. She wasn't dead; she'd been guarding Promise Larsen from the evil that her father would do, as any good Daughter of God would have done. I knew then that Desmond had been right. If he was right about that, then he was right about the rest. As were you wonderful, brave women. Unique, powerful, and necessary, every one."

Now the women of the circle wore actual smiles. The world burned around them, but they showed no fear.

"We returned to God's Hill," Caitlin continued. "Here for the end, but just in time. We found Desmond guarding the compound from Johnny Larsen, a machine gun in his hand and the fire of God at his fingertips. He told me there was still time to become a Daughter."

Even Gwendolyn smiled at this point.

Caitlin pulled off her dirt-covered T-shirt, revealing her bra underneath. If she couldn't beat them, she'd have to join them.

"But I have to fulfill the Climb," she said, pulling down her shorts. "And the southern route is on fire. I've been told there's a northern route."

Lily Kramer stepped forward. "There is. We can take the road down to at least the washout. I can show you."

Magda looked at Caitlin with tears ringing her eyes. There was no time to pull her aside and make sure they were on the same page, but Caitlin thought they were.

After everything, we have to be.

Magda smiled her way, then addressed the daughters. "We all will show you," she said, putting her hand on Gwendolyn's bare shoulder.

Gwendolyn nodded, then raised her bloody hand, leading the believers in another refrain.

"We climb God's Hill together, now and at the end of days."

Lily Kramer grabbed a tiki torch from the path, then led the way down the northern steps. Caitlin handed Magda her clothes and the satellite phone.

"Get Promise to the truck and meet us down at the road. Check in with 911 and see how close they are."

Magda threw her good arm around Caitlin.

"I don't know how to thank you," she said, bursting into tears.

Caitlin hugged her mother as if for the first and last time. "I understand."

Her mother pulled back. "Understand what?"

A thousand words wanted to come out. She understood that sometimes the best thing a parent could do was recognize that they'd make a terrible parent. That in Maya's crazy way, she really had believed that joining the Daughters of God would save the world, including her own daughter, and that saving the world meant abandoning it to do so. How the need to feel special and wanted made people worship anyone who saw them as unique, even to the point of blind acceptance of their flaws—the same way she'd worshiped her own father.

More words came, more revelations. Caitlin shook her head and walked toward the stairs, answering with only one. "Why."

Full of hope and song, the naked women marched Caitlin down the asphalt road, not noticing when Magda and Promise detoured at the garage, nor slowing when Caitlin led them down the steep and uneven surface of the landslide.

The sight of Stupid Tom's body stopped the singing, the joyful noise replaced by curious but still-hopeful conversation. A tiki torch near the window of the red town car stopped the hope.

"It's one of ours," someone said.

The fire couldn't be far behind, but Caitlin fought the urge to guide their discovery. She'd taken them this far; they had to have their own revelations. She took another step down the hill.

"Wait," Gwendolyn called. "Let me through."

They'd started to clump in front of the broken window. Gwendolyn pushed her way forward.

"It can't be," she said, then turned and vomited onto the dirt. Rather than stopping to help her, the rest pushed closer, sweeping dirt away with their hands until the whole car door was clear.

"The Five," someone else said. "These are the Five."

Caitlin watched each woman witness the tomb, each processing the sight alone. Some chattered nervously; others went silent, sitting in place or staring off into the distance.

"But if they're here . . ." someone started.

Another woman picked up the thread. "Daya said . . ."

One Daughter wobbled away from the window, searching for eye contact. "Maybe the Five betrayed us," she said, holding her own arms. "They had to have betrayed us, right?"

Again, Caitlin fought the urge to interfere. Luckily, one of the others stepped forward.

"What the hell's wrong with you? All they wanted was to leave, and Daya killed them."

A woman screamed, not in blood-curdling terror but a wail of utter hopelessness. The others shifted from clump to clump, looking for any-one to explain anything.

"My brother's money," someone said. "He gave them so much money."

Caitlin saw a woman on the edge of the group turn and start kicking a tree trunk with her bare foot. No words, just pure, skin-splitting anger.

"But the miracle was witnessed." The arm-holding, still-devout woman cornered Gwendolyn. "You told us they ascended, Sunrise."

The others who'd already looked into the car, the ones not screaming into the night or bloodying the remains of their feet on a tree trunk, turned toward their last leader.

"You saw it, right, Gwendolyn? You told us you witnessed the miracle."

Gwendolyn prostrated herself in the dirt, speaking, but not to them.

"I saw the miracle," she said. "I saw the face of God. I am unique and necessary."

For a second, Caitlin thought the circle around Sunrise might turn violent, but faced with Gwendolyn's complete submission, the lost women turned away without focus.

Finally, Lily Kramer, the last to leave the window of the town car, turned Caitlin's direction and asked the obvious. "Was any of it true?"

The high-pitched whine of a Boeing 747 SuperTanker soaring overhead drowned out any need for Caitlin to answer. A massive plume of retardant fell from the plane's tail, and the Eternal Flame at the top of Ceremony Peak went dark.

CHAPTER

66

A T FIRST, THE people milling around the gymnasium floor seemed indistinguishable from each other; men, women, and children wandering about dressed in clothing donated from Coquille's resale shops and restaurants. Lost eyes and dreams shuffled from table to cot, cot to aid station, wearing T-shirts with the Red Devil mascot of the local high school, hoodies from Mr. Zach's, and ball caps from the Broiler. Watching a woman in an oversized Trail Blazers sweat shirt towel off her hair, Caitlin honestly couldn't guess whether the night's fires had taken the woman's home, her faith, or both.

Of course, the first responders had clothed the naked Dayans, administered first aid, and split the multiple smoke inhalation sufferers between the hospitals in Coos Bay and Coquille. Caitlin and six of the women from the hill had been grouped with the county's other victims in the makeshift shelter of a high school's gym.

After hours of restless, impossible sleep, the natural dichotomy between the Dayans and the citizens of Coos County became apparent. Not by actions, for the townspeople handing out towels and sandwiches gave everyone the same hug regardless of tragedy, but a long strip of police tape suspended through the center of the room separated usual from unusual.

With the taped barrier came the county's deputies, officers from local municipalities, and state troopers, as if someone had sent up the Bat signal and every hero in the Justice League had come running.

Caitlin had to laugh. First no one would come; now they wouldn't stay away.

Finally, a deputy raised the tape, looked around, then settled on Caitlin.

"Mrs. Bergman," he said. "Sheriff Martin is ready to see you."

"It's Miss, actually."

He held the tape up for Caitlin to walk under. "What's that?"

Caitlin shook her head, grabbed the travel toothbrush some angel had handed her in a prepackaged Dopp kit, and followed the deputy out.

Safe in the passenger seat of the deputy's SUV, Caitlin spoke for the first time in hours. "Did you see the women? On top of the hill near the fire pit?"

The deputy cleared his throat. "I'm not really supposed to talk about it."

Caitlin nodded. "But were you there?"

He parked his truck in front of the same building Caitlin had visited a week earlier to identify the remains of her mother, who DNA had finally confirmed hadn't been her mother after all but the infamous Daya Sperry. "I was there."

"How many women died from the poison?"

"I can't say."

Caitlin leaned in. "Off the record."

He shook his head. "I mean they're still counting. Over twenty, maybe more. You need help getting out?"

Caitlin reached for the door. "No, I got this."

Over twenty, maybe more.

If she hadn't stopped for Stupid Tom's gun, or wasted time finding the Five, or . . .

She let the unresolvable thought go and beat the deputy to the sheriff's department, leading the way to the closed door of Sheriff Martin's office and walking in on a heated discussion between Boz and Anders Larsen.

"Here's the bitch now," Anders said, puffing up and turning in Caitlin's direction. "Arrest her for my boy's death, or I'll wait for her outside and get some real justice, State of Jefferson–style."

Caitlin put both hands out and pushed the old man backward, full force. He fell onto the side of Martin's receiving chair and caught himself against the office wall.

"Christ," Martin said, trying to move around his desk.

Caitlin closed in on the elder Larsen. Even at five foot six, she towered over the cowering bully. "This bitch has the justice you want right here."

Sheriff Martin pulled her back, corralling her behind his desk. "Easy, Bergman."

Caitlin pushed against Martin's hand, happy to see a look of terror in Anders Larsen's eyes. "We can talk about your perfect son's relationship with his daughter and your five generations of family values."

Martin got Anders to his feet, then shuffled the man out into the lobby, where the deputy who'd driven Caitlin over hovered awkwardly.

Anders tried to find his anger again. "She assaulted me, Martin. If you let her get away with this, I can guarantee you won't see reelection."

"Sit tight," Martin said, pointing the deputy toward Anders. "We'll talk about that."

The deputy grabbed Anders Larsen by the arm.

Martin straightened his shirt, resting his hands on his gun belt. "And we'll talk about how the most destructive wildfire this county's ever seen happened to start on your Powers ridge property one day after Land Management issued a cease order."

Larsen looked ten years older and a foot shorter. "Because that ridge was a tinderbox."

Martin nodded. "Exactly. It's not official yet, but preliminary findings from the ODF suggest spent incendiary rounds at the flash point. You and I are gonna talk about how the same type of rounds fired at the Dayan compound were loaded in a rifle found in your son's lap."

Larsen staggered backward, took a seat. "I'm calling my lawyer."

"You do that," Martin said, pulling the door shut and returning to Caitlin. He took a deep breath and exhaled. "You okay?"

Still standing behind Martin's desk, Caitlin felt her heart pounding through her ribs. She copied his deep breath, finally letting a small laugh escape. "I didn't think I had any adrenaline left."

She started to move to the other side of the desk, but Martin collapsed into the reception chair.

"I thought I'd seen everything," he said, scratching his head. "I mean, I've seen some messed-up stuff—"

"How many?" Caitlin took the chair behind his desk.

"John Larsen, Gunner Garrett, Tom Edwards—all shot. Another three Dayans, same. Then there's a car at the bottom of the landslide that looks like it's been there for a year—"

"The Five," Caitlin said. "From the letter in the box we opened with the butt key."

Martin shook his head in disbelief. "Who would've thought a key in a dead woman's bottom wasn't the worst thing I'd see in this life?"

"The hill?"

He looked up at the ceiling. "Thirty maybe. They're still sorting that horror out, but we have no idea what we're looking at. You've got to tell me everything."

"Who knows everything?" Caitlin started, mentally piecing the week's events together like an air-accident investigator without a black box. "But I'll try."

Martin started a recorder, and they switched spots.

It took twenty minutes for Caitlin to get him to the SuperTanker's arrival.

He turned off the recorder and sat back. "So Promise Larsen shot her father?"

"Well, I got him once in the Kevlar, but that only pissed him off."

"What about Garrett or Stupid Tom?" Martin caught himself. "I mean, Tom Edwards?"

"No idea, though lots of those women were carrying guns."

He nodded. "Two of the deceased were found with weapons. Topless, but still armed."

He sighed, then leaned forward. "You mentioned being trapped in one of the rooms in the main house with some sort of magnetic lock system."

"That's right. The first night I was up there."

"Were you aware of anyone else trapped in one of those rooms?"

Caitlin sat back. "No idea. Was someone found?"

He tilted his head side to side. "Remains. Well, almost cremains at that point. You said their leader—"

"Desmond." She hadn't thought of Desmond once since escaping the hill. He'd knocked her down, then disappeared down the hall. Was the door she'd heard slam one of the containment rooms?

"Right. You said that Desmond Pratten dropped his satellite phone."

"That's correct, running away from Johnny Larsen's assault. I found it in the hall while trying to revive Magda. Were the remains his?"

Martin laced his fingertips on the desktop. "You tell me."

They had to be Desmond's remains. It was the only thing that would explain how he'd disappeared in such a short distance. Had she known that then? Of course not. How could she have? Her mother was shot, possibly bleeding to death, and after two decades of loyal servitude, Desmond had poisoned his followers and planned to run away with thirteen-year-old Promise Larsen. Yes, Caitlin had known about the containment rooms and that he was still in the building, but if Desmond had hidden in one of his own detention cells, he would have known how the locks worked, giving him a better chance of escaping than any of his previous captives.

Judging from the unspoken excuses rushing to her defense, Caitlin knew the case could justifiably be made that she had murdered the guru known as Desmond. By her own admission, she both knew about the rooms and had beaten him and taken his phone. Would a wealthy local like Anders Larsen want revenge enough to force the authorities to look closer? Would Gwendolyn Sunrise, or one of the other still-somehow devout survivors, put missing pieces together that didn't quite fit but could create the picture they wanted to see? Might Sheriff Martin, feeling the certain pressure of impending international media coverage, grasp at the chance to pin some small bit of responsibility on someone not associated with Coos County, Oregon? Most of all, was she lying to herself, like the Dayans had for years? Hiding some part of her subconscious that knew damned well that Desmond Pratten had dived into the room to the right, before the entrance to the gallery, the same room she'd been in that afternoon—and that she'd let him do it? Had the clattering of the satellite phone skidding across the hall made the same sound as a magnetic door lock sealing a man in a tomb? She didn't think so. Wouldn't think so.

Sometimes it's better to face the truth, Matthew Bergman had told her on her thirteenth birthday. *It'll come out anyway. Better to get it over with.*

Back then, she'd thought he was talking about meeting Mama Maya. Now she knew he'd been ready to tell her he was her real father, and she'd said no. He could have insisted and told her anyway, possibly ruining their relationship, but hadn't.

Her father wasn't perfect after all.

He'd never said he was, but she'd spent her life following the man's words like scripture.

She took a breath and followed his example one more time. "I have no idea who would have been in one of those rooms, Sheriff. Between Johnny Larsen's assault on the compound and finding all of those women choking on poison, plus the fires—"

She paused, closed her eyes, and took a breath. Maybe the truth would come out in time, but like her father before her, Caitlin could live with the wait. She opened her eyes and finished.

"I barely got out of there alive. If I had to guess, it was all part of Johnny Larsen's plan to get his daughter back."

The sheriff nodded. "Thank God that didn't happen. Now, about your mother—"

"How is she? She'd lost a lot of blood before the ambulance arrived. They took her and Sunrise to Bay Area Hospital, I think. Promise too, because of whatever Desmond gave her."

"She's gone."

Caitlin hadn't heard from anyone in the hours since the ambulances left the scene, but she'd never considered that their parting had meant they might never see each other again.

Her chest shook, and her body convulsed with surprise. Her voice trembled through unexpected tears. "She died from a shoulder wound?"

Sheriff Martin's eyes widened. "What? No, God, I'm sorry. Your mother didn't die."

Caitlin wiped her eyes. "Promise? She seemed to be coming out of it when—"

"No," Martin said, stopping her. "They're both alive, or were this morning. They disappeared from the hospital, haven't been seen since."

Caitlin's jaw might have dropped a foot. She put a hand on her chest, then laughed. "Dammit, Sheriff. That's the second time in a week you made me think my mother was dead."

"Sorry," he said. "Little overwhelmed here. I need to speak to Magda, or Maya, or whatever she's calling herself."

Caitlin stood up. "I'm sure you'll find her."

He rose as well. "Miss Bergman, wait, I have more questions."

"I bet you do, Boz, but that's your job, right?"

She thought back to the words he'd said the last time she left his office and opened the door. "I'll go back home. You've got everything covered."

"You can't leave, Miss Bergman—"

She turned to face him. "Are you arresting me?"

"Well, no, but—"

She walked out.

"Wait." Martin followed her out, but a tired-looking receptionist stepped between them and grabbed the sheriff.

"Boz, the press are here."

"Good lord, already? Where from?"

"International, I think. This English girl seems to know everything."

Caitlin raised a hand to hide her smile and kept walking. Across the bustling office, an anxious deputy failed at holding back a determined young woman with dark skin and a distinct British accent.

Not determined, *intense.*

CHAPTER

67

IT TOOK ALL of Lakshmi's willpower to restrict her contact with Caitlin to a quick nod on her way past. Instead, she started her phone's voice recorder and fired question after question at Sheriff Martin over the reception desk, relenting only after the words *no comment* were replaced by the announcement of an official press conference at six that evening.

While not exactly great sound bites, the denials gave her enough material to pitch something to her boss. She threw her phone into her bag and went outside. Caitlin sat on the sidewalk two spots down from her rental pickup, her eyes tracking a sheriff's department SUV pulling up to the end of the block.

A middle-aged blonde in scrubs coming out of the government building rushed past Lakshmi, then ran to meet the SUV. A deputy helped a young woman in her late teens or early twenties out of the passenger side. The blonde in the scrubs stopped feet away from the young woman.

Lakshmi grabbed her phone, opened the camera app, hit record, and waited.

The young woman took a small step. Scrubs did the same, but hesitantly. A second passed, then two; then the younger woman rushed forward, throwing her arms around the woman in scrubs and resting her head against the woman's shoulder.

Lakshmi turned and saw Caitlin stand up and wipe tears from her eyes. She stopped the recording. "Gross."

Caitlin looked her way, broke into a smile. "What's gross?"

Lakshmi laughed. "It's like seeing Wonder Woman cry."

Caitlin laughed as well. "I'm choosing to hear the part of that sentence where you think of me as Wonder Woman."

She beat Lakshmi to their own hug.

Lakshmi fell into Caitlin's arms, only slightly aware that it was the first time they'd hugged where she hadn't instigated the contact.

When they finally stopped, Caitlin wiped another crop of tears away and looked back down the sidewalk to the mother-daughter pair.

"One of the Dayans?" Lakshmi said.

The women separated, and Caitlin nodded. "The medical examiner's daughter."

"Should we—"

"Yes." Caitlin headed toward the rental truck. "But not now. Let's get out of here."

Lakshmi unlocked the truck and went for the passenger door, but Caitlin had already climbed in and shut the door, leaving Lakshmi to drive. Another first.

She got in and found Caitlin looking through the things on the back seat. "My suitcase, my bag." She reached into her laptop bag and pulled out her phone. "Oh, sweet technology, where have you been?"

She glanced up and pointed down the street. "Turn right here, then right again on the Forty-Two."

Lakshmi pulled out, following her directions. "There's a press conference at six, unless you want to get to the airport, which I'd totally understand."

"Are you kidding? This is your big break, Lakshmi. Maybe even the story of a lifetime."

Lakshmi turned onto the main road that led from Coquille to Coos Bay. "I'm not sure how far I can take it. I don't even know if NPR will let me pitch it."

"Let me worry about that." Caitlin ran a power cord to her phone, dialed a number, and let it ring on speaker. A man answered in a huff.

"Bergman, where the hell have you been? I thought you wanted to make this work, but you left me high and dry for three days, and I'm supposed to have a follow-up piece for the three-states thing—"

Caitlin smiled. "I missed you too, Stan."

Stan Lawton. Lakshmi recognized the name of Caitlin's editor.

"I'm not kidding. You won't believe the stress I'm under—"

Caitlin started the pitch. "I'm going to save your ass. I've got the best damned investigative reporter you've never heard of, and she's got a story that'll win awards, regardless of politics. Real news, Stan, like we both used to do. Not only that, it's a scoop and she's got access to the biggest witness to it all."

"And who's this reporter I've never heard of?"

"Lakshmi Anjale," Caitlin said. "She's been slaving away for peanuts at NPR, and she's ready for the big time."

"Jesus," Stan said. "The name alone's gonna—"

"Gonna what, Stan?"

"Nothing, just want to make sure I spell it right."

Caitlin shot Lakshmi a smile. "Be sure that you do. Between the hits and shares this story will generate, it'll have legs for weeks. Might even go viral, as the kids say."

Stan Lawton said nothing for a bit, then finally returned. "Well, what's it about?"

"Motherhood."

"Christ, Bergman, are you kidding?"

"Fine," Caitlin shook her head. "It's about a cult, a mass grave, child molesters, an aging porn star, kidnapping, and corruption, all in a beautiful town in coastal Oregon."

"And why aren't you're writing it?"

"Because I lived it. Now I'm gonna put Lakshmi on the phone, and you're gonna make her an offer that shows you're the editor in chief, Stan, no matter what your overlord wants you to print."

"Fine," he said. "I'll talk to her. By the way, who's this Anjale girl to you, anyway?"

Caitlin looked over and smiled. "Family. Treat her like she's my daughter, Stan."

Lakshmi smiled back, then chimed in like she hadn't been on the phone the whole time.

"Mr. Lawton, my name is Lakshmi Anjale, and I'd like to pitch you the story of your career."

Ten minutes later, she pulled into the parking lot of the Mill Casino and Hotel with a new job, a deadline, and Caitlin Bergman, a woman who thought of her as a daughter.

68

CAITLIN SPENT THE next two weeks in Coos Bay with Lakshmi, helping the young woman shape the story and pointing her toward sources. Her predictions rang true; not only did the *LA Voice* have a hit, but they scooped the rest of the nation. Broadcasters and wire services alike came to Lakshmi for access. She even negotiated a podcast exclusive between the paper and NPR, just to mend any bridges burnt by her sudden departure.

Of course, she and Caitlin left Beverly Chandler, her private jet, and Tanner out of the conversation. While local outlets picked up on the disappearance of Promise Larsen and Magda, their incomplete stories couldn't compete with the intrigue surrounding the survivors of God's Hill, or the legend of Desmond Pratten, who made the whole tragedy possible by abusing the contrast of agony and release.

As days went by, Caitlin spent less time supervising Lakshmi and more time by the ocean, hiking through groves of coastal oaks to watch the majestic sea combat the wooded shores. Eventually she bought a new pair of running shoes, even ran through Coos Bay in tribute to Steve Prefontaine.

"Doesn't staying where it all happened terrify you?" Lakshmi asked her.

"Not at all," Caitlin replied. "It's beautiful here, and the people are great. You know, without the Larsens around."

After all the threats, Anders Larsen never attempted any kind of rogue justice, Jefferson-style or otherwise. If anything, he followed the typical old-white-man playbook and had his lawyer file libel and slander suits. They'd linger for years, ultimately doing nothing but draining bank accounts and keeping lawyers employed, but such was the way of the seventy-year-old bully who no longer had a son with anger management issues to abuse.

A week later, tipped by one of her LAPD connections, partly to keep Lakshmi's presence at the Sperry mansion out of the story and partly because Caitlin had sat on the sidelines for long enough, she left Lakshmi in Oregon and returned to Los Angeles in time for the official identification of Linda Sperry's skeletal remains, indeed found on the Laurel Canyon property. The articles both she and Lakshmi wrote led to complementary pieces about the Dayans' Southern California origins. Those pieces brought forward former Dayans willing to speak about their time in the group and answered Caitlin's lingering questions, including their name change from the Dayans to the Daughters of God.

The wild sexual exploration of the Dayans at their height led to some spectacular jealousies and more than one involvement with underage women, which meant more than one interaction with the authorities. To stave off future police investigations and any public perception that the Dayans were a wild sex cult, Daya decided that all men but Desmond must leave, and Desmond didn't complain. Of course, many of the women had formed monogamous relationships with male members and followed their exits, cutting the numbers in half.

Since the majority of the enterprise had been funded by Linda Sperry's investments, Daya and Desmond maintained the Laurel Canyon property, using Tanner as a caretaker who would handle simple banking tasks without ever declaring Linda dead. In addition, they made group members pool their financial ties for the betterment of the organization, allowing Daya and Desmond to siphon from those with outside investments, social security, or trust funds. Anyone who'd wanted to leave the group after that, like the Five, disappeared. When the final accounting had been completed, Daya and Desmond had been cashing checks for sixteen women, none of whom had been found to date, dead or alive.

"What about the *Knowing*?" Scott Canton asked, after hearing Caitlin's account of the story during their first phone call post-cataclysm.

She laughed. "After that whole story, that's what you want to know about?"

"I do this for free," Scott replied, "and you carry more baggage than a freight train. I want to know why these women believed they'd seen the face of God. Was it Reiki, qigong, faith healing?"

Scott wasn't the only one interested. After interviewing several of the former members and consulting psychiatrists, neurologists, and hypnotherapists, Caitlin published an article centered around the prevailing theory that Desmond had combined sleep deprivation, extreme physical activity, deep breathing, dietary restriction, fasting, and neurolinguistic programming with the art of the stage hypnotist's speed trance. While no experts could reproduce the experience, they happily agreed with each other's hypotheses rather than allowing for any spiritual connection between Desmond and the God he'd claimed to channel.

As for Caitlin, even a month out, she was aware that interest in her mother's story, and subsequent outcome, had grown. Whether that meant follow-up calls from Oregon law enforcement, a friendly visit from FBI agents, or the occasional black car with tinted windows parked outside her place, the fate of Maya Aronson and Promise Larsen remained a question mark people wanted to make a period.

She'd been back on the bench in front her father's plaque in the Abbey of the Psalms mausoleum for only a minute, not even long enough to get out his pack of cigarettes, when a voice she didn't recognize surprised her from behind.

"Caitlin Bergman?"

The woman, a well-dressed, young-looking sixty-something in a bright floral dress, sat beside Caitlin on the bench. Her face had the creaseless perfection of a fair amount of work done by a skilled hand.

"You must be Beverly Chandler," Caitlin whispered.

Beverly looked around, then nodded. "Thank you for meeting me—and keeping me out of the story." She looked toward Caitlin's father's memorial. "Maya spoke about Matt a lot, before our Dayan adventures."

"Really?"

Beverly smiled. "Not all good, but then, who among us can say we've done no wrong?"

A million questions came to Caitlin's lips, but Beverly had already risen and turned toward the exit.

Caitlin stood. "Maybe we can speak more, when all of this goes away."

Beverly stopped near the exit. "Maybe, but all of this doesn't really go away until we go away." She smiled again, then walked out.

Caitlin looked down at the bench and saw that Beverly had left a brand-new copy of *She Taught Me to Fly* by Carol Rusnak and the kind of prepaid cell phone bought at a drugstore. She double-checked that she was alone, then flipped through the pages of the book until she saw yellow highlighter on the familiar phrase. Unlike in her original copy, there was handwriting at the bottom of the page:

1-888-CNF-CALL #5423376

Caitlin stood and walked to the mausoleum's central corridor. Confident that no one else was around, she picked up the disposable phone, dialed the toll-free conference call number, punched in the meeting code, and listened.

"One party is waiting on the line," the automated operator informed her, but Caitlin didn't hear anyone.

"Magda?" she said, still not hearing anything from the other end.

She looked down, checked her phone's signal, then brought the handset back to her ear.

"Maya, are you there?"

"Sorry." Magda's voice came through. "I was muted, apparently. Promise had to show me how to use this thing. The gong here is very loud, so I tried to . . ." Caitlin heard ruffling. "Anyway, I got confused."

Caitlin smiled. For a second, she felt like any one of her friends with a senior parent troubled by technology.

"They have a loud gong, huh? Sounds foreign. So I shouldn't expect to run into you anytime soon?"

"I'm afraid not, not until we know Promise is safe, and I don't think I'll be able to return to the States anytime soon."

"I think you'd be surprised. No one here's trying to put the Larsen family back together again. Promise's mom dropped off the map. Anders got caught up in arson investigations, had to sell his lumber mills. Some people even think of you as a hero—"

"I killed Daya."

Caitlin sat back down on the bench. It was her turn to not speak.

"Caitlin? Did you hear—"

Caitlin cleared her throat. "I guess I figured that out. The police as well. Once they saw you with teeth, and alive."

"I'm not sorry I did it," Magda continued. "It happened fast and I hit her hard, harder than I thought, but she was going to sell Promise back into a life of hell. My only regret is that a life on the run means I'll never see you again."

Caitlin looked up toward the mausoleum's skylights. "May never."

Magda moved the phone on her line enough to make a muffled noise. Maybe she was fighting back tears as well. "I want you to know, you never were a 'crystalline bird.' I was. Maybe I still am. When I left you with Matt, any single day of my life would have broken us into a thousand pieces, all three of us. I don't blame him for not telling you what he and I had done, or keeping you from whatever message I'd scribbled while tweaked out of my mind."

Caitlin reached into her bag for a Kleenex. Sure enough, a tear escaped while she wrestled with the tissue pack's plastic wrapper.

Magda continued. "I know you don't believe in God—"

"I don't not-believe in God," Caitlin said. "I just—"

"Right," Magda overlapped. "I don't know what I believe in anymore either, but thank you."

Caitlin sniffled. "Thank me? For what?"

"For being mad enough at me after all these years to tell me to my face. Anger and love are both sides of the same coin."

Caitlin laughed. "Well, shove a key in a lady's butt, and you get a girl's attention."

Magda laughed on the other end, the way someone in tears would. "I don't know when the end of days will come, but know that I will be there, looking forward to the time we'll spend together in the Light."

"Magda." Caitlin stopped herself. "Maya? I don't know what you'd like to be called now."

"That's up to you, my darling. Neither is the name I go by now."

Caitlin shook her head and laughed, louder than anyone in a mauso-leum should. "You're kidding, right?"

A loud shush came from her left.

She looked over and saw the same woman who'd lectured her about smoking more than a month earlier, once again dressed in full-mourning black.

"There's no talking on phones here," she said, with just as much righteous judgment as she had shown during their previous interaction.

"Yeah," Caitlin answered, covering the microphone. "I'm talking to my mother."

"Is there someone there?" Magda said.

Caitlin waved the old mourner away. "Uh-huh."

"Then this is good-bye, my darling."

"What? She's walking away—"

"Be well, Caitlin. Be strong and be true. The Daughters of God walk with you."

"Magda—"

It was no use. The line went dead.

Caitlin called the number and entered the meeting code again, but no one answered.

"Damn it," she yelled.

The old mourner returned. "This is a hallowed place of calm reflec-tion. If you can't—"

Caitlin stood up. "Lady, you shush me one more time and I'll make sure you haunt this hallowed place for eternity."

The old mourner took a step back, then went for the exit, yelling for security.

Caitlin threw her head back and laughed.

She stood up and touched her father's plaque.

"Well, Dad. I was gonna do a whole heart-to-heart thing about how I can't believe you never told me the truth, and how much I would have loved you, probably even more, if I'd have known you were my real father for my whole life. Then I probably would have said that 'I know you were flawed, but to me, that's what made you the perfect father.' And I'd add some sort of joke, so I didn't seem too emotional, like 'And I should know, because I turned out perfect.' You know, something classy and well thought out. But that lady's definitely calling the cops, and I doubt you want anyone from the LAPD finding your only daughter talking to herself like a wackjob. So this one's for you, Daddy."

She gave his metal plaque a pat, reached into her bag, found the cigarettes and lighter, then lit one in his memory.

After one big drag, she erupted into a coughing fit, which turned into a laughing fit, which ended in two really deep and painful coughs. "See? Perfect daughter."

She walked out, laughing again, her father's laughter loud and alive in her ears. She couldn't smoke anymore, but she could drive over to Canter's Deli, down a bowl of kreplach soup in his honor, a plate of pickles for Mama Maya, and a side of fries, just because.

ACKNOWLEDGMENTS

The writing of this project coincided with the release of my first book, *Come and Get Me*: A Caitlin Bergman Novel. Therefore, any acknowledgment of the many people behind this title must also include the army of friends, family, and complete strangers behind the first book's successful release—including the reviewers who took the time to let the world know about Caitlin, the independent bookstores and libraries that ordered copies, and every reader who took a chance on a debut author. Special thanks to David Bell, Lisa Brackmann, Christine Carbo, Simon Gervais, Steena Holmes, Lydia Kang, Gale Massey, Barbara Nickless, and Thomas Shawver for lending your names and reputations by contributing promotional blurbs. In addition, thanks to official publicist Justin Hartgett, and un-official publicists Ruthann Stevens and Tawnya Bragg, for getting the word out at every opportunity; Mystery Ink Bookstore (Huntington Beach, CA), Mysterious Galaxy (San Diego, CA), Barnes & Noble Booksellers (Burbank, CA, Bloomington, IL, The Villages, FL), LA Times Festival of Books, The Story Tavern (Burbank, CA), Books & Brews South Indy (Indianapolis, IN), Sisters in Crime OC (Orange County, CA), & Lit Up OC (Tustin, CA) for hosting events that brought me face to face with readers; the Santa Barbara Writers Conference, the Southern California Writers Conference, Thrillerfest, Magna Cum Murder, & Bouchercon for allowing me to speak on panels, teach, and hang at the bar; the International Thriller Writers Association, Mystery Writers of America (National and SoCal), & Sisters in

Crime (National, Los Angeles, OC) for the support and resources; Mystery Scene Magazine, CrimeReads, Criminal Element, Suspense Magazine, the Bloomington Herald Times, the Thrill Begins, the Big Thrill Magazine, the Santa Barbara Literary Journal, Center Grove Magazine, Advice to Writers, Writers Read, KRL News, Michael Bradley, Elena Hartwell/Elena Taylor, PJ Bodnar, Gwen Florio, My Detective Stories Podcast with John Hoda, DIY MFA Podcast with Gabriela Pereira, & the Character Floss Podcast with Maddie Margarita for the interviews, reviews, and ridiculous fun. Every social media post, email, cover photo, and signing appearance made my heart stretch to its fullest, which I've been assured is a good thing. I'd be remiss if I didn't single out Lauren Miller, JC Meunier, Tommy Bechtold, Mike Hughes, Janis Thomas, & Frank Gonzales Jr. for being the loving eyes at that first pre-release appearance, despite the hour and a half drive. Please let me know if you need anyone killed (in fiction).

My career began and continues with the efforts and support of my agent extraordinaire, Eric Myers, who fights for his clients like they're his family, while maintaining a professional's critical eye and bon vivant's flair and style. I'm always honored to sit at your table.

Despite a world in flux, the team at Crooked Lane Books once again helped produce a Caitlin Bergman novel I love, starting with the hard work and dedication of Chelsey Emmelhainz and transitioning smoothly to the helpful hands of Melissa Rechter, with support along the way from Jenny Chen, Terri Bischoff, Ashley DiDio, Madeline Rathle, and Matt Martz.

My friends and mentors from the Santa Barbara Writers Conference also did their part through workshops, critique, and support, including but in no way limited to: Ara Grigorian, Trey Dowell, Chase Moore, Matt Pallamary, Lorelei Armstrong, Avery Faeth, Tawnya Bragg, River Braun, Jenny Davis, Andrea Tawil, Robin Winter, & Grace Rachow. Trey Dowell and Stephanie Gold actually flew to Los Angeles just for a signing, thereby winning the ultimate honor through personal expense... though Chase Moore and Kelly did house them...

This project's core beta readers gave useful and necessary criticism without destroying my ego. Eternal gratitude to the keen eyes of this novel's first line of defense: Ara Grigorian, Jeremy Kryt, Derek Miller, Hilary Ryan Rowe, & Rebecca Stevens.

Mentioned twice already, mentor and mensch, Ara Grigorian continues to be both an amazing friend and guide, whether discussing writing or life. Similarly, journalist and author, Jeremy Kryt challenges me to strive for literary excellence, in both prose and concept. Actor and writer Derek Miller, despite the ocean between us, keeps the smile on my face and the dream in my heart.

Screenwriter, forensic specialist, and author of the *Coroner's Daughter* series (also by Crooked Lane Books), Jennifer Dornbush, was kind enough to make sure my creepy dead body stuff was accurately creepy. Apologies to her expertise if there are parts that I didn't clear with her.

The character of Caitlin Bergman began in a screenplay in 2007. While based on several of the strongest people this author has known, the part was written specifically for my college friend—and later Broadway, TV, and film actress, as well as wife and mother—Karen Walsh Rullman. While Karen's life and problems did not parallel Caitlin's, I hear her voice whenever I write a line of Caitlin's dialog.

This novel deals with complex family structures, contrasting the families we're born into with the families we choose. Unlike Caitlin, my own legal and biological family of Normans, Thoemings, Wensings, Rusnaks, Michaleks, Stevens', & Burns' continue to amaze me with their love and support, despite all the F words. As for the family I've chosen, which includes iOWest, Second City Hollywood performers, the cast of Opening Night: The Improvised Musical!, cruise ship friends, ADS employees, circus folk, authors, college buddies, and high school friends & teachers; an amazing motley crew continue to reach out and help in ways I couldn't have imagined.

This novel also deals with religion, and cults in particular. While I consider myself a religious person and attend an organized church on a semi-regular basis, I understand the damage that a malicious manipulation of faith can wreak on the world, especially when coupled with the abuse of cognitive dissonance, as in the affirmation of ludicrous beliefs after they've been proven demonstrably false. For research, I turned once again to my personal therapist, Annie Armstrong, multiple documentaries, and several books; most notably *When Prophecy Fails: A Social and Psychological Study of a Modern Group that Predicted the Destruction of the World* (Festinger/Riecken/Schachter, 1956, University of Minnesota), and *Apocalypse Child: A Life in End Times* by Flor Edwards (2018, Turner).

While informed by those works of non-fiction, in no way should this fictional account be construed as an attempt to downplay or profit from someone else's traumatic experiences, or to be representative of any existing theology. Recovery from religious zealotry and manipulation, especially at the cult level, should be done under the supervision of trained mental health professionals.

In a similar vein, like Los Angeles and Pasadena, the towns of Coos Bay, North Bend, Bandon, and Coquille are all real locations in Coos County, Oregon, USA, and the sheriff's department and office of the medical examiner are staffed with real people doing real law enforcement work. In no way is this work meant to disparage their worthy occupations or to insinuate any parallel to the hard-working people in those positions in that beautiful locale. As far as the white supremacy alleged in the area, while Oregon has a fair amount of documented history on that front, sadly that issue still pervades every state in the union, including my home states of Indiana and California.

Finally, this novel, and much of my life, couldn't exist without my brilliant, gorgeous, generous, and hilarious partner-in-crime; my wife, Rebecca Stevens. The adventures we conquer together make even the most daunting task seem possible—and sexy for some reason. Between the writing of this story and the release by the publisher, we will have brought a son into our household. Of course, little Jamison will face his own stresses, pains, and sorrows as he finds his way in the world. I can only hope that we teach him to laugh as hard—and love as honestly—as we do, and to always—even when the world seems to be ending—fight for friendship, honor, and the last French fry.